we all looked ^{up}

we all looked up

tommy wallach

SIMON & SCHUSTER BFYR

New York London Toronto Sydney New Delhi

SIMON & SCHUSTER BFYR

An imprint of Simon & Schuster Children's Publishing Division

1230 Avenue of the Americas, New York, New York 10020

For information about special discounts for bulk purchases, please contact Simon & Schuster
Special Sales at 1-866-506-1949 or business@simonandschuster.com.

The Simon & Schuster Speakers Bureau can bring authors to your live event.
For more information or to book an event, contact the Simon & Schuster Speakers Bureau at
1-866-248-3049 or visit our website at www.simonspeakers.com.

Book design by Lucy Ruth Cummins

The text for this book is set in Garamond.

Manufactured in the United States of America

2 4 6 8 10 9 7 5 3 1

Library of Congress Cataloging-in-Publication Data

Wallach, Tommy.

We all looked up / Tommy Wallach. — First edition.

pages cm

Summary: The lives of four high school seniors intersect weeks before a meteor is set to pass
through Earth's orbit, with a 66.6% chance of striking and destroying all life on the planet.

ISBN 978-1-4814-1877-5 (hardcover : alk. paper) — ISBN 978-1-4814-1879-9 (eBook)

[1. Meteors—Fiction. 2. Self-realization—Fiction. 3. Friendship—Fiction.
4. High schools—Fiction. 5. Schools—Fiction. 6. Science fiction.] I. Title.

PZ7.W158855We 2015

[Fic]—dc 3

2014004565

FIRST
EDITION

To my mom,
for a lifetime of encouragement,
counsel, and inspiration

And the meteorite's just what causes the light
And the meteor's how it's perceived
And the meteoroid's a bone thrown from the void
That lies quiet in offering to thee

You came and lay a cold compress upon the mess I'm in
Threw the window wide and cried, Amen! Amen! Amen!

—Joanna Newsom, "Emily"

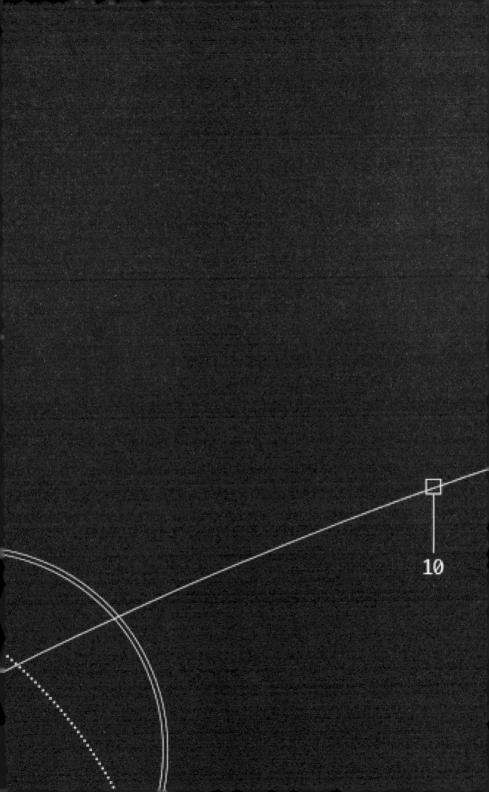

Peter

"IT'S NOT THE END OF THE WORLD," STACY SAID.

Peter looked down. He'd been staring vacantly at the sky, replaying his brief conversation with Mr. McArthur in his head. He still wasn't sure what to make of it.

"What?"

"I said it's not the end of the world. So one person doesn't like you. Who cares?"

"You really think he doesn't like me?"

Stacy groaned. They'd already been talking about this for fifteen minutes, which, in Peter's experience, was about fourteen minutes longer than his girlfriend liked to talk about any serious subject.

"I don't know. Maybe he's jealous of you or something."

"Why would he be jealous of me?"

"Because, like . . ." She flipped her hair to one side of her head, then back again. Peter had never understood why she did that; maybe she'd seen it in a shampoo commercial or something. She did have great hair, though—a shoo-in for best in school, when yearbook time came around—long and latte brown, the same smooth, glossy texture as a basketball jersey. "You have all this potential, you know? Like your whole life in front of you. And he's stuck in this shit school teaching the same shit history over and over again. If I had to do what he does every year, I'd probably end up hanging myself in a supply closet or something."

"I guess."

The thought had never crossed his mind, that a teacher might be jealous of a student. As a little kid, Peter had figured that once you reached a certain age, somebody just handed you all the knowledge you'd need in order to be an adult. But it turned out that wasn't how it worked at all. Peter's dad had recently admitted that even at the age of fifty-two, he sometimes woke up with the absolute certainty that he was only twenty-four, with his whole life still spread out before him like an untouched Thanksgiving dinner. It was just one of the many mysteries of getting older, along with male pattern baldness, midlife crises, and erectile dysfunction. Of course the only alternative to going through all that stuff, to slowly losing your looks and your teeth and your hair and finally your mind, was to bite the big one early, which *nobody* wanted to do.

Mr. McArthur was bald. Maybe he had erectile dysfunction, too. And really, what right did Peter have to be pissed at some aging high school history teacher, when his own life was so freakishly, criminally good? In his three and a half years at Hamilton, he'd started on the basketball team four times. He'd been to state twice and nationals once. He'd lost his virginity to Stacy, been given a sweet Jeep for his sixteenth birthday, and ended up good and wasted at about a hundred crazy-fun parties. And now he was eighteen. In the fall, he'd be off to sunny California (technically, acceptance letters wouldn't come until March, but the Stanford athletic department said he was as good as in). And seriously, how sick was college going to be? Pledging some frat and playing ball all over the country and partying with his teammates and frat brothers every weekend. Stacy would be sure to get into SF State, so they'd see each other all the time. Then he'd go pro if he were lucky, or else get into coaching or something, and he and Stacy would get married and raise some kids and hit up Baja or TJ over Christmas breaks and buy a kick-ass summer place on Lake Chelan with a Jacuzzi. That was what life was supposed to do, right? Just keep getting better and better?

But Peter knew it wasn't like that for everyone; he watched the news (or at least saw it out of the corner of his eye when his parents turned it on). People starved. People lost their jobs and then their homes. People came down with messed-up diseases and they had ugly divorces and their kids got in motorcycle accidents and ended up in wheelchairs. Maybe Mr. McArthur's life had just been getting worse and worse since he left high school. Maybe he really *was* jealous.

And if not, then what the hell point had he been trying to make in class?

"Baby, stop worrying about it." Stacy gave him a dry kiss on the cheek. "If I got all bent out of shape whenever someone didn't like me, I'd be, like . . ." She thought for a few seconds, then shrugged. "I don't know. Seriously bent out of shape."

"Yeah. You're right."

"Of course I am. And I'm also *starving*. Come on."

It was chicken fingers day in the lunchroom, traditionally a day of joy (because the Hamilton chicken fingers were mad good). Peter loaded up his tray with two paper boats full of them, a lemon-lime Gatorade, a chocolate pudding, an apple, a granola bar, and a finger-bowl's worth of wilted green lettuce and shredded carrot. He crossed the lunchroom, catching sight of his little sister's newly dyed hair (the sink in their shared bathroom still looked like a leprechaun had thrown up and then died in it). She was eating lunch with her freak boyfriend over at the freak table. In his mind's eye, Peter could still see a younger version of her sitting next to him on the living room couch, playing with her Legos, back before she transformed into something feminine and unfathomable.

"Dude, you okay?" Peter looked up into the waving hand of his best friend, Cartier Stoffler. "I've already eaten, like, three of your chicken fingers."

"Yeah, sorry. I'm having a weird day. Something a teacher said."

"You in trouble?"

"Not like that. It's hard to explain."

"Here's my trick with teachers, right? Don't ever listen to them in the first place."

"Brilliant."

"It's got me this far," he said, then popped a whole chicken finger into his mouth.

Peter laughed as convincingly as he could. Cartier was generally pretty good at cheering him up, but it was no use today. Mr. McArthur's question had created a black hole that sucked in everything good around it. Or more like it made everything around it suck. Like, it sucked that high school was almost over. And it really sucked that Cartier had applied to WSU to study beer brewing instead of trying to go to college somewhere in California. They'd been friends since the first day of high school, so inseparable that Coach Duggie named them Cookies and Cream (Cartier, though black, insisted that he had to be the cream, on account of his smoothness). They'd shared their first bottle of beer, their first blunt, their answers to homework questions, and even, for a few weeks in tenth grade, Amy Preston, who managed to convince them it was perfectly normal for a girl to have two boyfriends at the same time. And sure, there'd still be the holidays—Thanksgiving and Christmas and the long, long weekend of summer—but it wouldn't be the same. Already, they'd stopped hanging out as much as they used to. The most painful part of it wasn't that they wouldn't be friends, but that they wouldn't even care that they weren't friends.

And if he and Cartier couldn't manage to stay tight, then who was to say that he and Stacy wouldn't break up too? Peter would be off playing away games every weekend, and she'd be left on her own. Would she really stay faithful to him? Would he stay faithful to her? Would any part of the past four years matter at all four years from now?

These black-hole thoughts wouldn't leave him alone for the rest of lunch period, but then there was chemistry and precalc to get through, followed by two exhausting hours in the gym, mindlessly running lines and doing passing drills on instinct. So it wasn't until he found himself under the steaming beam of the locker-room shower that he really had time to think again. And there was Mr. McArthur's question—"Would that be a Pyrrhic victory?"—stuck in his head like one of those crappy pop songs that you only knew the chorus to.

He'd stop by the history department in Bliss Hall. If Mr. McArthur had already left for the day, then that would be the end of it. And if he hadn't, well then at least Peter could get this dumb song to stop playing in his head.

It was the last week of January, and in Seattle, that meant traitorously short days. You'd step into the gymnasium in full daylight, and by the time you got out, the sun would be slipping behind the horizon so fast you'd think it was getting away with something. Peter left the locker room just after six, and all that was left of the day was that fugitive red glow on the horizon. He zipped up his North Face jacket and put his hands in the fleecy pockets. His mom had bought him leather gloves for Christmas, but he'd stopped wearing them after Stacy said that they made him look like the kind of guy who offered to show children the lollipops he kept in his van. The only students left on campus were those who inhabited the extremes of the work-play spectrum: overachievers laboring late at the library and the skater/slackers who didn't have anywhere better to go. You could hear the faraway *click-snap-skittle* of their skateboards even from inside Bliss Hall.

Peter knocked on Mr. McArthur's door, half hoping no one would answer.

"Come in."

The office was so cramped that the door stuck on a footstool in the corner, and Peter had to squeeze through the gap. Mr. McArthur was on his own—his two office mates must have already gone home for the day—sitting in a brown plastic chair in front of a narrow desk piled high with ungraded essays. Peter had never felt confident in his ability to guess the age of anyone between twenty-five and sixty, but he figured Mr. McArthur was somewhere in his late forties; his forehead had a few permanent creases in it, but they didn't make him look old so much as perpetually concerned. He was popular with the students, engaging but not pushy. Peter had always liked him well enough—until today anyway.

"Hello, Mr. Roeslin. Make yourself at home."

"Thanks."

Peter sat down on a small sofa. A ragged stuffed bunny lay upside down on one of the cushions. Its once pink places had gone gray with age. Mr. McArthur wrote *B+* on the essay he was grading, circling it twice. His pen wasn't the typical felt-tip marker, but something slimmer and more elegant, with a diamond-shaped metal nib. He capped it and set it aside.

"So how can I help you?"

Peter hadn't really thought through what he was going to say, and now the possibilities backed up in his head, tripped over themselves like a defense falling apart in the face of a solid drive. "I just, well, we were talking today, right? And you asked me this question about a sports star or something, and you were talking about stuff I do, you know? Or might do. I mean, I think you were. Do you have any idea what I'm talking about?"

"I might," Mr. McArthur said, with a patient smile.

Peter idly patted the stuffed bunny, trying to remember exactly what had happened. They'd been learning about the phrase "Pyrrhic victory," which came from Roman times and meant that you'd won something, like a battle, but in order to win, you had to lose so much that you really hadn't won at all. Mr. McArthur asked the class if anyone could come up with some examples from real life. Nobody else was going for it, so Peter raised his hand and said that if you won a basketball game or a football game or something, but your best player got injured, that would be an example. Mr. McArthur nodded, but then he stared hard at Peter with the combined intensity of his earnest eyes and that inquisitorial forehead and said, "What about if you were a big sports star, and you made loads of money, and you bought big houses and you drove fast cars, but when your time in the limelight was over, you ended up unhappy because you didn't know what the point of your life had been? Would that be a Pyrrhic victory?"

He'd let the question hang out there, like some big old rainbow of a three-pointer. And then Andy Rowen said, "I'd take it anyway," and the whole class laughed and they moved on to Caesar.

But Peter couldn't help thinking that Mr. McArthur was probably right: It *would* be a Pyrrhic victory. Because when the golden days were over, and you were lying on your deathbed, watching the instant replay of your life, wouldn't it be pretty depressing to think you'd wasted your best years playing a *game*?

That was the thought that had plagued Peter for the last six hours, though he didn't quite know how to put it into words. Thankfully, Mr. McArthur finally came to his rescue.

"Peter, I'm sorry if it seemed like I was criticizing you today. I like you. And I've seen a lot of popular kids go through this school. The ones at the top of the pile, I mean. Most of them let it go to their heads, but I don't think you do."

Flattery embarrassed Peter; he looked over toward the wall, where an empty Advent calendar still hung, open windows counting down the days until Christmas. He'd expected a lecture from Mr. McArthur, not a recitation of his good qualities. "I guess."

"Most kids wouldn't have given a second thought to what I said. So why do you think it's made such an impression on you?"

"I don't know."

"Okay. Then let me ask you this—what is it that makes a book really good?"

"I don't really read that much. Outside of homework, I mean."

"Then I'll tell you. The best books, they don't talk about things you never thought about before. They talk about things you'd *always* thought about, but that you didn't think anyone else had thought about. You read them, and suddenly you're a little bit less alone in the world. You're part of this cosmic community of people who've thought about this *thing*, whatever it happens to be. I think that's what happened to you today. This fear, of squandering your future, was already on your mind. I just underlined it for you."

Something inside Peter thrummed along with this explanation. "Maybe."

"It's a good thing, Peter, to worry about having a meaningful life. Are you at all religious?"

"I guess so. I mean, I believe in God and stuff."

"That's some of it, then. Religion is all about making meaning for yourself. And you'll have to excuse me if this is too personal, but have you ever lost someone? Someone close to you, I mean."

"Yeah," Peter said, a little awed by Mr. McArthur's intuition. "My older brother, a couple years ago. Why?"

"My father died when I was very young. It forced me to confront things that many of my peers had the luxury of ignoring. The big questions. Does that sound familiar?"

"I'm not sure."

Mr. McArthur left some space in the conversation, waiting to see if Peter would say more, then shrugged his caterpillar eyebrows. "My point, Peter, is that you're one of those people who've been blessed not only with talent, but with self-awareness. And that means you get to choose what you want to do with your life, instead of life choosing for you. But having that power, the power to choose, can be a double-edged sword. Because you can choose wrong."

"How do you know if you're choosing wrong?"

"You tell me. Do you think it's better to fail at something worthwhile, or to succeed at something meaningless?"

Peter answered before he realized what he was saying. "To fail at something worthwhile." The implications of his answer hit him like an elbow to the sternum.

Mr. McArthur laughed. "You look positively tragic!"

"Well, you're saying I should stop doing the only thing I've ever been great at."

"No. I'm not saying stop. I'm saying *evaluate*. I'm saying *choose*. You can ignore everything I said today if you want."

"Can I?"

"I suppose that depends on what kind of man you want to be." Mr. McArthur stood up and put out a hand. "I'm sure you'll figure it out. Come talk to me anytime."

Peter stood up too. He was a few inches taller than Mr. McArthur, but he felt smaller than he had in years. They shook hands. As Peter was leaving, the teacher called out after him.

"Hey, Peter?"

"Yeah?"

"The bunny."

Peter looked down. Sure enough, he was clutching the old stuffed animal in his left hand, so tightly that its face had been squashed down to a nub.

"Sorry," Peter said, and tossed it back onto the couch.

Back outside, darkness had set in. Peter felt like a different person; his certainties had all disappeared with the daylight. Almost too perfect then, that the sky was suddenly unfamiliar: Against an eggplant-purple backdrop shone a single bright star, blue as a sapphire, like a fleck of afternoon someone had forgotten to wipe away.

Peter heard the click of a door opening nearby. Someone was coming out of the arts building, a swirl of multicolor scarf that he knew for a fact she'd knitted herself—Eliza Olivi. It was the first time they'd been alone together in almost a year. And it was happening today, of all days? What did they call that? Serendipity?

"Eliza," he called out. "Do you see that star? Isn't that crazy?"

But even though she must have heard him, she just kept on walking.

Eliza

IT HAD ALL STARTED A YEAR AGO.

Eliza was working late in the photo lab, as usual. She spent most of her free time there, alone with her thoughts, her favorite music, and her vintage Exakta VX (a kind of reverse going-away present from her mother, who moved to Hawaii with her new boyfriend just a few weeks after Eliza turned fourteen). It was the same camera that Jimmy Stewart used in *Rear Window*, with a black leather grip and a polished silver band running down the center. The dials on top were thick with machine-tooled hatchings and spun with heavy, satisfying clicks. Eliza kept the camera in a side compartment of her bag at all times, so she could get at it easily in an aesthetic emergency. Quick draw, like a cowboy with a six-shooter, always ready to capture that fleeting frame.

She believed photography to be the greatest of all art forms because it was simultaneously junk food and gourmet cuisine, because you could snap dozens of pictures in a couple of hours, then spend dozens of hours perfecting just a couple of them. She loved how what began as an act of the imagination turned into a systematic series of operations, organized and ordered and clear: mixing up the processing bath, developing the negatives, choosing the best shots and expanding them, watching as the images appeared on the blank white paper as if in some kind of backward laundromat—a billowing line of clean sheets slowly developing stains, then hung up until those stains were fixed forever. And then there was the setting, crepuscular and shadowy, everything about it perfectly calibrated for creativity, from the sultry red glow of the darkroom lights to the still and shallow pool in which her prints rested like dead leaves on the surface of a pond. If no one else was around, she could put her phone in the dock and blast Radiohead or Mazzy Star loud enough to make the room tremble with each downbeat, to erase the world outside. Immersed in that cocoon of sound and crimson light, Eliza could imagine she was the last person on Earth. Which was what made it so startling to be touched gently on the shoulder as she was examining a developing print for the first hint of beauty.

She whipped around with a hand out, as if slapping at a mosquito. A boy, bent over, holding his palm to his face.

"Ow! Shit!" he said.

She ran to the dock and turned down the music. The boy shook off the slap, unrolling his impossible height. Eliza felt annoyed that she recognized him, in the same way that you can't help but recognize Hollywood actors on the covers of magazines, even if you despise everything they stand for. He was Peter Roeslin, of the Hamilton basketball team.

"You surprised me," she said, angry with him for having been hurt by her.

"Sorry."

He stood there in the semidarkness, tall and slim as the silhouette of a dead tree.

"Hey, what are those?" he asked, noticing the prints drying on the line.

"Pictures. Can I help you with something?"

He took her curtness in stride. "Oh, just the music. We're having a meeting upstairs. Student council." He leaned in close to one of the photographs. "What are they pictures of?"

"Nothing really."

"I totally suck at art. I'm super jealous of people like you."

"Thanks, I guess."

"Why are they all black and white?"

"Why do you care?"

"I don't know. I'm just interested. Sorry."

But now she felt bad for being so abrupt. "No, it's okay. It's just hard to explain. I think black-and-white photos are more honest. Color has no . . . integrity." That was the best she could do with words. To really answer, she'd have to show him how the blacks in a color photo were always tinted red or speckled with yellow. How the whites were creams. How the grays were so often contaminated with blue. Eliza had always felt that fiction described reality better than nonfiction (or *her* reality, at any rate); in the same way, black-and-white photographs mirrored the world as she saw it more faithfully than color photographs did. Sometimes she dreamed in black and white.

"Look at that kid," Peter said, pointing at one of the pictures. "Poor little guy!"

"Yeah, he's kinda amazing."

The photograph Peter was looking at happened to be her favorite. It had been taken outside a private elementary school just a few blocks from Hamilton. By chance, Eliza had passed by just as the kids were struggling to arrange themselves in alphabetical order for a fire drill, and one boy had immediately caught her attention. He was smaller than the others in his line, and dressed about ten years too old, in pressed chinos and a button-down shirt with a little red bow tie—an outfit that wouldn't have been cool even if he *had* been ten years older. Every school had a kid like this. He stood in the very center of the line, exactly where he was meant to be—a point of stillness—as the students diffused into a buzzing, slow-exposure swarm at either end of the frame. You could already see the tough years of puberty stretching out before him, a minefield strewn with awkward rejections on dance floors and lonely Friday nights. He was imprisoned within his upbringing. Doomed.

"I feel like that kid sometimes," Peter said.

"Are you joking? In what possible way are you like that kid?"

"You know. Just keeping it together. Being good."

"And what would you be doing if you didn't have to be good all the time?"

She hadn't meant it to sound flirtatious, but everything was flirtatious in a darkroom. Peter looked down at her, and Eliza felt her pulse quicken. This was crazy. She didn't know the first thing about him. And sure, seen from a purely objective standpoint, he was a handsome guy, but she'd always preferred the artsy delinquent types—the ones who'd already ponied up for their first tattoos and would be walking walls of graffiti by the time they were twenty-one. Or at least that's what she preferred in her head. In reality, she'd never had a serious boyfriend, and she'd lost her virginity practically by accident at a summer camp for blossoming artists, to a pale Goth boy who only painted wilted flowers. But standing there in the unnatural bloodred twilight, only a few inches away from a beautiful stranger who happened to be Hamilton royalty, she felt the inner twist of desire, or at least the desire to be desired.

"I don't know," he said softly. "I just get sick of it sometimes. Going to practice every day. Doing enough homework to get by. Dealing with my girlfriend."

Eliza could picture this girlfriend. Stacy something. "I've seen her. Brunette, right? More makeup than face?"

Peter laughed, and even in the darkness Eliza could make out the moment when he realized he shouldn't have been laughing. He distracted himself by looking back at the photos. "I wish I could do stuff like this. I wish I could . . ."

"Could what?"

His eyes were auburn in the red light. Too close. He reached around behind her and drew her toward him, and then their mouths were mashed hard together and he was lifting her up off the ground. She heard the fixer fluid sloshing over the edge of the bath and splashing onto the floor. He sat her back down on the table, still kissing her, his tongue rough in her mouth, and his hands were making their way up her shirt when the lights flickered on.

A skinny blond girl stood between the black curtains in the doorway, her mouth agape, like some cartoon character expressing shock.

"Are you an idiot?" Eliza said. "This is a darkroom! Turn the light off!"

The girl turned and ran, her heels clicking on the tile like a snicker.

"Shit!" Peter said.

"Who cares?"

"She's a friend of Stacy's." He was already chasing after her, but he stopped just in front of the curtains. "Listen, I'm sorry about this."

Eliza pulled down her shirt. "Don't worry about it."

He started to say something else, then gave up and left.

Eliza was surprised by her behavior, not to mention the suddenness of the kiss, but she wasn't particularly worried. Assuming word even got back to Stacy, what was the worst that could happen? A confrontation? A catfight? Was one kiss really that big a deal, in the grand scheme of things?

Yes, was the answer. Yes it was.

By the time Eliza got to school the next morning, someone had already spray-painted her locker, one huge black word with four capital letters: S-L-U-T. The same word had been written on a few hundred scraps of blue-lined notebook paper, which came pouring out of her locker when she opened it up, a flood of little anti-valentines. Suspicious eyes greeted her from every corner of the lunchroom, and a few girls went out of their way to slam against her shoulder when they passed her in the halls.

The first day it was shocking. The second day it was infuriating. And every day after that, it got a little bit sadder, a little more isolating. With all the tools of social media at their fingertips, Stacy and her friends spread the word far and wide, even to the freshmen and sophomores, so that everywhere Eliza went, there were whispers and points and pointed smiles. The girl who'd prided herself on always staying under the radar was suddenly thrust into the spotlight, cast as the lead in a crappy high school production of *The Scarlet Letter*.

It totally, incontrovertibly sucked, in all possible ways, shapes, and forms.

And then everything got much, much worse.

"Hey, Judy," Eliza said to the nurse working the front desk. "My dad awake?"

"Should be. Go on in."

"Thanks."

She walked past reception and down the hall, but was so distracted that she passed right by her dad's room. For some stupid reason, she couldn't stop thinking about Peter calling out to her across the quad that afternoon. She'd been so focused on ignoring him that now she couldn't even remember what it was he'd said. Something about the sky?

"Hey, Dad."

"If it isn't Lady Gaga," he said, sitting up in bed. She'd gotten used to seeing him like this, gaunt and hairless, studded with tubes, wearing nothing but a flowered dressing gown.

"Once again, I'd like to formally protest the use of that nickname."

"You know I'm kidding. Gaga's a fucking hag next to you." (For as long as Eliza could remember, her dad had sworn like a sailor around her. There was footage of baby Eliza's first steps accompanied by the repeated cry: "Look at that kid fucking go!" And though Eliza's mom had waged a pretty serious campaign against the constant stream of vulgarity, she'd lost the right to judge anyone for anything when she skipped town.)

"Untrue. But thanks anyway."

Eliza took her usual seat by the window and started in on her homework. Her dad watched TV and flirted with the nurses. He still had a charming shred of an accent left over from his childhood in Brooklyn, and though a few women had taken an interest in the years since the divorce, they all fled the scene when they realized that he wasn't over his ex-wife.

"I just need a little more time," he'd always say.

But time had run out on him. Hard as it was to believe, the ladies weren't exactly lining up at the hospital door.

Up until her dad got sick, Eliza had believed the universe to be a fundamentally balanced place. She figured that, excepting the super lucky and the super unlucky, most people ended up with about the same amount of good and bad in their lives, when all was said and done. Which meant that if you happened to be ostracized by the majority of your high school because of one stupid kiss, you were owed some good news. It was only fair.

But not long after Eliza's illicit moment with Peter in the darkroom, her dad checked into the hospital with a weirdly tenacious stomachache and a low-grade fever. And after a lab rat's worth of tests had been administered, the diagnosis was delivered by a matter-of-fact oncologist with all the empathy of a GPS system correcting a wrong turn—stage III pancreatic cancer. Might as well have been a guy in a black robe with a scythe. At first Eliza couldn't even believe it, considering all the other shit she was dealing with. But that diagnosis was her first taste of what she now recognized as the fundamental rule of life: Things were never so bad that they couldn't get worse.

She cried for about a month straight, in classes and on buses, in her bedroom and in waiting rooms, alone and by her father's side while he got the chemo treatments that doctors said were unlikely to do much of anything other than make him nauseous. The grief was so profound that it transformed her; she went hard and numb as a frozen limb. Before, she'd walked around school like a leper, gaze perpetually set on the floor. Now, if some bitch tried to stare her down in the lunch line, Eliza would just stare back, dead-eyed, until the other girl got so unnerved she had to look away. The strangest thing was that her frosty attitude earned her a sort of prestige (the difference between coldness and coolness was, after all, simply a matter of degree). She was befriended by Madeline Seferis—a.k.a. Madeline Syphilis—a famously promiscuous senior, who introduced her to a new way of expressing disaffection, by putting on a tight skirt and a lot of makeup and heading out to the clubs where the bouncers didn't card and the college boys bought the drinks. "If you're going to have the reputation," Madeline said, "you might as well get the fun."

But Madeline had gone off to college last September, and Eliza was left on her own again. The chemo did end up slowing the growth of her dad's tumors, but good news was a weird thing when you were dealing with a fatal illness. Instead of a few months, the doctors gave him a year. That was how you could be lucky without being lucky. That was how you could be a winner and still lose.

"Dinnertime," a nurse said, balancing a tray in each hand, like a waitress.

They dug into their overcooked penne and overly sweetened pudding. Eliza realized that she now ate the vast majority of her meals off of cafeteria trays.

"Doc says the stent is good to go, so I'll probably be home tomorrow."

"Great."

"So what about you? Anything juicy happen at school today?"

"Not really. Well, sorta. Do you remember Peter?"

"You mean the Peter from last year?"

"Yeah. He tried to talk to me today. First time since . . . you know."

Her dad shook his head. He knew the whole story. "That asshole. Didn't know a good thing."

"Yeah."

"Wait." He poked her chin gently with his fork. "You're not interested in him, are you?"

"Are you kidding? He, like, wrecked my life."

"I know. But your mom wrecked my life too, and you know my feelings about her."

"I do." Eliza knew them, she just didn't understand them. How could you keep loving someone who cheated on you and then ran away? "But the answer is no. I'm not interested. He can fuck off and die for all I care."

"There's my sweet girl."

After dinner, she gave her father a kiss and grabbed ten bucks from his wallet to pay for the hospital parking lot. She couldn't handle being alone at home right now, so she headed out to the Crocodile to have a drink and maybe dance a little.

The guy who chatted her up at the bar was probably twenty-two, with a nicely trimmed blond Afro and the easy confidence of the stupid. They danced. They made out. And all the time, Eliza was thinking about Peter. Peter who sometimes felt like a little boy in a red bow tie. Peter who'd let his girlfriend ruin Eliza's reputation. Peter who was still with that same girlfriend.

Screw him.

"So you wanna go back to my place?" the blond Afro guy asked.

"I don't go home with strangers," Eliza said. "But you can come home with me."

He said he'd be cool with that. They always did.

Outside the Crocodile, a group of punkers was standing around in a haze of warm breath and cigarette smoke. Eliza recognized one of them from Hamilton—Andy Rowen. He had long brown hair, down to his shoulders, and was finally beginning to triumph over the volcanic acne that had plagued him since puberty. She'd bought pot from him once, and he'd given her a discount.

"Eliza!" he said. "Holy shit!" His excitement at seeing her off campus was so sincere she was almost embarrassed for him.

"Hey, Andy."

"Where you going? You guys should sit down and hang out."

"Sorry, we were just leaving."

Andy looked at her, then at her date, connecting dot A to dot B. She would have introduced them, but she couldn't remember the name of the guy she was about to take home. Something with a *J*?

"Hold up, though. You wanna see something amazing?"

"Sure."

Andy pointed upward. She followed the line extending from his index finger out into the dark distance. A single spark of bright blue, like a puncture in the black skin of the sky. And hadn't Peter said something about a star?

"Wicked, right?" Andy asked.

Eliza knew what he meant by the word; it was one of a million different synonyms for "cool": sweet, ill, rad, dope, sick. But for some reason, she felt like he had it wrong. The star seemed wicked in the original sense. Wicked like the Wicked Witch of the West. Wicked like something that wanted to hurt you.

Eliza had been labeled a slut by an entire high school. She wasn't speaking to her mom. Her dad was dying. But if she'd learned anything in the past year, it was that no amount of suffering could save you from more of it. And that star looked like a sure sign that more was coming.

Wicked indeed.

Andy

ON THE OTHER HAND, IT WAS GOOD TO BE OUT OF CLASS.

Andy threw down his deck and hopped on, letting the pavement carry him effortlessly down toward the other end of campus. If only everything in life could be like that—effortless. If only there weren't all this school to get through, and homework, and all these expectations. If only you could get up when you wanted and eat some Cinnamon Toast Crunch and play some music and smoke a bowl and drive to school whenever and maybe take a class if you felt like it, if you were actually *interested* in it, and then just chill with your friends the rest of the time. If only . . .

"Andy Rowen!"

Midge Brenner: freshman and sophomore English teacher, and one of Andy's many faculty nemeses. Clearly, she missed having him in class, where she'd reamed him out on the daily for his controversial stance on homework (namely, that it represented a blatant transgression of every man's God-given right to life, liberty, and the pursuit of happiness). Now the only way she could get her authoritative jollies was by killing his buzz *outside* the classroom.

"Yeah?"

"As a senior, I would have expected you to know that skateboarding is not allowed on campus."

"Totes forgot, Ms. Brenner. That's my bad."

Andy did a little ollie in place before hopping off and kicking the board up into his hand, earning an extra-strength frown from Midge. Not that there was anything she could do about it. You couldn't get sent to the principal's office when you'd already *been* sent to the principal's office. That shit was called *double jeopardy*.

"Thank you, Andy."

"Don't mention it."

Actually, even though he'd been sent there, Andy wasn't going to the principal's office. Last year he and Mr. Jester had come to an agreement. Andy's infractions were frequent but minor, and the principal didn't have the time or energy to deal with every single one. Instead, whenever Andy got in trouble, he was to report to Suzie O, the student counselor.

In other words, he'd been outsourced.

Suzie O's office was located on the second floor of the library, far from the fascist administrators who worked out of Bliss Hall. It was quiet there, because nobody hung out in the library if they could help it. That is, no one other than the librarians, toddling about behind the desk and in the circulation room, begrudgingly lending out their precious books. They seemed to see students primarily as things to be shushed; you could have a whole conversation with one of them that consisted of nothing *but* shushing sounds. Andy gave a fancy salute to the librarian behind the front desk as he walked up the stairs and out of her jurisdiction.

As he reached the second floor, he saw Anita Graves come out of Suzie's office, wiping at her eyes. Anita was pretty much the most clean-cut, put-together girl in the whole school. Her family had crazy money, and she was crazy smart—word was she'd already received her early decision acceptance from Princeton. So what the hell was she doing crying at Suzie O?

The counselor gave Anita a quick hug. "You think about what I said, okay?"

"I will." Anita sniffled, then shook her head with a single violent snap. Suddenly all the sadness was gone. She looked her usual self— sharp, focused, unflappable.

"Hey, Andy," she said, even smiling as she passed.

"Hey."

He turned to watch her go. Cute, in the way of certain high-strung girls, like a perfect pile of raked leaves you just wanted to dive into and scatter back over the lawn. He called out after her, "Yo, whatever it is, it's not worth it."

She didn't look back, but she did break her stride for half a second, which was really the most you could hope for with a girl like that.

"Eyes over here, Rowen." Suzie was leaning against the door frame. "I'm gonna guess you're not here in the middle of fourth period because you missed me."

Andy grinned. "That doesn't mean I *didn't* miss you."

"Come on in."

Suzie's office was actually pretty sweet, for an office. There was a fluffy brown couch long enough to lie out on, a mini-fridge stocked with soda, and a big basket with a layer of fruit hiding a secret stash of real snacks—what Suzie called her "childhood obesity facilitators."

28

Best of all was the television in the corner, available for the occasional midday movie screening, if Suzie was in a good mood.

To say they were friends might have been a stretch, but they got along pretty well for a high school senior with "behavioral issues" and an overweight counselor in her forties. Andy could talk to her about anything: drinking, drugs, girls, his shit parents, whatever. It hadn't come straightaway, of course. The first few times he'd been forced to meet with her, he didn't say a word, just sat there staring at the wall until the bell rang. But Suzie was smart. One day, instead of trying to talk to him, she put on the first season of *Game of Thrones*. And as if that weren't enough right there, she'd started to recite the words along with the characters. It was too much. How could you hate someone who had memorized entire episodes of *Game of Thrones*?

"And to what do I owe the pleasure today, Mr. Rowen?"

"Same old. I was too funny for Ms. Holland. She got jealous."

"I should've known. You want something to eat?"

"Oreo me, dawg."

Suzie tossed him one of the blue packets of cookies. "So, only five months left. You psyched?"

"About getting out of this shithole? You know it."

"And what's your plan after graduation?"

Andy didn't like talking about stuff like *plans*. Why were adults always so obsessed with the future? It was like the present wasn't even happening. "I don't know. Get a job. Move into an apartment with Bobo. Skate. Smoke. Enjoy life."

"Sounds nice. Any thoughts about college?"

"You know, I totally forgot to apply. That's on me."

"What about Seattle Central? You could take a few classes, see how you feel." Andy made a face, and Suzie raised her hands, like a criminal caught in the act. "I'm just being real with you. A high school diploma used to be enough in this country. Now you'll be lucky to make minimum wage with it."

"I don't care about money."

"It's not about money. I'm glad you don't care about money. I'm talking about boredom. You think school is bad? A minimum-wage job makes school look like freaking Burning Man. Unless you have some kind of fetish for doing the same rote physical task eight million times a day."

"Maybe I do."

Suzie laughed. "Yeah, I know you probably get this all the time from your parents—"

"I don't," Andy said. "They don't give half a shit."

"I'm sure that's not true."

"Believe what you want, man."

"What I believe is that you shouldn't waste your potential flipping burgers."

Andy unscrewed an Oreo and licked the creamy center. "Suzie, no offense, but you are stressing my shit *out* today."

"That's my job."

"I thought your job was to help people deal with the stress they already have."

"Strung-out people need to be chilled out. But chilled-out people maybe could use a good kick in the ass." She mimed a kind of seated kung-fu ass kicking.

"Stressed people like Anita Graves? What was she doing here, anyway?"

30

"Everyone's got their troubles."

"I'd trade mine for hers."

"Don't be so sure."

"Why don't you do me a real favor?" Andy said, popping the last Oreo into his mouth and talking while he chewed. "Teach me how to get laid. Bobo calls me Mary now, like the Virgin Mary. It's humiliating."

"All right. Lesson one, don't talk with your mouth full. It's gross. Lesson two, go to college. Girls like guys with plans."

"Oh yeah? Well, you've got a job and shit, and I don't see the dudes beating down your door, do I?"

He'd only meant it as an observation, but as soon as he said it, the vibe in the room turned cold. Suzie wasn't smiling anymore. "You're a good kid," she said, "but you've got a mean streak in you."

Andy wanted to apologize, but he didn't know how to put it into words. Just the thought of trying exhausted him. "Whatever," he said, standing up. He pushed Suzie's door out of the way like it was somebody trying to hassle him.

After school, Andy found Bobo already waiting for him in the parking lot, flicking the top of his lighter open and shut. He was wearing tight black jeans and a black Operation Ivy hoodie—both of them studded with patches and rips and safety pins.

"Mary!" he said, pulling a pair of headphones as big as coconut halves off his ears. "You made it! I was afraid we'd lost you for good when you got kicked out of Holland's class."

"I'm a survivor. So what's on tap today?"

"Same old. We hang out here till we get bored, then we leave. I told everybody we'd meet them at the Crocodile at seven. The Tuesdays are playing." Bobo pulled a rumpled pack of cigarettes out of the pocket of his hoodie, lit two, and handed one to Andy.

"You sure you don't wanna rehearse a little?" Andy asked.

"You know I don't believe in that shit. We gotta book a show first anyway."

"Never hurts to be prepared."

Bobo shook his head. "Don't be a bitch, yo. Let's just skate."

Together, they prowled over the Hamilton campus, hopping up on rails and jumping benches and sideswiping trash cans, until the sun started to go down and Hamilton's athletes slumped sweaty and worn-out from the gym. Then they hopped into Andy's station wagon, picked up some McDonald's, and headed downtown.

The Crocodile was an all-ages club with a decent sound system and a delightfully scuzzy clientele. By seven, the heavy, distorted belch of the Bloody Tuesdays was already blasting out of the place like a weapon of mass destruction. Andy and Bobo ordered a couple of Cokes (improved immeasurably by the flask of rum Bobo kept in his back pocket) and sat down at a table. Halfway through the set, the rest of the crew showed up: Jess, Kevin, and Misery, Bobo's girlfriend. She'd dyed her hair green last week, and it looked good.

They buried themselves deep in the moshing crowd and danced, though for Bobo and Misery, that basically meant grinding and making out. Somehow Andy could hear the click of their tongue rings even over the music. He did his best to tune it out.

Andy had met Misery on the very first day of junior year and had a crush on her pretty much right away. She was a freshman, but already confident and cool and unapologetically punk rock. Unfortunately, before he could make a move, she met Bobo. Within hours, they were a couple. It had pissed Andy off at first, but what was he gonna do? Bobo had always been the alpha dog in their little pack—funnier, crazier, more willing to get in trouble. He'd been suspended from school twice already; it'd be a miracle if he made it to graduation.

The set ended and they all went back to their table, soaked in their own sweat and the sweat of strangers.

"So when is Perineum gonna play again?" Misery asked.

"When this dude writes some new songs," Bobo said, punching Andy in the shoulder.

Perineum was their two-man punk rock/death metal band. They'd opened for the Bloody Tuesdays a couple of times over the summer but hadn't performed since. Andy had actually written a lot of songs in the past few months, but none of them were right for a lead singer who thought that music:eardrums = boxer:punching bag.

"Let's go outside," Misery said. "I wanna smoke."

The lead singer of the Tuesdays, a big ginger guy who called himself Bleeder, was already out there with his bassist. They were both staring up at the sky.

"That's some crazy-ass shit," Bleeder said.

Andy looked up. The star was bright blue, like the center of the flame off a chemistry-class Bunsen burner.

"What is it?" he asked. "Like, a comet?"

"It's probably a satellite," Bleeder said.

Jess shook his head. "Satellites move."

"Not always."

The door of the club opened, disgorging a wave of beer smell and feedback. Andy noticed her even before he recognized her—Eliza Olivi, on the arm of some blond dude with a ridiculous Afro. He was way older than her, and totally shitfaced.

"Eliza!"

"Hey, Andy."

She seemed eager to get away, but when he pointed out the icy blue star, she stared at it for a long time. Then she walked off without even saying good-bye.

"You're so into that," Bobo said.

"Shut up."

"Come on, it's inevitable. You're the biggest virgin at Hamilton, and she's the biggest slut. You're just working the odds."

"Dude!"

It was a stupid point, anyway. Of course he had a thing for Eliza. Everybody did. The only difference was that he'd liked her from the beginning, back when she was just a quiet presence in the back row of classrooms. But everything changed after she hooked up with Misery's older brother, the basketball player. Story was they'd been having sex in the photo studio for, like, six months before his girlfriend caught on. Andy had always figured the rumors about Eliza's promiscuity were mostly made up, but then what was she doing going off with some rando from the Crocodile on a weeknight?

Sometimes Andy wondered if he understood anything about anyone. Like, he'd thought his parents were totally fine right up until the moment they split. And though he still saw Bobo as a kind of brother, stuff between them had been totally fucked up since Andy had "broken the pact" last year. They never talked about it, but it hung over them like one of those sky-wide Seattle clouds that just drizzled down on you for days and days. Only in this case, it wasn't rain that Andy had to put up with, but a constant stream of insults, dead legs, and general disdain.

"Mary," Bobo said, snapping his fingers. "You're thinking pretty hard over there. Should I call an ambulance?"

Andy breathed out a stream of smoke and tried to release all his anxiety along with it. So what if Bobo was still pissed off at him? So what if Suzie O thought he was a dick? So what if Eliza was giving it up to some loser with an Afro when Andy probably wouldn't get laid until he was thirty? None of it really mattered. Today was just another shit day in a life that sometimes felt like a factory specializing in the construction of shit days.

"Life sucks," Andy said. A cliché, sure, but that didn't make it any less true.

Bobo nodded. "Blame it on the blue star," he said, purposely misquoting Radiohead.

Andy figured it was as good a scapegoat as any. He raised his middle finger toward the sky.

"Fuck you, star."

Anita

IT WAS A BOLD PLAN. EVEN AS ANITA PASSED OLD STEVE AT THE BROADMOOR GATEHOUSE, she hadn't decided if she would really go through with it. She clicked a button on the Escalade's sun visor to open the private gate that led to her house. The driveway was long and straight, lined on either side with oak trees. They'd recently been pollarded, which made their upper halves look grotesque—the arboreal equivalent of the Venus de Milo, with dozens of severed limbs instead of just two. *Better be careful*, they seemed to say, *or you'll end up like us.*

Anita shut the front door behind her. The housekeeper, Luisa, was ferrying a huge pile of linens toward the laundry room.

"*Hola*, Anita."

"Hey, Luisa."

"*¡En español!*" Luisa insisted.

Anita was studying Spanish at Hamilton, and Luisa occasionally gave her lessons on the subtle mysteries of the subjunctive mood, the differences between *ser* and *estar*, and, when no one else was around, a smattering of never-to-be-repeated slang terms "straight from the streets of Bogotá."

"*Hola, Luisa. ¿Cómo estás?*"

"Not so bad. I am going to clean out the guesthouse now your grandparents are gone back to Los Angeles. Not that there's much to do. They are so clean!"

"*Yo sé.*"

"My grandparents are coming like a hurricane," Luisa said. "But yours, I am hardly telling that they are there."

"*Si. Son locos.*"

"*Están locos.*"

"Right. *Lo siento*, Luisa, but I'm a little distracted. Have you seen my father?"

"*En la oficina.*"

"*Gracias.*"

Her father's office had all the warmth of a refrigerator. Basically, he'd built a corporate boardroom in his house, complete with a wide glass desk and an expensive space-age chair behind it. A dozen metal filing cabinets topped with gray plastic binders were lined up against the walls. The only object in the room with any life in it (both literally and figuratively) was a large dome-top cage of stainless steel. Inside, Bernoulli, the world's saddest hyacinth macaw, jumped from perch to perch, squawking and pooping and gazing longingly (or so it looked to Anita) out the window.

When she came into the office, her father was reading that weird pink newspaper that only people whose lives revolved around money bothered with. She thought it was funny that a paper like that would be pink, of all colors. Better khaki, or plaid, or whatever color a good power tie was. Seeing her father reading from those pink pages made her think of Barbie dolls and Hello

Kitty backpacks and Claire's. Of course, she kept this observation to herself.

"You're back early," he said, folding the paper up and placing it on his desk.

"Student council. There isn't much on the agenda this time of year."

"I'm sure you could've found something to work on, if you'd really applied yourself. Hamilton is hardly perfect."

Funny, it was just one more droplet of negativity in the vast ocean of criticism she'd been drowning in since birth, but it was one droplet too many. Suzie O was right: Something had to change.

"I got a C," she blurted out. Then, watching the anger rush into her father's face like an invading army, she hastened to explain. "It was just one calculus test, so my overall grade will still be fine as long as I keep everything else up. Even Mrs. Barinoff said it was a rare misstep. That's what she called it: 'a rare misstep.'"

When her father finally spoke, he had the quiet gravitas of a faraway mushroom cloud. "Anita, do you understand what a conditional acceptance is?"

"Yes."

"Do you understand that if your grade point average drops, Princeton could retract your offer?"

"It was just one test."

"If it can happen once, it can happen again."

"Well, the world wouldn't end if I didn't go to Princeton," Anita said, and cringed inwardly in preparation.

Her father stood up. He wasn't a particularly tall man, but when he got this worked up, he looked like a giant. "Young lady, we made our decision as a family, and every time you question that decision—"

"I'm not—" she tried to say.

"*Every time* you question that decision, it shows a lack of respect for everything this family has done for you. Everything we've sacrificed so that you could be in the position to attend a good university. Are you really that ungrateful? Do you really have that little respect for the investments we've made in your future?"

That was the funny thing about her father. He made investments for a living, and somewhere along the line, he'd started to mistake his daughter for just one more of them. And how did an investment work? You put some money in up front, and then, somewhere down the line, you expected a return. Hence the SAT tutors and the weekly reading assignments and the Saturday-morning French classes. Hence the curfews and the lectures and the "dictionary dinners" (during which Anita's father asked her to reel off the definitions of obscure words while her food got cold). In fact, the only reason Anita had attended Hamilton High in the first place was because the admissions adviser her father had hired insisted she'd have a better chance of being accepted at Princeton if she graduated from a public school. Every single thing Anita did had to be about the bottom line: jacking up the return on her father's investment. Only it wasn't more money he wanted. It was success. It was prestige. It was a good little black girl with an Ivy League degree and a serious career—doctor, politician, entrepreneur.

Well, maybe I don't want any of those jobs, Anita wanted to scream. *Maybe I don't think I should have to do whatever you say just because I live under your roof!*

Most people her age were already engaged in the difficult task of transforming the parent-child relationship, of turning a strict

39

dictatorship into something more like a democracy. But Anita still couldn't help but see her father as a kind of god. A petty, arbitrary god, but a god nonetheless. And on any other day, if she'd had to stand there, listening patiently while a god called her a disappointment and a disgrace and a delinquent, she would have been in tears. But not today. Today, Anita was strong. Today, Anita was composed. Because today, Anita was lying. She'd never gotten a C in her life.

It had been Suzie O's idea. Anita had gone to see her because she'd felt herself teetering on the brink of a mental breakdown. The past three years had been one oasis-less desert of excruciating effort. Anita had hoped it would all end when she got into Princeton, but it hadn't. If anything, expectations had only risen to keep pace with her newly enhanced prospects. It was as if someone had challenged her to hold her breath underwater for as long as she could, and when she finally broke all the world records and started swimming back up to claim her trophy, she discovered that the surface had frozen over.

"Maybe you need to disappoint him," Suzie had said.

"What do you mean? Like, flunk something?"

"You don't even have to do it. You could just pretend."

"What for?"

"Because then you'll see that the world doesn't end if your dad doesn't approve of something. And maybe he'll see that too."

"He won't, though. I know he won't." The tears had come before she could remember to hold them back. And then that slacker kid, Andy Rowen, had caught her in the act. He'd looked so surprised, like he never would have guessed that she was capable of normal human emotions.

"Whatever it is, it's not worth it," he'd said.

Wise words, in spite of the source. They were what gave her courage now, to walk out of her father's office right in the middle of his denunciation.

"Young lady?" he called out after her. "Young lady, where are you going?"

She escaped to her bedroom and stood very still, waiting for her father to chase her down and continue to berate her. But he didn't come; the only explanation was that he was paralyzed with shock. Anita closed and locked the door, then took Amy Winehouse's *Back to Black* off the shelf. It was her secret de-stressing ritual—switch on the turntable, turn up the volume as loud as it would go without bleeding downstairs, and, finally, shut herself in the closet.

She didn't do it to be alone, though it was nice to be alone. And she didn't do it because the closet was dark and warm and cozy, though it was all of those things. She did it because the closet was the only place—in the entire world, it sometimes felt—where she could sing without being overheard.

Since the age of eight, Anita had dreamed of being a singer. And ever since her parents had discovered that dream, they'd been hell-bent on thwarting it. There had been piano lessons, but only until Anita's teacher made the mistake of allowing an Alicia Keys song into the repertoire. Within a week, the piano in the sitting room had been replaced with a solid oak table, and Anita was taking ballet. In middle school, chorus had been mandatory, but somehow there was always an important family event scheduled for concert nights, so the choir director never gave Anita any solos. As a freshman at Hamilton, she'd tried out for the school musical—*Into the Woods*—and had been cast as the Witch. But when her father found out, two weeks into rehearsals, he marched into the school and took the director aside, explaining that they had a strict rule in their house—curriculars before extracurriculars. The part ended up going to a skinny white girl named Natalie.

Anita's father knew he couldn't afford to give her so much as an inch, because music ran in the Graves bloodline. Anita's uncle, Bobby, was a professional saxophonist, touring the country with whatever band would have him. He had no roots, no family—no investments at all. Benjamin Graves would have set fire to every jazz club in Seattle before he'd let his daughter end up like that.

But no one could stop her from singing in the closet. In the closet, there was no distinction between dreams and reality, no need to choose one path or another. There was just the heavenly lift of the strings, the sharp shriek of the horns, the twinkle of the guitar, Amy Winehouse's iniquitous voice blasting its way across the divide between life and death to duet with Anita's. And high school and college and the ponderous, bloated look on her father's face all faded away. She sang through the whole record—every verse, every chorus, every bridge—high as a heroin addict until the last note warbled and died.

Whatever it is, it's not worth it.

Anita felt something strange overtaking her, a sense of self-determination that had been swelling ever since Andy made that off-hand comment outside Suzie's office. It was a bit like how she felt on those nights when there was a full moon and suddenly she was manic or depressed or pissed off and there was just no other explanation for it but the stars. Before she could second-guess herself, she slipped back downstairs, past her father's office, past Luisa and her mother and the smell of roast chicken, out the front door, and into her car.

Her father hadn't *technically* grounded her, but that would be scant defense when she got home.

She drove slowly past Swedish hospital and down into the city, windows open even though it meant drops of rain prickling her arm. Esperanza Spalding was playing all this week at Jazz Alley, and Anita was going to go see her. Anita knew about Esperanza from YouTube. She'd been a musical prodigy, teaching at the Berklee College of Music by the age of twenty. Now she was a star.

The crowd at Jazz Alley was older, mostly in their forties and fifties. Anita took a seat at a small round table and ordered a Shirley Temple.

She'd hoped that watching Esperanza perform would fill her heart with resolve and inspiration, but as the show went on, she only got more and more depressed. Here was this ridiculously talented artist living her life as loud as a bullhorn. And here was Anita, watching from the darkness, destined for an insignificant and utterly silent existence. At the beginning of application season, Anita had suggested she might apply to a couple of music schools alongside all the Ivy League universities her father was so excited about. The resultant tantrum had been so huge that Luisa later swore she'd picked up the phone and dialed the first two-thirds of 9-1-1.

When Anita got out of the club, she realized she hadn't looked at her phone in hours. Sure enough, there were two dozen missed calls and almost as many messages, all from HOME. She listened to one, but stopped it after the first few furious words and cleared her in-box with a tap.

It was a weeknight, so there weren't many people out on the streets. Anita wandered down toward the water, into the heart of homeless Seattle. Cardboard boxes and sleeping bags. Unkempt hair and hollow faces and clothes the color of pigeon wings. From under the bench of a bus stop, a white fragment of eye followed her across First Avenue. She went all the way down to the wrought-iron fence, bent into curlicues and spirals, beyond which Puget Sound sparkled blackly, and grabbed hold of the smooth metal bars. She lifted herself off the ground, imagined rising up and up and over the topmost prong and out into the water.

"Hey, sister."

She turned around, for some reason expecting to find a friend. But the man standing behind her was a stranger, tall and black, with a long scar snaking across the bottom half of his face.

"Hey," she said.

"You looking for someone?"

"No."

"You shouldn't be alone out here this time of night. It's not safe."

Before she could say anything else, there was the sound of a car door slamming, and a cop was making his way toward them with a long, aggressive stride.

"There a problem here?" he asked.

"No problem," the stranger said.

The cop looked at Anita.

"No, sir."

He didn't seem to believe it. "Why don't you come along with me, miss? As for you"—he pointed at the stranger—"you stay there. My partner wants to talk to you for a minute."

"Whatever, man."

Anita and the cop walked across the street, past the festive flicker of the cruiser.

"What are you doing on your own down here, young lady?"

"Nothing."

"You need a ride?"

"My car's just up the street."

He put a hand on her shoulder. "You go straight there, okay? Pretty girl like you should be more careful."

"Thanks."

She climbed back up to First Avenue; the incline was so steep that it bent her backward, pointed her at the sky like a telescope. A lone blue star floated out among all the white ones, like a mutation. Anita felt pinned in place, caught between the dead eye of that star and the cold care of the police officer behind her. She didn't want to go back to the car, but she didn't want to stay where she was, either. She would have been happy just to disappear.

Whatever it is, it's not worth it.

She said the words aloud, but they were hollow now, no more meaning in them than in that distant will-o'-the-wisp adrift in the sky. Suzie O was wrong. Anita wasn't miserable because of the way things were. She was miserable because she kept hoping things would change. If she could eradicate the hope, she could eradicate the sadness.

It was time to go home.

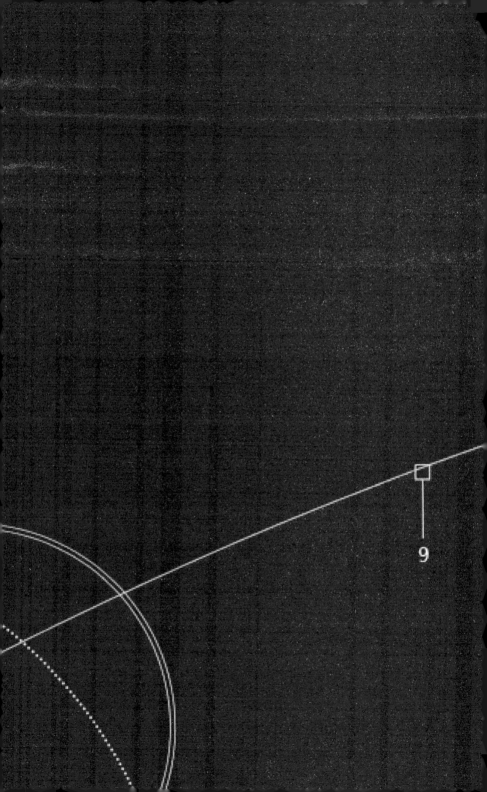

9

Eliza

WAS THERE ANYTHING IN THE WHOLE ENTIRE WORLD WORSE THAN WAKING UP NEXT TO someone you didn't want to wake up next to?

His name was Parker—at least she could remember that much. He was asleep on his stomach, blond hair curling around his ears like cotton candy, another little patch at the base of his spine. Eliza was careful not to wake him as she rose from the bed and got dressed. It took her fifteen minutes in front of the bathroom mirror to scrape away the telltale signs of an alcohol-fueled one-night stand. She brushed her unwashed hair into a wild bun and stuck it with a pair of black chopsticks. The result was presentable enough, though all the primping in the world would do nothing for the pounding headache. For that, there was only her traditional mixture of coconut water and Red Bull—what her friend Madeline used to call a Bull Nuts. Breakfast accomplished.

Which only left the question of what to do about Parker. With all the discharge forms and final check-ups, Eliza's dad wouldn't be home before two or three in the afternoon, but this skeeze had to be gone by then. And he'd have to go on foot, because Eliza had driven him here. She left a note on the bedside table: *If you're reading this, you should be out of my house.* Too mean? Maybe. But she was way too hungover to care.

It wasn't until she saw the digital clock in the car that she realized how early it was. Still, spending an extra hour at school was way better than spending it alone in the house with a passed-out mistake. She turned the radio to the news—a monotonous recitation of international catastrophes—then flipped the station. Eighties music was undoubtedly better for the soul.

The parking lot at Hamilton was mostly empty. Eliza turned up the radio, got a blanket out of the trunk, and laid it across the warm humming heat of the hood. She leaned back against the windshield . . .

Someone was shaking her by the foot. Eliza opened her eyes to a gray-white sky, uniform but for that wicked blue speck of light. What was it still doing up there?

"Good morning, Mr. Magpie."

She sat up and practically collided with the implacable grin of Andy Rowen. He was wearing baggy jeans and an unzipped gray hoodie over a T-shirt featuring the pale, spaced-out faces of the Cure.

"Rough night?" he asked.

"A little."

"Didn't Blondie deliver the goods?"

She ignored the question. "What time is it?"

"By my watch"—he pulled up his sleeve and stared hard at the empty white expanse of his wrist—"about halfway through first period."

"Seriously? Fuck!" Eliza jumped down from the hood.

"What's the big deal? I always get to school around this time, and lo, the world continueth to spin."

Her book bag wasn't in the backseat, or in the trunk. In her rush to get away from Parker, she must have left it at home.

"Shit!" She slammed her fist into the side of the car.

"Whoa," Andy said. "Chill out, man. It's just class."

Eliza took a deep breath, then spoke with quiet scorn. "This may come as a shock to you, but some of us actually care about stuff. I'm sure you think that's lame or gay or whatever, but we can have another talk about it ten years from now, when you're still living in your mom's basement and working at Chipotle and the rest of us have lives."

She stormed off toward campus, already feeling guilty for lashing out; it wasn't Andy she was pissed at.

"Jeez," he said, "that must have been some shitty sex."

"It was," Eliza said, without stopping.

But she was glad to hear him laughing behind her.

She couldn't focus during chemistry class. The blue star kept popping back into her head, like the memory of a bad dream. And every time it did, her heart began to race.

She didn't think to ask about it until lunch, and only then because she happened to pass by the table in the corner of the lunchroom, farthest from the windows. Maybe it was judgmental, to think of it as the "nerd table," and yet there was no getting around the fact that a school had its factions, and one of those factions happened to consist primarily of intelligent, not very attractive, not particularly socially capable boys, along with a few girls who hadn't yet learned how to dress or put on makeup or pretend to be dumber than they were. It was the girls who eyed Eliza with suspicion when she sat down at the table, as if she were an emissary from a tribe of Amazon women sweeping in to steal the menfolk away. The boys tried to look blasé, but they couldn't hide a bubbling undercurrent of fandom.

"Hey," she said. "I'm Eliza."

A boy with thick brown hair styled in an unfortunate mullet reached out a hand. He had an air of authority about him, confident in his element.

"Hello, Eliza. I'm James."

"Hi, James."

He introduced the rest of the table, but Eliza didn't absorb any of their names.

"You're here because of Ardor, aren't you?" James's eyes had the bright, almost manic intensity of extreme intelligence. Eliza knew she was reasonably smart, but brilliant people still freaked her out. She didn't like the idea that somebody might be seeing more of her than she wanted them to see.

"What's Ardor?"

One of the girls answered without looking up from some Japanese comic. "It's JPL's name for the asteroid. ARDR-1388."

"Ardor," James said, "is a near-Earth object, or NEO, a category including asteroids, meteoroids, and comets that orbit close to our planet. The Jet Propulsion Laboratory keeps tabs on all of them. It's part of their job."

"Is it big?"

"Big enough to wipe us all out."

"So why haven't I heard about it before?"

James raised his eyebrows. "You regularly visit the JPL website for updates on NEOs? You keep up with contemporary astronomy journals?"

"I do not."

"So there you go."

Eliza did her best to smile through this meteor shower of condescension. "Thank you, James. That was very helpful." She stood up. Across the lunchroom, Peter Roeslin and his still-girlfriend Stacy looked over at Eliza at exactly the same time. She pretended not to see them.

"Hey," James said, waving to get her attention, "if you're wondering whether or not to be afraid of Ardor, you shouldn't be."

"I'm not afraid."

"Sure you're not," he said, as if conceding a point he knew he'd already won. "But just in case you were *considering* being afraid at some point in the future, I wanted you to know that there's little rational basis for it. The odds of collision are very slim. In reality, everything we ought to be concerned about is already right here on planet Earth."

"I thought you said not to be afraid."

"I said don't be afraid of the asteroid. This is the twenty-first century. The oceans are rising. Mad dictators have access to nuclear weapons. Corporatism and the dumbing down of the media have destroyed the very foundations of democracy. Anyone who isn't afraid is a moron."

There was something violent in the way James said that last word—"moron"—as if he were at that very moment surrounded by them, and they were his enemies.

"Thanks again, James."

"Don't mention it. Stay safe."

After school, a few dozen students assembled on the grass outside the refectory to sky watch. Someone had brought a telescope from the science building, though it was being used primarily to look down people's throats and up into the offices on the top floor of Bliss Hall. Everyone was joking around and having a good time, but Eliza couldn't shake a sense of foreboding. Even if James was right, it wasn't easy to be relaxed about a giant rock flaming through the sky at a gajillion miles an hour.

When she got back to the condo, her dad was sitting in front of the TV, watching the news. Even though she knew he was equally sick wherever he happened to be, Eliza always thought her dad looked about a million times healthier at home than he did in that beige, fluorescent hellhole they called a hospital—all beeping machinery and mechanical beds and death smells.

"Hey, Dad."

"Hey, Gaga. Looks like someone left a love letter for you on the kitchen table."

A piece of notebook paper with a childish scrawl on the front was propped up like a little tent: *Thanks for stranding me in the suburbs, bitch.*

"You wanna talk about it?" her dad asked.

"Not even a little."

She sat down in a puffy red chair next to the couch. On the TV, a couple of news anchors were talking about the asteroid, which appeared in a CGI rendering as a colorless rock pocked with craters, like a small misshapen moon.

". . . our conspicuous new friend will be with us for at least a few more weeks. Labeled ARDR-1388 by the scientists who first discovered it, the asteroid is now affectionately known as Ardor."

The CGI disappeared, replaced with a white-bearded man with wire-rim spectacles and altogether too much enthusiasm. The subtitle said he was Michael Prupick, professor of astronomy and astrophysics at the University of Washington.

"If Ardor has broken its orbit, we'll be able to watch it blaze across our sky on its way out of the Milky Way and into deep space. Near-Earth objects may get a bad rap in Hollywood blockbusters, but they're incredibly useful to astronomers, not to mention the fact that mining companies are researching ways to exploit asteroids just like this one for rare elements in the very near future. In short, we could not be more excited about Ardor's appearance."

The news anchors popped back up onto the screen.

"Sales of telescopes at local camping and toy stores are already up twenty percent this week—"

Eliza's father muted the television.

"So what poor slob did you strand in the suburbs?"

"Did I not say we wouldn't be discussing that?"

"Did I agree?"

They sat there in silence for a few seconds, while the talking heads on the TV continued their Muppet-y mouthing, but Eliza could feel her dad building up the energy for another push.

"It's just that I need to know you're gonna be able to take care of yourself. With me heading toward, you know, the margins of the picture, and your mom and everything—"

"Don't start."

"I'm just saying that stuff like this is on my mind, all right? Fucking sue me."

Eliza thought the rules were understood, even if they'd never been stated explicitly. She and her father were never to bring up either (1) the fact that, within a year, he'd almost certainly be dead, or (2) the fact that Eliza's mother had fallen in love with another man and moved to Hawaii with him. And now her dad was breaking both rules at once. She got up and sat down next to him on the couch.

"Dad, what's going on?"

"Nothing. I don't know. I think it's that fucking rock. It's got me all worked up."

"I asked some kids at school about it. They said we shouldn't worry."

Her dad shrugged. "Maybe. But just in case, could you humor me on one thing?"

She already knew what he was going to say. "No."

"Come on!"

"We've been through this. If Mom wants to talk, she can call."

"She tried that."

"Not since last year."

"Because every time she tried to talk to you, you'd just tell her what a shitty person she was and hang up!" Her dad was actually shouting at her; Eliza couldn't remember the last time he'd done that.

"She deserved it."

"No, she didn't! I told her she could go, Eliza!" His voice got quiet again, and he put his hand on top of hers. "I told her she could go. Because she was in love. And arguing with that is pointless. It would be like"—he gestured toward the TV—"trying to stop that asteroid with a fucking BB gun. But I know it tore her apart to leave."

"She still did it."

Her dad nodded. "Yeah. She did."

"And I don't forgive her."

"Well, that's another thing. I'm just asking you to talk to her."

Eliza rolled her eyes. "Jesus. Fine. I'll think about it."

"Good." He patted her hand. "So what's for dinner?"

"I was thinking I'd make something."

"Oh yeah?"

"Yeah. Like, make a call to Pagliacci's for delivery."

Her dad smiled, one of those wistful smiles, like he was already missing something that wasn't gone yet. The kind that made her want to cry.

"Works for me," he said.

Anita

ANITA HAD PREPARED HERSELF FOR THE INTERROGATION. SHE HAD PREPARED HERSELF FOR the lecture. She had prepared herself for the threats, the grounding, the silent treatment, the wagging finger, the shaking head, and all the general parental bullshit that was bound to result from her unprecedented escape from Casa Graves the previous week. What she had not prepared herself for, however, was the loss of her car key. With it went the very soul of adulthood—the freedom to be alone. She was under constant surveillance now. Every morning her father drove her to Hamilton on his way to work, and every afternoon her mother would arrive promptly at three forty-five to take her home. Even inside the house, Anita wasn't left to herself. Every twenty minutes or so, someone would knock on her bedroom door to ensure she hadn't pulled some kind of Rapunzel or Juliet and shimmied out the window.

An only slightly lesser evil was the talk radio her father listened to in the car.

"A trickle of news about our friend Ardor from the eggheads over at NASA today," said some loudmouth host that you could practically hear getting fatter and dumber as he spoke. "You'd think they'd have something better than this, given that all they do these days is spend our tax dollars and complain about how they don't get enough of our tax dollars, but hey, what do I know? Anyhoo, initial estimates placed the asteroid about two million miles away from Earth as it passed through our solar system. But now they're saying it'll be more like half a million miles, which in terms of deep space is a pretty close shave. And it's funny, you know, those NASA guys have been drowning us, *literally* drowning us in all this talk about man-made climate change and holes in the ozone layer and all these problems that we know aren't really an issue, and now we've got this asteroid that we're gonna be dodging like one of those bullets in *The Matrix*, and the eggheads just say, 'Oh well, we didn't quite see it, sorry about that.' So maybe these guys need to adjust their priorities a little bit, is what I'm saying. Back in five after this."

"Are your science teachers talking to you about global warming?" Anita's father asked, turning the radio down.

"A little."

He shook his head. "Of course they are. I'll give you some books to read when you get home. And you'll read them."

"Okay."

The only good news was that today was a Wednesday, which meant there was a student council meeting after school. These meetings could last anywhere from twenty minutes to two hours, and Anita's mother could hardly be expected to just sit around the parking lot waiting. That meant Luisa would be coming, and Luisa could always be counted on to help Anita out. The goal was to get the meeting over with as quickly as possible. If Anita were lucky, she might end up with enough time to get a burger at Dick's on Capitol Hill. Though it had only been a week, she yearned for a taste of the outside world like a prisoner ten years into a life sentence.

Hamilton bylaws required that student council be made up of one boy and one girl from each class. Anita represented the seniors along with Peter Roeslin, the basketball player. The juniors were Damien Durkee and Krista Asahara. Krista was one of those hyper-earnest over-achievers who couldn't understand why anyone would ever disagree with her about anything ever. Also, she was pretty obviously in love with Peter. The sophomore class was represented by Charlie Howard and Julia Whyel, and the freshmen by Ajay Vasher and Nickie Hill. All the underclassmen pretty much deferred to Krista on everything.

Anita called the meeting to order, ran over the minutes from the previous session (on the plausibility of once-a-month vegan lunches and fielding a Hamilton foosball team), and laid out the agenda. The only pressing issue was Olot, the schoolwide formal dance where the girls invited the boys, which was in need of a theme. As usual, Krista was the first one with a Statue-of-Liberty raised hand and the idea to go with it.

"So the newspapers are saying that Ardor—you know, the asteroid?—is going to pass by us around the same week as the dance. So what if we went with some kind of space thing? Not science fiction-y, but more, like, astronomy, all planets and stars and stuff."

"Sounds great to me," Anita said, already seeing the light at the end of the tunnel.

"We can cover all the pillars and the walls in black felt," Nickie said, picking up on Krista's theme. "And we can use Christmas lights to make stars. It'll be super pretty but also cheap."

Ajay always chimed in when budgeting was at issue. "We could ask people to bring lights in from home. Everyone has a box in their basement, and usually even if they're dead, it's just a bad bulb."

Krista was bright as a new bulb herself at these promising signs that her concept was a hit.

"Shall we vote on it?" Anita asked, glancing around the room. "All in favor of the theme of Olot being something space-related, say aye." There was a chorus of ayes. "Perfect. Let's brainstorm ideas on our own, and then we can decide on the best ones at our next meeting."

Krista gave a couple of weak, thudding high fives to Nickie and Ajay.

"Well, that's everything on the agenda. Is there anything else anyone wants to discuss?"

Anita was afraid Charlie would bring up his favorite subject: the impossible, irreverent, and yet strangely divisive issue of allowing marijuana use on school grounds, now that it was legal in the state at large. But he seemed just as eager to get out of there as she was.

"Then it looks like we're done," Anita said. "Thanks, everyone, for coming—"

"What we're doing here is a joke."

Heads turned. Peter sat slouched in his chair, looking uncharacteristically morose. He didn't tend to say much in student council meetings, unless the conversation turned to something involving athletics or nutrition.

"What are you talking about, Peter?"

"I mean, aren't we supposed to care about stuff other than just dances and foosball? Could we maybe try to do one thing that actually matters in the real world?"

"Like what?" Anita said, unable to keep the frustration out of her voice. The truth was, she actually agreed with him. Sometimes it seemed like all they did in here was pad out their résumés while enjoying some pizza on Hamilton's dime. But did he have to choose today of all days to develop a conscience about it?

"I don't know," Peter said. "It's just that the world's so messed up. Even here at school, we've got all these kids who are probably gonna drop out at some point, or at least not go to college. Can't we do something about that?"

A long silence. Then, from the deep well of her crush, Krista hoisted up a fresh bucket of enthusiasm: "Totally, Peter."

Anita took a deep breath. The meeting wasn't over anymore. Not by a long shot.

"Ideas?" she asked.

Peter was exactly the kind of guy that Anita's parents wished she would date. Or maybe "wished" was a little strong—her parents probably would have been pleased as punch if their daughter never even spoke to a boy until after she'd graduated from college. But if she *were* to get involved in the dating scene, Peter would have been their first-draft pick. He was an athlete, which wasn't great, but an athlete who was going to Stanford, which meant he'd have a career no matter what. He looked the part too—tall, attractive, and as white as the day was long (not that her parents were self-hating or anything, just that they associated white values with material success, while they seemed to suspect most black kids of being, at worst, drug dealers and, at best, freeloading bohemians). Anita could almost see herself with a guy like that. She would have bet good money that Peter was stellar at the whole "impressing the folks" thing, and probably looked damn good with his shirt off. The only problem, and it wasn't a small one, was that he was just a little bit stupid. Not direly stupid. Not pushing-on-the-pull-door or 2 + 2 = 5 stupid. Just not quick to get the joke. Not sharp. And without that spark, for all his Abercrombie & Fitch looks, he did less than nothing for her.

The student council meeting lasted for two hours and fifteen minutes, in which time they discussed everything from a soup kitchen in the refectory, to weekly after-school lectures on subjects like world hunger and climate change, to an old-fashioned bake sale. Peter was uniformly psyched about each new idea, along with Krista and the underclassmen, which left Anita to be the voice of reason.

"We won't get an okay from the administration on bringing homeless people on campus."

"You can schedule all the lectures you want, but you can't make people go."

"Bake sales don't make money."

By the end of the session, the only thing they'd managed to agree on was drafting a group of volunteer tutors to help struggling kids with their homework. It wasn't exactly saving the planet or inspiring world peace, but it was something. Krista was so excited by their collective progress that she hugged everyone good-bye after the meeting.

Anita practically sprinted out of the building. There wasn't time for burgers anymore, but she could at least get a snack and a few minutes to herself.

Luisa, waiting patiently in the roundabout, rolled down the window of the Audi.

"Hey, Luisa, you mind if I run to Jamba Juice?"

"You don't want me to drive?"

"I'd rather get the excercise, if that's okay."

"Of course. And your friend will go too?"

Anita turned around to find Peter standing right behind her.

"That's a great idea," he said. "I could totally go for a Berry Razz-matazz."

"Oh. Uh, sure. See you in a bit."

Luisa smiled so broadly at Peter that Anita was actually embarrassed.

They began to walk. It was raining, but the kind of rain where the droplets are so light that they float around like snowflakes in a blizzard, without any discernible slant. Anita knew there couldn't be anything romantic behind Peter's desire to hang out with her. He had a girlfriend, a paragon of the kind of bland and curveless beauty advertised on the cover of just about every magazine in the country. And though there'd been a rumor going around that he'd cheated on her somewhere along the line, Anita didn't put much stock in gossip. People were always trying to bring down the folks on top. Still, it was weird to be alone with him, given that they'd hardly ever spoken outside of student council.

"That was so energizing, wasn't it?" he said.

"What was?"

"You know, trying to make a difference."

Anita couldn't help but laugh. "Peter, what is going on with you today? You've basically slept through student council all year, and now you're giving speeches about social responsibility? What's your deal?"

Peter smiled sheepishly. "Yeah, I guess I must seem sorta nuts, huh? I'm just . . . working out some stuff."

"What kind of stuff?"

"It's hard to explain." He paused, then: "Anita, do you ever worry that you're wasting your life?"

Out of the mouth of babes, it was said, though that was probably meant to refer to babies, rather than attractive teenage boys. But of course Anita worried about whether she was wasting her life. She worried about it all the time. Maybe it was blasphemy, but she felt like God had intended for her to be a singer. Otherwise, why had she been born with both the talent and the passion for music? And if she allowed her dream to die on the vine, wouldn't it be the same as disobeying a direct order from God? Was that really so much better than disobeying her father?

"I think everybody does," Anita said. "But we're only eighteen. You can't have wasted your life at eighteen. We haven't even *lived* our lives yet."

"But you have to decide, you know? It's like that poem with the road in the woods. You don't want to end up running down the wrong road, because you'll probably never get back to that place again. The place where the road splits, I mean."

"Actually, the point of that poem is that it doesn't really matter which road you pick."

Peter looked confused. "Are you sure?"

"Yeah. But hey, poets don't know everything. If they did, they wouldn't always be dying of syphilis in garrets in Paris."

"Right."

Jamba Juice was mostly empty, but Anita's attention was immediately drawn to the girl making drinks behind the bar. She moved smoothly between the tubs of frozen fruit and the industrial-strength blenders, all the while bouncing along to a different beat than the Top 40 crap blaring from the overhead speakers. She was black, slightly overweight, but with an easy arrogance that Anita felt pretty sure slightly overweight white girls weren't capable of. A pair of in-ear headphones snaked up from her jeans pocket and disappeared into her dreads.

"What are you listening to?" Anita asked.

The girl pulled out an earbud. "What's that?"

"What are you listening to?"

"Myself," she said, grinning widely. "Why? You into music?"

"Isn't everybody?"

The girl pointed to a little table by the door. "Grab a flyer on the way out. My band's playing the Tractor Tavern next week. You and your boy should come down. I'm the best thing since sliced bread."

"He's not my boy," Anita said, but the girl had already put her earbud back in. "Can you believe that?" she asked Peter, but he was staring hard at the smoothie girl, his forehead creased and his eyes all squinted up, as if he suspected her of something. It was a second before Anita realized he was *thinking*. He was the kind of guy who had a unique facial expression dedicated to *thinking*.

"What is it?" she asked.

He stepped close to her, speaking quietly. "I always figured that working some crappy job like this would be the worst thing that could ever happen to me. But I've got a funny feeling that this girl knows what she's doing a lot better than I do. I mean, can you remember the last time you felt *that good*?"

It was true, the girl did seem to be amazingly cheerful and self-assured. And though Anita knew Peter's question had been rhetorical, it suddenly came back to her: the last time she'd felt *that good*. Ironically, she'd been standing in front of an open coffin at the time. It was her aunt's funeral, and Anita had been asked to sing "Abide with Me" at the service—the one performance her parents had no excuse for canceling. Afterward, her uncle Bobby had told her she ought to think about studying voice in college.

Anita had laughed. "I don't think my parents would like that very much."

"But you'd like it, wouldn't you?"

"I guess."

"So do it. You can make your own decisions, Anita."

But that was easy enough for him to say. He wasn't Benjamin Graves's greatest investment. And investments weren't supposed to make their own decisions; they were just supposed to *mature*.

Anita watched the smoothie girl—the best thing since sliced bread—as she tapped the side of the blender, filling the paper cup just up to the rim. All the while, her head traced a sinuous figure eight to the beat of the music. The beat of *her* music.

Peter

"SO WHERE EXACTLY ARE WE GOING?" MISERY ASKED.

Peter put on his FBI-agent voice. "That's classified information, missy."

From the passenger seat, Stacy took a break from texting long enough to say, "I don't like secrets."

"Have some faith," Cartier said. "My boy wouldn't steer us wrong."

Peter was pretty sure that none of them would have been there if he'd told them where they were actually going. That was why he'd only dropped some vague hints about food: for Cartier, he casually mentioned the possibility of spicy chicken wings; for Stacy, the single magic word "macrobiotic." Misery, however, wasn't so easily tempted (he wasn't sure she ate anything at all, unless inhaling a pack a day of Camel Lights counted), so he'd needed his parents' help to "young lady" her into acquiescence.

Their destination was in Belltown, where most of the city's best restaurants were located. It was one of the strange ironies of Seattle, that the nicest and the shittiest neighborhoods somehow coexisted in the same physical space, like parallel dimensions. Peter parked in front of a trendy coffee shop as brightly lit as a sports stadium and led his three oblivious charges past the electric screech coming out of the Crocodile. They stopped in front of a typical-looking restaurant called Friendly Forks. Inside, waiters were scurrying around between the empty tables, adjusting place settings and lighting candles.

"Wait a minute," Misery said. "Is this that place where they get all the drug addicts and criminals and stuff to make the meals?"

"Well, they also accept noncriminal volunteers, but yes."

His little sister smiled. "Wicked."

"Are you sure it's any good?" Stacy asked. "What if they put razor blades in the lasagna or something?"

"We didn't come here to eat," Peter said.

A gorgeous girl with honey-colored skin and a shaved head stood just inside the door, looking over a reservation book the size of an atlas.

"Volunteers?" she asked.

Peter nodded. "I'm Peter Roeslin. This is Samantha Roeslin, Cart—"

Peter's sister interrupted, "I go by Misery."

The hostess looked Misery up and down—from her Sharpie-embellished sneakers to the wisps of emerald hair sticking out from under her black woolen cap. "Nice to meet you, Misery. I'm Keira. Everyone follow me."

Stacy tugged at Peter's sleeve. "What's going on?" He just smiled innocently and shrugged.

Keira led them across the restaurant floor and into the kitchen, which was already about a thousand degrees and bustling with people who didn't look remotely pleased at the arrival of a bunch of high school students. A radio played something Spanish-sounding—all plinking guitars, piercing trumpets, and tight harmonies. Keira tapped the shoulder of an enormous mound of human being, who turned around as if pushing his way through a heavy revolving door. Where most people were made up of ovals and circles, he appeared to have been constructed out of cubes—a cube head on a cube body. He had a small goatee and long sideburns, and delicate vines of ivy-green tattoo spiraled from the top of his white collar halfway up the trellis of his neck. He held a large, gleaming knife made small by his huge cubic hand.

"Kids, this is Felipe, our head chef," Keira said. "Felipe, these are your kids. Enjoy."

Cartier watched her go, unconsciously letting out a low whistle. He turned back into the unsmiling mug of the head chef.

"You checkin' out my girlfriend, *ese*?"

The room went silent. In the years Peter had known Cartier, he'd never seen his friend physically intimidated by anyone. But staring into the eyes of an enormous, knife-wielding chef with more tattoos than a player for the Denver Nuggets, Cartier seemed to shrink.

"Dude, I'm sorry. I didn't know she—"

Suddenly Felipe emitted a laugh proportional to his size, and the rest of the kitchen joined in.

"I'm just messing with you, man! You shoulda seen your face, though. Woo!"

One of Cartier's best qualities was the ability to laugh at himself, and his smile was genuine as he took the knife that Felipe offered him, handle first.

"Does that mean she's not your girlfriend?" he asked.

"She's like my little sister, man, which still puts her out of your league." Felipe led them over to a low counter of white plastic, gouged and stained and gored with tomato pips. "So we're gonna be moving you around a lot tonight, station to station, depending on what we need. Most of the work you'll be doing won't be for dinner, but this catering gig we've got tomorrow. For now, you're all on vegetable duty. You wash, you dry, you peel, you chop. Basically, whatever I or anyone else in this kitchen tells you to do, you do." He handed a black hairnet to Stacy, who held it as if it were a dead spider.

"I have to wear this?"

"Health regulations," Felipe said.

"Just me?"

"Your friends got hats on already. Speaking of which, any of you touch your hair, your face, your ass, or anything other than a knife or a piece of food, you wash your hands. You're gonna be washing your hands all the time, starting right now. And use some fucking soap, yeah?"

Felipe waddled off toward the range.

"I like him," Cartier said.

"I can't believe this," Stacy whispered, wrapping her hair up into a bun and slipping the hairnet over the top. "It's probably, like, *never* been cleaned."

"Very white trash chic," Misery said.

"Shut up."

"Make me."

They cleaned and chopped vegetables for close to an hour; then Felipe split them up. Peter and Misery were given a half-dozen ingredients and a simple recipe for vinaigrette, while Cartier and Stacy were taught how to close out tabs and run credit cards on the computer. Doors opened at six thirty, and as soon as the first few customers had put in their orders, the kitchen went nuts. Someone was always yelling at Peter to do something—usually just to get out of the way. The radio was turned down slightly, but the manic energy of mariachi music still permeated the room. Stacy cut her finger while peeling a potato and looked like she might pass out. After that, they put her on dish duty. There was a slight letup around eight o'clock (time enough for Stacy to take Peter into the alley behind the restaurant and ominously inform him of the "long talk" they were going to have later), and then everything started up again. Peter was crushing peppercorns with a mortar and pestle when the music gave way to a short news bulletin in Spanish. Felipe was closest to the radio, and he was the one who shouted for quiet.

Beneath the sizzling and spattering, the announcer's voice was barely audible. He spoke Spanish at that rapid clip that made Peter wonder how even a native could understand it. Only a couple of words stood out from the gibberish: *presidente*, Ardor, *emergencia*.

"What's he saying?" Stacy asked, and was immediately shushed.

The segment wrapped up, and a commercial jingled to life in its place. Everyone looked dead serious.

Felipe shut off the radio. "Back to work," he said. "We've still got customers."

By the time the last guest called for the check, the four volunteers were sweat-swollen, smoke-soaked, and sore all over. They shook hands with Felipe ("Come back soon," he said, in a tone of voice implying that he didn't expect to see any of them ever again) and, after Cartier got shot down by Keira ("I have a boyfriend in grad school, player"), walked on throbbing feet back to Peter's car.

"Turn on the news," Stacy said. Peter flicked through the stations until he heard the calm cadences of public radio.

"—numerous examples of the president speaking to the American people simply to allay the possibility of panic. This kind of thing has become something of an action-movie trope, so the very idea of something like Ardor is frightening to the average person. But any astronomer can tell you that there's more chance you'll be struck by lightning in the next thirty seconds than that an asteroid will collide with the Earth. The simple fact of a press conference is not a reason to worry."

"Thank you, Mr. Fisher."

"My pleasure."

"That was Mr. Mark Fisher, one-time director of FEMA, now a professor at Georgetown University. Whether there's any true cause for alarm will probably not be known until the president delivers his speech. Join us here at NPR for live coverage of the event tomorrow night."

"Jesus," Stacy said. "Do you think something's going to happen?"

"Nah," Cartier said. "That's crazy. Space is so freaking big. It would be like throwing a penny up in the air and hitting an airplane."

"Maybe this is our punishment for trying to destroy the planet ourselves," Misery said.

Stacy scoffed. "Don't you get tired of being so gloomy all the time?"

"I don't know. Do you get tired of being so dumb all the time?"

"Miz!" Peter said.

"What? She started it."

Peter and Stacy had been dating for more than three years, but the animosity between his girlfriend and his sister had never been worse. And while he didn't exactly blame Misery, there was no getting around the fact that Stacy was basically the same person now that she'd been at the beginning of their relationship, whereas Misery had completely transformed. Ever since she fell in with Bobo at the beginning of freshman year, she'd been on a downward slope: drinking, smoking, blowing off her homework, and God only knew what else. She and Peter barely ever talked to each other like friends anymore; he inevitably ended up sounding like some kind of third parent, or else a PSA about drugs.

"Well, that was a weird night," Cartier said when Peter dropped him off. "But it was worth it just to meet that Keira chick."

"You'll get her next time."

"No doubt, brother. See you tomorrow."

Peter wished he could have just gone inside with Cartier, to watch some TV and maybe sneak a beer or two out of the fridge, but he had a date with an argument. At least Stacy was good enough to wait until they were standing alone at her front door before she started yelling.

"So what the hell was that?"

"What was what?"

"Taking me to that . . . place."

"I don't know. Just a change of pace, I guess."

"We already applied to college, Peter. We don't need to do shit like that."

"I thought you might enjoy it."

"Well, I didn't! I hated it!" Stacy's cheekbones were all sharp and serious, and there was that familiar little cinder in her eyes. She was prettiest when she was angry, and that was saying something, because she was pretty all the time. Peter couldn't believe it when they first got together, when they first touched, when he first saw her naked. What had he ever done to deserve something so beautiful? But his sense of gratitude had faded over the years, giving way to a constant low-grade irritation. That was the reason he'd kissed Eliza in the photo lab last year. Because for just a second there, he hadn't wanted the beautiful social queen. He'd wanted something different. Something more peaceful or pensive. Or maybe just something *more*.

"Why?" he asked, and the exhale of that one syllable felt huge, like smashing through a window with his bare fist.

"Why what?"

"Why did you hate it? I mean, we did a good thing tonight, and you should feel good about that."

"I can't even deal with how much of an asshole you're being right now," she said, then stalked into her house and slammed the door.

Peter walked slowly back to the car.

"She looked pissed," Misery said.

"She was."

"Yeah. I'm sure she would have had a better time torturing puppies or something."

Peter didn't have the energy to bother defending his girlfriend. "Did you have a good time at least?"

Misery slouched down in her seat, pulled her black cap over her eyes. "Yeah. But only because ex-cons are badass."

Peter smiled. And totally unbidden, totally unfairly, a thought came to him: Eliza wouldn't have been bothered by a night like this. He could picture himself working next to her at the vegetable station, quietly slicing up beets, then going out afterward to some foreign film or something. Sitting alone in the back row of the movie theater, their fingers interlocked, and then leaning over, turning her face to his . . .

Peter knew that thinking about being with Eliza was a kind of cheating, but he couldn't help it. The fantasies fell like dead leaves from somewhere above his conscious mind, more and more often every day. And no matter how often he swept them away, they always came back.

That night, when he gasped awake sometime in the hours before sunrise to find Ardor framed perfectly in his bedroom window, gleaming like the eye of some sleepless demon, his defenses dropped away, and he allowed himself to imagine Eliza slipping into bed beside him, kissing him like she had that first time. The fantasy led him gently back down into his dreams.

It was the last good night's sleep he'd have for a long time.

Andy

THEY MET UP TO WATCH THE SPEECH AT ANDY'S PLACE, A.K.A. THE MA-IN-LAW, WHICH everyone agreed was the sickest crib in the greater Seattle area. Basically, after his parents split, Andy's mom married some dude named Phil, who worked for Microsoft and made bank. Phil had a couple of other kids from a previous marriage, both of whom were already done with college and making bank themselves, so he figured he was more or less done with being a dad (a conclusion Andy's *actual* dad had come to right after the divorce). Meanwhile, Andy's mom just wanted to chill out and spend Phil's money in peace. Their house, a big old wood-frame built in the sixties, had a separate apartment below it, which Andy's mom called a "mother-in-law apartment" (now simplified to "the ma-in-law"). It was a split-level deal, with kitchen, bedroom, and bathroom upstairs, and the small bottom floor devoted to passive entertainment: a couch, a couple of beanbag chairs, and a TV with a PS4.

Everybody else was already there by the time Andy got home (Bobo had a key, and basically came and went like an honorary roommate). Kevin and Jess were in the beanbags, passing a pipe back and forth.

"Yo, Andy," Jess said. "You drinking or smoking?" He was wearing a backward baseball cap and a Nets jersey, holding the pipe in one hand and, in the other, a can of Monster that was probably spiked. Jess was biologically a girl, but he'd started dressing like a dude last year, and told everyone he was now a "he." After high school was over, he planned to get a job and save up for gender-reassignment surgery. For now, he was taking some kind of testosterone supplement every few days; a couple of thick black hairs had begun to grow on his chin. Whatever, Andy figured. To each his/her own.

"Maybe in a bit."

"Hey, Andy." Misery was stretched out along the couch like a cat, a thin belt of white skin visible below the hem of her T-shirt. She'd dyed her hair orange a couple of days ago, and it made her look like a Creamsicle.

"Hey, Miz. Where's Bobo at?"

"Kitchen."

Andy climbed the half set of stairs. Bobo was standing in front of the stove, reading the instructions on the back of a package of macaroni and cheese.

"Hey, man. You making dinner?"

"I'm straight-up sick of this," Bobo said, holding up the box. "Let's order."

"I'm broke."

"So hit up Kevin."

"Dude, you do it. I feel like shit when I ask him."

"You drink his beer same as me."

"I know, but—"

Without warning, Bobo whipped the box of mac and cheese

straight at Andy's head. It slammed into the wall and exploded into a firework rattle of uncooked shells, peppering Andy's neck like shrapnel.

"I said go hit up Kevin," Bobo repeated.

Andy groaned. "Fine. But I'm not cleaning this macaroni up."

"That makes two of us, yo."

Andy crunched over the pasta on his way back downstairs.

"Hey," he announced, as if he were talking to the whole room. "Cupboard's bare up there. Maybe we should order some pizza or something. Anybody wanna make the call?"

Kevin, who was holding down a massive hit from the pipe, raised his hand. His parents were totally loaded and, unlike Andy's stepdad, were happy to spread the wealth around. They owned a car dealership in South Seattle, and their last name, Hellings, adorned the plastic license-plate frames of half the cars in the city. In other words, Kevin was *set*. Bobo said that if they all played their cards right, they could be mooching off him for decades. Andy felt bad about it sometimes, but every friendship involved some kind of transaction, right? They let Kevin hang out with them, and in exchange, he kept them in video games, Dick's burgers, and weed.

"I'm on that shit," Kevin said, finally exhaling. He was one of those guys who got mystical and hazy when he was high, and his conversation with the pizza place was one for the ages: "Do we want pepperoni? Oh, man, I don't even know. Hold on. Guys, do we want pepperoni? No, we don't want pepperoni, even though I have no idea why, because pepperoni is delicious. Actually, I'm going to ask one more time. Guys, do we really not want pepperoni? No? Man, that's *crazy*."

Andy sat down at the absolute edge of the couch, so that he wouldn't be in contact with any part of Misery's body, but she scooched over and clung onto his arm.

"You making a move on me?"

"I'm kinda freaking out," she said.

The television displayed an empty podium with the blue crest of the president of the United States of America behind it. A couple of premature flashbulbs went off.

"Bobo," Andy shouted, "it's about to start!"

"Coming!"

Misery leaned the other way as soon as Bobo sat down, leaving Andy's left side cold.

"What do you think he's gonna say?" she asked.

"The usual," Bobo said. "Move along. Nothing to see here. I don't even know why you guys wanna watch. There's this movie on Netflix where these people get stuck on a chairlift and die. It's sick."

"This is history right here," Kevin said. "Don't you wanna be informed?"

"Sure. But it'll be up on YouTube in twenty minutes, and that way we can skip the boring parts."

Some hipster-looking dude with glasses came up to the podium only to say, "Ladies and gentlemen, the president of the United States of America." Then he stepped aside for good old Obama, climbing to the stage with his wife and children in tow. Andy dug President Obama; there were pictures of him smoking a blunt in college, and he wanted to help out poor people and immigrants and shit. Plus, the guy always looked chilled out, even when he was angry; his anger was the anger of someone who was mostly angry because he had to get angry. *I'd rather just shoot some hoops and light up,* his expression seemed to say, *but a bunch of uptight assholes are making me act all serious and presidential.*

"There's something weird about him today," Jess said.

It was true. The president didn't project the same cool, I-got-this-covered attitude that he usually did. The giveaway was right there on his face: no smiles. No smile for the crowd. No smile for the camera. No smile for his family even.

"My fellow Americans," he said, "I come to you today in humility, and in hope. A lot of people have been saying a lot of things over the past couple of days, and I'm here to separate the rumors from the realities. As most of you know, an asteroid called Ardor was spotted in the sky a few days ago. It was our own astronomers at the Mount Wilson Observatory in California who first located the asteroid, though since then the study of Ardor has been a truly international effort. Folks, there's no easy way to tell you that the most recent estimates made by scientists around the world put the asteroid roughly on course with our own orbit."

The press room exploded with noise, and Obama waited patiently until it died down. "Now, I promised, when I was sworn in as your president, that I would be as transparent with you as possible. But when you're dealing with these kinds of velocities and distances, it's impossible to determine anything for certain. Truth is, we aren't gonna know more for a while, maybe not until Ardor is right on our doorstep, which I'm told should be somewhere between seven and eight weeks from today."

The First Lady, standing statue-still behind the president, appeared to be weeping. Andy looked around his little apartment—suddenly everything seemed to have changed. Who were these strange people? Were they really the best friends he'd ever have? Misery was shaking, her eyes wide and wet.

"Holy shit," Kevin said. "Holy shit."

The president went on. "I can't sugarcoat the result of a collision. The asteroid is almost eight miles wide at its thickest point. If it lands, it will unleash the force of more than one billion nuclear bombs. But this collision is far from assured, and two months is too long for us to be holding our breaths, or acting as if our lives were no longer of consequence. When this danger passes us by, as I know it will, we cannot afford to have let fear run our country, or ourselves, for even a single day. The only thing we can do now, the only *American* thing to do, is to continue on with our lives, hold our loved ones close, and trust that God will keep us safe. Thank you all, and God bless the United States of America."

A veritable strobe light of flashbulbs went off as Obama walked away from the podium. Andy realized that Misery was holding on to his hand so tightly that the tips of his fingers had gone white. This was real. This could really happen.

"What are our chances?" some reporter shouted, but there was no one left onstage to answer. Meanwhile, Kevin had pulled out his MacBook and was scouring the web.

"What are they saying online?" Misery asked.

Kevin didn't answer, only clicked and swiped and typed, opening up a dozen tabs in his browser. Why was it, Andy wondered, that no matter what color appeared on the screen, computer monitors always shone with the same shade of blue-white light—the exact color of Ardor? The panes of Kevin's glasses reflected two squares filled with tiny text.

"What are they saying?" Misery asked again, and there was a desperate edge to her voice that sent a shiver down Andy's spine. "Kevin, what the fuck are they saying?"

"I was hoping to find something different," he said, looking up from the screen. "They're saying two-thirds."

"Two-thirds? Like, sixty-six percent?"

"Yeah."

"So two-thirds we all live, and one-third we all die?"

Kevin hesitated, checked the screen again, then slowly shook his head. "The other way," he said.

Misery stood up, turned around in place like some kind of cornered animal looking for a way out, then fell down onto her knees and put her head in her hands. Nobody went to comfort her.

"Does it bother you?" Bobo asked.

"Does what bother me?"

"You know. Dying a virgin." He laughed.

Everyone else had left about an hour ago. Soon after that, Andy's mom had paid a rare visit to the ma-in-law to announce that she and Phil would be leaving first thing in the morning for Phil's cabin in eastern Washington, where they'd wait out "all this hysteria." Andy told her that he'd sooner jump off the Space Needle than spend his last days on Earth cooped up in the middle of nowhere with her and Phil. She called him an ungrateful little punk, then slammed the door.

"It's been nice knowing you!" Andy shouted after her.

He and Bobo turned out the lights, but they were both way too keyed up to fall asleep. So they nuked a bag of popcorn and played a couple wordless hours of PS4, instead.

"Suck it," Bobo said under his breath, racking up yet another kill. He was kicking Andy's virtual ass.

"How can you focus on this?" Andy asked.

"What do you mean?"

"I mean I'm losing my shit over here. How are you not?"

"I don't know. I guess the idea of death doesn't really scare me."

As if on cue, Bobo's avatar took a plasma ball to the face. Half the screen went black. Bobo threw the controller down and leaned back on the couch.

"Aren't you gonna respawn?"

"Nah. You kinda blow tonight. It's no fun."

Andy kept playing on his own for a while, until he noticed that Bobo had pulled back the sleeves of his hoodie. A thin pink line ran upward from each wrist, disappearing under the black fabric bunched around his elbow. Andy felt something clench up inside him. He looked away.

"You have to do that?"

"Relax, man. I'm proud of 'em." He admired his scars. "We could try it again, you know. If shit gets real."

Andy didn't say anything.

"I don't blame you," Bobo said. "So you pussed out. I get it. It was a big thing."

"I didn't puss out."

If only they'd been in the same room, everything would have been different. But when they made the pact, they decided to do it separately and alone, synchronizing the alarms on their phones like something out of a James Bond movie. Andy couldn't even remember now why he'd agreed to it. Bobo had just broken up with Misery (temporarily, as it turned out), and his dad was in some kind of alcohol treatment facility, so he had plenty of reasons, but Andy hadn't been going through anything worse than the usual shit. Crazy as it sounded, he just didn't feel right saying no. He called Bobo's cell as soon as he realized he couldn't go through with it, but there was no answer, so he called the police. Later on, a paramedic told him it had come down to just a few minutes. "You're a hero," the guy said.

But Andy knew that wasn't true. He'd abandoned his best friend. He *had* pussed out.

Bobo finally pulled his sleeves back down, like dropping a curtain on the past.

"I'm just saying think about it, all right? Just in case."

The clock blinked over to four thirty.

"We should get to bed," Andy said. "School's gonna be a bitch on three hours of sleep."

"I already Googled it. School's canceled tomorrow. They're giving us a three-day weekend. As if we were gonna go anyway."

Andy hadn't even considered skipping out on school, but Bobo was right. There was no reason left to show up at Hamilton. For that matter, there was no reason left to do much of anything. Andy thought about making the same old drive, sitting through some pointless sad assembly, seeing a bunch of people he didn't really give a shit about and who definitely didn't give a shit about him. Was there even one person there that he'd actually miss?

"Eliza," he said, and the word was like a doorway stumbled on in the dark.

"What?"

"Eliza Olivi."

"What about her?"

What was it that made you keep playing a video game, hour after hour, day after day, no matter how terrible the writing was or how boring the story? You kept going because you had a quest. It didn't even matter what it was—saving a princess or conquering an alien world or assassinating a king. Andy pictured Eliza as she used to be: shy and spectral, quiet as a painting. It was as noble a quest as any.

"I'm going to sleep with her," Andy said.

Bobo laughed. "Bullshit."

"A hundred bucks says I do it by the time Ardor gets here."

"Fine. But make it a thousand."

"A thousand?"

"It's the goddamn end of the world, Andy. And you have to have sex with her, okay? We're talking hard-core, sustained intercourse here."

"Sustained?"

"Sustained. None of that premature ejaculation shit."

"Deal." They shook hands—a gentleman's agreement. Sure it was immature and stupid and probably impossible. But you had to have something to get you out of bed in the morning. Something to hope for. And for Andy, that something would be Eliza.

In a landslide, running unopposed, she'd just been elected his reason to live.

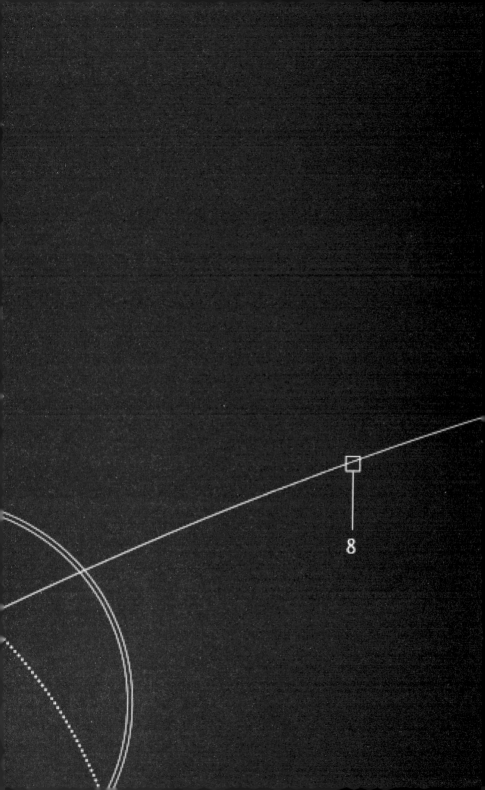

8

Peter

AFTER IT WAS OVER, PETER SAT ON THE COUCH AND LET HIS MOM HOLD HIM. HIS DAD KEPT changing the channel on the TV, hoping to find someone able to contradict some part of the president's speech. Both of them were crying, his mom steady as a stream, his dad like an imperfectly sealed pipe— just a slow drip around the edges. Peter loved his parents, but right now, he would have given anything to get away from them. Their anxiety burned away all the oxygen in the room; his own feelings couldn't breathe. He was only eighteen! There were so many things he hadn't experienced yet—world travel, bungee jumping, sushi. And what the hell had he been waiting for? Why had he assumed time was some sort of infinite resource? Now the hourglass had busted open, and what he'd always assumed was just a bunch of sand turned out to be a million tiny diamonds.

Peter could feel the moisture of his mom's tears bleeding through his T-shirt. He shivered. His parents had always been pretty miserly when it came to heating the house. The wisp of a funny thought: Why not keep the thermostat at a balmy eighty degrees from here on out? Odds were good they'd never have to pay the bill. And how many nest eggs and trust funds would get blown in the next couple of months? How many secret grievances would finally see the light of day? How many neighbors would finally go ahead and shoot the yipping Chihuahua that had been keeping them awake every night? Or, come to think of it, why not just shoot the inconsiderate neighbor who wouldn't keep his damn dog in the house? All of a sudden, the world seemed like a very dangerous place.

"I'm going to go find Miz," he said.

His mom actually moaned—one long, ghostly note—as Peter peeled himself away from her.

"Good idea," his dad said. "But come right home, okay?"

"Sure."

Misery would be over at Andy Rowen's place—the ma-in-law—where her crew always hung out. He texted her to come outside in twenty minutes; for some reason, he really didn't want to see her boyfriend right now. The news about Ardor seemed to affirm the *Why bother with anything?* philosophy that Bobo and his friends had always championed. Peter couldn't help feeling like a sucker for having sided with the seekers and the strivers of the world.

She was waiting for him when he got there, standing on the sidewalk in a round puddle of light. Impossibly slim, like an orchid. Her pumpkin-colored hair and crazy ripped-up clothes seemed like some kind of futile existential gesture, and Peter felt freshly responsible for it. He'd always suspected that his sister's rebelliousness was, in some way, a response to his own mainstream triumphs. And though he'd come to terms with the sarcastic attitude and the slacker ethos and the freak-show fashion sense, the one thing he still couldn't understand was why a smart, pretty girl like her chose to spend all her time with a drug-dealing creep like Bobo.

"Hey, Miz."

"Hey."

They hugged in that awkward space between the front seats.

"Mom's freaking out," he said.

"I'm sure." His sister pulled a pack of Camel Lights and a red Bic from her purse. Peter considered chastising her, then figured that lung cancer was yet another of the million things that no longer mattered. "Hey," she said, breathing out a cloud of smoke, "would you mind if we didn't go straight home? I can't really handle being in that house right now."

"I would the *opposite* of mind."

It was a clear, quiet night. The news had emptied the streets. Peter didn't have any destination in mind as he started driving, but when he saw the sign for Beth's Cafe—a pig with wings atop the old DRINK NESBITT'S ORANGE marquee—he pulled off and parked.

The door jingled as it opened, wafting a breath of warm air that smelled of pancakes and bacon. Beth's had always been Misery's kind of place, rather than Peter's, but it felt right to him tonight. The twenty-four-hour greasy spoon hearkened back to a time when the freaks of the world didn't feature in every prime-time drama and on every street corner, when they really *needed* their own places to congregate. Tall red stools were evenly spaced along an L-shaped counter. The waitress at the register—a smileless Goth monster with a face comprised mostly of holes filled with metal—greeted Misery by name. Nobody in the restaurant looked particularly tragic or hysterical. Was it possible that none of them had heard, or were they all still in shock?

Peter and his sister were seated in the passageway between the restaurant's two rooms, just across from the jukebox and the little nook where the pinball machines lived. The tinny digital effects almost disguised the sound of Peter's phone ringing: Stacy.

"You gonna get that?" Misery asked.

He hadn't even thought about his girlfriend since the announcement.

"Not right now."

"So you're finally gonna break up with her?"

"What?" But Peter hesitated a little too long before answering, "No!"

Misery smiled hugely. "You are? Really?"

"I said no, Miz."

"Yeah, but you had to think about it. That means it's just a matter of time. Start the countdown."

His sister seemed so genuinely pleased at the thought of his dumping Stacy, he was tempted to do it just for her. But that would be even more awful than doing it in the hopes of getting together with a girl he barely knew.

Misery ordered black coffee and hash browns. Peter decided there was no time like the present to tackle Beth's famous twelve-egg omelet. The song on the jukebox kept saying something about a bomb, over and over again.

"So, while we're on the subject of breaking up," Peter said, "what about you and Bobo?"

"Why would I break up with Bobo?"

"Because he's a punk. And he's too old for you."

"Two years is nothing. Plus, I love him, even if he is a punk."

There was another jingle as four men entered the cafe. They were classic Beth's—all leather and studs and the reek of stale cigarette smoke—and brought with them the kind of generalized menace that made you cross to the other side of a dark street. As they passed by the table, one of them did a double take. He couldn't have been older than thirty, but his skin was prematurely leathery—drugs, probably. He was smaller than the others, five-foot-five tops, though something about the way he moved marked him as their leader. Peter noticed the tattoos on his knuckles as he placed his hands on the tabletop: LIVE on the right, ONCE on the left.

"Misery," he said, "you're looking good."

"Hey, Golden."

"And who's this guy? You stepping out on Bobo?"

"This is Peter, my brother."

Peter put out a hand to shake, but Golden didn't take it. His pupils were steel gray, dilated so far that there had to be some kind of amphetamine in his system. He fingered the thin gold chain looped a dozen times around his neck.

"Hey there, Peter my brother."

"Hey."

"You take good care of this one, yeah?"

"That's what brothers do."

Peter's phone rang again. Golden glanced down and saw the screen, smiled a mouthful of gold teeth. "Better talk to mommy," he said, then walked away.

It took Peter five minutes to convince his still-weepy mom that he and Misery would come home right after dinner. Meanwhile, the waitress dropped off their food, looking with tired distrust toward the hysterical laughter and thumping already coming from the game room, where Golden and his friends had ensconced themselves. Peter took one bite of his omelet and realized he wasn't hungry. It was time to discuss the elephant in the room.

"So," he said, "death."

"Yep."

"How are you feeling?"

"I don't even know. It doesn't seem real yet. I mean, what are we supposed to do? What's going to happen?"

"Nothing good."

A raucous cry, then the sound of something shattering. A sickle-shaped fragment of coffee mug slid across the floor from the game room to knock against Peter's sneaker.

"So those are Bobo's friends, huh?"

"Friends would be pushing it."

"Well, I can see why you'd want to be involved with such classy people."

"Leave it alone, man."

But he'd seized on something important now, and he wouldn't let it go without a fight. Even if he accomplished nothing else before the end of the world, at least he could set his sister straight.

"Listen, Miz. I know you've never liked Stacy, and I know I've never liked Bobo, but that doesn't make them equivalent issues." He could see her eyes beginning to glaze over. "Bobo's a thug. It's his fault you weren't with the family tonight. It's his fault your grades this year have been a train wreck."

Misery leaned back against the window at the far end of the booth. "Can you even hear yourself? Who cares about grades anymore?"

"It's not your grades that I'm worried about."

"Then what?"

"Your . . . soul," Peter said, and wondered where the hell *that* word had come from. "I know guys like Bobo, Miz. They don't give a shit about anything."

"He gives a shit about me. And you don't know him. You don't know how fucked up his life has been. That's why he acts the way he does. And every time I make him happier, I feel good. He makes me feel good."

"Misery, you weren't put here on Earth to cheer up a scumbag."

As soon as he said it, he knew he'd gone too far. Misery struck back hard. "You're the one with a girlfriend you don't love," she said. "And I've never cheated on Bobo." She slid out of the booth. "Not that you'd care, but he and I *did* break up once. And he tried to kill himself. So, you know, there's that."

His sister stormed out of the café, while Peter sat back and tried to process this new information. It did clear up one thing; now he could understand how Misery had gotten hooked. The prospect of rescuing someone from death itself—what was more compelling than that?

There was another loud crash from the game room. A member of Golden's crew came out, wincing and grinning at the same time. His hand was covered in red streamers of blood, and a shard of glass protruded from between his knuckles like a shark fin. "My ball got stuck in that fucking machine," he said, by way of explanation.

Misery refused to talk to him on the way home, so Peter just watched the road. He counted three ambulances, two fire engines, and seven police cars. It had already started. . . .

Home again, Misery ran straight upstairs, ignoring their parents, who'd waited up in the living room.

"Is she okay?" his mom asked.

Peter laughed bitterly at the ridiculousness of the question—at the fact that, for the next two months, all such questions would be ludicrous and insensitive and insane.

"Yeah, Mom," he said. "She's fantastic."

Andy

THEY RAN AROUND LIKE CHICKENS WITH THEIR BALLS CUT OFF. TEACHERS. ADMINISTRATORS. Officials. An all-shook-up ant farm of adults, so used to being in control of everything that they didn't even realize the days of control were over. Next to them, the students looked downright chill. Andy figured that was probably because kids were always getting thrown into shit they had no control over. Then again, he wasn't feeling particularly chill himself; after a long weekend spent getting stoned and avoiding anything that so much as resembled a thought, he was now undergoing the mother of all comedowns. Question: How could you look the end of the world in the face and not go crazy? Answer: You couldn't. The only sane thing to do was seek out enough distraction to numb the terror. Andy scanned the room for Eliza—his princess in a castle. Usually, assemblies were packed solid, but today, every row had a few truant teeth knocked out. Of course, Andy wouldn't have bothered to show up either, if it weren't for the quest.

A bright flash momentarily blinded him. After blinking the little purple motes away, he saw her, hidden behind her camera, facing the back of the room. Another flash. For a second, he wondered if she was taking pictures of him. But then he turned around and saw her real quarry. Hamilton had invited some guests to today's assembly—two members of Seattle's finest, one stationed in front of each of the auditorium doors.

So it was happening here, too—Big Brother on the march.

All weekend, Andy had walked the streets of Seattle with Bobo, getting a feel for their new city. He'd expected some kind of bunker mentality—the streets zombie-apocalypse empty, tumbleweeds rolling by, and Mad Max tooling around on a Harley. But the vibe turned out to be more music festival than Thunderdome. Everybody had come out to play, from the druggie psychotics to the white-bread suburbanites, all doing their best to wring some enjoyment out of the wet February weather. It might have been enough to make you forget what was really going on, if it weren't for all the cops. They were everywhere now. No matter which way you turned, some fat-necked, buzz-cut blue boy was looking at you with that *just give me a reason* glare. On the radio, they talked about how the SPD might start deputizing unemployed civilians. ("Of course, none of them will be given guns," the chief of police said—so they'd be a ton of help when shit really went down.) Kevin, their crew's historian-in-residence, said this was how it always started. A few people were granted extraordinary power—just for the sake of public safety, of course—and before long, those well-meaning civilians were lobbing gas canisters and flipping on the fire hoses and driving the trains to the gulags. Andy had figured Kevin was talking out his ass, but now, seeing those cops standing at the back of the auditorium, he wasn't so sure.

Mr. Jester, Hamilton's principal, took the stage, sweating like a guilty killer after three hours of interrogation. How he'd become the principal of anything was a mystery to Andy. Leaders were supposed to be the kind of guys you'd follow into battle. But if there were ever a battle at Hamilton, Mr. Jester was the kind of guy you'd ask to hang back and maybe sweep up the barracks or something.

"Good morning, Hamilton."

The student body answered back, "Good morning, Mr. Jester."

"I'm going to keep this short, if I can. I think it's going to be very important that we maintain our usual routines as much as possible. That being said, there are certain inevitabilities resulting from the tragedy that we have to address. That is, the *potentially* tragic, uh, nature of things."

Mr. Jester said a whole lot of nothing with a whole lot of words. Every couple of minutes the flash of Eliza's camera would briefly bleach the room.

Bobo leaned over the armrest. "Yo, if you wanna get her attention, you gotta do something to stand out."

"Like what?"

"What's the point of calculus?" Bobo shouted, stopping Mr. Jester midsentence and earning a laugh from the room. A good principal would have immediately ordered him out of the auditorium, but Mr. Jester looked to be just a couple of seconds away from a full-on Fukushima-style meltdown. Bobo had always had a sixth sense when it came to the weaknesses of others.

The principal did his best to ignore the interruption. "As I was saying, school is still technically mandatory, though this policy is being reviewed at the federal level as we speak. Please continue to attend your classes as scheduled."

"Say something," Bobo whispered.

"Dude, why are you helping me? There's money on the line."

"Because, Mary, I want a real competition here, and you're already blowing it." Bobo raised his voice again. "Answer the question! What's the point of calculus?"

Mr. Jester squinted into the audience. "Calculus is important, sir, because it's a part of mathematics. And mathematics are important because numbers, you see, are the cornerstone of an education, along with science and history and, uh . . ." He swallowed the rest of his meandering sentence. Another flash went off, right in Andy's eyes this time—Eliza had just taken *Bobo's* picture! His dumb yelling had actually managed to prick the thick bubble of her awareness.

"Listen," Mr. Jester said, "I'm trying to tell you some important stuff here, so if you could just cut me a little bit of slack, we can—"

"What are these cops doing here?" Andy shouted.

"That's not important right now. It's just regulations."

"What regulation says we need armed police officers at a high school? What are you afraid of?"

"Nothing, and that's quite enough, Mr. Rowen."

Andy ignored him, electrified by the attention. "Yo, Hamilton, if you care at all about your personal rights, come to the bleachers after school. We gotta stand up for ourselves. This is how fascism starts—"

He felt something tighten around his shoulder; one of the cops had grabbed hold of him and was trying to lift him out of his seat.

"What the hell?"

"That really isn't necessary, officer," Mr. Jester said.

"Get off me, pig!" Andy wrenched himself out of the cop's grip, but his momentum sent him careening forward into the metal rim of the empty seat in front of him. A white flash of pain, then a slow trickle of blood tickling the follicles of his right eyebrow. Outrage rippled through the room like a murmurous earthquake. Another white flash, only this one came from Eliza's camera. Andy looked right at her and smiled. Blood leaked into the corner of his mouth.

"Bleachers after school if you value your freedom," he shouted one last time, as he was dragged up the stairs and out of the auditorium.

At lunch they considered their next move. Kevin insisted that they had momentum now, politically speaking—Andy's injury was all anyone could talk about—and they had to strike while the iron was hot. Of course, none of them really knew what *striking* would entail. Bobo offered to take point at the bleachers, and Andy was only too happy to agree. He'd never really liked the limelight, and the last thing he wanted was more trouble. He was lucky to have gotten out of that assembly with just the head wound. ("Let's not make some kind of federal case about this," the cop had said, holding a soggy ball of paper towels to Andy's forehead, "and we'll forget about the scene you caused in there. Deal?")

Almost a hundred people were waiting out on the bleachers after school, their hoods pulled up against the drizzle like a monastery's worth of monks who'd neglected to color coordinate. A lot of different crews had answered the call. There was James Hurdlebrink—he of the hideous mullet and the stratospheric IQ—along with the gamer kids and mathletes he ran with. The slackers from pretty much every class had shown up, though good luck getting them to actually do anything. Finally there were the artsy types—girls who dressed like Joan Baez and played acoustic guitar, boys who dressed like Kurt Cobain and played electric guitar, mega-gay theater kids, the staff of the school paper, the menagerie of monstrosities that made up the Hamilton orchestra. Lending gravity to the occasion was the cop who'd roughed Andy up, watching them from the far end of the football field. He reached down toward his Batman-style utility belt, and for a second, Andy half expected him to whip out his sidearm and mow them all down. But he just unsnapped the radio and said something into the microphone.

Andy stood behind Bobo and tried to look grave and traumatized. Misery had wrapped his head in an Egyptian mummy's worth of bandages, to make his injury look worse than it was, but now they were heavy and cold with rainwater and smelled like a musty hospital.

"I know you all saw what happened today," Bobo said, addressing the bleachers from the middle of the track that circumscribed the field. "Maybe it surprised you, but it didn't surprise me. The assholes who run things want us to think that we're in danger from people like us, but you and I know that the real enemy's already in our midst. I'm talking about them." He pointed across the field, right at the cop. "They're as scared as the rest of us, only they've got guns. You think they'll stress over shooting some kid who's giving them a hard time? They can do the math: sixty-six point six percent chance that they won't have to answer for shit. And even if we're still alive two months from now, you know that every cop on the street will be called a hero, whatever he did. Extraordinary circumstances, they'll call them. We're at their mercy, unless we stand together."

"What are you suggesting?" James Hurdlebrink asked.

"Nothing hard-core for now," Bobo said. "We gotta sit back and see how things develop. But we need to be ready. We need a chain of command to organize shit."

"And you'd like to be at the top of that chain?"

"Why not?"

James laughed a harsh, condescending laugh—one that had probably cost him a lot of friends over the years. "Because this is moronic. What are we going to do against a bunch of armed cops?"

"There's plenty we can do."

"Like what?"

"I know people," Bobo said. "People who get things done. You'll just have to trust me on that."

James spread out his hands in temporary surrender. "As you wish, fearless leader."

"Anyone else have something to say?" Bobo looked over the crowd. "Good. I'll make a private Facebook page later tonight, so friend me and I'll send you an invite. Now Misery has one more brief announcement to make."

Misery stood up at the back row of the bleachers. "You're all invited to the Crocodile at ten o'clock this Friday for the Perineum reunion show. Wait, I take that back. Not invited. *Required*. Consider it your initiation. Cover's five bucks."

"Isn't that Valentine's Day?" someone asked.

"So what?" Misery said. "Bring a fucking date."

The crowd dispersed, but not before Andy noticed Anita Graves watching from behind the bleachers; she turned and walked off the moment he made eye contact. That girl was getting weirder and weirder.

"Come on," Bobo said. "We should probably rehearse or something."

"Why didn't Eliza show up?" Andy said. "That was the whole point of this."

"She showed. I saw her taking pictures from the other side of the quad."

"Really?"

"Don't get excited, Mary. It's the closest you're ever gonna get to nailing her."

"Sticks and stones, asshole."

They walked across the football field, passing close by the cop. Bobo spat right at his feet, but the guy either didn't notice or didn't care.

"You could have told me you booked a show," Andy said.

"Fuck the show, man. The show's just the bait."

"What does that mean?"

"It means"—and Bobo took a deep breath, as if preparing for an argument—"that we're inviting Golden."

"Golden? Like, your boss Golden?" The first little disembodied finger of doubt took hold in Andy's mind. What had he set in motion by making that scene in assembly today?

"He's my *distributor*, yo. And he's got a crew behind him."

"A crew of drug dealers."

"What's your problem with dealers? You get along with me just fine."

"Yeah, but you only sell weed."

Bobo made an imaginary gun with his hands and trained it on Andy's forehead. "You saying I'm not for real, bitch?"

"I'm saying that Golden freaks me out."

"That's exactly why we need him. Right now, this is just about Hamilton. With Golden, it could be citywide! We could actually make a stand, if we needed to."

"Can't we do that without him?"

Bobo shook his head. "When the real shit goes down, we'll need more than a bunch of kids from marching band on our side."

"I don't know, man—"

"Fuck that," Bobo suddenly snarled. "Fuck your weak-ass maybe-ing all the time! Can I count on you to help me with this, or are you gonna let me down?"

An unsaid word floated at the end of Bobo's question: *again*. Or maybe that was just Andy's guilty conscience talking.

"Fine. Golden can come to the show—"

"I know he can."

"But only if you let me play one song solo."

Bobo laughed. "Is this about Eliza?"

"Maybe."

"Well, assuming she comes, I say go for it."

"Thanks."

"Don't mention it." Bobo clapped him on the back. "Once she hears your shit voice, that grand is as good as mine."

Eliza

SHE WAS STANDING IN THE SHOWER WHEN THE THOUGHT FIRST OCCURRED TO HER. JUST an idle question—how many more showers would she be likely to take?—followed by a quick calculation. Even if the water and electricity stayed on until the end, and even if she took one every morning and another every night, she'd only end up with about a hundred more showers. And that statistic led her to seek out others. Twenty more shampooings. A hundred more tooth brushings. And what about all the stuff that didn't take place in the bathroom? Fifty sunrises. Twenty-five furtive masturbation sessions (or fewer, if extreme terror had a negative effect on her sex drive). One more skim through *To the Lighthouse* ("The very stone one kicks with one's boot will outlast Shakespeare."). People talked about their *days* being numbered, but really, *everything* was numbered. Every movie you watched was the last time you'd watch that movie, or the second-to-last time, or the third-to-last. Every kiss was one kiss closer to your last kiss.

It was a truly terrifying lens through which to see the increasingly terrifying world.

She and her dad spent most of that first long weekend on the couch, watching the bad news roll in. Riots everywhere from Amsterdam to Los Angeles. A record number of homicides reported in a single day. Half the shops and restaurants in major cities lacking the manpower to open (how many more times would she eat in a restaurant?). Eliza's dad suggested they bet on what continent the next calamity would hail from; he won twice, both times with Asia. On Saturday night they chose to forgo the news in favor of a diversionary James Bond binge. Eliza thought it would help get her mind off things, but without the constant feed of real-world information, her imagination took over. All through *Thunderball* (and was this her last time watching *Thunderball*?), she was envisioning America's prisons breaking open like overripe fruit, releasing the seeds of chaos. Even now, some serial killer was probably skulking toward their apartment building, machete drawn, slaughter in his heart.

It didn't help that her dad seemed to be taking the apocalypse in stride; she could've used him on Team Terrifying Existential Dread. That was the problem with a death-sentence cancer prognosis—the end of the world was already coming. But didn't it bum him out a little bit that his daughter would never grow old enough to have kids, or see Europe, or drink legally? Wasn't that worth a few tears?

"It's not going to happen," he said. "I'm calm because I know it won't. Now, shall we move on to the Roger Moore era?"

So it wasn't any sense of social responsibility that got Eliza out of the house and onto the downtown 982 that Sunday night. She just needed to get away from her dad's claustrophobic optimism.

There were way more people out on the streets than usual, and they weren't the usual people either. Subcultures that had flourished underground, scared into hiding by the vitality of the world, had decided that the surface was safe for their kind again. Whole colonies of sightless nematodes were blinking to life in the moonlight: the punks and the bikers, the nutjobs and the druggies. They were everywhere, with their tats and their piercings, their jackets emblazoned with the bloodred *A* for anarchy, laughing too loudly and drinking fearlessly from paper bags. They walked from corner to corner and back again, aimless, as if they were waiting for a leader to show up and direct them.

Eliza's first photo was of a girl with a crazy face tattoo and a baby asleep in the fabric sling between her breasts. The girl raised her middle finger just as the flash went off, which only made the shot more perfect. Next was a legless veteran with a sign that read YOU'LL BE DEAD SOON, SO GIVE ME SOME GODDAMN MONEY. After that, Eliza spent an hour transfixed by the balletic loopings of the hollow-cheeked skater kids at SeaSk8. A fight broke out and went on for twenty minutes before some cops came and broke it up. She got a lot of pictures of the police, who still looked fresh and capable. It would probably be a very different story a month from now.

She took photos of a couple of hip, expensive restaurants in Belltown that had already shut down, and then she happened to pass by Friendly Forks, the charity place where ex-cons and ex-addicts came to get work experience. Ardor didn't seem to have affected anyone inside just yet; the place was a whirlwind of preparation for the dinnertime rush. Some guy was kneeling at the front wall of windows, spraying Windex and then wiping the spritz away with a rag. Behind him, waiters scurried to and fro, folding napkins and adjusting chairs. It was incredible, the way that people kept on going, whether they were dying of pancreatic cancer or drug addiction or the apocalypse itself. Just the thought of it made her want to cry. And as she lifted the viewfinder to her face, the guy who'd been scrubbing the windows stood up. She snapped the photo, but it wasn't until she wiped the tears from her eyes that she recognized him. He waved, and she waved back, and something crackled warmly around the edges of her somewhere, like the inexplicable satisfaction you get stepping on an icy puddle after a freeze.

The following Monday Eliza came to school prepared, with her Exakta VX and a backpack full of Ilford Delta 120 film. She knew the first day back would be worth documenting, but she could never have guessed just *how* worthy it would turn out to be. The assembly alone was a gold mine: poor, flustered Mr. Jester, the gargantuan cops at the back of the room, all those empty seats. Then Andy, unsteady on his feet, forehead dripping with blood, being roughly dragged toward the exit. Police brutality in a high school, gorgeously rendered in black and white? Next stop, Pulitzer Prize.

And that wasn't the end of it either. After Andy had been removed from the auditorium, all eyes turned back to Mr. Jester. He cleared his throat. "To continue, we will be eliminating all off-campus privileges, including during free periods." The crowd, primed for protest now, responded with loud boos and catcalls. Someone threw a pencil at the stage. It bounced off the lectern and clattered onto the floor. A moment later, the floodgates opened, and Mr. Jester suffered a veritable stoning of teenage paraphernalia: loose change and crumpled notes, tubes of lip gloss and squares of Starburst, tampons and Kleenex, and even one long fluttery confetti strand of unopened condoms that Eliza caught smack in the center of her viewfinder just as it connected with Mr. Jester's forehead.

The principal backed away from the podium, shielding himself from the bombardment. Mr. McArthur, a well-liked history teacher, stood up and ran to the stage. Eliza had taken his Eastern Society, Western Influence course as a junior; she could still remember the story he'd told about living in China in the mid-nineties, and how he'd offended his host by confusing the word for "mother" with the word for "horse." He was in his late forties, handsome in a teacherly sort of way. Word on the street was he'd just married some guy named Neil, though he still showed up to Hamilton events on his own. He whispered something to the shell-shocked principal, then stepped up to the lectern himself. After a few moments, the students—maybe a little scared by what they'd just been allowed to get away with—quieted down.

"I can only imagine how all of you must feel," Mr. McArthur said. "This is an impossible amount for anyone to take in. For all of us, too. And now, on top of everything, it seems like your school is turning into some kind of police state." He shook his head, gave a little whistle. "I certainly can't blame you for taking a few potshots at Mr. Jester here. But before you load up your spitballs and your paintballs and your blue balls again, there are two things you have to know. First, these are not our decisions. We're just passing on the rules handed down to us from the school board. Second, nothing we do is meant as a punishment. It's only to ensure your safety. No one can say exactly what's going to happen in the next two months, but this world is full of desperate people even at the best of times. Bob Dylan once said—you kids still know Bob Dylan?" Eliza laughed along with the rest of the room. "Thank God for that. I have a theory that if the day ever comes when the students and the teachers don't listen to any of the same music, the entire educational system will collapse.

Anyway, Dylan wrote that when you got nothing, you got nothing to lose. And Edmund Burke, who was kinda like a more boring version of Dylan back in the eighteenth century, said that those who have much to hope and nothing to lose will always be dangerous. Well, a lot of people in the world have just started thinking that they don't have anything left to lose, and it's our job to protect you from them. I don't want to scare you, but history tells us that whenever there's panic, there's death. It's the way of the world."

He gave this morbid prediction a bit of time to sink in, then went on. "But to my mind, the physical threat is less of a danger than the psychological threat, which is why Suzie O and I have decided to start a discussion group entitled 'The Consolations of Philosophy.' It'll meet every day, during eighth period. And I do realize how incredibly lame it sounds, but if you feel the need to talk about what's happening, please come." He leaned into the mic and added, "And in answer to Mr. Boorstein's question, Ardor has probably not altered the relevance of calculus to most of your lives, which asymptotically approaches zero as you approach adulthood. Thanks, everyone."

After assembly Eliza headed toward the arts building. She could feel her phone vibrating in her backpack, but she didn't bother to fish it out. Her mom had called about a hundred times in the last few days, but Eliza had yet to answer.

In the empty photo lab, she put on her favorite Sigur Rós record (how many more times would she get to listen to Sigur Rós?) and let her mind slip into that strange space of both total focus and total unconsciousness that was necessary for making art. Images dissolved into being on the line.

The woman with the baby, baring her middle finger more as an act of desperation than an act of anger. The beggar with the sign, his upturned hat glittering dully with dirty change. The skateboarders fighting for absolutely nothing and absolutely everything at the same time. Cops standing sentry at street corners. Cops helping some homeless drunk into the back of a squad car. Cops everywhere, like a blue-sky promise of trouble to come.

At first Eliza worried she was kidding herself, because the photos felt important in a way that nothing she'd ever done before had felt important. But someone had to watch the watchmen, as the saying went, and why *not* her? Here was Bobo, screaming a wordless, animal challenge at the principal. Here was Mr. McArthur, standing silent as his heavy words hit home. The image of the students throwing all their junk at Mr. Jester managed to be both celebratory and menacing at once—a cross between Mardi Gras and a gladiatorial arena. The sweat reflecting off the principal's forehead in one picture found its parallel in another, with the slick black blood that streaked across Andy's face like war paint.

And though Eliza had promised herself that she would never, ever, *ever* start a blog unless someone held a gun to her head and said, *I'll seriously shoot you right now in the head if you don't start a blog* (and even then, she wouldn't have been happy about it), she knew she'd have to break her rule. She wanted to share these photos with the world. She had to.

The school day had just ended when she finally emerged from the photo lab; she'd spent more than five hours inside, skipping out on all her classes (how many more classes would she actually bother to go to?). A surprisingly large crowd had gathered on the bleachers—all the freaks and geeks of Hamilton, perched like a murder of silent crows, cheerless in a place meant for cheering. She took a few photos of them from the other side of the football field.

Her phone was vibrating again. By tomorrow morning, she'd have seven new messages on her voice mail: six wordless hang-ups bearing an area code from Honolulu, Hawaii, and one long, drunken screed from a certain Andy Rowen, throwing around words like "karass" and "duprass" and "wampeter" that Eliza would only vaguely recognize. But that was tomorrow.

Tonight she would post her twenty-five favorite photos to her newly designed Tumblr, *Apocalypse Already*. She'd tell the whole story of that morning's assembly in the captions, then juxtapose the photos from school with those from downtown to demonstrate how the police officers walking around the outskirts of Hamilton gave off the same vague air of threat as the thugs walking the city streets. She couldn't have explained why she felt compelled to add yet another blog to a 66.6-percent-doomed world, other than that she didn't know what else to do, other than that there was nothing else *to* do. Nor could she have explained why that blog would go viral over the course of the next forty-eight hours, or how that would instantly transform her into a kind of minor celebrity—a little star—sliding as easily and frictionlessly into the public consciousness as Ardor was just then sliding through the cosmos, bearing down a little closer every moment, like the end of a story.

Anita

EIGHT DAYS AFTER THE ANNOUNCEMENT, ON A MISTY VALENTINE'S DAY MORNING, ANITA clandestinely packed a small suitcase. She included a week's worth of clothes (good for even longer if she mixed and matched), her toiletry kit (this was to be a grand gesture in the name of independence, not a stand against personal hygiene), and a sleeping bag and pillow (in case she ended up spending the night in the back of the Escalade). In her view, the jailbreak was equal parts running *away* and running *toward*. The first half of this equation was pretty obvious; in the last few days, her parents had totally lost the plot. At dinner on Wednesday, her father had thrown a full plate of food at the wall, then dabbed at his mouth with a napkin and politely excused himself from the table. Her mother was acting out in a different way, hiding all her anxiety behind a creaky facade of sunniness, like that thick cake of foundation some girls tried to use to cover up their acne. Anita saw her parents now as if from some stupendous, galactic distance. For the first time in her life, she felt sorry for them. They were both so stuck in their ways, so unhappy without knowing it. But it wasn't her job to fix them. The only person she could save was herself.

As for the running *toward*, that was harder to explain. She only knew that something was out there, calling to her, and if she didn't go now, she wouldn't get another chance. This was (according to her mother, at any rate) the end of days. The Rapture. The Second Coming. Anita had heard it all described in the most lurid detail on any number of groggy Sunday mornings. The book of Revelation—"revelation" being the English translation of the Greek word *apokalypsis*, as some minister or another had taught her—said that the end times heralded the return of Jesus. But that seemed unlikely in this case, unless he was planning to ride in on an asteroid like a white-robed space cowboy. Anita never thought the last book of the New Testament fit in very well with the rest of it. You started off with this incredibly nice guy who spent his time with prostitutes and preached forgiveness, and you ended up with eternal damnation and the Whore of Babylon. That was the first thing that had shaken her faith, followed soon after by ninth-grade biology. And according to a fair number of sermons she'd heard, those doubts meant she had an eternity of hellfire to look forward to. Good times.

Anita knew she was supposed to be terrified at the thought of death. So then why did she feel this unbelievable lightness of being as she zipped up her suitcase? Why couldn't she stop smiling and humming to herself as she slipped out the front door? Why did she find herself laughing as she drove past the Broadmoor gatehouse, as the stiffness of eighteen years of pretense and submission suddenly fell away from her, golden chains snapping as easily as uncooked spaghetti? It scared her a little; she didn't know whether madness was the kind of thing you could actually watch overtaking you, or if being aware of your developing insanity was enough to prevent it.

The mood at Hamilton was understandably subdued, so Anita had to keep her exhilaration on the DL. Only a little more than half the student body was bothering to show up anymore, which left the halls strangely wide and quiet. Certain classes, specifically the ones in which Ardor was never referenced, became surreal exercises in trying to ignore the unignorable. Anita's mind, usually a faithful partner, began to cheat on the chalkboard equations with random thoughts and daydreams. It stole out of the present moment and into the future, wondering what tonight's show at the Crocodile would be like. Though she couldn't imagine enjoying Andy's music (based purely on the way he dressed), she still felt confident that she was meant to be there to hear it.

When eighth period rolled around, Anita went to the discussion group that Mr. McArthur and Suzie O had put together. It had already become her favorite part of the school day. This week they were discussing ancient philosophers; Anita had spent the last couple of nights reading about the Stoics and Cynics, the Epicureans and the hedonists. Socrates believed that in a perfect world, every person would be doing the thing that they were born to do. Which meant that if you really believed your true calling was as a singer, to do anything else would be to break the most fundamental rule of the universe.

The subject today was happiness—an appropriate one, given Anita's current state of mind. Having read all the relevant texts, she still wasn't sure where her sudden joy had come from.

"Some people think happiness is impossible in the face of death," Mr. McArthur said, "but Epicurus tells us that there's no reason to fear death, because we don't get to meet it. While we exist, there is no death. And when death comes, we're not there anymore."

"That's stupid," some junior boy said. "Waiting for something is the worst part. Like when you have to get a shot or something."

"Epicurus would argue that anticipation is the stupid thing. Why spend your life worried about something that hasn't happened yet?"

"I didn't get the hedonists," said Krista Asahara, Anita's chipper student-council nemesis. "What kind of life would that be, just pursuing pleasure all the time?"

"An awesome one," somebody joked.

"Actually," Suzie O said, "the hedonists weren't as selfish as most people think. Sure, they valued pleasure above all else, but they also thought that most people didn't understand what true pleasure really was. The hedonists believed that justice and virtue were the real pleasures of life, while sex and meals were only good for a couple hours."

"Even that's pretty optimistic," Mr. McArthur said.

"Depends who you're with," Suzie answered, and everyone laughed.

Mr. McArthur had been right—there *was* consolation to be found in reading the works of all these dead people who'd struggled to figure out what life was about. The first day of the discussion group, Suzie O said that the secret goal of all philosophy was to figure out the best way to die. Weird how the most depressing stuff could turn out to be the most comforting.

Anita didn't say much at the meetings; a few dozen students usually turned up, and in any group that size, there would always be a couple of people willing to speak for everyone else. But that Friday, after the discussion was over, she followed Suzie back to her office in the library.

The counselor was already Skyping with a pretty girl in a dorm room when Anita came in.

"Hey, Suzie. Are you busy? I can come by tomorrow or something—"

"No, it's fine." She turned to the girl on Skype. "I'll call you back in a bit."

"Okay," the girl said, and shut off her camera.

"Who was that?" Anita asked.

"My daughter. She's a senior at Rutgers."

"I didn't know you had a daughter."

"Well, now you do. So what's up?"

"I had a sorta weird question."

"I love weird questions."

Suzie sat there expectantly as Anita figured out the best way to word it. "I guess I was just wondering if I should be worried. About myself."

"Why?"

"Because I'm . . . happy."

Suzie frowned. "You're worried because you're happy?"

"Yeah."

"Do you feel hysterical?"

"No. I feel peaceful, actually."

"And why do you think that is?"

"I guess because I realized that nothing really matters." A few bars of Freddie Mercury's "Bohemian Rhapsody" played in her head.

"Are you sure about that? We've still got a shot at surviving."

"I know. But I don't mean that nothing matters *anymore*. I mean nothing *ever* mattered. Like, if it's all so fragile anyway, then it was never really real, you know? Even if there weren't an asteroid, I could still die tomorrow. So why worry? It's like Andy said. 'Whatever it is, it's not worth it.'"

"Andy's a good kid, Anita, but I'm not sure I'd pick him as a philosophical role model. We all have to believe in *something*."

Anita shrugged. "I guess." She wasn't exactly sure what she'd expected to get out of this conversation; it wasn't as if Suzie was going to tell her not to be happy. "So what's your daughter studying at Rutgers?"

"Economics."

"It must be hard to have her so far away, huh?"

Suzie smiled. Then, without any warning, her face crumpled up like a paper bag. "Shit, I'm sorry," she said, and let her head fall into her hands.

"Oh, it's okay."

Anita put her arms around Suzie's wide shoulders and held on until the shaking stopped, as if the emotion were just a bit of turbulence. She tried to remember the last time she'd seen her mother cry. Had she ever?

"It's just a sore spot right now," Suzie said, pulling a Kleenex from a box hidden inside a porcelain turtle. "I thought she'd come right home, but she's got this boyfriend who lives in New York that she doesn't want to leave. And we haven't always gotten along." She blew her nose. "I'm really sorry, Anita."

"Don't be."

"What a load of good I'm gonna be, huh? The students need to see someone keeping it together."

"Are you kidding?" Anita said. "I think you should cry in front of everyone who comes in here. Then they'll know it's okay not to be okay."

"Thanks." Suzie shook out her hands and blinked away the last of the tears. "All right, I think I'm stabilizing. And even if I've lost all credibility as a counselor, at least I proved my point."

"What point was that?"

"There's still time for you to do things that matter. Even if it's just being there for someone who's freaking out." Suzie took hold of Anita's hand and gave it a squeeze. "Don't forget that."

Anita hadn't been downtown since the night of Esperanza Spalding's show, and things had definitely changed. There were so many people out on the streets, as if a big concert had just gotten out and nobody wanted to go home. The Crocodile was packed wall-to-wall with Seattle's misfits—aging rocker types in studded leather pants, pairs of spiky-haired girls holding hands, big-bearded metalheads with arms as densely decorated with tattoos as the venue's bathroom stalls were with graffiti. Anita sat at the bar, alone with her suitcase and a glass of orange juice, feeling scared and lonely and excited all at once. She was really doing it. She was running away from home.

Now all she had to do was find a place to stay.

The first band was made up of four guys who might have been contestants in a Dracula look-alike contest. One of them played a synthesized church organ. Next up came a group of skinheads; the lead singer liked to take the whole microphone into his mouth while screaming into it. The dance floor looked like a breakout at a mental hospital for the criminally insane.

Around ten, Andy and Bobo stumbled onstage and began to set up. Both of them had clearly been drinking. Their music was messy, bland, and painfully loud all at once. Over the feedback and the constant shimmer of crash cymbal, it was impossible to make out a word of Bobo's manic screech. He was a decent front man—struttingly confident and unafraid to look crazy—but the songs themselves were incomprehensible.

Anita was disappointed. In spite of herself, she'd been expecting magic. All she was getting out of Andy's "band" was that special sort of despair she always felt after listening to truly terrible music. Well, that and a ringing sound in her ears.

After a period of time which might have comprised two songs or two dozen, Andy stumbled out from behind his drum kit. He was so thoroughly wasted that you could see it in every part of his body; his limbs moved like overfilled water balloons, and he almost dropped the guitar when Bobo handed it to him. He grinned goofily out at the crowd—kinda cute, actually.

"This is a song of mine, about not wanting to deal with other people's shit. Maybe you can relate to that. Or not. Whatever. It's called 'Save It.'"

He hit a couple of wrong notes before locking into a slow arpeggio, clear and quiet, reverbed like a rubber band. And what came out of the speakers after that was, without a doubt, the craziest thing Anita had heard since the news that an asteroid might soon blow them all to kingdom come. The little skater punk, with his too-tight jeans and bangs that wouldn't stay out of his eyes, was playing soul music. His voice was frail and unsure, and the audience was thrown by the sudden shift in tone, and even Andy himself didn't seem to totally understand what he was doing, but Anita got the message loud and clear, like neon runway lights pointing the way toward her future. Like second star to the right and straight on till morning. Like fate.

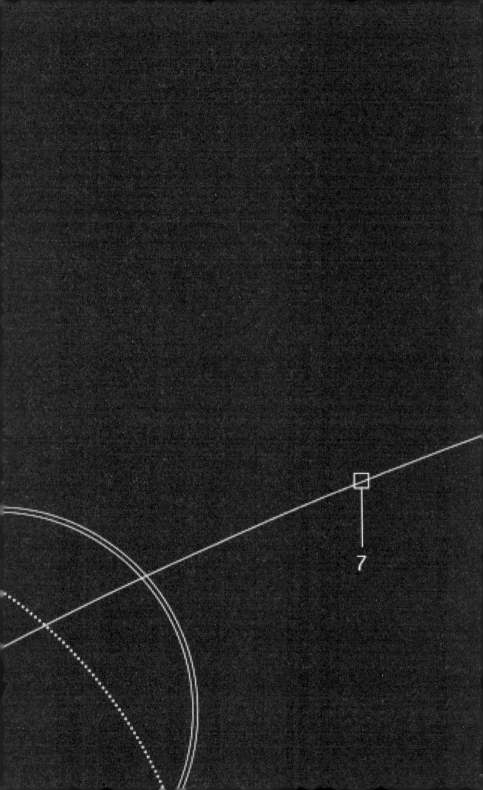

7

Andy

SAY WHAT YOU WOULD ABOUT BOBO, BUT THE DUDE KNEW HOW TO DRAW A CROWD. THE Crocodile was jam-packed by the time Perineum took the stage. It had been a few months since their last show, and as Andy climbed onto the throne behind the beat-up house kit, he felt the prickle of butterflies drowning in the four beers (delivered by a sympathetic bartender) he'd already put in his stomach. The lights were too bright, and he couldn't seem to find a good distance from the snare.

"Hello, Crocodile!" Bobo said. "We're Perineum, and this is our first song!" Andy counted it off. Somehow, without consciously ordering his body to start drumming, he was there right on time, and then the flow of it, the crazy speed trip that was punk rock, swept him out from the chorus to the verse and back again. One song became another. He was immediately soaked in sweat—a well-oiled machine keeping the beat coming and going like a set of windshield wipers—and through the rainbow glare he could see that the moshing was intense, a jumble of limbs and leather. Was Eliza out there? She had to be. Anything else would be a failure on the part of the universe. They made it through about ten of their two-minute songs before Andy noticed that the room had gone silent. Bobo was offering up his guitar.

"Hey," Andy said into the mic. "I'm gonna do something a little different here. Hope you don't mind."

"I mind!" someone shouted. Andy shielded his eyes and saw Golden standing right at the lip of the stage. The light glinted off the links of his necklace.

"This is a song of mine, about not wanting to deal with other people's shit. Maybe you can relate to that. Or not. Whatever. It's called 'Save It.'"

He started playing. It wasn't a song you could mosh to. It wasn't punk. It wasn't even rock. He'd written it a little more than a year ago, about this freshman girl he'd started dating only to find out she was batshit crazy (she claimed to brush her teeth for an hour and a half every night because she "liked the sensation"). Nobody booed him offstage, so they couldn't have hated it too much, even if the applause was sparse and the cheer loud when Bobo returned to the mic. He gestured to Andy to start the beat for their last song.

"Thanks for coming out on this fine Valentine's Day evening," Bobo said. "As you may know, tonight's concert is about more than music. This is the beginning of a movement. Unless we're all ready to stand up when the time comes, we'll get trampled into the dirt." The crowd cheered. "If any of you give a shit about your civil liberties, pass your e-mail to my girl over there." He pointed to Misery, momentarily spotlighted at the edge of the stage. She'd dressed up for the occasion like a true punk-rock slut—short pink-and-black tartan skirt and spiderweb tights, tight pink tank top, and a black bow in her hair. Maybe it was just because they wanted to talk to a pretty girl, or maybe it was because there was a giant ICBM of a rock bearing down on them, but Andy saw people start to crowd around her.

They finished their set. Andy felt the molten lava of performance anxiety draining from his bloodstream, and he quickly replaced it with a couple of the tequila shots Golden was buying by the dozen. He was shoving his way through the crowd, searching for Eliza, when he ran face-first into Anita Graves.

"Heeeeeeeeeeey!" he shouted. "It's Anita Bonita!" He hugged her, coating her in a layer of 60-proof sweat.

"Hey, Andy. I liked your set."

"Really? Awesome!"

"Well, not your whole set. Just the one you sang. The rest of it kinda sucked."

"Oh. Cool." He felt flattered and offended at once. "Uh, have you seen anyone else here?"

"Anyone else?"

"From Hamilton, I mean."

Anita looked around the room. "Half of this crowd's from Hamilton."

"Yeah, but I mean, have you seen anyone specific? Like, a specific girl?" Andy wasn't sure how to ask about Eliza without actually asking about Eliza.

"You're drunk, Andy. I think it's time to call it a night."

"No way! The guys are all going to the Cage. Golden said he can get us in."

"Is that an invitation?"

"You wanna come? That is so great! Anita Bonita at the Cage!" He hugged her again.

"I'm definitely driving," she said.

The outside air sobered Andy up a bit, enough for him to realize how weird it was that Anita had come to the concert. He would have asked her about it, but she didn't give him the opportunity.

"So do you have any other songs like the one you sang?" she asked.

"A couple. But I'd—"

"Have you ever considered having someone else sing your songs?"

"I guess, as long as—"

"And how do you feel about collaborating on new songs?"

"Well, Bobo and I tri—"

"Who are your musical idols?"

It was like being interviewed for *Rolling Stone* by a journalist with ADHD. Eons seemed to pass before Anita found a parking space and Andy could escape the interrogation.

"We're not done talking about this," Anita warned.

"I'm sure we're not."

The Cage was Seattle's most famous biker bar. A huge black guy in an orange trucker's cap sat outside a door built into a spiked wooden palisade. As Andy and Anita approached, he looked up from the book he was reading—*Man's Search for Meaning*—and emitted a single dry chuckle.

"What are you? Sixteen?"

"We're with Golden," Andy said.

"And you're already wasted, aren't you?"

Andy looked guiltily to Anita. "I'll keep him on a short leash," she said.

The bouncer sighed and picked up his book again. "Whatever, man. I'm quitting tomorrow anyway."

There was a wide-open patio space on the other side of the palisade. Golden and his crew were seated at the centermost table, already festooned with a half-dozen foamy pitchers of beer. Bobo had positioned himself at Golden's right hand and seemed to have captured the drug lord's attention. Andy had always been impressed by his best friend's familiarity with the street scene; even back in middle school, Bobo had been able to chat up the crackheads and the gangbangers and even the homeless, as if he were one of them.

"Which one's Golden?" Anita asked.

"Head of the table. Dude's one of the biggest dealers in the city. Sweet, right?"

"Dealer? You mean a *drug* dealer? And you think that's cool?"

"I don't know. Dealers make bank. Even Bobo can pull down a couple hundred bucks in a good week."

"Musicians are way cooler than drug dealers, Andy. They don't end up in prison. Usually."

But Andy wasn't paying attention. He wanted to find out what Golden and Bobo were talking about. "Wait here a second, okay?"

"I'm thinking we do the same kind of thing, only on a bigger scale," Bobo was saying. "That way, you've got people when the time comes. But we've got to move on it. Like, next weekend or something."

Golden nodded sagely, a general in consultation with his lieutenant. His necklace was the exact same color as the glass of beer in front of him. He noticed Andy lingering nearby.

"Andy, nice set tonight."

"Uh, thanks."

"So Bobo here wants to put together a little fiesta next week. You think that's a good idea?"

"Bobo's full of good ideas," Andy said, but he was so drunk he'd already half forgotten the question. "I mean, whatever he says, I'm in. I just want to enjoy myself before the end, you know?"

"I do, Andy. I really do." Golden gestured for Andy to come closer. "You wanna hear a secret?"

"Fuck yeah."

"You ever heard someone talk about having greatness thrust upon them?" Andy shook his head. "Fucking Shakespeare wrote that."

"Whoa."

"Exactly. As soon as I heard about that asteroid, Andy, I made a decision. This was my chance to be great. Ardor is thrusting greatness upon me. Maybe upon you, too."

"Okay."

Golden lifted his glass. "To greatness."

A shot materialized in Andy's hand. He downed it—vodka, maybe?—and then, for all intents and purposes, he ceased to exist. He didn't remember sitting down at the other end of the table and talking with Anita. He didn't remember leaving a few minutes later, or vomiting out the passenger-side window of her Escalade. He didn't remember telling her where he lived. He definitely didn't remember using his phone to visit Eliza's Facebook page (and had she always had 4,254 friends?) in order to get her phone number so that he could leave a five-minute message on her voice mail. In fact, pretty much *everything* that occurred after he'd climbed down off the stage at the Crocodile was gone the next morning, as if someone had taken the mad pencil sketch of those few hours and rubbed at it with a big pink eraser.

He woke up with a hangover so pure and perfect that it awed

him. He groaned one long wordless groan—the sound of absolute suffering.

"Good," a voice said, "you're finally awake."

"Eliza?" Andy sat up in bed like a shot. Sitting on his futon, a book open on her lap, was Anita Graves.

"No," she said, stating the very obvious, "I am not Eliza."

Peter

HE STOOD TRANSFIXED FOR A GOOD THIRTY SECONDS AFTER SHE WALKED AWAY, HIS ARM up like some cardboard cutout of a guy waving. It was the Sunday after the announcement, and the first time Eliza had acknowledged Peter's existence since they'd made out in the photography studio a year earlier. She was wearing a chunky pair of headphones and carrying some kind of antique camera, its big black eye replacing her brown ones as she raised it to take his photo. A little kaleidoscopic spin as the iris opened, a brief wave, and then she was gone.

Felipe saw the whole thing happen.

"That a friend of yours?"

Peter finally dropped his hand. "Sorta. Do you mind if I say hi?"

"Go get her, champ."

But by the time he untied the tight knot of his apron and went outside, Eliza was gone. He felt a stab of anxiety on her behalf, then felt stupid for worrying. What was she to him, or he to her? Nothing at all.

Peter volunteered at Friendly Forks every night that week. It wasn't just that he hoped Eliza would come back and find him;

he liked the camaraderie in the kitchen, the satisfaction that came from accomplishing something practical. Many of Seattle's restaurants had already closed their doors, so Friendly Forks had more customers than ever. Peter's presence had only been tolerated at first, but now the guys in the kitchen were getting used to having him around, and they'd come to treat him like an annoying but ultimately lovable little brother. They'd even taught him a few words of Spanish, just enough so that he could understand the full extent of their vulgarity when they made fun of him for being, as Felipe put it, "*El lavaplatos mas gringo en todo el continente americano*," which translated roughly to "The whitest dishwasher in all of the Americas."

Peter wasn't just doing it out of the goodness of his heart; he was desperate for distraction. The whole "two-thirds chance of everything he knew and loved disappearing just a few weeks from now" was really getting to him. He couldn't sleep more than a few hours a night. Every time he closed his eyes, he saw the asteroid looming just above the house, his sister framed in her bedroom window, eyes wide, as the light grew brighter and brighter and then everything went white. He would wake from these half dreams and run to his own window, finding nothing but the usual stars, distant and disinterested as ever (Ardor had lost its telltale blue tint, and now it was well hidden in some innocuous constellation, like a sleeper agent). Peter would then return to his regularly scheduled tossing and turning. The only effective sedative was sunrise; somehow, seeing the world spinning its way back into day temporarily interrupted the dark thoughts. As the sky colorized, Peter would finally pass out, only to wake up a couple of hours later to the shrill cry of his alarm. There was no way he was going to skip out on school, no matter how much his mom hinted that she wished he'd stay at home. What would he do all day? Sit around comforting her? Wait for his dad to get back from work, later and later every night, as fewer and fewer people came into the office to share the load?

No, the key was to make sure there was a never a free moment in which to think. That first weekend after the announcement, Peter spent Friday and Saturday with his family, and on Sunday he took Stacy out for a nice brunch. He apologized for forcing Friendly Forks on her, and she forgave him. With everything else that was going on in the world, the last thing he needed was a lot of arguing or a messy breakup (however happy it might make his sister). He'd even managed to get Stacy's endorsement of his own volunteer work ("I don't get it, like, at all, but I think it's pretty amazing that *you're* willing to do it"), which had become his favorite part of the day. At the restaurant, there wasn't time to ponder the ephemeral nature of life or imagine your loved ones melting into puddles. From the moment the first guest sat down until the moment Felipe judged the kitchen "fucking spotless," there was only the work.

On Valentine's Day they closed up shop a little after midnight, gracefully escorting the last tipsy couple out the door. So many people were out on the streets that it looked like some kind of citywide block party. Peter was standing on his own outside the restaurant, taking it all in, when someone punched him on the shoulder.

"What's up, Whitey?"

It was Felipe, and behind him, Gabriel, his sous chef. Peter had yet to actually speak with Gabriel, who was one of those "all business, all the time" kind of dudes. Word was he'd been offered a job as a chef at Starfish, an upscale seafood restaurant on the Sound, just before Ardor showed up and shut the place down. It was an impressive accomplishment, considering that he was a black ex-con with a long, Bond-villain scar stretching across his face from cheekbone to chin.

"You heading home?" Felipe asked.

"I'm supposed to see my girlfriend. Valentine's Day, you know? I promised we'd do a late-night dessert thing."

"Come get a drink with us first."

The truth was, he *did* have a better time with Stacy when he was a little buzzed. "You sure it's cool?" He looked to Gabriel, for some reason, who nodded. "All right. One drink."

Unlike Gabriel, Felipe was the kind of guy who could just talk, on and on, and didn't even seem to care whether anyone was listening— the perfect thing for keeping your mind occupied. He told some crazy story about a rich girl he'd dated in high school, and it lasted them all the way to their destination. Down a narrow alley, a red light was set into a wooden palisade illuminating a small wrought-iron sign: THE CAGE.

The patio was clouded over with more smoke than the stage at a heavy metal concert, produced by a crowd of grizzled bikers in studded leather and beefy, tattooed Hispanic dudes fresh off the late shift somewhere. There were maybe a dozen women there, and most of them could've passed for men in a pinch.

"Find a seat," Felipe said. "I got the first round."

Peter was left alone with Gabriel. "So, you guys come here often?"

"Sure."

"Seems like a cool place."

"It's okay."

A raucous explosion of laughter from a group of punkers nearby. Peter recognized a couple of them: Golden, the thug he'd met at Beth's Cafe, and Bobo, his sister's slacker boyfriend. Thankfully, Misery wasn't with them.

"You know those guys?" Gabriel asked.

"A little bit."

"Those guys aren't good guys." He pulled a joint from his back pocket and lit up. "You want a hit?"

"No, thanks."

"Six bucks for three Buds," Felipe said, back from the bar. "Best deal in town."

The bubbly coolness trickled down Peter's throat and into his stomach, loosening up everything along the way. It was probably the best beer he'd had since his very first, enjoyed at the end of a dock on Lake Washington. He and Cartier had tossed back a whole lukewarm six-pack (secured by Cartier's older brother) and talked shit until dawn.

The possibility of actual relaxation was just coming into focus when a hand landed heavy on the table, rattling their glasses.

"Big man slumming it in the city," Bobo said. His voice was an alcoholic slurry. Golden stood a few feet behind him.

"Just having a few with my friends," Peter said.

"Why didn't you come to my fucking show tonight, yo?"

Peter vaguely recalled seeing some flyers around school, but he didn't really go in for punk rock. "Didn't know you had one."

"Well, I did. And I kicked ass. Misery was there. Your sister. My girlfriend. But she already went home. Said you were all up her ass about not staying out late. And now here you are. What's that about?"

"She's younger than we are. Anyway, I'm glad to hear she actually listened."

"Eh, maybe you're right." Bobo squinted up at Ardor. "You can feel it up there, can't you? It's coming for us. It wants blood."

"You trying to kill our buzz, *ese*?" Felipe asked, just friendly enough to break the tension. "We're trying to forget about that shit."

Bobo smiled. "Sorry. It's my fucked-up head, I guess. Good to see you, big man."

Golden stepped closer as the others were walking away. He put a hand on Gabriel's shoulder. "We miss you round the Independent, G. You ever wanna get back in the game, you let me know."

Gabriel's answer was a long, cool plume of smoke.

"Drug dealers," Felipe said, after they were gone. "They're always assholes. It's because they got no friends. Everybody wants something from them. Turns 'em mean."

"You and Golden known each other a long time?" Peter asked Gabriel.

Gabriel shook his head. "He doesn't know me. He knew a guy who looked like me. I got the next round."

He stood up and went to the bar.

"Man's got stories," Felipe said. "Took him a long time to straighten out."

Peter would have liked to hear some of those stories, only just then there was an eruption of shouting on the other side of the palisade. A few of the guys on the patio looked up from their drinks, but nobody actually moved. Even Felipe only paused for a moment, bottle of beer halfway to his lips, before knocking it back.

A girl screamed.

Peter stood up, but Felipe grabbed him by the wrist. "Nah, man," he said. "It's not our business."

Peter shook him off. In the alley just outside the Cage, Golden's crew was clustered around something. Peter pushed through them to find Golden with his hand around the neck of some street girl, her hair a tangled mess and her eyes sunk deep as land mines in her head.

"What the hell are you doing?" Peter said.

Golden was momentarily distracted, and the girl took advantage, scratching at his arm with a wicked claw of sparkly painted nails. He dropped her, and straightaway she was up and running, throwing bony elbows in every direction. Bobo got knocked back on his ass and came up with a gushing nosebleed. *I should be running too*, Peter thought, but too late. The circle had re-formed, and he was at the center this time.

Golden stepped deeply into his personal space. "Are you stupid?" His irises were huge and black, with only a thin rim of gray around the edges, like two eclipsing suns. "Don't answer that," he said. "Just from looking at you, I can tell you haven't worked a day in your life, so maybe you don't understand the concept of making a living. That girl owed me money."

"That's not a reason to get violent with her."

Golden smiled. "You think that was violent?" He reached up and unclasped his necklace. It unspooled, sinuous and shiny, long as a magician's handkerchief. "I bet you've never seen violence outside of movies—that's why you can't recognize it. What you just saw wasn't violence. It was intimidation." Golden began to wrap the chain around the fingers of his right hand, covering up the LIVE tattooed on his knuckles. "Intimidation is a *threat* of violence. Good intimidation is like torture; it can go on for years. But violence is different. Violence is like lightning. It's over as soon as it starts."

Peter wasn't used to being afraid—a six-foot-tall athlete seldom is. But then Golden squeezed his fist, now fully encased in the chain, and the muscles in his wiry forearms shifted and rippled, veins rising like some secret maze that had been hidden beneath the surface of his skin. Peter understood that a blow from that fist would be grievous. It would be meant to crush his nose and break his jaw and shatter his teeth. It would be meant to annihilate him.

And the one crazy thought in his head was that Eliza would never kiss him again if he lost all his teeth.

"Where would you like me to hit you?" Golden asked.

Before Peter could answer, there was a single, simple click from somewhere close by. Everyone turned to see Gabriel and Felipe standing by the door of the Cage. Felipe was red-faced with anger, but it was the tranquil-looking Gabriel who held the gun. Such a strange thing, Peter thought, a *gun*. It was a toy he'd been playing with for most of his life. And when it wasn't a toy, it was a prop, popping up in TV shows and movies about cops and robbers and heroes saving the day. It was easy to forget that guns existed in real life, too.

Golden looked straight down the barrel. "Only a pussy brings a piece to a fistfight," he said. Still staring directly at the weapon, he lashed out and caught Peter in the cheek with the back of his hand. The chain bit hard, but Peter knew it was only a gesture. Golden wanted to give up the field without giving up his dignity. Peter's greatest fear at that moment was that Gabriel would shoot anyway, and then all hell would break loose.

But there was no gunshot. Golden uncoiled the necklace from his fist and wrapped it around his neck again, taking his time. Without another word, he walked off, holding tight to the wall of the alley.

"There's more coming for you than an asteroid now," Bobo said. The blood was already drying to a crust around his nose, and it crackled when he smiled, fell away like flakes of crimson snow.

What was it Mr. McArthur had called it?

A Pyrrhic victory.

Three days later Peter stood waiting outside the Hamilton refectory, shaking with fear. But it wasn't Golden he was afraid of, and it definitely wasn't Bobo. It was a slight brunette girl in a pale-green tank top. She waved at him from across the quad, flipped her hair over her shoulder, and smiled—totally oblivious.

Could love really disappear so quickly? Or did that mean it had never been there in the first place?

There was no safety left in the world. If Peter hadn't known it before his run-in with Golden, he definitely knew it now. And after another weekend of sleepless nights spent imagining his last few moments on Earth, he realized that when he looked up at Ardor as it came streaking down through the atmosphere, turning scarlet with the heat of entry, it wasn't Stacy's hand he wanted to be holding. Whether the asteroid blazed past them like a bad overhead pass, or landed like a huge fist wrapped in chains of fire, Ardor had already delivered its stale but necessary message: Life was just too goddamn short.

"Hey, baby," Stacy said, then noticed the lattice of scabs on his face. She reached up to touch his cheek. It was the very same spot she would soon slap with all her strength, reopening most of the tiny wounds, leaving a checkerboard of blood on her palm. "Is this why you haven't been answering your phone? What happened?"

He took hold of her hand for what would turn out to be the last time. A few days later, she and her parents would decide to leave Seattle for their family cabin on Lake Chelan. She wouldn't even bother to call him to say good-bye.

"A lot," he said. "And we need to talk about it."

Anita

"ELIZA?"

Anita looked up from her book—Immanuel Kant's *The Critique of Pure Reason.*

"No, I am not Eliza."

Andy blinked like a baby bear coming out of hibernation. He was still wearing the clothes he'd worn at the concert, and his hair was an avant-garde sculpture, all curves and sudden outcroppings. "You're Anita," he said.

"Well done. Now get out of bed and take a shower before you kill somebody."

Andy sniffed at his armpit and grimaced. "Good call."

Anita retreated into the living room, where she'd spent the night on a couch that sagged so deeply it might as well have been a hammock. A couple of times in the middle of the night, her hand had fallen into crevices that somehow managed to be both sandy and moist at once. Now, in the cold light of day, she removed the cushions, fluffed them, and swept away the dust, pennies, and crushed Skittles that had collected underneath.

After ten minutes or so (oh, to be a boy!), Andy emerged from the bedroom in a pair of jeans scribbled all over with colored marker and a T-shirt bearing a portrait of George W. Bush above the words *The Decider.*

"My head feels like a My Bloody Valentine song," he said. "Coffee time."

They drove to a nearby Denny's and were seated in a booth with a panoramic view of the parking lot.

"So that was something else last night," Anita said.

Andy ran his hands through his hair, transforming the sculpture (which had survived his two-minute shower practically unscathed). "I really left Eliza a message?"

"Oh, you wish it were just a message. This was a monologue. This was an epic poem."

"Jesus."

"Hey, if I got something like that, I'd be flattered. Or disturbed. Definitely one of the two. What's your thing with her, anyway?"

The waitress, a matronly sixty-something with bleached-blond hair and exposed roots, dropped off Andy's coffee. "Thanks, Claire," he said. Anita wasn't sure if it was really sweet or really sad that he was on a first-name basis with the Denny's staff. He blew on the top of his coffee, sipped it. "I don't know. Eliza's cool."

"That's your whole reason? She's cool?"

"Stop grilling me, yo! Anyway, *I* should be the one asking questions here."

"Why's that?"

"Because *you're* the one being a weirdo."

"No, I'm not," Anita said, but she was secretly pleased. It made for a nice change to be seen as a weirdo for once, instead of some uptight mega-prude.

"Yeah, you are. Like, what are you doing here right now? Since when do you go to punk rock concerts and biker bars and spend the night at some boy's house? That's not the Anita Graves I know."

"So maybe you don't know Anita Graves."

"I know the Anita Graves I had to work with on that physics project back in the day."

"If I remember correctly, you didn't do much of that project."

"Exactly my point. You were, like, seriously . . ." He tightened his hands into fists, then shook them a little.

"Spastic?"

"High-strung. You wouldn't smoke a single bowl with me that whole week."

"I'm not into drugs."

"Yeah, but even when I wanted to, like, take a snack break, you acted as if I said we should drop out of school and go score some heroin or something. And aren't you going to Harvard next year?"

"Princeton. Conditionally."

Andy laid his hands out on the table, like he'd just proven something. "There you go. So why are you suddenly spending your time with a fuckup like me? Is this just an asteroid-coming-to-kill-us-all thing?"

Anita shrugged. "Maybe. I mean, probably. But that doesn't make it a bad idea. You know, I think I'm the only person out there who's actually been happier since we all heard about Ardor. It was like a wake-up call, you know? I've spent my whole life doing the stuff I was supposed to, and all because I thought that people like you, people who just did whatever they wanted, were the dumb ones. But now I'm thinking, who's dumber? The guy who does his own thing, or the girl who does someone else's thing?"

"So what's your thing?"

"I want to sing," she said, without hesitation. "That's why I came out to your show."

"You want to join Perineum?"

Anita laughed. "No! God, no!"

"Well, you don't have to be a dick about it."

"Sorry. I'm just not really much of a punk girl. But the song that *you* sang? That was amazing! I mean, I couldn't believe my ears."

Andy smiled into his coffee. He clearly wasn't used to praise. Anita wondered if that was how kids became slackers. Nobody ever built them up when they succeeded, so they started to wonder why they should bother trying in the first place.

"Which song was it?" he asked.

"What do you mean?"

"Which one did I play?"

"Seriously? You can't remember?"

Andy shook his head sheepishly, and then both of them were laughing. Their food came: hash browns and wavy bacon strips and flapjacks with a swirly flame of butter in a little paper cup. Anita couldn't remember the last time she'd eaten at Denny's. It was delicious.

"So can I ask you something else?" Andy asked, his mouth full of food.

"Sure."

"Why were you crying that day, in the library?"

Anita had never told the truth about her family to anyone other than Suzie O, but maybe that was just because no one had ever asked. "In a nutshell? Because my dad's an asshole, and my mom just goes along with him on everything. They have these huge expectations of me, but even when I meet them, they still aren't happy. I thought getting into Princeton would change things, but it's only made everything worse."

"My parents don't expect anything out of me," Andy said.

"That must be nice."

"You'd be surprised."

The waitress came and refilled his mug. "I can't believe you can drink so much coffee," Anita said. "I get jumpy after my first cup."

"I've built up an immunity."

"Sometimes I worry I don't have enough vices to be a musician. My uncle plays saxophone for a living, and I've watched him drink ten cups of coffee in one go. Also half a bottle of bourbon. Maybe it's time I developed a drug habit or something. Or started sleeping around, like—" She cut herself off, but it was too late.

"Like Eliza?"

"Sorry."

"It's fine. She does have a bit of a rep."

"You're not just interested in her because of *that*, are you?"

"No! I like her. For real. And I just needed *something*, you know? I needed to need something."

"I totally get that," Anita said. "I need some things too. From you."

"Like what?"

"First thing, I want to make music. I can sing. You can play. Deal?"

"Deal. What else?"

"I need you to help me plan a party. Which means you'll have to come to student council."

Andy mimed hanging himself from a very short rope. He spoke while swinging slowly to and fro. "I guess I can do that. For a party."

"Thanks." She took a deep breath. "And there's one more thing."

"Hit me."

"I sorta need to move in with you."

That Wednesday, Anita dragged Andy along to the eighth-period discussion group, so as not to lose track of him before student council. She worried he might act out like he had in assembly (or else fall asleep), but actually, he got along just fine. He hadn't done any of the reading, of course, but that did nothing to diminish his passion for argument. They spent the hour debating between something called the "categorical imperative," which said that you shouldn't do anything that you didn't believe ought to be a law, and "utilitarianism," which was the theory that the best choice in any situation was the one that would lead to the most happiness for the most people.

Andy raised his hand. "So if I, like, kicked someone in the nuts, but it made a lot of other people laugh, that might be all right?"

Mr. McArthur considered. "Assuming that we could quantify the enjoyment versus the . . . groin pain? Then yes."

"And even if Ardor wiped out ninety-nine percent of the people on the planet, it could be a good thing, if the survivors and their kids and stuff ended up way happier?"

"Yep."

Andy sat back in his seat, shaking his head. "That's some fucked-up shit right there."

In this brave new post-asteroid world, you could actually get away with talking like that in front of your teachers.

After class, Suzie O gave Andy a fist bump. "Anita, are you responsible for bringing this malcontent here?"

"Guilty. He's my end-of-the-world project."

"Hey, Suzie," Andy said, looking down at the carpet, "I'm sorry about last time, in your office. I was being messed up."

"Don't mention it. Emotions ran high. Anyway, I hope you keep coming to our little meetings here. You had a lot to add."

"Thanks. It was actually way less boring than I thought it would be."

"Andy!" Anita said.

But Suzie only laughed. "From anyone else, that would be faint praise, but from Andy Rowen, for whom almost everything is boring, I think it's a pretty serious compliment."

"Exactly," Andy said, grinning. "Suzie, you just get me."

After a snack break in the lunchroom (during which Andy introduced Anita to the peanut butter and Ruffles barbecue-flavor potato chip sandwich), they headed to student council. It was the first meeting since the announcement of Ardor, and the council had already shrunk from eight members down to five. Unfortunately, Krista Asahara was not among the absentees.

"What's *he* doing here?" she asked, pointing at Andy.

"I invited him," Anita said. "We're short today anyway."

"Our bylaws say we need two freshmen and another sophomore."

"I think the bylaws are moot at this point. And Andy is here because he and I have put together some new ideas for Olot that we want to share with you."

"Olot?" Damien Durkee asked. "Are we even still doing that?"

"Of course we are," Krista said. "The students need it, for morale."

"Actually, we had a different plan," Anita said. "The dance is scheduled for three weeks from now, but we want to hold it the night before Ardor comes."

Krista looked horrified. "We don't even know when that is!"

"We will."

"But how could we plan it? It's totally unfeasible!"

Andy leaned onto the back two legs of his chair. "Hey, Krista, no offense, but you're being, like, *super* annoying right now."

"I'm not sure that's a helpful comment," Anita said, trying to hide her smile.

"Sorry. It's just, she's whining so loud, and it's, like, right in my ear. Besides, all we have to do is throw the party in a place that we can use whenever we want."

"Olot is held in the gym," Krista said. "Or is it annoying for me to mention that?"

"This isn't fucking Olot anymore! It's the Party at the End of the World! And it doesn't happen in the gym, because it's too *big* for the gym, yo, because everyone is allowed to invite whoever they want. Invite your whole family. Invite strangers in the street. Invite your dealer. It's the fucking Party at the End of the World."

"This is crazy," Krista said, looking to the rest of the room for support. "Peter, you can't approve of this, right?"

But Peter didn't answer. He was staring out the window, totally unaware of what was going on inside the room. There was a weird pattern of red marks on his cheek, as if he'd fallen on a tennis racket strung with razor wire. Rumors were he'd broken up with his girlfriend this week. Maybe she'd gone at him with her perfectly manicured nails.

"Peter!" Krista said.

He blinked back into his body. "Sorry, what's happening?"

"They want to cancel Olot and replace it with some random party!"

"Oh yeah? Right on. Olot's the worst."

Krista was totally speechless, and for the first time, Anita actually felt bad for her. What was a suck-up to do when the whole hierarchy of the universe broke down?

"Let's vote on it," Anita said. "All in favor?" Hands up in the air from everyone, even Krista, who knew a lost cause when she saw it. "The Party at the End of the World passes unanimously."

"Fine," Krista said, already adapting herself to the new status quo. "So who's gonna DJ this super-party?"

Andy slammed his hand down on the table. "No goddamn Top Forty R and B, I'll tell you that much. This party has to be more than the same old shit."

"What do you suggest?"

"I'm glad you asked—" Andy was interrupted by the plinky sound of a digital marimba. He pulled a busted-up Nokia from his pocket.

"We turn off our cell phones in student council," Krista said.

But Andy was just staring at the screen, eyes wide.

"Didn't you hear me? We turn off our phones—"

Andy looked up at Anita. "It's her," he said. "She's calling me."

It was another couple of rings before Anita realized who Andy was talking about—Eliza, responding to the legendary voice mail he'd left on Friday night.

"Help me! What do I do?" Andy was looking at the phone as if it were a magic lamp that had just offered him three wishes, only he had to decide on all of them in the next three seconds.

146

"Answer it, genius! And don't be a freak."

"Right." He stood up so fast that he knocked over his chair.

"So?" Krista said, after Andy had left the room. "If we can get back to business here, tell me—what's our entertainment going to be if not a DJ? You have an in with the Seattle Symphony or something?"

"No," Anita said, and she felt like she'd been waiting her entire life to say it. "I'll be the entertainment."

Eliza

ELIZA ADJUSTED THE ANGLE OF THE LAPTOP SCREEN, CENTERING HERSELF IN THE FRAME. Seeing your own face as other people saw it was a bit like repeating a word over and over again until it lost its meaning and became just a collection of sounds. If Eliza looked in the mirror for too long, she wouldn't see a human being anymore, just some weird space alien, all bushy eyebrows and wide mutant nose and creepy pygmy ears.

"Still there, Eliza?"

Out from the laptop speakers zinged the super-peppy voice of Sandrine Close, editor of *Closely Observed*, a popular website devoted to young photographers and their work. Sandrine, a gorgeous twentysomething hipster with fireball-red hair, had invited Eliza to "appear" on the site for a live-streamed video interview on the subject of *Apocalypse Already*. She wore a pair of stylish emerald-green glasses that came to points at the corners and a matching blouse that revealed a plunging triangle of pale skin, the final vertex of which was cut off by the bottom of the frame.

"Yeah."

"You ready to go?"

"I feel a little underdressed."

"You look great. All right, it's six. We're going live in three, two, one . . ." Sandrine smiled hugely. "Hello, Observers! I'm here with a very special guest, photographer and blogger Eliza Olivi. We've been featuring Eliza's work for the past week, but if you haven't visited her blog, *Apocalypse Already*, you can click the link farther down the page. Eliza has been photoblogging about the effects of Ardor on Seattle, using her own high school as a metaphor for society at large. And if I may say so, it's brilliant."

"Uh, thanks."

"So, Eliza, you've certainly blown up fast. Tell us what that's been like."

"It's surreal. I mean, everything is pretty surreal these days, so I guess by that standard, it's kinda normal." She laughed, but was thrown off by the fact that she couldn't tell if anybody was laughing with her. "I never expected anyone to care about what I was doing. Maybe they wouldn't have, if not for those pictures of Andy."

"Andy is the boy who was assaulted by the police officer?"

"Yeah."

Sandrine glanced down at a piece of paper hidden offscreen. "So do you see what you're doing primarily as an aesthetic or a political activity?"

"I'm not sure what you mean."

"Like, the photo you call 'Friendly Forks.' Some commenters are seeing it as a piece about the empty nobility of volunteerism in a world on the brink of destruction. Other people think that it's been staged, with a handsome young model and a set, as a purely formal exercise."

People really thought Peter was a model? Eliza imagined he would have found that funny, though she didn't really know anything about his sense of humor. They still hadn't actually spoken to each other, but since the day she took that photograph, she'd felt something brewing between them—a destined collision, or a doomed one. Either way, the symbolism wasn't lost on her; the only question was which of them was the world-destroying asteroid, and which the blue planet peacefully minding its own business.

"First of all, none of my photos are staged. And as for what it all means, I try not to think about it too much. I mean, sure, I want to help publicize the stuff that the police or the government or the school wants to keep private, but that's only a part of it. Like, people have always said that photography is an attempt to capture something fleeting. And suddenly everything is fleeting. It's like Ardor is this special tone of light we've never had before, and it's shining down and infusing every single object and person on the planet. I just want to document that light, before it's gone."

"Isn't that a lovely thought?" Sandrine said. "Moving on. With the National Guard being called in to help L.A. and New York, to say nothing of the bombings in London and across much of the Middle East, we don't hear too much about Seattle. But your photographs show that the Emerald City hasn't escaped unscathed. Many of your pictures feature looters and drug dealers caught in the act. My question is this—aren't you ever scared? I don't imagine those folks much like having their picture taken."

"What's to be scared of? The world's probably going to end in, like, six weeks."

"What about your parents? Don't they worry?"

Eliza hesitated. She was still dodging her mother's calls, and as for her dad, he'd taken one look at the photos on her website and said that she had to keep going with the project, no matter what. And the weird thing was that a little part of her wished he'd asked her to stop. Not that she would have or anything. She'd just wanted to be asked.

"I live alone with my dad, and he's a graphic designer and a photographer himself, so all he really cares about is that I'm making something good."

"Lucky you. One last question, Eliza. Given what a beautiful girl you are, I'm sure everyone wants to know—is there a special someone in your life?"

And what did it say that her mind flashed straight to Peter, like some kind of Pavlovian response mechanism?

"No. There's nobody."

"What a shame. Well, that's it for me. Let's turn things over to our listeners."

Eliza answered one question about the blog ("I'm a big Francis Ford Coppola fan"), three questions about her personal life ("Straight but looking forward to my experimental phase," "Does 'bad for me' count as a type?" and "Missionary, I guess, but they're all pretty good"), three questions about her technical process, and two questions about her favorite photographers. Then Sandrine thanked her invisible audience and shut down the live feed.

"Great job, Eliza."

"Was it?"

"Sure! You've really got a future in this. If, you know, you have a future at all. And hey, if you ever make it out to New York, I'd love to launch you on that experimental phase."

"Oh. Thanks."

Sandrine winked and closed out the session. Eliza shut the lid of her laptop. Across the table, Andy looked up from the book he was reading—by Immanuel Kant, of all people.

"Someone's got a secret admirer," he singsonged.

"Shut up."

He'd gotten lucky, was all. When Eliza first got Andy's drunken ramble of a voice mail, she didn't even bother to listen to it all the way through. It wasn't until a few days later, when she was talking to Madeline on Skype, that she thought about the message again. Eliza had been hoping that her best friend would come back to Seattle after the announcement, but apparently Madeline had fallen in love with some senior boy at Pratt, and because most of her family still lived on the East Coast anyway, her parents decided to move out that way.

Eliza wasn't sure which was stranger, the fact that she might never see Madeline again, or the fact that Madeline was actually in a relationship.

"You have to have enough fun for the both of us, okay?" Madeline said. "Tell me stories. Any crazy end-of-the-world sex yet?"

"Not quite. I did, however, receive the mother of all drunk dials from a boy."

"Do you still have it?"

"Yeah. But only because deleting it would involve looking at all the voice mails my mom's left me. It's getting ridiculous."

"We can talk about that later. First I wanna hear the epic drunk dial."

"Really? You wouldn't rather talk about my deep emotional issues with my mother?"

"Nope."

"Fine." Eliza scrolled quickly—Mom, Mom, Mom, Mom, Mom, Mom—until she found the five-minute-and-forty-two-second message left by an anonymous 206 number.

"It's actually sorta sweet," Madeline said, once it was over.

"But he's totally wasted."

"So what? He sounds . . . romantically insane."

"I agree with exactly half of that."

But once she turned off Skype, Eliza listened to Andy's message again. This time she noticed something she hadn't before—a particular word that he used, odd but familiar. She Googled "cuirass," and then "corass," and finally the search engine got her drift and pulled up results relating to "karass." The ever-helpful Urban Dictionary defined it as "a group of people linked in a cosmically significant manner, even when superficial linkages are not evident." How could she have forgotten? It was from Kurt Vonnegut's *Cat's Cradle*, one of her favorite books back when she was a sophomore, with its promise of a world religion that owned up to its own ridiculousness, and an apocalyptic ending that was more than a little relevant to current circumstances.

Maybe it was just a lucky guess on Andy's part, but it got her attention. A couple of days later, she decided to call him back.

"I'm not interested in anything romantic," she told him. "If you can handle that, meet me at Bauhaus at six thirty. And don't you dare bring any fucking flowers."

He was already waiting for her when she got there, so she snuck around the table to order a drink and do a little reconnaissance. Her primary fear was that he might still misinterpret this as some kind of date. The end of the world was coming, after all, and a lot of people were doing a lot of crazy things. In the past few days, the scientists had nailed Ardor's arrival time down to the wee hours on Tuesday the first of April—April Fool's Day. It was T-minus forty days, which meant humanity as a whole was living in the existential equivalent of last call at a dive bar, when people's standards started dropping like panties at a Justin Timberlake concert. Andy had obviously cleaned himself up for the meeting—his hair was freshly cut and combed, and he was wearing a pair of jeans that actually fit him and a sweater instead of a hoodie. It was way too dramatic a change for him to have pulled off all by himself. A woman's hand, or at least a gay guy. Was this really the outfit of a boy who'd gotten the hint?

"Well, you got me here," she said, gently setting her saucer down on the table.

Andy had a cup of black coffee in front of him, already nearly empty. "I guess so. Everyone's a sucker for a good drunk dial."

"One thing first, just to ensure we are definitely, one hundred percent on the same page—we will not be having sex now, or at any point in the future. Understood?"

"Understood. Any hand holding?"

"None."

"No cards on Valentine's Day?"

"I'd kill you. Plus Valentine's Day probably won't come again."

"Okay, last question. Does no sex also mean no kinky role-playing, wherein you play the mature professor and I play the naughty student in need of a good spanking?"

"It does."

"Got it. I forgot to bring my Catholic schoolgirl outfit anyway."

Eliza laughed, and Andy looked pleased with himself for making her laugh, and the awkwardness between them let up a little bit.

"So you think we're in a karass together, do you?" she asked.

"Sure. It makes sense, right? We're basically living in a Vonnegut novel now anyway."

"Those don't tend to end well."

"That is true."

Eliza sipped her coffee—about forty cups left, assuming her usual one-a-day regimen. She hadn't told anyone about her morbid new habit, but she figured Andy would probably get a kick out of it. "So I've started doing this weird thing in my head," she said. "Like, when I put on socks, I think to myself, well, I'll only put on socks forty more times. And when I look at the moon, I think about how many more times I might look at the moon. Even when I ordered this coffee, I couldn't help counting how many more coffees I'd probably get."

Andy held up his mug. "I think I can fit in a good two hundred, if I stay focused. Which the coffee should help with. Now if only I had something to focus on other than my own imminent demise."

"Actually, that reminds me, I could use your advice about something."

"Really?" He seemed genuinely surprised.

"Why not? We're karass-mates, aren't we?"

"Damn straight."

"So I started this blog a few days ago, and it's already turned into a bit of a thing. But I think I might be totally full of shit, in which case I should probably shut it down."

"Are you talking about *Apocalypse Already*?"

"You know it?"

"My friend Jess found it on Reddit. It's kickass."

"Really?"

"Totally. You gotta keep doing it. Bobo says it's important that everyone knows about the messed-up shit that's going on at Hamilton."

"Yeah, well, Bobo seems pretty messed up himself, as far as I can tell."

Andy stiffened, as if someone had just insulted his mom. Eliza remembered how she used to feel when her dad gave her grief for hanging out with Madeline, whose sense of style he once described as "a stripper dressed up as a prostitute for Halloween."

"Bobo's smarter than people think."

"I'm sure he is," Eliza said, backtracking. "But he does seem a little, I don't know, loose-cannon-y."

"I guess." Silence as Andy downed the rest of his coffee. He slammed the mug down on the table. "Hey! I just realized, you could probably help *us* out too!"

"With what?"

"This party that me and Anita are planning."

"Anita Graves? Wait, are you guys a thing?"

"What?" Andy looked almost offended. "Dude, no! We're just collaborating on this party. And also I think we're a band now."

"She sings?"

Eliza didn't know much about Anita, other than a collection of adjectives: rich, ambitious, smart, aloof. "Musical" was not to be found on that list.

"Like Janelle Monáe and Billie Holiday had a baby. It's crazy."

"You listen to Billie Holiday?" Eliza asked.

"What? Because I dress like a punk I'm only allowed to listen to the Cramps or something? Don't be a bigot, yo. Anyway, that wasn't my point. My point was that we're planning this party for the night before Ardor comes. I'm talking *massive*. Not just Hamilton. All of Seattle. All of anywhere, maybe. But we weren't sure how to get the word out. And suddenly you've got this big audience, right? It's, like, fate or something." Andy looked down into his coffee mug. "Hold up. I need a refill here if I'm gonna get my two hundred cups in."

One thing you could say for Ardor, it was definitely bringing out the weird in everyone. The school's foremost slacker teaming up with a girl who probably couldn't *slack* in a hammock on a Cancún beach while sipping a margarita laced with Valium. And now it came out she was some kind of secret soul singer, and the slacker was probably the next Paul McCartney. Weird and weirder.

Up at the counter, Andy joked with the barista—a pincushion Goth girl who seemed to know him.

I like him, Eliza thought. Not the way he wanted her to, maybe, but at least as a friend. Since Madeline left for college, Eliza hadn't really let herself get close to anyone. When she needed to be around people, she'd hit up a party or go out on her own. Pretty girls never struggled to find someone to talk to, as long as they didn't need to say anything important. But she did need to say important things. She'd needed that for a while, actually.

When Andy got back to the table with his coffee, he pulled a small silver flask from his backpack and unscrewed the top.

"Wanna make it Irish?"

"Why not?"

He spiked their drinks—once, twice—and at some point in the next hour she just started opening up: about the nightmare her life became after what happened with Peter, about her dad's illness, even about her mom, whose messages continued to build up on her voice mail like plaque on some hard-to-reach molar.

"You should call her," Andy said.

"Why?"

He shrugged. "Because at least she gives a shit."

"She didn't give a shit for the last two years."

"Maybe. But she does now. Trust me, that's worth something. Besides, it's the apocalypse, right? It's your last chance. Get on the tearful reunion train already."

Eliza, buzzed on the Baileys and having a surprisingly good time, thought how crazy it was that just a month ago, she wouldn't even have *spoken* to Andy unless some teacher had forced her to. And now she was actually thinking of listening to him.

That Friday, Eliza got the tap on her shoulder she'd been expecting ever since *Apocalypse Already* took off. Ms. Cahill, the office receptionist, stood above Eliza's desk, casting a dour administrative pall over the whole AP Chem classroom.

"Ms. Olivi," she whispered, though the room had already gone quiet. "The principal would like to see you."

Walking upstairs with Ms. Cahill, Eliza couldn't help but imagine herself a convict, traipsing the long corridor toward the electric chair. Each classroom she passed was a prison cell; from inside came the desperate screams of chalk on chalkboard and the sighs of tortured teenagers spending what might be their last hours on Earth learning about the causes of the Peloponnesian War and the best way to ask for directions in German.

"Am I in trouble or something?"

"You'll have to ask Mr. Jester."

When they reached the main office, Ms. Cahill pointed out the principal's door and then disappeared into her cubicle, as if she were just an appliance, like a vacuum cleaner, that would sit patiently in a corner until it was needed again.

Mr. Jester didn't even notice her come in. He was staring out the window, past the dusty stripes of the blinds, toward the Hamilton parking lot. His outfit was decidedly non-principal-esque: wrinkled cargo pants and a ratty T-shirt with a picture of Jim Morrison on the front.

"Hey," she said.

He jumped. "Jesus, you scared me." His eyes were sunken and sleepless, and even the ring of hair atop the naked atoll of his head was wild and greasy. She watched him attempt the Herculean task of hauling up the heavy corners of his mouth. "How are you, Eliza?"

"Okay, I guess, considering."

"Where are you hoping to head in the fall? New York, right?"

"If there's a New York to go to. How'd you know?"

"I read the blog, of course! New York's pretty crazy, though. I couldn't take all that noise and traffic, but a young thing like you, you'll do fine."

A long silence. "You want me to take down the site, don't you?" she asked.

The whole Botoxed cheer of Mr. Jester's face went slack. "It's not about what *I* want, Eliza. I believe in the arts. Free speech and all that." He pointed to Jim Morrison on his T-shirt, and Eliza wondered if he'd put it on just for her sake. "But those pictures you're taking have already caused a lot of trouble for this school. And I promise you that if you keep going like you're going, it'll turn out badly."

"Is that a threat?"

The principal put his hands down flat on the desk. His voice was desperate, almost manic. "No! It's a plea! Look . . ." He scrabbled through the mess on his desk, coming up with a week-old copy of the *Seattle Times*, whose presses had stopped rolling a few days back due to employee attrition. The headline read VIOLENCE INCREASINGLY TARGETS KIDS AND TEENS. "It's not safe out there, Eliza."

"But it's safe in here? At Hamilton?"

Mr. Jester waved the question away. "Listen, my superintendent says he got a call yesterday from the DOE. That's the Department of Education, Eliza. That's federal-level stuff! They think there's some kind of corporal punishment going on here because they saw the picture you took, with that slacker kid all covered in blood."

"His name's Andy," Eliza said.

"I know his fucking name!" The obscenity reverberated around the room like a gunshot. When Mr. Jester spoke again, it was with controlled fury. "I could get in real trouble, Eliza. Please. This is my life we're talking about."

For years now, Eliza had felt a captive to the whims of adults, whether they were acting voluntarily (her mom, leaving), or involuntarily (her dad, dying), or just ordering you around (pretty much all of them, all the time). She thought she'd always feel that powerless. Then she met Madeline, who taught her one way to exercise some modicum of control over the world: by making a weapon of her body. It took Eliza a year to realize that, while that kind of power was real enough, the exercise of it sapped some internal resource, one that took a long time to recover, if it ever did. Today, for the first time, she felt like her power was based on something other than sex. The fear in Mr. Jester's eyes was the fear of a small man come face-to-face with something bigger than himself. And maybe it was cruel, but Eliza told him the truth—that she wouldn't take the website down just because of what might happen if she didn't, because she felt that what she was doing was good, and so only good could come of it, even if it wasn't immediately clear how. And when the principal began to sputter and threaten and shout, she calmly reached into her bag and pulled out the Exakta. It was the only thing about that whole meeting that truly surprised her: As she fit the viewfinder to her eye, Mr. Jester froze. She pressed the shutter button, replaced the camera in her bag, and left the office. All the while, the principal stayed perfectly still—resigned to his final pose.

He was fired the following week.

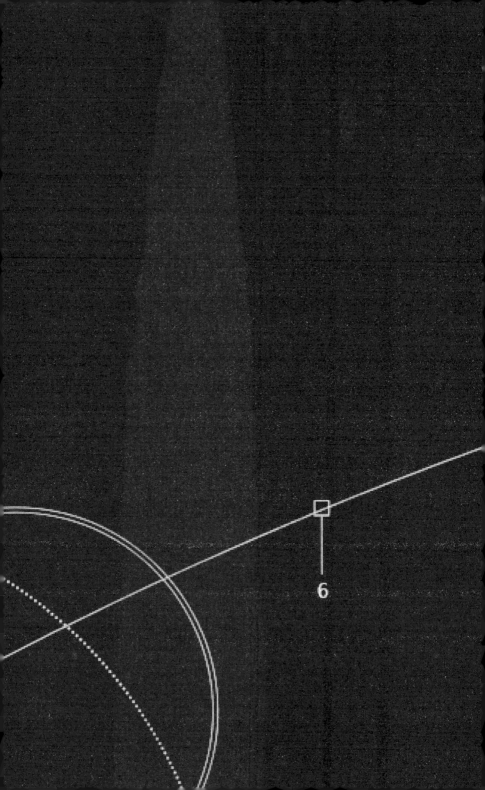

6

Anita

FOR THE FEW HUNDRED STUDENTS WHO STILL CAME TO SCHOOL EVERY DAY, THE MORNING now began with a mandatory twenty-minute assembly, presided over by Officer Foede, their government-appointed interim principal. He'd pass along the newest information about Ardor (as if they weren't all compulsively checking it online a hundred times a day), then hand the proceedings over to student council, who'd been tasked with organizing a five-to-ten-minute daily "pep rally." The remaining members of the Hamilton improv team, Sudden Infant Monkey Death Syndrome, claimed Wednesdays, while a group of boys who sang a cappella versions of female pop songs—Miley Cyborg—performed every Friday. The other three days featured a rotating cast of the talented and talentless, proving that ten minutes could feel like two or two hundred. Today, however, Anita had claimed the slot for herself; she and Andy were going to officially unveil the Party at the End of the World.

"Good morning, Hamilton," Officer Foede said, stepping up to the podium. He was the quintessential cop—stalwart and ruddy-skinned and self-important.

"Good morning, Mr. Foede."

"Today I have something very important to talk to you about. It's come to my attention that a political gathering is planned for this upcoming Saturday at Cal Anderson Park. I am here to tell you that it is expressly forbidden that any student attend this event."

Anita heard a clicking sound from somewhere nearby. Two seats over, Eliza Olivi was taking photos of the proceedings. Her dark-brown hair hung loose and a little curly, reaching just to the top of a silver ankh that drew the eye down into the vortex of her prodigious chest. So this was what Andy had himself all worked up about. It wasn't as if Anita didn't get it; the pretty airheads like Stacy Prince you could always write off as so much plastic, but Eliza was different. You could tell she'd actually be a beautiful woman, not just a beautiful girl. Still, Anita wondered if Andy recognized the insecurity balanced perfectly between the push-pull of Eliza's two protective shells: the bitchy attitude and the skimpy clothes. Or maybe only other girls could see it, like those frequencies only dogs could hear.

Eliza noticed Anita watching her. She stood up and displaced the junior boy sitting between them with a word: "Move."

"This might sound crazy," she said, after she was seated next to Anita, "but I think I'm the reason this douche bag is our principal. Mr. Jester asked me to take my website down, because it was going to get him in trouble, and I said no."

"What website?"

Actually, Anita knew all about *Apocalypse Already*, but for some reason, she didn't want Eliza to know that she knew. "It's this blog I started. And it's gotten a lot of attention, I guess, and so has Hamilton. Like, not *good* attention."

"Huh."

Foede was still going strong on the subject of dangerous political activity, glaring around the room as if he wished he could interrogate the whole place at once. Eliza snapped another photograph.

Anita looked over her shoulder. Andy and Bobo, seated in the otherwise empty back row of the auditorium, were laughing quietly at Foede's impassioned prohibition. If anything, the dumb cop had only made it *more* likely that students would go to Cal Anderson on Saturday. Anita didn't know much about the event—some kind of demonstration involving that creepy Golden guy (and what kind of second-rate hip-hop name was Golden, anyway?)—but she hoped it wouldn't dilute the impact of her own announcement vis-à-vis the Party at the End of the World.

"I want to be very clear about this," Foede continued. "The Seattle Police Department and various other law enforcement agencies have reason to believe that this rally represents an incitement to violence against the state. For your own safety, and for the good of the community, do not attend. That is all. Please proceed to your first-period classes." He released the lectern as if he'd just finished waterboarding it.

Anita stood up. "Hey! I have an announcement to make!"

"You can make it tomorrow!" Foede shouted, over the murmur and shuffle of liberated teenagers.

"What was it?" Eliza asked.

"The Party at the End of the World. I had a whole speech prepared."

"Oh, don't worry about that. Andy asked me to start writing about it on my blog. You'll reach a lot more people that way than in here."

Anita had an uncharitable thought—*I didn't ask for your help*—then swallowed it and smiled. "Thanks, Eliza."

"No problem. Hey, we should hang out sometime. Maybe with Andy?"

"Sure."

"Cool."

Eliza wafted off in a bubble of floral shampoo smell, drawing stares as she went, along with a few more uncharitable thoughts.

The music room was located on the ground floor of the arts building, separated from the main hallway by two sets of swinging doors. You entered on the topmost level, and as you moved toward the center of the room, the floor stepped down like an inverted ziggurat—wide enough on each step for one stratum of orchestra players. The great black heart of the room was an old Steinway grand, lid lifted to reveal the crisscrossed coils and struts that were its innards. Andy had replaced the wooden bench with a leopard-print drum throne. He was already sitting there when Anita came in, picking out the melody to a song they were working on and sampling harmonies in the left hand. They met here every day now, one fifteen-minute snack break after the Consolations of Philosophy.

"Afternoon, Mr. Ray Charles."

"What's up, Aretha?"

Anita leaned into the curve of the piano—her favorite spot. "I spoke to your girl today."

Andy stopped playing. "Eliza? When?"

"She sat down next to me in assembly."

"You talk me up?"

"I didn't get the chance." Anita chose her words carefully. "You ever feel like she's a little . . . full of herself or something?"

"Maybe, but that's only because she's so awesome."

Anita laughed through her annoyance. So what if boys always went in for the ones with the big boobs and the reputation for putting out? Didn't matter to her.

"What are we working on today, Ms. Winehouse?" Andy asked.

"Let's do 'Seduce Me.' I thought we were getting pretty close yesterday."

"On it."

Anita more or less ran their rehearsals, but Andy wasn't afraid to speak up when he thought she was wrong about something. They already had a couple of songs in good shape—"Bloodless Love" and a retooled version of "Save It"—and a few more that were coming together. "Seduce Me" was probably Anita's favorite, because it was a collaboration. Andy had written the melody months ago, but he hadn't been able to sort out the lyrics. "You should take a run at it," he'd said. Anita had never considered herself a writer, but as soon as she set pen to paper, she realized how desperate she was to express herself somehow. She could spend hours working on a single line, poring over a rhyming dictionary and a thesaurus, even going back to some of her favorite songs to see what made them tick. She'd already developed two fundamental rules of songwriting: (1) Every word that rhymed with "love" was a cliché (and anyone who wasn't Prince who used the word "dove" in a song deserved to be shot), and (2) Clichés were sometimes okay. Otherwise, how could you have songs like "Stand by Me" and "I Can't Stop Loving You" and even "Love Is a Losing Game"?

Andy composed on piano, but once they had something solid, he'd switch over to guitar. His playing reminded her of Amy Winehouse's, actually—nothing showy, but always clean and tasteful. And his sense of rhythm was, for lack of a better term, exceptionally not-white.

"Don't try to sound sexy," Andy told her after the first run-through. "The song already does that."

"I wasn't trying. That's my natural sexiness."

"Then tone it down, porn star."

They worked "Seduce Me" for an hour or so, then finished up the basic melody of a new one, "Countdown." That night, back at Andy's apartment, he'd finalize the chords while Anita sat on the couch, cleaning up his lyrics. They were together practically 24-7 these days, like sudden siblings. She knew his wardrobe, his breakfast cereal preferences, even his smell—a musk of sweat and deodorant and cigarettes and old cotton.

It was hard to believe she'd been staying with him for almost three weeks now, ever since that Perineum concert on Valentine's Day. Her parents weren't happy about it, of course, but there wasn't much they could do. Her father had come to Hamilton just once, a couple of days after she ran away, and they'd argued each other to a draw in the hallway outside U.S. history. Anita hadn't been kidnapped. She was still going to school. And the police were way too understaffed and overworked to bother getting involved. It was fun, seeing her father utterly powerless to command her, walking away in a childish huff.

She quickly replaced her family with Andy's. Well, not his *actual* family, who'd long since abandoned ship, but his friends. And while Bobo still hadn't grown on her (or vice versa), she got along well enough with the rest of them—the exploited rich kid Kevin, Jess-who-used-to-be-a-girl, and Misery, who seemed way too messed up to be Peter's sister, but not quite messed up enough to be dating a sociopath like Bobo.

Anita didn't have any friends for Andy to bond with; she'd always kept way too busy for that. And though she had no particular desire for him to meet her parents, she did have to pick a couple of things up from the house, and she really didn't want to go alone. After rehearsal, she ran the idea by him and got pretty much the response she'd expected.

"Andy, how would you like to meet some parents even worse than yours?"

"About as much as I'd like a kick in the balls."

Anita slapped him on the back. "Then you better strap on a cup, kid, 'cause this is happening."

It was strange—after only a few weeks away, the house no longer felt like home. Anita had never noticed how pointlessly big the place was. Why in the world did three people need so much space, except to escape from one another, to be more alone? Andy hummed the chorus to "Hotel California" as they drove up the long driveway.

Just on the other side of the front door, Anita's mother stood mopping the marble floor. She looked up when they entered, nervous and suspicious at once, like a wildebeest trying to ascertain whether the approaching lion was hungry.

"You're back," she said simply.

"Just for a few minutes." It struck Anita that she'd never actually seen her mother clean before. "What are you doing? Where's Luisa?"

"She quit. We offered to double her salary, but she said she wanted to spend time with her family."

"Go figure." Anita laughed experimentally.

Her mother replaced the mop in its red bucket and leaned the handle up against the stairs. There was hesitance in her eyes, a softening toward the thought of softening. Then a decision was made and everything went hard again. "Do you have any idea what you've put us through, Anita? Where are you even staying?"

Judgment. Disapproval. How could she have hoped for anything else?

"With Andy. He's a friend."

Andy raised a hand. "Yo."

Anita's mother swept her eyes over him like a grocery clerk scanning a bag of potato chips, ascertaining his worth, then brushing him aside. "You should talk to your father. He'll have some choice words about this."

"No, thanks. I just came back to get some things."

She walked past her mother and up the stairs. Her room had been dusted and polished and arranged. *Nothing wrong here!* it said. *No daughter on the run or anything!* Anita took a duffel bag out from under the bed and hurriedly filled it: clothes, jewelry, a stuffed cat worn down to a matrix of gray thread from all the times she'd tried to squeeze some human warmth out of it. And then she was crying—hot, angry tears—and Andy was there, supporting her as she slumped against him, letting the weakness pour out of her. It felt so good to be held; even after she was strong enough to stand on her own again, she didn't immediately step away.

"I used to sing in that closet over there," she said.

"Good acoustics?"

"Thick walls." She walked to the closet and shut herself inside. "Fuck you, Mom!" she shouted.

Andy said something in response, but Anita couldn't make out the words. She looked around the little room, pinched the hem of a red velvet dress she'd grown out of years before. "Good-bye, closet," she whispered.

Back in the bedroom, Andy was looking over her music collection. She threw a last pair of shoes in the duffel bag and zipped it up. "Let's get out of here."

Her mother was still mopping when they came back down.

"I'll meet you outside," she said to Andy, passing him the bag.

"All right. Nice to meet you, Mrs. Graves."

Anita's mother didn't say anything until Andy had shut the front door behind him. "What are you and that disgusting boy getting up to?" she asked, fire in her voice.

Anita wanted to shout back, but she checked herself. Who knew when she and her mother would see each other again? Maybe never. She didn't want to leave on bad terms.

"We're just friends," she said.

Her mother scoffed. "Friends?"

"Yeah. But it's none of your business anyway."

Her mother threw the mop onto the floor. "The Bible says to respect your elders, Anita! Maybe that doesn't mean anything to you, but it meant something to me and your father when we were kids. We had respect then. Not like this. Running away from home. Shacking up with some boy who looks like a drug addict."

"Doesn't the Bible say something about supporting your children? About loving them unconditionally?"

"The commandment is honor thy mother and father. Not the other way around."

"Then the Bible is fucked!" Anita said.

A terrible shroud of detachment seemed to fall across her mother's face—a cloud passing over the sun. Her voice went flat as a gravestone. "I don't think you understand what's going on out there, young lady. This is the final reckoning. They may not discuss it that way at that school of yours, but those of us who are right with God know what's going on. It's the separation of the saved and the damned. So you go, if that's what you want to do. You go and damn yourself."

Anita felt the tears coming again, and it seemed one and the same with holding them back to march deeper into the house, into her father's office. He rose from behind his desk, silent as a monument, as Anita went straight to the polished metal palace in which he kept Bernoulli, the world's saddest hyacinth macaw, and opened the hatch. She expected a fluttering flush of blue to erupt into the room, but the bird didn't move. Bernoulli had no idea what to do with freedom; even the desire for flight had been bred or beaten out of him.

"Get out of there!" she screamed. "Are you stupid?"

Bernoulli tilted his head, squawked once.

"Where would he go?" Anita's father asked.

It was true, Anita realized, and her mind reeled with the weight of that truth. Even if the bird escaped his cage, he'd just be stuck in the office. And if he got out of the office, he'd just be stuck in the house. And if he got out of the house, then where could he go to be safe? He'd be every bit as trapped outside the cage as he'd been trapped inside it. And Anita was afraid it would be the same for her. All the world was a cage.

"Fine," she said, and stormed back out of the office. Somewhere along the line, the dam had burst again; tears streamed down her face. One drop fell onto the polished marble floor of the foyer, a salt stain Anita knew her mother would mop away before it even had time to dry.

Eliza

Eliza checked the printout again. "He calls himself 'Chad Eye.'"

"Eye? Like an eyeball?"

"Yep."

"Sounds like hippie nonsense."

"I think it's badass," Andy said. "Like Sid Vicious or something."

"Well, he can call himself the reincarnation of Tupac, as long as he's got something for us," Anita said.

They'd posted requests everywhere—from actual flyers on the Hamilton bulletin board to Craigslist's "community activity" forum—but when the offer finally came, it came through *Apocalypse Already*. Eliza put out the word that they were seeking a venue for the Party at the End of the World, and within a few hours, she got the e-mail from Chad. He said he had a proposition for them but wanted to meet in person to discuss it. They were told to come by his house at five thirty on Thursday morning, and also "to abstain from heavy foods or sexual activity for the previous twelve to twenty-four hours." In other words, the guy was certifiably crazypants. But a Zillow search of his address—just on the other side of the 520 bridge—turned up a house valued at four million dollars. So here they all were.

The ride turned out to be oddly uncomfortable. Eliza was getting a distinct passive-aggressive vibe off Anita, and she had no idea why. It wasn't as if they were competing or something. Neither of them were interested in Andy, and Eliza was as bad at singing as Anita probably was at taking photos. Maybe it was inevitable—one of those rivalries that so often sprout up between girls, like mushrooms in the crevices of a forest, craning up toward whatever attention filters down through the canopy.

"The pictures you put up on the blog yesterday were wicked," Andy said. "How long did it take for that place to burn down?"

"Well, the fire department got there after an hour, so it didn't really burn down. But I doubt anybody's going to be living there anytime soon."

"Couldn't you have helped out somehow?" Anita asked. "Instead of standing around taking pictures?"

"What was I supposed to do, run inside and start carrying people out?"

"You're listening to KUBE 93," said the radio DJ. "Let's keep this best of the eighties countdown rolling with 'Lucky Star' by Madonna!"

Anita turned down the volume. "Gross. At least the end of the world means no more eighties music."

"You don't like Madonna?" Eliza asked, then immediately regretted it. Of course Anita didn't like Madonna; that would be way too mainstream and predictable.

"Girl, Madonna is nothing but an old shoe."

"What the hell does that mean?"

"She's got no *soul*," Andy said, and both he and Anita cracked up.

Eliza snorted. "That's stupid."

"*Madonna* is what's stupid," Anita said.

Eliza was preparing a less civil rejoinder when she was interrupted by the voice of the unflappable GPS lady.

"You have reached your destination."

They parked on the shoulder of a wide suburban street, surrounded by vaguely Germanic mini-mansions and mailboxes shaped like vaguely Germanic mini-mansions. It was all pretty cookie-cutter, except for the house directly across the street, which just happened to be where they were going.

Chad's house had been built in the style of a Japanese temple, all terraced spires and bloodred wood inlaid with bronze. The yard wasn't dirt or lawn, but raked gravel and smooth rocks, littered with trees that looked like giant bonsai. At the far end of the garden, a couple sat cross-legged in a small pagoda, facing each other. The path from the street led across a short, steeply curved bridge, arcing over a pond in which the moonlight caught an occasional flicker of a fin or glittering plane of scales. There was no doorbell or knocker at the front door, only a small gong with a mallet attached to its base by a length of leather cord.

"Is this a joke?" Andy asked.

Eliza grabbed the mallet. "Only one way to find out."

The shimmer of the gong crescendoed and died out, like a coppery koi swimming up from deep water and then descending again. A few moments later the door opened.

Standing on the threshold was a monk holding a beagle.

Or maybe not quite a monk, Eliza thought, never having seen one in the flesh before. He wore saffron-yellow robes, his head was totally shaved, and he wore a couple of necklaces made out of huge wooden beads. What he resembled most of all was one of those guys who hang around in airports handing out flyers that say things like *Experience Love!* or *Happiness Can Be Yours!* The beagle stared out at the new guests with an inscrutable calmness, both canine and Buddhist at once.

"You made it," Chad said, making eye contact with each of them in turn. "Come in, please."

They followed him into the house, through an atrium with nothing in it but a small pyramidal fountain trickling water through a pile of rocks. The living room was equally spare—one low table on a thin tatami mat, and in each corner, a massive ceramic urn supporting a bouquet of curling bamboo shoots. Above them, a skylight displayed a black square of firmament, prickled with stars. A girl walked in carrying a gray cast-iron pot and four porcelain cups in a wobbly column. She was in her twenties, dressed entirely in off-white hemp, with natty blond dreadlocks and a pound of sterling silver perforating each ear.

"Steeped and ready for takeoff," she said.

Chad accepted the pot and the cups. "Thank you, Sunny. Would you mind taking Sid?"

"Of course not!" Sunny reached down and picked up the beagle, who immediately took one of her dreadlocks into his mouth. "You kids are in for a *tree-eat*," she half sang on her way out of the room.

They all sat down around the table as Chad poured the tea. He set a cup in front of each of them, giving a little bow as he did so. When

Eliza returned the gesture, her hair fell down around her face. She felt a hand reach over and tuck it back behind her ear.

"It was gonna get in your cup," Andy explained.

Warning lights went off in her head. She might even have said something—a brief reminder of their definitive platonic status—only at that moment, she got a whiff of the steam off the tea and nearly gagged.

"What the hell is this?"

Chad smiled. "A very weak brew of hallucinogenic mushrooms."

That was all the recommendation Andy needed. He tossed back his portion, fought to keep it down, then grimaced. "Yum."

"Is this safe?" Anita asked.

"Completely," Chad said. "At this level of dilution, it may have no effect at all. But hopefully, it'll cause you to see things in a slightly different light. Of course, you're free to abstain."

Eliza looked down into her cup. The liquid was reddish brown, the same color as English Breakfast. This was crazy. They'd just come into a total stranger's house, and now they were going to get high with him? Hadn't she watched about a million videos in elementary school whose only purpose had been to convince her not to do exactly this?

Eliza saw Anita hesitate at the rim of her own cup, like a diver suddenly realizing exactly how high up the board was.

"Hey, Anita," Andy said. "Whatever it is, it's not worth it."

Anita smiled. "Screw it," she said, then drank. "Woo! That is foul."

Eliza had no choice now; she wasn't about to be shown up by Anita Graves, of all people. The concoction tasted like rotten vegetables steeped in mud.

Chad drank last. "It'll be a while before it kicks in," he said, "but

I'll get right to the point. You're looking for a location for this party of yours. You have no money and hardly any ideas. Right so far?"

No one disagreed.

"Now, allow me to tell you a bit about myself. Once upon a time, many lives ago, I worked for a little company called Boeing. I made a lot of money there, before I realized I didn't believe in what we were doing."

"Building airplanes?" Andy said.

"Defense," Chad answered, putting air quotes around the word. "Which is actually a polite way of saying 'offense.' So I quit my job and started wandering. I built a boat and sailed it between Australia and New Zealand. I lived in a yurt in Costa Rica. I studied at a monastery in Tibet. And at the end of it all, I found myself in a strange position—loads of money, and no real need of it. I considered giving it all away and disappearing to some tiny cabin in the woods, but I decided I could do better than that. I wanted to set an example of responsible, community-based living. And that's what I've done." He uncrossed his legs and stood up. "Let's take a little tour."

They followed him through the spacious halls of his gigantic house. Most of the many rooms were occupied, and the occupants, each of whom Chad introduced by name, ranged from college-age to nursing-home-age. All of them were undaunted, if not downright excited, by the prospect of hugging a few strangers.

"How many people live here?" Eliza asked.

"About twenty, usually."

"And this is what you spent your money on?"

"Actually, living like this is relatively cheap. We grow a lot of our food in a garden plot a couple miles away, and I own the house outright."

They finished their tour and returned to the tearoom. Chad looked up at the skylight. "It's almost time," he said. A sliding door opened onto a wooden balcony overlooking the water. They sat down in cushioned deck chairs, facing out toward the lake.

"I'm up at this hour every morning now," Chad said. "I find the juxtaposition of sunrise and the asteroid so beautiful. Alpha and omega. Beginning and end."

Eliza looked up. Logically, she knew that the sky was the same as ever, but her perception was shifting. The tiny gradient of blue just visible at the bottom of the mountain range suddenly contained within it the full spectrum of color—pinks and greens and yellows and silvers and the infinite legion of nameless shades in between, all blending together like the watery rainbow of an opal. And now, ever so slowly, the sun began to lift itself over the chalk outline of the Cascades. It was like some sort of exercise, a single quick pull-up, that the heavy sphere did every day purely as a favor to the inhabitants of Earth. That was its purpose, to rise and shine, just as every person it shone down on had a purpose. Eliza felt as if her heart were a prism, refracting that magic light into Andy and Anita and Chad's hearts, into the hearts of everyone who was watching this harlequin sky, and then onward, to every human being and every animal and every object that had ever existed. Even Ardor—a white freckle on the blushing face of the heavens—was deserving of her love, because the asteroid was doing nothing worse than what it was meant to do. Time passed. When the sun was safely pinned to the lapel of the horizon, Chad spoke again.

"The best thing we can give people is a moment of true connection before the end. And I'd like to help you do that. I have friends who specialize in bringing people together in temporary communities.

They'd like to create a celebration for the coming of the asteroid. I've also spoken with my old boss, and he's volunteered Boeing Field as a venue. It covers ninety-two acres, roughly one-sixth the area provided at Woodstock."

"Andy and I want to perform," Anita said. Her voice was somehow dreamy and resolute at once.

"I'd have to hear you first," Chad said. "I've got a piano inside."

"I'm not sure I could find the notes," Andy said, and giggled.

"You'd be surprised what you can do on shrooms."

Chad led them back through the house, into a large, low-ceilinged room with a grand piano standing like some proud, sable-skinned animal in the corner. Andy sat down on the bench and launched right into a song.

"I'm not warmed up," Anita said.

"You're always warmed up, Lady Day."

The notes of the piano rang out louder and fuller and more present than any music Eliza had ever heard. Anita sang, and her voice was everything Andy had said it would be, full of bite and ache and despair. For a while, Eliza floated along with just the sound, until a few of the lyrics clarified in her conscious mind—something about the number of lovers someone would get in a lifetime, followed by a countdown: *Ten, nine, eight, seven, six, five, four, three, two, one—and you're on your own.* Eliza realized that Andy had written this song for her, for the way she'd started seeing the world in terms of countdowns. He loved her and she didn't love him back. And before the world ended, he'd learn that.

Eliza was crying, at the song and the drug and the sunrise and the inevitable future she'd predicted.

"He'll hate me," she whispered to no one.

Chad put a warm hand on her shoulder. "Hate is only a temporary failure to perceive our absolute interdependence. It's not real."

Before she could ask him what he meant, the song had ended. Chad was applauding. "Absolutely wonderful! You're hired. Now your only job is to convince people to come to the party."

"Eliza can manage that," Andy said, fixing her with a huge smile. "She's famous now."

"So it's real then?" Eliza asked. "We're really doing this?"

"I'd like to think so. Of course, no one can say for sure what's going to happen in the next few weeks. We might lose touch."

"So then how will we know the party's still on?"

Chad shrugged. "You won't. You can't. Just like I can't ever know for certain if Sid will come when I call him." He cupped his hands around his mouth. "Sid!" After a moment, the beagle sauntered into the room. His attitude wasn't that of a dog responding to a call so much as one who'd coincidentally decided to come of his own volition at just the right moment. He pooled himself on top of Chad's bare feet.

"That," Chad said, "is what faith is for."

Andy

IT WAS A 1965 GIBSON ES-175D IN A SUNBURST FINISH. HOLLOW-BODY, WITH A TRAPEZE tailpiece, Tune-O-Matic bridge, and vintage humbuckers. Usually only jazz guys went in for that kind of sound, but Andy had played the guitar a few times in the store and convinced himself that it had just the right tone for the songs he was writing with Anita—fat and rich and crunchy (when played through an original-issue Fender Twin Reverb and an OCD overdrive pedal, natch). The only problem was that it cost seven grand.

Though all of Seattle's print newspapers had stopped their presses, the website for the alternative weekly *The Stranger* was still running. It was there that Kevin learned about the closing of Bellevue Mall. The manager cited "asteroid sickness"—a combination of not enough customers and not enough employees. What he should have said was, "Come and get it, gentlemen."

Bobo, Kevin, Misery, and Jess had all come along for the ride, so the station wagon was fully loaded. Andy had told Anita he'd be spending the afternoon skating with Bobo, to avoid the inevitable hour-long ethics lecture. It wasn't as if he felt great about looting, but it would be a tragedy for an instrument of such quality to go unplayed for a whole month. Besides, he could always bring the guitar back in the event of non-apocalypse.

They drove up to the top level of the mall's huge spiraling parking garage. Andy had expected the place to be empty, but there were a few other cars already parked in the lot.

"What do you think they're doing here?" Kevin asked.

"Same as us, probably," Andy said.

"Or they could be security. We sure this is a good idea? The cops are arresting everything that moves these days."

Bobo slapped Kevin on the back of the head. "Nut up, man. And Andy, pop the trunk for me."

Bobo withdrew the sledgehammer he'd brought along like Excalibur from the stone, then gave it a few whooshing practice swings. Misery and Kevin sat in the backseat, strapping on roller skates. The rest of them had brought their skateboards, so everyone could be mobile in the case of an emergency.

It wasn't going to be a very subtle break-in. Their many squeaking wheels, echoing through the parking garage, would have served any nearby security guards about as well as a homing beacon. Just behind Macy's, they found a pair of double doors at the bottom of a long ramp marked EMPLOYEE ENTRANCE. A chain was wrapped around the handles, with a busted padlock still dangling off one of the links.

"Goddamn it," Bobo said. "I wanted to break something."

Misery massaged his shoulder. "There'll still be things to break, baby."

"Whoever's in there could be, like, real criminals," Kevin said.

Bobo slammed the head of the sledgehammer into the door, denting the metal. "We're the real criminals, yo! Whoever's in there should be afraid of us!"

The lights on the other side of the door switched on as they entered, cued to proximity sensors. A sad employee lounge and a busted soft-drink machine later, they found themselves in the home furnishings department of Macy's. Andy threw down his board and took off, weaving between old-lady couches and patio furniture and tables set for some Mormon-scale family dinner. A clangor erupted behind him, as Bobo knocked one shelf of kitchenware into another.

"Stink bomb!" Jess shouted. He was riding at top speed toward the perfume department. Shifting his weight backward, he kicked the deck up and javelined it into a display case of heart-shaped bottles, smashing them to pieces. The room filled with the same smell you got off that one table in the lunchroom, where all the girls had curly burned hair and press-on nails and velour pants with writing on the ass. Andy dodged the broken glass and pulled up at the spot where the white tile of Macy's gave onto the red tile of the mall. From somewhere far away came a wavecrash of shattering glass. They definitely weren't alone.

"I'm gonna go upstairs and upgrade my wardrobe," Misery said. "Can you boys live without me?"

"I'll hang back with you, Miz," Kevin said.

Bobo pulled up next to Andy. "Good call. Jess, you stick around too."

"Me? Why?" Jess got majorly offended whenever anyone hinted that he might still be a girl in anything but rank biology.

"Because if shit gets real, I don't want Miz to be alone with a pussy like Kevin."

"Hey!" Kevin said, but Jess seemed content with the explanation.

"Aw, you're worried about me?" Misery skated over and kissed Bobo on the cheek. "Go find me something nice and sparkly." A smooth glide toward the escalator was followed by an awkward roller-skate ascent. Jess and Kevin followed her up and out of sight.

"Race you to the other end of the mall," Bobo said.

Their decks hit the ground at the exact same moment. Then they were rushing over the ribbed tile, past the airy whiteness of the Apple store and the iridescent blue of Tiffany's and the brownish check of Burberry. The floor sloped downward toward the food court, lending them extra speed. Orange Julius was just an orange blur. There was some movement inside a Champs Sports—a few kids picking out sneakers and baseball caps. They glanced out as Bobo and Andy blazed past. The floor began to angle upward again. Momentum gave out, and Andy had to kick hard to keep moving. By the time they reached the Nordstrom at the other end of the mall, neither of them even noticed who'd won the race. Andy collapsed onto a metal bench across from an LCD screen displaying the mall directory. Two seconds later Bobo transformed it into a spiderweb of cracks and a couple of spastic pixels. He left the sledgehammer wedged there, wobbling like an arrow just sunk into a bull's-eye.

"You got a cig?" Andy asked.

"I got something better than that." Bobo pulled a joint from behind his ear.

"Hot damn. Is that why you got rid of everybody?"

"I hate sharing. Anyway, you better enjoy this—supply's mad low. I've doubled prices out on the street, and people are still paying. That's the end of the world for you."

"Golden's hooking you up?"

"He fucking loves me. I could talk to him if you want, get you a little product to sell."

"Thanks, but Anita and I are practicing twenty-four/seven these days. I'm booked solid."

"Whatever. But you better be at the rally tomorrow."

"No doubt."

"I'm serious. I mean, it's cool that you've finally got some girls in your life, but if you're not even gonna get laid—"

"I will."

"So you say."

"I have to, yo. It's my quest. If I can't get Eliza, I might as well not even be alive."

"I'll smoke to that," Bobo said.

The sound of shoes slapping on tile, then two guys sprinted past the bench. They were black, maybe in their mid-twenties, and carried so much jewelry that their whole bodies seemed to glitter. A chunky security guard in a gray uniform chased after them, losing ground with every step.

"Look at Humpty Dumpty go!" Bobo said.

The guard turned around, still jogging backward as he did so. "You kids get out of here!"

"We totes will," Andy said.

"Looting is a criminal offense. You'll end up in jail."

"Go get the bad guys, Humpty!" Bobo shouted.

The security guard disappeared around the corner of a Gap Kids. Andy actually felt a little bad for him.

They finished the joint, then headed up the paralyzed escalator to

Kennelly Keys. A metal curtain, padlocked to a loop in the floor, was the only security the shop had. They traded off sledgehammer blows, like convicts on a chain gang, while spitting game at the lock.

"You like how I do it?" Bobo asked.

"You like it like yo mama like it?"

"Spread them legs, girl."

"The safe word is motorboat."

After a few dozen blows, the tumblers gave out. Andy rolled up the grating and Bobo shattered the glass door.

Kennelly Keys was a pretty small music shop, catering mostly to suburban families who wanted to get their kids playing "Für Elise" for the grandparents. The store made its money off cheap violins and Casio keyboards and an ugly plywood mini instrument called My First Guitar.

"Look at me," Bobo said, raising two of the tiny guitars over his head at once. "I'm Pete fucking Townshend." He smashed them together. "Rest in peace, my first and second guitars."

Andy made a beeline for the back corner of the shop, where lived the one object that saved the place from total irrelevance—the 1965 Gibson ES-175D in a sunburst finish. The case wasn't even locked. And then Andy had it, heavy and solid in his hands—like a sledgehammer you could make music with. He powered up an amp, plugged in, turned the dial hard to the right, and strummed the open strings. *Shit yeah.*

"Too clean," Bobo said. "That guitar sounds like a girl who won't even take her shirt off."

"Nothing wrong with a good tease."

"At least it's loud. Let's do this. One, two, three, four . . ."

Bobo brutalized a child's drum kit with a pair of xylophone mallets. Andy turned up the drive knob on the amp and played power chords as fast as he could. After about thirty seconds, Bobo kicked the drums over one by one, then stood up.

"Good night, Seattle!"

As the guitar's reverb died out, they both heard it: a long, low wail. At first, Andy thought it was some kind of alarm. But soon the wail resolved into words—"Someone, please!" The voice was that of a sad old man who'd only been trying to do his job.

"Looks like Humpty fell off the wall," Bobo said, sniggering. "Hey, what are you doing?"

Andy leaned the guitar against the amp. "I don't want it," he said.

"Dude, don't be fucking stupid. That thing almost makes you sound like a real musician."

"Nah. I'm not feeling it."

Bobo picked up the sledgehammer and raised it over his head. He looked crazed. "Take that guitar or I swear to God I'll break it in half right now." Andy imagined the moment of contact, when the head of the hammer would sever the neck of the Gibson at one of its glistening silver frets, shattering the pearlescent inlays, leaving only the tendons of strings to hold the whole thing together. Such a waste.

"Why do you even care?"

"It's a symbol, yo! Some fucked-up stuff is about to go down in this world, and we gotta have each other's backs."

"I've still got your back," Andy said.

Bobo shook his head. "Ever since you started hanging out with those girls, you've changed. I need to know it's not gonna be the pact all over again. I need to know my best friend isn't gonna puss out on me."

And for just a second, Andy saw the fear at the heart of all Bobo's bluster and bullshit. That was the problem with understanding someone too well—you couldn't help but forgive them, no matter what they did. He picked up the guitar and threw the strap over his shoulder.

"Whatever, man. Let's go make sure Humpty Dumpty can put his shit back together."

Bobo rolled his eyes. "All right, Mother Mary. Lead the way."

They skated across the mall, following the wail of the security guard. With the guitar around his neck, Andy found it hard to build up any momentum. Every push made his muscles burn. He felt so heavy.

Peter

PETER HADN'T BEEN PLANNING TO GO TO THE RALLY. BOTH BOBO AND THAT CREEP GOLDEN
had been responsible for organizing the event, which was two strikes
against it right there. And when Peter's parents expressly forbade him
and his sister from attending, that seemed to settle it for good. But
everything changed when he woke up on Saturday morning.

Misery's room was already empty, the wrinkles in the sheets of her
unmade bed like a scrawled *fuck you* to the very idea of imprison-
ment.

His mom and dad were waiting for him at the kitchen table, fully
dressed and looking solemn. His breakfast had already been arranged
on a plate—scrambled eggs, bacon, whole-grain toast glistening with
butter. So he was literally getting "buttered up" here—but why? Were
they going to ask him to take their side in the next episode of "Misery
gets reprimanded and still doesn't give a shit"? Or maybe they were
sending him out to the rally to drag her back home.

"We're worried about your sister," his mom said.

"What else is new?"

His parents didn't so much as smile.

"She's barely ever at home anymore."

"She's in love."

Peter's mom actually gave a little yelp of a laugh. "Love? At her age? Please. And now I can only assume she's gone to this rally, even though we told her not to."

Peter had heard this all before. "Yeah, but you know what she's—"

"We can't go on like this!" his dad shouted. "It's totally unsustainable!"

Peter sensed now that he'd underestimated the scale of this intervention. It was an easy mistake to make, if you allowed yourself to forget about Ardor, which turned all existence into a soap opera. "You want to leave Seattle," he guessed.

His mother took hold of his hand. "We can always come back, if we regret it."

"We're thinking we'd go camping first," his dad said, "to really bond as a family. Then we can stay with your grandparents in Mendocino and see how it feels."

"What about school?"

"I think school is the least of our worries now."

Peter felt gripped with a sudden sense of panic. They couldn't be serious, could they? Seattle was their home. Why would they want to let go of it, to let go of *everything* safe and familiar, at the most terrifying moment in any of their lives?

Then again, most of the people who mattered to Peter had already jumped ship—Cartier had gone to Oregon for some epic family reunion just a few days after the announcement, and Peter hadn't heard a word from Stacy since her family moved to their lake house. Really, what was left for him here?

Only a fantasy. Only a shred of a hope.

"I need to think about this."

"It's not up to you—" Peter's dad started to say.

"Of course," Peter's mom interrupted. "Take the day to process. We're going to need your help in making Samantha understand why it's the right decision."

And that was where Peter found his angle. "Actually, I think I should go find her now, at the rally. It'll give us a chance to talk one-on-one. Besides, it's not safe out there." He didn't mention his ulterior motive: Eliza would definitely be at Cal Anderson Park, in her role as documentarian of mayhem. *Apocalypse Already* was growing more popular every day. Peter had opened a Tumblr account just to be one among her 405,242 followers. He felt a little embarrassed by his crush now, as if he were stalking a movie star or something. But he'd never forgive himself if he left Seattle without at least speaking to her one more time.

His parents shared a glance—the telepathy of the long-term couple.

"Fine," Peter's dad said. "But in and out, okay? You get your sister, then you leave."

"Deal."

There were only a few cars out on the freeway, and most of them were busted up in one way or another: windshields with concentric circles of shatter around a central impact point, lightning-bolt scratches and dents in the body, rearview mirrors hanging like eyeballs torn from their sockets. Innumerable black columns of smoke rose from behind the highway walls, as if supporting some great invisible structure floating up above the cloud line. Arson had become a pretty major problem in the past week or so; *The Stranger* had reported that a few dozen buildings were going up in flames every day. When the view opened up south of 45th Street, Peter could see out over the whole city, to the piecemeal conflagration raging like so many signal fires all signaling the same thing—chaos.

He pulled off the freeway and turned toward Capitol Hill. From every corner of the city came the sounds of police sirens and car alarms, like a choir of babies crying out for their mothers. Only a few hundred feet up Denny Way, two cars were stopped perpendicular to traffic, blocking the road. Their emergency lights were on, but no one was inside. Peter pulled the Jeep onto the sidewalk and parked.

A light rain fell from a sky the color of wet cement—the Seattle winter status quo. It pattered gently on his jacket.

As he walked up the hill toward Broadway, he began to see more people. A group of four men came out of an apartment building, each one struggling beneath the weight of a large flat-screen television. They moved slowly but fearlessly, and their eyes dared anyone to step to them. Peter crested the hill and came in sight of Broadway. Here were the crowds missing from the rest of the city—the poor, the homeless, the immigrants and minorities who'd fallen through the gaping holes in the national safety net (Felipe always had a lot to say on that subject). The vibe was somewhere between a gang fight and a refugee camp. Almost everyone carried some kind of weapon, usually a crowbar or baseball bat. Across the street, a bunch of kids were laying waste to a tricked-out Hyundai.

Inside Cal Anderson Park, at least a thousand people were standing around or sitting on the grass in front of the stage, watching a group of purple-haired punkers who seemed to be competing to see which of them could make the most noise. The power cables from their speaker stacks ran across the street and through the broken window of Dick's Drive-In.

Peter bought tacos from a food truck for fifteen dollars each (that was an apocalypse economy for you) and sat down on the edge of a fountain to eat. And there, just across the water, he saw Eliza walking arm in arm with Andy Rowen. Peter wasn't jealous exactly, but he wasn't *not* jealous either. Andy had always seemed like one of those kids who just hung around class to say dumb stuff, who'd end up working minimum wage at a gas station or a Starbucks for the rest of his life. But now Anita had taken him under her wing, and if she was as good at rehabilitation as she was at everything else, Andy just might turn out okay.

But there was no way that Eliza could be into him, right?

"Big man!" someone said. Peter looked away from Eliza, directly into a consummate Bobo smirk. "I don't remember sending you an invite to this party."

"I'm looking for Samantha. You know where she is?"

"Are you sure that's who you're looking for? 'Cause I coulda sworn you were staring at Eliza."

Peter stood up. "See you, Bobo."

"Hold on! I might know something that'll help. Your sister ever tell you why we call her Misery?"

"No," Peter said, and he felt pretty sure he didn't want to know.

"Because she loves company."

Bobo performed a lascivious mime of doggy-style sex. Peter couldn't help himself; he grabbed Bobo by the collar of his T-shirt and pushed him hard into a tree.

"Shut the fuck up."

Bobo's laughter turned to a sneer. "Think this out, big man. Is this really the place to get into a fight with me?"

Peter looked around. A sea of slackers and thugs and freaks: Bobo's people. Peter was the preppy jock with a target on the back of his polo shirt.

"Why do you have a problem with me?" Peter asked.

"You got it backward. I couldn't give a shit about you. You're the one with the problem."

"What?" Peter laughed, but his heart wasn't in it.

"Misery told me about how you can't sleep."

"So what?"

"So that's why you've got a problem with me. Because I never expected life to hand me anything, so I don't mind seeing the whole thing go up in flames. Because you know that while you're staring out the window at three in the morning, shaking like a little bitch at what's coming for you, I'm sleeping like a baby. That's why you hate me. 'Cause I'm not scared."

At some point during this little monologue, Bobo had grabbed hold of Peter's forearms. Now, glancing down, Peter caught sight of the long delicate lines that ran upward from each of Bobo's wrists, like colorless veins. Scars.

"Yeah, I'm scared," he said, "but not for myself." He threw Bobo back against the tree and walked away. Suddenly the whole crowd seemed sick and menacing. The air was heavy with pot smoke, and here and there a couple of guys were fighting at the center of a cheering circle—pressure-release valves. The band had stopped playing, and now some guy Peter didn't recognize stood before the mic, speechifying about civil rights. Golden sat at the edge of the stage, cheering along with the crowd after every sentence.

"The SPD has locked up so many people that it's had to find new places to put them." Cheer. "Everything's a fucking crime now." Cheer. "Everybody out here today has friends who've been put away, without trial, without appeal." Cheer. "And if we stand by, it'll only get worse." Cheer. "The world hasn't ended yet." Cheer. "I'm not giving up my liberties just because those fuckers are afraid of us. I'll die first!" The guy pulled a gun out of his jeans and pointed it at the sky, earning the loudest cheer of all.

Peter had to find his sister right now.

There was a big oak tree next to the stage, with a few people perched in the branches. From there, Peter figured he'd be able to see out over most of the park; Misery's orange hair ought to be easy to find. He reached the bottom of the tree and gazed upward. A pair of skinheads drinking Olde English, a black kid with a pair of binoculars, and highest of all, on a branch that looked about as thin as one of her arms, Eliza Olivi.

"Hey!" he cried out.

She looked down, squinted to recognize him. "What are you doing here?"

"I'm looking for my sister. But I'd like to talk to you, too."

"Oh yeah?"

"Yeah. I think it's about time."

One of the skinheads threw an empty beer can at Peter's head. "Shut up, dude. I'm trying to listen."

Eliza climbed down the tree. It took a long time, as her sweater kept getting stuck on branches. He felt as if he were her prom date, waiting at her door with a corsage as she slowly descended the stairs.

"So, Peter," she said, brushing the dirt off her hands, "what shall we discuss?"

After imagining this moment for so long, he had no idea what to say first. His heart was pounding, and his head was brimming with the memory of the last time they'd stood this close together. If he hadn't thought it would make him sound like a total freak psycho, he probably would have said *I love you* right then and there.

"Shit, it's happening!" the guy at the microphone shouted. "It's a bust!" He knocked the mic over, leaving a high whine of feedback to hang in the air like a scream. The park began to collapse in on itself; hundreds of people were running toward the stage like animals trying to escape a forest fire. Puffs of pinkish smoke filled the air like little fireworks: tear gas.

"You should get out of here," Peter said.

"Can't we leave together?"

"I have to find my sister."

"Then I'll come with you."

"You shouldn't—" he started to say, but then she'd taken hold of his hand, and he didn't want to argue anymore. They rushed head-long into the gas; the burn was like the one he'd get chopping onions at Friendly Forks, only a hundred times worse. Everyone was screaming, a hellish dissonance punctuated by the hiss of gas canisters and what was either the popping of balloons (though Peter couldn't remember seeing any balloons) or gunfire. He and Eliza broke out into a space of clear air and saw the line of riot police, dressed all in black, with thick visored helmets and Plexiglas shields as big as their whole bodies.

"There!" Eliza said.

Misery's flame of hair disappeared behind a cloud of vaporous pink. Peter tried to run to her, but something was holding him back.

"Let go of me, Eliza!" he said. But when he looked over his shoulder, it wasn't Eliza who had hold of him; it was some young cop, his eyes full of fear and threat.

"Sir, my friend's just looking for his sister," Eliza said. She put a hand on the officer's elbow. "He's not trying to start anything."

The cop wrenched Eliza's arm behind her back, and then he was carrying her away, back beyond the wall of shields. Peter would have gone after her, but the riot cops were moving forward in lockstep now, forcing everyone back the other way. He ran with the mob, toward a second line of cops waiting on the opposite side of the park. They were grabbing up anyone who came close. Peter was one of the lucky ones, sprinting through the line and out of the park. His eyes were still burning when he got back to the Jeep, as much from shame as the lingering effects of the tear gas. He'd escaped, but what was that really worth, when he'd lost everything else?

In the end, the rally wound up provoking the exact thing it had set out to prevent.

Early the next morning, the government declared an official state of emergency. The National Guard was called in, and a curfew was instated. Leaving the house for any reason other than to stock necessities was forbidden. Being out at all after dark was forbidden. It had happened just as Bobo and Golden said it would—which somehow made it that much worse. Exactly twenty-three days before Ardor was to either spare or slaughter them all, martial law had finally come to the city.

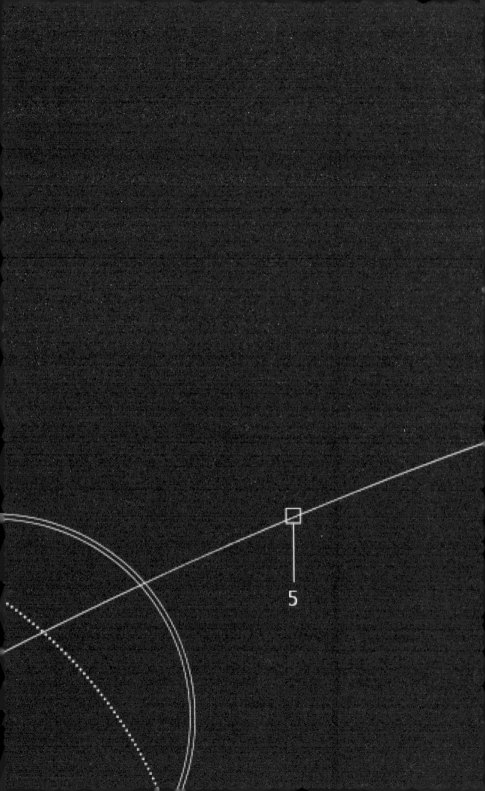

5

Eliza

PRISON WAS A LITTLE BIT LIKE SLEEPAWAY CAMP, IF SLEEPAWAY CAMP WERE POPULATED exclusively by people who really didn't want to be at sleepaway camp. The place was coed, probably because the police didn't have the space or resources to provide a separate facility for each gender, and everyone slept in a single enormous room filled wall-to-wall with cheap, creaky bunk beds. One wall was just windows, but they'd been covered up with a single piece of canvas so thick that it only let in light at the very edges, like a thin white frame.

An average day consisted mostly of sitting around the dormitory and eating in the mess hall. Breakfast was cereal, lunch was a sandwich, and dinner was a combination of leathery meat, vegetables so overcooked that they dissolved on the tongue like baby food, and bread rolls with the cloying consistency of McDonald's hamburger buns. Twice a day the inmates were let out onto a cement lot that had once been a couple of basketball courts, where they could mill around, trade their quickly evaporating store of cigarettes and chewing gum (for reasons unknown, though likely related to Ardor, they'd been allowed to keep these items upon entry), and absorb some gray sunlight. Their prison-mandated outfits were pale blue jumpsuits and white slip-on canvas sneakers, which made them all look like Smurfs.

Though there were always tons of people around, the detention center was a weirdly lonely place. Eliza didn't have any friends there, so she spent most of her time agonizing over all the things she should have done differently. Why hadn't she spoken to Peter weeks ago, after she found out he'd broken up with Stacy? Why hadn't she bothered to answer a single one of her mom's phone calls? Why hadn't she spent more time hanging out with her dad instead of working on her blog all the time? Eliza kept herself awake with these regrets, watching each one jump over a little fence in her mind, like those sheep you were supposed to count to bring on sleep—but the counting only made her more restless. That was why she was still up in the middle of her third night at the center, when a weight landed gently on the mattress alongside her. At first she thought it was her imagination—but no, someone was actually climbing into the bottom bunk with her. She was about to scream when he spoke.

"You don't know me," he said, "but I'm a really nice person. And I think you're absolutely beautiful. If you tell me to go, I'll go. But I'd love to hook up with you, and because it's the end of the world and we're stuck here, I figured I might as well ask."

Eliza knew it was just about the least feminist thing she could do (Madeline would have thrown a fit—ethical slutdom was supposed to be about self-empowerment, not altruism), but the boy seemed so sad and sincere, and if she couldn't make herself happy, it seemed the least she could do was bring a little joy to someone else.

"I'm not going to have sex with you," she said. "And this is a one-time thing."

"That's cool."

And then what happened happened. When it was over, the boy said a husky thanks and disappeared. She never found out who he was.

But the next day, freshly reminded of the significance of human contact, she decided to try and start a conversation with the only group of people there that she knew. Four days was a long time to spend alone with your thoughts, particularly when those thoughts were mostly about death, the parents you'd never get to say good-bye to, and the boy you'd never get a second chance with.

Bobo, Misery, and the nerdy one, Kevin, were leaning up against a cement wall in the recreation lot, passing around a single cigarette.

"Can I get a drag?" Eliza asked. Kevin looked to Bobo, who nodded. "Thanks." She breathed in deep, felt her lungs open up. "So, do we have any kind of plan here?"

"What kind of plan would we have?" Bobo asked.

"I mean, are we gonna sit around here until the end? Just watch the sky and hope for the best?"

"What else can we do?"

"I don't know. Get a message out somehow? If anybody found out where we were, they'd raise holy hell. Somebody in here must have parents with some pull, right? And I bet these guards don't want to be here any more than we do. There's fewer of them coming in every day. All we'd have to do is give them a reason—"

Bobo cut her off. "You got your drag. Now leave us alone."

"Don't be mean," Misery said. "She's Andy's friend."

"No, she's not. She's just stringing him along, because she likes the attention. That's why she does everything she does. For the attention."

Eliza felt an unexpected prickle of tears behind her eyes. "Pay attention to this," she said, giving Bobo the finger.

She heard him laughing as she walked away. "Oh dear. Did I make the princess mad?"

Eliza hid on the other side of a big metal Dumpster and breathed deeply. She hated Bobo, but more than that, she hated herself for showing weakness in front of him. If only there'd been anyone else here to talk to, she wouldn't have even bothered. . . .

A tap on her shoulder. Eliza spun around, ready to deliver a hard knee to a soft crotch (she'd been getting a lot of untoward attention from her fellow inmates, in spite of the fact that the blue jumpsuit was just about the least provocative thing she'd worn in the past year).

"Hey," Kevin said. "You okay?" He had this perpetual look of apology on his face, as if he were trespassing on everyone's time and space just by existing.

"I'm fine."

"Sorry about Bobo. He's just protective of Andy."

"That's what you call being protective?"

"It's complicated, because Andy likes you and everything. You know, it's a shame you don't like him back. He's a good guy."

Eliza shrugged. What was there to say?

"Anyway, I didn't come over here just to apologize. I wanted to know, if you *could* get a message to the outside, what would you say?"

"I'd tell them whatever I could about where we are, and hopefully they'd find us. Why?"

Kevin looked around, then leaned in close. "I've got an Android phone under my foot right now."

"Seriously?" Eliza said, a little too loudly. Then, whispering, "How?"

"They were carting so many people out of Cal Anderson, they only had time for really quick pat-downs. Nobody thought to look inside my socks. Then when I got here, I told the guard I had bad circulation in my feet, so he let me put the new socks on over my old ones."

Eliza couldn't help herself. She gave Kevin a huge hug and a kiss on the cheek. "You're a genius!"

His face reddened. "Not really. And there are some problems. Turns out cell reception's pretty much nonexistent here. I don't know if it's down for good, or if we're in a dead zone, but I can't get a single bar."

"So the phone's useless?"

"That's what I thought at first. But it turns out there's an unprotected Wi-Fi network upstairs."

"I didn't even know there *was* an upstairs."

"Me either. But I saw a couple guards go through that door between the dorm and the cafeteria, and figured there might be some kind of office back there. If there were, they'd probably have Internet."

"So you snuck in?"

"Not exactly. The only way in was to get sent there. Like, to get in trouble."

Eliza laughed. "How'd you do that?"

"I kept throwing food at one of the guards until he snapped. He took me to meet the guy in charge of this place, who's actually kinda cool, if you can believe that."

"So did you get a message out?"

"They were watching me the whole time. I didn't have the chance. Besides, I wasn't even sure what to say. There are windows up on the second floor, but I didn't see anything that I recognized, so I still don't know where we are." Kevin glanced over his shoulder. "I think

I should get back. I told them I'd only be a second. But if you want, I can pass you the phone and you can figure out what to do with it."

"I already know what to do with it. But I'll need your help."

"I doubt I could help much."

Eliza liked Kevin, more than he liked himself, at any rate. She wanted to tell him that high school was a little like a play in which everybody got cast prematurely, and he'd ended up with a pretty crappy role. If he could just survive until college, he'd get to try out for a new play, one with plenty of good parts for people like him. She wanted to tell him that she'd already met the kind of boy he would eventually become—still a dork, but in a hip, unapologetic way. Hell, she'd even *slept* with a couple of boys like that.

But all that touchy-feely shit would have to wait. They had schemes to scheme.

"Kevin, you ready to get sent back to the principal's office?"

They spent the next twenty-four hours brainstorming various ways to get themselves in trouble, and each one sounded more fun than the last. There was *The Gladiators*, a scenario in which they'd try to start a prison-wide pillow fight. There was *The Arsonists and the Pea*, which involved setting an unoccupied bunk bed on fire. There was *The Nudists*, the name of which really spoke for itself. But in the end, Eliza decided to go with *The Overzealous Seductress*. The plan required a specific guard to be on duty in the dormitory—the one who looked more like a kid playing dress-up than an actual soldier—so it was another day before they could put it into action.

Eliza waited until nobody nearby was paying attention, then sauntered up close to the guard. "I like your little hat," she said.

"Thanks." His tone was of the *I'd like to be friendly but I'm not supposed to be* variety.

"Take it off for me, will you?"

"It's my uniform, miss."

"I know. But you can take it off for just a second, can't you? For me?"

The guard attempted to quell the violent revolution of a smile. "I can't."

"Pretty please." She fluttered her eyelashes. The guard checked around for his superior, then briefly doffed his cap and replaced it.

"Happy?"

"Very. Now take off your shirt."

"I definitely can't do that."

Eliza stepped closer and put her hands on his camouflaged chest. She unbuttoned the topmost button, revealing a few curly hairs poking out just above a little triangle of white cotton T-shirt.

"Stop that," the guard said.

"Stop what?"

She undid the next button, and the next. Finally he grabbed her by the wrists.

"I'm serious."

She laughed, pulled her hands free, then tore his shirt the rest of the way open, sending buttons skittering over the tile floor, drawing the attention of Kevin, who just "happened" to have wandered into the vicinity.

"I saw it!" he said. "You're sexually harassing that girl!"

The guard had no choice now. "Come with me!" he barked at Kevin, while dragging Eliza roughly out of the dormitory and through an unmarked metal door that opened on a narrow set of stairs.

"Both of you. Get up there."

The upstairs hallway was just as Kevin described it—bright and airy, lined on one side with wide rectangular windows. Eliza looked out for some kind of landmark, but there was nothing special in sight. She could only hope that someone else would recognize the view. Otherwise, all of this was for nothing.

The three e-mails were already written. One would blast the soon-to-be-taken photo out to every single person in her address book, another was a private message just for her dad, and the third was for Peter (she'd searched out his e-mail address that day she'd seen him at Friendly Forks, just in case she ever felt like getting in touch with him). It was this last message that had required the most attention, the most writing and rewriting and general creative anxiety. Her first draft had been coy and subtle, so subtle that it really didn't convey any message at all. She'd gone for a flirtatious vibe next, but that came off sounding shallow and oblivious. In the end, she tried to be as candid as possible, given the circumstances.

It was funny, but she didn't even realize what she was writing until she'd already written it—her very first love letter. First and last, probably.

The guard disappeared behind a door at the end of the hallway. Eliza slid the phone out of her sleeve and turned on the camera app, but the guard was back a second later, and she had to hide it again.

"Send one of 'em in," said a voice from the office.

Kevin was standing closer to the door (just as they'd planned), so he went in first. They'd hoped the guard would go along with him, giving Eliza a minute or two alone in the hallway, but no such luck. *The Overzealous Seductress* included a provision for such a situation, but Eliza was still a little embarrassed to put it into action.

"I guess it's just the two of us," she said.

"I guess so."

"Listen, I know we don't have long here, but would you mind holding me?"

"What?"

"Just one hug. Please. It's now or never."

The guard glanced toward the office. "Only for a second."

Eliza wrapped her arms around his neck. He smelled strongly of some kind of too-fresh body spray, probably with a name like "Mountain Air" or "Glacial Breeze."

"Mmm," she murmured, gently spinning his back toward the window. She went up on tippy-toe so as to see over his shoulder. It wouldn't be a great shot, but it would have to do.

"I'm Eliza."

"Seth," he said. "And I hate this job."

Eliza laughed sincerely, then placed a gentle hand on the back of Seth's head. A moment later the door at the end of the hallway opened up again.

"Your turn," Seth said softly.

Eliza winked at Kevin as they passed each other, to signal that she'd successfully taken the photo. Now all she needed was a few seconds alone with the phone, to attach the image and send the e-mails.

Inside the office, a massive mound of man sat behind a simple wooden desk, lit by an old-school banker's lamp with a green glass shade. He was totally bald, though the hair had only migrated else-where—to his thick red mustache and his hairy knuckles. CAPTAIN MORGAN, according to his nameplate.

"Is that a joke?" Eliza asked, shutting the office door behind her.

"Well, technically I'm *Major* Morgan now, but my staff gets a kick out of the old title." He had a slight accent—something Southern. "But wait, it gets better." He opened the bottom drawer of his desk and took out a bottle of Captain Morgan Spiced Rum and a tumbler. "You want some?"

"Sure."

"Ha! Nothing doing, darling. Now, why don't you take a seat and tell me your name."

"Eliza."

"Eliza." Captain Morgan poured himself a substantial glass of Captain Morgan. "So, Eliza, our mutual friend out there says you attempted to undress him. Is that true?"

"Yes, sir."

"What are you? Sixteen?"

"Eighteen."

"Well, I know every eighteen-year-old woman loves a man in uniform, but your buddy told me you were just messing around. Is that the case?"

"Yes, sir."

"That's what I thought." Captain Morgan sat back in his chair, swirled his drink. "How are you all holding up down there? It's pretty boring, yeah?"

"Yes, sir."

"Just so you know, I would not have done something like this. All these kids locked up, with that big ol' rock coming. I mean, I don't know exactly what you're in here for, but if it was just because you happened to be at that concert thing—well, that's crazy, in my opinion. If it were up to me, we'd shut the whole thing down."

"It could be up to you," Eliza said.

Captain Morgan seemed to consider this, then shook his head. "That's not how it works, darling. I have to keep doing my job, the way I'm supposed to. Otherwise, what's left, you know?" He looked down into his glass, as if the ruddy dregs might tell him something. "All right, you get on out of here, Eliza. And keep your chin up."

Back in the hallway, Kevin and Seth were standing by the stairwell.

"Come on," Seth said. "It's almost time for dinner."

But she hadn't had a chance to send the e-mails yet. She needed to play for time. "Hey, is there a bathroom up here?"

"You can use the one downstairs."

"That one's coed! The boys leave it disgusting. Please?"

"Sorry. It's not my call."

"Then I'm sorry too," Eliza said.

"For what?"

"Grab him!" she shouted. Kevin slid to the ground and wrapped himself around Seth's legs like some kind of human barnacle. Eliza blitzed past them, turning into the first room she could find and slamming the door shut behind her. There was a twist lock on the knob, and she spun it just in time.

She let the phone slip back into her palm and clicked the icon for e-mail. Seth's keys were already jangling in the lock. Eliza added the photo to the prewritten message in her drafts folder and clicked send. The loading bar dashed across to the 90 percent mark, then stopped. Seth must have used the wrong key, because the doorknob only jiggled against her back.

"Where you gonna go, Eliza?"

"Isn't this the bathroom?" she said, then to the phone, "Come on, come on."

She looked up for the first time and noticed her surroundings. It was an office, empty but for a few posters on the walls. A still frame from a familiar movie, in which a shirtless man with a wide-brimmed black hat stared off into the distance, with a little speech bubble coming out of his mouth: I LOVE THE SMELL OF NAPALM IN THE MORNING. A kitten trying to climb up a ball of yarn. A yellowing newspaper article with a picture of a plane taking off and the headline 3-2-1-BLASTOFF: SAND POINT NAVAL AIR STATION CLOSES ITS DOORS FOR GOOD.

Sand Point Naval Air Station! That had to be where they were. And if she'd only had another minute, she could have added it to the e-mails. But Seth had fit a second key into the lock, and this time the knob turned. Eliza ran toward the windows at the other end of the room. The loading bar was moving again. 91 percent. 92 percent. Seth was inside the office now, brandishing something that looked like a cross between a gun and a grocery-store bar-code scanner. Eliza pulled one of the windows open and dangled the phone outside; she didn't want Seth to know what she was sending.

"What is that?" he asked. 94 percent. 95 percent. "Give it to me!"

"What? This?"

96 percent. 97 percent. He was only a couple of feet away now. She tossed the phone as hard as she could, straight up. 98 percent, and then it was flipping too fast to read, up and up, then plummeting down toward the cement. She looked back to Seth just in time to see him squeeze the trigger. A strange flickering sound, like one of those old film projectors, and then her whole body was pumped full of fire. She blacked out.

Peter

PETER HAD KNOWN FAILURE BEFORE. HE'D FLUNKED A COUPLE OF MATH TESTS HERE AND there, choked at the line at state championships (going three-for-twelve, to his eternal shame), and worst of all, he'd cheated on Stacy, which was the sort of failure he'd never even imagined himself capable of. But all of it was nothing next to watching Misery and Eliza disappear behind that line of riot cops, as implacable and impassable as a row of pawns on a chessboard. If he hadn't let himself get distracted by Bobo, he might have found Misery in time. If he hadn't secretly wanted Eliza to stay by his side, he probably could have convinced her to leave the park once the riot started. But he'd made all the wrong decisions, and now both of them were gone.

As a sort of punishment, he sat up in his bedroom doing exactly nothing. He didn't try to call Cartier or any of his old friends. He didn't exercise. He didn't check the web to keep up with Ardor's murderous progress through the heavens. His circadian rhythm capsized; the night teemed with too many terrors for sleep. Unconsciousness came only in fits and starts during the pale, misty days, when that toxic star was swallowed up in the brightness of the sun. His parents started leaving food outside his door; he ate just enough to keep the hunger pangs away. Once, in the middle of the night, he snuck downstairs and grabbed a handful of trash bags from under the sink. He wanted to get rid of all of the junk in his room: the trophies and the ribbons celebrating a bunch of victories that counted for nothing now; the love letters and keepsakes from a relationship that he'd sacrificed on the altar of a delusion; the old toys and stuffed animals left over from more innocent days. He didn't want to look at any of it anymore. When the bags were full, stacked on the floor of the closet, there was hardly anything left in the room but the furniture. *That's what my life adds up to*, Peter thought. *Nothing at all.*

Four days disappeared in a fog of depression and regret. Then, late on a Thursday morning, there was a firm knock on his bedroom door.

"What?" Peter was in bed, and though he was only half-asleep, he didn't get up.

"I'm giving you ten seconds to get out of there," his father said. "Ten, nine, eight, seven—I'm not kidding around here—six, five . . ." But Peter still didn't move. Part of it was the paralysis of despair—he found it hard to build up the energy for *any* sort of movement right now—but there was more to it than that. Deep down, he knew he needed whatever it was that his dad had planned for the end of the countdown—the grand gesture that only ever came at zero. ". . . four, three, two, one. That's one, Peter! All right, then. Zero."

With a crash, the door flew open, sending a slim shard of wooden frame sliding across the floor. His dad stepped into the room with the majestic air of a knight who'd just slain a dragon. Did that make Peter the fair maiden?

"Your mom and I have come to a decision," he said.

"Good for you." Peter turned over, toward the window.

"We spent most of the past few days down at the police station, screaming along with all the other parents, but there's nothing we can do. It looks like your sister threw a beer bottle at a cop, or at least they're saying she did, and that means they can basically hold on to her for as long as they want."

"That's your big decision? You're giving up?"

"The police promised us that Samantha is being held only with other juveniles, and that the facility is very safe, but they're not saying where it is. I think they're afraid that if people knew where their kids were, they'd go blow a hole in the wall or something. Given the circumstances, they're probably right."

"I could have brought her home, Dad. She could be here right now. We could be on our way to California, like you wanted."

"Peter?" The squeak of old coils as Peter's dad sat down on the other side of the bed. "Peter, look at me."

Peter turned back over. He wasn't ready to accept the forgiveness in his dad's eyes; he wanted someone *outside* his head to berate him, so he could stop doing it to himself. "It's my fault. Don't try to tell me it isn't."

"Fine. Then I'll just tell you that it doesn't matter whose fault it is. Blame is just a way to keep score, and adults don't play games like that. So grow up, Peter. Get your butt out of bed."

With a groan, Peter lifted himself to a seated position.

"Hey!" his dad said, noticing the state of the room. "You cleaned up in here! I like it. Very spare."

"Thanks."

"Now come on. It's grocery day. You'll feel better with a little bit of fresh air."

But Peter did not feel better with a little bit of fresh air.

"Grocery day" meant a day spent waiting in lines. At the gas station, cars had to alternate with men and women filling up iron jerry cans, plastic jugs, and, in one case, an empty beer keg. The air was rife with angry shouts and the raucous honk of car horns.

"Why do they want extra gas?" Peter asked.

"Generators," his dad said.

"Do you think the power's going to go out?"

"It's already gone out twice. Didn't you have the computer on in your bedroom?" Peter shook his head. "Honestly, I'm surprised they've kept the juice flowing this long."

Almost an hour passed before it was their turn at the pump. The price of gas had jumped again and again in the last few days; it hovered now at twenty-three bucks a gallon.

"What a racket," his mom said. "If the world doesn't end, remind me to buy some Exxon stock."

After filling up the tank, they drove over to Safeway, where the line stretched across the parking lot and a block and a half up the street. It moved at a grass-growing, paint-drying, watched-pot-of-water-boiling pace, while the winter sun hovered at just that angle where it seemed to slice straight into your brain. You could try to turn your back on it, but then you wouldn't notice when the line moved, and everyone would yell, as if that next two or three feet were the only thing standing between them and a miraculous rescue from cataclysm. At one point, a fistfight broke out near the front of the line, and nobody bothered to break it up; the fight ended when one of the guys went down and stayed there.

A couple of hours of pained familial conversation later ("How's Stacy doing?" his dad innocently asked), they passed through the double doors and the suspicious stares of four armed National Guardsmen. A small bald man in a red T-shirt and chinos greeted them. MANAGER was stenciled onto his name tag.

"Welcome to Safeway," he said, while the rest of his face said, *I'm no happier to be here than you are.* "Please be aware that we're asking everyone to limit themselves to fifteen minutes inside the store, so we can keep the line moving. Now, you're a family of three, so—"

Peter's mom interrupted. "We're a family of four."

The manager counted them with one nod of his head each. "I'm seeing three."

"Usually we're four," Peter's dad explained, "but today we're three."

"Then that makes you three, doesn't it?"

Peter wondered if he could punch the manager hard enough to shatter his blanched, egg-shaped skull and make the golden yolk spill out.

"Families of three are allowed up to two hundred and fifty percent of the individual limit listed on any item, rounded down. So, if the card says one each, you're only allowed two, okay? Not two and a half."

"That doesn't seem fair," Peter said.

"Fairness is a matter of opinion, sir. We're trying to ration. Now please move along. You're slowing everyone down."

"*You're* slowing everyone down!" Peter said, but his dad already had him by the arm and was pulling him through the second set of doors.

He would have kept arguing, but his anger evaporated as soon as he saw the state of the supermarket. Here was the real apocalypse, missing only a few tumbleweeds and a cow skull bleaching in the sun to complete the image. One glance at the decimated produce department shattered a childhood fantasy—it turned out that those huge pyramids of fruit, which Peter had always assumed were solid all the way through, rested on hollow wooden skeletons that gave them their shape and the illusion of abundance. The display stand of bananas had been picked clean but for a few lime-green pygmies that probably wouldn't ripen by the time Ardor came. The apples and pears had been just as savagely culled. All that remained were the most obscure fruits and vegetables—kiwis and kumquats, bok choy and chard. And if you didn't grab something the moment you saw it, you wouldn't get another chance. This wasn't a leisurely day at the grocery store; it was mortal combat. Like the doomed minor characters in a slasher movie, Peter and his parents split up, grabbing the maximum allowance of anything remotely edible—bacon-flavored potato chips, wasabi soda, off-brand animal crackers, gluten- and dairy-free oven-bake pizzas. The glass case in front of the butcher counter was empty, but there were still some weird-looking layered cheeses up for grabs.

They ended up with a pretty serious haul of second-rate food, lugging it back to the car with a mixture of triumph and disappointment, like Vikings who'd just conquered a village of penniless pacifists.

"That wasn't nearly as bad as I thought it would be," Peter's dad said. He set his bags down on the pavement and reached into his back pocket for the car keys.

A rustling sound from a nearby hedge, followed by a burst of color—

the three kids had grabbed a bag each before Peter even realized what was happening. He took off after them, a massacre on his mind.

"Peter, no!" his mom shouted.

"But I can catch them!"

"Please!" The note of desperation in her voice was just enough to stop him. "I bet they need it more than we do anyway."

Peter sighed. She was probably right.

"Let's get home," his dad said. "These bacon-flavored potato chips aren't going to eat themselves."

The Internet was still technically around, but whole swathes of it had gone down in the past week. You could no longer spend the day skimming videos on YouTube. Facebook gave up a single, strangely cheery error message: *Uh-oh, seems like something's gone wrong on our end. We're looking into it.* Peter's e-mail account was still active, but he hadn't checked it since the day of the riot.

There were only two unread messages in his in-box, both of which had come in earlier that day, and both of which had been sent by a certain ApocalypseAlready@gmail.com.

To Whoever's Getting This:

This is Eliza Olivi, of the blog Apocalypse Already. *Attached is a picture taken from the window of the detention center where I and a few hundred other juveniles are currently being held. None of us know where we are, but hopefully this picture will mean something to someone out there. Don't bother writing back (I won't get your response), just bust us out, okay? I have a party to plan.*

Eliza

Peter checked out the second e-mail before opening the attachment. Unlike the first message, this one was addressed only to him.

Dear Peter,

Hello from sunny jail!

If all has gone well, I've just blasted out a message to every e-mail address I could remember. Hopefully it'll help someone find us. But I wanted to send this message just to you, because there's something I wanted to tell you that's been eating away at me in here. Except I'm not going to say it, because you should already know what it is. And you should also know that I wish I'd told you when I had the chance. Okay. That's the best I can do. Hope to see you sometime.

—xE

Peter felt bubbly and out-of-body, capable of flying into space and stopping an asteroid with his bare hands. He opened Eliza's attachment with an unshakable faith that he would recognize the location. Otherwise, how could he rush in and save her, as the universe so clearly wanted him to?

Or not. The photograph was pixelated and dark. All Peter could make out was a nondescript road and a chain-link fence topped with coils of barbed wire. It could have been taken anywhere. For now, the best he could do was drag it into iPhoto, raise the brightness and contrast a bit, and print it out.

And it was a good thing he did. Just a couple of hours later, the power finally died for good. The timing couldn't have been worse: only a handful of people were likely to have downloaded Eliza's attachment, and probably none of them had bothered to print it.

Which meant it all came down to him. He needed to show the picture to someone who really knew Seattle, down at the street level. And there was only one person he knew who fit the bill.

"I think I'm going to turn in early," he announced.

His mom was running around the house, lighting candles and putting batteries in flashlights. "Really? You haven't even had dinner."

"I'm just super tired all of a sudden. I'll see you in the morning, okay?"

"Okay. Sweet dreams."

He gave it half an hour or so, then stole quietly out the front door.

His street was darker than he'd ever seen it; the houses looked derelict and dead. He was already sitting in the driver's seat of the Jeep when he remembered the curfew. Crap. The last thing he needed was to get hauled off to prison himself.

It was nearly an hour later when he let his old twelve-speed drop onto the lawn outside the ma-in-law. It didn't look like anyone was home. The doorbell only clicked—no power. He knocked. Silence. He knocked again. This time he thought he heard something. Or maybe that was just the wind in the trees. He put his ear to the door. No, there was definitely someone moving around in there . . .

The door swung open, and Peter found himself face-to-face with the barrel of a gun. "Don't shoot!" he said.

Andy squeezed the trigger.

A bright orange Nerf dart bounced off Peter's forehead and landed, suction cup down, on the tile walkway.

"Got you," Andy said, then turned and retreated into the house. "Come in, I guess."

Andy

ANDY HAD ALWAYS SUSPECTED THAT PETER MIGHT BE A MEMBER OF HIS KARASS, SO HE wasn't completely surprised to find him standing out on the doorstep in the dark. The only problem was that he didn't really like Peter. They'd always inhabited different dimensions of the social universe, seeing each other not quite as people, but as blurry people-shaped shadows floating around the periphery of classrooms and dances and parties. More to the point, they were obviously competing for Eliza, and Peter, having already made out with her once, was winning.

"So you know what happened at the riot, right?" Peter asked, stumbling around the underlit room (just a single flashlight on the coffee table, pointed straight up) until he fell into the beanbag chair.

"Yeah. They got Eliza."

"Not just her. My sister, too."

"And Bobo," Andy said, *while we're talking about people other than the one we're really talking about.* "So what?"

"Well, I got an e-mail from her. From Eliza, I mean. Just a few hours ago. I thought you might have gotten it too."

"I didn't check my messages today," Andy lied. He felt as if someone had poured a cold glass of water directly into his chest cavity.

"Well, I don't know how she managed it from inside, but she attached this picture. I brought it with me."

Peter flattened a piece of paper out on the table next to the flashlight. It was a photograph of a nondescript street, probably unrecognizable to anyone without a deck.

"That's the old navy base, out at Sand Point," Andy said.

"You're sure?"

"Definitely. We used to go out there to skate, before they fenced it off."

"Holy shit! This is great!"

"How so? You planning a jailbreak?"

"I was thinking more like a protest."

"And who's coming? The web's down, yo."

Andy enjoyed the look of disappointment on Peter's face, his heroic locomotive stopped in its tracks.

"But you've got friends, don't you?" Peter asked. "Maybe you can talk to that Golden guy, who put the rally at Cal Anderson together."

Andy laughed. "If you want to talk to Golden, you can do it yourself."

"I can't. He hates me."

"Well, he doesn't like me much either. Bobo's his point guy."

Peter threw up his hands. "So you just wanna do nothing? Do you even care that our friends are locked up?"

It was a reasonable question, but it only pissed Andy off more. Why had Eliza reached out to *Peter*, of all people? They weren't even friends! In fact, considering the whole Stacy slut-shaming fiasco last year, Eliza should have hated him. It was so unfair. *Life* was so unfair.

And maybe that was why Andy did what he did next—to strike a blow against the injustice of the universe. He sighed theatrically. "Maybe you're right. I mean, I wouldn't really be much of a boyfriend if I didn't at least *try* to get her out."

Someone with a little more cunning in him might have played it cool, but Peter wouldn't have known cunning if it came up and stabbed him in the back. He looked dumbfounded and perplexed and rejected all at once. Andy crumpled the guilty feelings up and kicked them into a dark corner of his brain. Even though Eliza wasn't his girlfriend, she *was* his friend. And the important thing here was to keep his *friend* from wasting her last few weeks on the planet with some cookie-cutter jock moron.

"How long have you been going out?" Peter asked.

"Just a couple of weeks."

"That's great. She's great."

Like that, it was done. Just one more lie in a world full of them. Between that and stealing the guitar, Andy was really knocking it out of the park these days, morality-wise. Whatever. None of that stuff mattered anymore. All that mattered was the quest.

Unfortunately, Andy had more to deal with than just his conscience. From the top floor of the split-level came a single loud cough. Peter jumped to his feet.

"Who's here?"

"No one," Andy said.

"So I'm no one now?" Anita came down the stairs, looking a little ghoulish in the shadows cast by the flashlight.

"Anita?" Peter said, now doubly confused. "What are you doing here?"

224

"I live here," Anita said. "For my sins."

It was true, though Andy hadn't really thought about it that way before. Anita hadn't been back to her own house since that day they'd picked up her stuff together. The cops had come looking for her once (her mom got Andy's last name out of the Hamilton yearbook), but Andy said that he hadn't heard from her in a week, and eventually they went away. And in spite of everything that was going on, the two of them had managed to have a pretty good time together— playing music, watching TV (until the power went out), eating a lot of canned soup. It was a bit like it had been with Bobo back in the day, before Andy broke the pact. Like he and Anita had become roommates in some shared mental space.

She climbed over the top of the couch and rolled down onto the cushions. "So what have you two been talking about?" she asked innocently. But Andy knew she'd heard everything, including his lie.

"Peter got an e-mail from Eliza. Now we know where she is."

"Wow," Anita said, putting a hand on Peter's arm. "She sent you a message from jail? She must really like you."

"I guess so," Peter said.

Anita glared knowingly at Andy. But was she going to give him away?

"Anyway," Andy said, "Peter thought we should stage some sorta protest, but I don't think we can get enough people to show up for it to matter."

"Sure we can! We know just the right people."

"I'm not talking to Golden, if that's what you mean."

"Not Golden. Better people. *Hippie* people."

"Oh yeah . . . them." Andy had almost forgotten about Chad and his little commune. If anyone would know how to put a protest together, they would.

"We'll head over there first thing tomorrow. Peter, why don't you come here as soon as you wake up and we'll go together."

"Sure. Good call." Peter stood up and went to the door, but he hesitated before opening it. "It's been really nice to see you guys. I've been on my own with my parents, and I think it's making me a little crazy." Even in the dark, Andy could see the sympathy flashing in Anita's eyes. *Don't do it*, he wanted to say.

"You wanna hang out here for a bit?" she asked. "You can even stay over if you want."

"Really? Thanks. I mean, if it's cool."

He was looking at Andy. Nobody spoke for a good five seconds.

"Of course it's cool," Anita said. "I'll go get you a beer."

Andy could remember watching a movie in European history class about this one Christmas during World War I when the two sides declared a truce and partied together between the trenches. Hanging out with Peter felt a little bit like that, like fraternizing with the enemy. They played Sorry!, a mindless dice-rolling game, and talked apocalypse: the kids who'd left town and the kids who'd stayed, the unlikely couples forming in the shadow of Ardor for want of better prospects, the surprising tribulations of impending doom.

"I figured everybody would be super sociable, you know?" Peter said. "Like we'd all come together or something. But it hasn't been like that at all."

Apparently, his best friend had moved away, and his ex-girlfriend (the famously lustworthy Stacy Prince) refused to speak to him.

Funny, it had been the exact opposite for Andy. Without Ardor, he wouldn't have made friends with either Anita or Eliza. Maybe the asteroid was turning the whole world upside down. The popular shall become unpopular. The freak shall inherit the Earth.

They stayed up talking for hours. Peter passed out first, on the carpet underneath the coffee table. Andy felt giddy and detached with sleeplessness.

"You shouldn't have said what you did," Anita whispered, "about you and Eliza."

"It was the only way to make him back off."

"What if he mentions it to her?"

"Why would he? Besides, he probably won't see her again anyway."

"Sure he will."

"What? You think this protest idea could work?"

Anita turned lengthwise across the couch, putting her legs over one of the arms. Andy could feel the warmth of her head against his knee. "You remember that morning with Chad, with the tea?" she asked.

"Of course."

"I saw things that day. Things I still can't put into words. Connections, you know? I felt that karass you're always talking about. We're all in it. You and me. Him." She pointed at Peter, sprawled out on the carpet like a giant fallen from his kingdom at the top of the beanstalk. "Misery and Eliza. Even Bobo."

"Wow. Even Bobo? How drunk are you right now?"

"I'm being serious. Chad said we had to have faith. So I'm going to. We'll get them out."

She didn't say anything after that, and a few minutes later, her breathing turned deep and even. Andy felt a fresh wave of shame wash over him. He didn't deserve Anita, who had kept his secret safe from Peter, who was so willing to help out even though there was no one in the detention center she particularly cared about saving (in spite of Andy's best efforts, she and Eliza had yet to really *bond*). She'd revitalized his music and made him feel like something other than a slacker and a misfit. Along with the quest, Anita had given him a reason to keep getting out of bed every morning. And why? What was in it for her? What reason had he ever given her to be so good to him?

He fell asleep with these questions orbiting endlessly around his head, like a hundred tiny asteroids.

The next morning, the three of them drove across the bridge to Chad Eye's house. Everything outside looked pretty much the same as it had the first time, clean and quiet and still.

A stranger answered the door-gong in only his underwear. He was very pale and very hairy and still half-asleep.

"Hello?"

"Hey, we're looking for Chad."

"Hold up one second." He walked away, scratching at his bare stomach. Through the open door, Andy saw that the house was a total wreck. Clothes and empty food containers were strewn all over, and a bunch of people were asleep on the floor of the foyer. Before, the place had felt like a Buddhist temple. Now it felt like an expensively decorated squat.

After a minute, a couple of familiar faces came to the door: Sunny, the dreadlocked blond girl, and in her arms, Chad's philosophical beagle, Sid.

"Hi," she said. "I'm Sunny."

Andy shook her ring-heavy hand. "Yeah, we've met."

"Oh yeah?" She nodded as if Andy had just told her something particularly interesting. "Cool!"

"So is Chad around?"

Sunny frowned. "Didn't you hear? He got busted at the riot."

"Seriously?"

It was terrible news. If Chad was in jail, who would be putting together the Party at the End of the World?

"This is perfect!" Anita exclaimed.

Everybody, Andy included, gave her exactly the sort of look that such an outburst deserved.

"I just meant that that's kinda why we're here. We need your help. A lot of our friends got taken away that day too. We're planning a protest at the detention center where they're being held. It's only for juveniles, so it wouldn't mean freeing Chad directly, but if we can get amnesty for the kids, it might start something bigger."

"Actually, that's not a bad idea," Sunny said. She leaned forward, dangling a single dreadlock in front of Sid, who batted it away. "Between you and me, we could really use a cause right now. It's gotten a little depressing in here. We can make, like, a festival out of it."

"Sounds great," Anita said.

"Okay then! See you soon!"

Sunny started to close the door.

"Wait!" Andy said.

"What?"

"You don't know where it is."

Sunny laughed. "Oh yeah!"

"We'll be at the old navy base at Sand Point, right by Magnuson Park."

"Cool. I'll round up some folks and try to get there in a couple hours. And hey, I'm sorry if I seem scattered. I'm, like, *super* high right now." She giggled, then shut the door.

"If there's still a *Guinness Book of World Records* a month from now, this shit should definitely go down as the smallest protest of all time," Andy said.

Anita nodded glumly. They'd been camped outside of the navy base for almost five hours, holding up signs they'd made over at Peter's house: ARDOR FOR AMNESTY (Anita), FREE SEATTLE'S KIDS (Peter), and THIS IS BULLCRAP! (Andy). But though they'd gotten a few friendly honks from passing cars, nobody else had joined the cause.

They were set up just in front of a wide gate in the chain-link fence that surrounded the base, centered so as to prevent any cars from getting past them. There was an empty gatehouse on the other side of the fence, guarding a huge cracked canvas of weed-choked tarmac. The actual navy base was a good half-mile away—too far for anyone inside to have noticed their tiny protest. The gate itself was held shut by a heavy-duty padlock, and the fence was topped with a sparkling helix of barbed wire.

Andy stood up and put his face up to the rusty diamonds of the fence. "Wait, I think I see something."

A car was moving across the tarmac. It came toward them, stopping a few dozen feet away from the gate. The driver's-side door opened up and a man in full camouflage stepped down. He had a jagged ball of keys in his hand.

"What the hell you all think you're doing?"

"Blocking the gate!" Anita shouted. "None of you get to leave until everyone does."

The soldier chuckled. "Are you crazy? Those are criminals in there. You want them out on the street?"

"They're just kids."

"Oh yeah? Well, so far this week, *kids* have shot at me twice. Believe me, every *kid* in there did something to deserve getting put away." He unlocked the padlock on the gate, then swung it wide open. "Don't even think about coming in here, by the way. We got snipers covering the lot."

"My ass you do," Andy said.

"Try it, punk. It's your funeral. I'd love to see your guts splattered all over—"

"Excuse me," someone said. "Are you threatening these civilians?"

Andy turned to find a clutch of strangers propping up their bicycles across the street. Most of them were wearing an inordinate amount of hemp and beaded jewelry, marking them as friends of Sunny's, but the one who'd spoken was dressed in a natty black suit and tie, as if he'd just come from a business meeting. He advanced on the soldier with a confident, professional stride.

"These *civilians* used threatening language themselves," the soldier said.

"Well, I look forward to telling your superior officer about that"—the well-dressed man read the soldier's name off his uniform—"Corporal Hastings."

"Knock yourself out." Hastings climbed back into his truck and restarted the engine. He revved it a few times, threateningly, but when the car finally moved again, it was in reverse, back toward the base.

"That was badass," Andy said.

The well-dressed man grinned. "Every good sit-in requires one guy in a nice suit. It lends an air of sophistication to the proceedings. Now let's talk strategy."

And with that, their protest had really begun.

Anita

BY THE TIME SHE WENT TO SLEEP THAT NIGHT, THERE WERE FIFTY OR SIXTY PEOPLE SITTING in front of the navy-base gate, with more coming all the time. They were black and white and Hispanic, toddlers and teenagers and grandparents. Most of them were friends of the commune, but some just happened to be driving or walking by and decided to join up. Those without sleeping bags or toothbrushes were provided for by Sunny's friends, who must have ripped off a camping store on the way to the protest, given all the supplies they "happened" to have on hand. They also prepared a delicious barbecue of veggie burgers, veggie hot dogs, and grilled vegetables, and someone even brought out a stumpy sugar cake that had been cooked in a wood-fire oven. Around midnight, a few police cars pulled up, lights flashing and sirens blaring, scaring everyone out of sleep. Someone on a megaphone ordered them to disperse, but when nobody moved, the cops gave up and left without a fight.

The next day was a Saturday, and the ranks of the protesters continued to swell: a hundred people, then two. Every few hours someone would go on a grocery run, collecting money with a hat or just taking the hit themselves. The protest was quickly becoming a community.

While Sunny's besuited friend Michael pounded the pavement to bring in new recruits, Anita took charge of managing the people who were already there. Food had to be fairly distributed. The drunk and disorderly had to be calmed down or else asked to leave. One guy showed up with a sawn-off shotgun and started screaming about how he was going to blow away whoever was responsible for imprisoning his son. It took an hour to convince him to hand over his weapon in exchange for a slice of pizza.

Anita had hoped that Andy and Peter would share in the responsibilities of leadership, but that turned out to be a pipe dream. In Andy's case, this was really a question of character—he just wasn't the administrative type (perhaps best exemplified by the fact that Anita had caught him sharing a joint with the hippie contingent first thing that morning). She put him on full-time sign-making duty, where his stoner creativity could really shine.

Peter, on the other hand, didn't seem to have the energy to do much of anything. Though Anita didn't know him very well, she could recognize the signs of a heavy heart. Late in the day, she found him standing alone at the chain-link fence, staring through the trees in the direction of the navy base. Night was beginning to fall, though the clouds were so thickly clustered that you could only track the setting sun as a vague sinking luminescence.

"What are you looking at?" she asked.

"Nothing."

"Are you in love with her?" The boldness of her question surprised Anita more than it seemed to surprise Peter, who didn't even pretend not to understand.

"I don't even know her. I didn't think she was the kind of person who could . . ." He shook his head.

Anita came closer and grabbed hold of the fence, digging the toe of her sneaker into one of the holes and raising herself up off the ground. She could make out a pale-green light shining in a top-floor window of one of the buildings across the tarmac.

"Who could do what?"

"I thought that she wanted to be with me, that's all. But I was wrong."

Sadness looked strange on Peter—too small, almost—like a sweater that reached only halfway down the forearm, that pulled up and exposed an awkward strip of midriff. With a word, she could eradicate that sadness. All she'd have to do was tell him the truth. Only then she'd be breaking trust with Andy, who was her best friend in the world. It was the lesser of two evils, then, to keep silent.

"And what about you?" Peter asked.

"What about me?"

"Are you in love?"

"Me? Who would I be in love with?"

Peter laughed.

"I'm serious. Who would I be in love with?" Anita let go of the fence, falling back to the hard earth. She really didn't know who Peter was talking about, but before she could press him, one of Sunny's friends came running from the direction of the main gate. Apparently, someone had tossed a whole bag of charcoal briquettes over the fence, and now they had no way to run the barbecue.

"To be continued," Anita said, but that first errand soon became a dozen others, and pretty soon she'd forgotten about Peter's question.

On Sunday spirits began to turn, and by Monday, a definitive mass depression had set in. The morning fog coalesced into Seattle's infamous drizzle, and there was a bite to the breeze that found the chinks in your clothing and led the rain inside. People had set up their tents just a few minutes too late to keep their stuff dry. Everything felt that way now—just a little bit too late. There were only two weeks left before Ardor was scheduled to arrive, and what were they all doing? Sitting around in the cold and the damp, waiting.

Anita watched the tarmac around the navy base turn slick and dark with rain. She'd hoped things would move more quickly than this; no one had so much as *tried* to get out of the gate since Corporal Hastings that first day.

Anita popped her head inside Andy's tent.

"Do you think there's some other way off the base?" she asked.

Andy sat up, blinking the sleep out of his eyes. "Anita? Why are you . . . who are you talking about?"

"The navy base! Do you think there's another way to get off it?"

"We already checked."

"Well, let's check again."

Anita let the tent flap drop, though she could still hear Andy whining. "You mean right now?"

Peter, who'd just gotten back from a visit with his parents, was eating a bowl of steaming oatmeal over in their makeshift kitchen area.

"Up for a walk?" Anita asked.

"Sure."

A few minutes later they were on their way, tromping down to the trail that led through Magnuson Park and all the way to Lake

Washington. Anita was grateful for the chance to get away from the crowd, which had begun to smell like one collective wet dog. The once festive strum of acoustic guitars had turned grating, and even Michael looked bedraggled and listless.

The three of them followed the chain-link fence around the outskirts of the base. The rain made conversation for them, pattering everywhere, filling the silence.

"Which do you like better, sun or rain?" Anita asked, hoping to kickstart a little communication.

"Rain, definitely," Andy said.

"Peter?"

"Sun. That's why I'm going to California. I mean, *if* I'm going to California."

Silence again. Well, it had been worth a try.

The tension between Peter and Andy was palpable, and it seemed to be getting worse by the hour. Every conversation had become a byzantine exercise in avoiding the subject of Eliza. And the truth was, it sort of sucked to spend all your time with two boys who were both in love with some other girl. Peter got a pass—he and Eliza actually had a history together—but Anita found herself more and more annoyed with Andy. Why was this stupid quest so important to him? He had to know that Eliza was totally wrong for him. Why couldn't he just drop the bullshit and let her be with Peter already?

"Remind me why we don't just cut a hole in the fence," Andy said, giving the chain-link a karate kick.

"We need to keep the driveway blocked off," Anita said.

"Yeah, but one person could do that. What if the rest of us went inside and got right up in their faces?"

"It doesn't matter if we're on this side or the other," Peter said. "It's not like we can just walk into the building. Plus, I'd rather not get shot."

The path they were walking on turned muddy; it darkened the white soles of Anita's sneakers. Fat globs of water fell off the branches of the evergreens, landing heavy as hailstones. Across the street, a building called the Western Fisheries Research Center stood dark and empty as a mausoleum. Anita wondered how many millions of things had stopped mattering in the last month. How many employees of the Western Fisheries Research Center were sitting at home right now, just praying they'd get another chance to continue their fishy research?

They reached the end of the fence, having failed to locate any secret exit off the navy base. They kept walking, though, following the pavement all the way down to where it met the lake. A wide parking lot gave onto a small lawn, where an old oaken park bench had been stained to mahogany by the rain. They sat down on the wet wood and watched the chop of the water for a while.

"Andy," Anita said suddenly, "say something nice about Peter."

"What?"

"Just do it. Right now. Don't think."

It was a trick that Anita's fifth-grade teacher had used whenever two of his students got in a fight. Andy probably wouldn't have played along if he'd had more time to think about it, but she'd caught him by surprise.

"Uh, you seem like a really good guy. Like, for real, though. Not like some kind of act."

"Thanks," Peter said, made shy by the compliment.

"Your turn," Anita prompted.

"Okay." Peter looked down at his hands. "You don't know this, Andy, but I heard you and Anita practicing once, in the Hamilton music room. You're really talented."

"Oh yeah? Thanks."

Anita exhaled heavily, letting her stomach unclench. She felt as if she'd just finished defusing a bomb. It was movement, anyway, which felt good after three days of total paralysis. But even turning Peter and Andy into best friends wouldn't turn their protest into a success.

She looked back out over the lake. "What do we do if this doesn't work?"

"It has to work," Andy said. And he surprised her by putting his hand over hers. She hadn't realized how cold her fingers were; now the warmth spread down her arm and out across her body, inexplicably fast. A moment passed; then Andy seemed to realize what he'd done. He pulled his hand away.

"It has to work," he repeated.

The next day Anita was taking an afternoon nap (more out of boredom than fatigue), when she was woken by a loud mechanical screech. She unzipped her tent and saw that a crowd had gathered around the fence near the gate. A lot of new protesters seemed to have arrived in the last couple of hours, and they were a very different animal from Sunny's commune crew. In fact, they looked like the kind of people who'd been at Andy and Bobo's gig a few weeks back—covered in piercings and tattoos, reeking of alcohol and cigarette smoke.

An enormous clang, as of a large piece of metal falling to the dirt, and the screeching abruptly stopped. A huge cheer went up, then people were lining up to crawl through the newly cut hole in the fence.

Anita pushed through the crowd and found Andy embroiled in some kind of argument with Sunny and Michael.

"But I talked to them about that!" Andy said. "They'll stay in line."

"You can't know that," Michael said.

"Maybe not. But we had to do *something*. It's been five days."

"You should have been patient. Given enough time, the ocean can turn a mountain to sand."

"It's the end of the fucking world, man! We don't have time to be the ocean."

"We won't be part of any happening that encourages violence," Sunny said. "I'm sorry." She took Michael by the arm and walked off in a huff.

"No one's encouraging violence!" Andy called after them. He turned to Anita. "Can you believe this? She's saying they're all going to leave."

"Andy, who are all these new people?"

"I brought them," he said, sounding both proud and guilty at once. "After you and Peter went to sleep last night, I biked over to the Independent. It's this apartment building that Bobo moved into a couple weeks back, 'cause Golden lives there."

"Does that mean Golden's here right now?"

"These people get shit done, Anita. And we need that now. But don't worry. I'll make sure nothing gets out of hand."

He jogged off toward the hole in the fence before she could berate him any further. And what else could she do but follow? The hole had been cut so low to the ground that she had to get down on her hands and knees to pass through it. The bite of gravel, then a patch of soft dirt, and finally the cracked cement of a derelict runway. A small commemorative plaque was mounted just on the other side of the gate: SAND POINT AIRFIELD WAS THE ENDPOINT OF THE FIRST AERIAL CIRCUMNAVIGATION OF THE WORLD IN 1924. Just another little piece of utterly irrelevant history, aspiring to permanence, doomed to oblivion. The end of the world revealed the futility of all commemorative plaques.

Everyone was running for the only building on the lot that had any lights on inside. It was some kind of barracks, but it looked less militaristic than academic—like something off the campus of a liberal arts college on the East Coast. Anita moved with the crowd, expecting sirens to switch on at any moment, followed by a hail of machine-gun fire, but they made it to the foot of the building without incident. The doors, unsurprisingly, were all locked.

Even if they'd lost Sunny and her friends, the people who remained seemed galvanized by the change of scenery, chanting and waving their signs with newfound enthusiasm. Golden's crew rolled a few kegs of beer across the tarmac, and they quickly succeeded in transferring the majority of the contents into their bodies. More than once, Anita plucked a cup out of Andy's or Peter's hand, but before long, the two boys were as red-faced and muddled as the rest of the protesters.

Decorum didn't last long. The nearly full moon was shining down like the bright, pupilless eye of some phlegmatic god when the first stone was thrown. The crowd was desperate for action, and pretty soon everyone had joined in, taking drunken aim at the barracks with whatever was close at hand. Anita saw Andy pull the commemorative plaque out of the ground and toss it onto the roof, where it stuck in a rain gutter. Within fifteen minutes, half the glass in the barracks had been knocked out. Not long after, a plump man in uniform appeared in the exclamatory comic-book bubble of a broken window on the second floor. The hailstorm momentarily ceased.

"How do y'all see this ending?" he called down.

Golden, standing on the steps of the barracks, had elected himself negotiator. "You let everybody out, including yourselves."

The man disappeared from the window for a long time, so long that Anita began to worry he was planning some kind of assault. But then, just as the crowd was getting restless, he reappeared. "You don't touch any of my men and women."

"Of course," Golden said.

"Your word."

"You've got it."

Like that, it was over. Within minutes, the tarmac filled with hundreds of kids, all of them dressed in pale-blue jumpsuits. Interspersed among them were a few soldiers in full camouflage, hurrying through the crowd toward the front gate. Anita saw Corporal Hastings pushed down onto all fours, but he only stood up again and kept walking. Parents called out the names of their children and reunited tearfully. The rain had begun to fall again, and as they were all too buzzed on their triumph to want to disperse just yet, the celebration moved indoors.

Anita had lost track of Andy and Peter in the hubbub, so she followed the crowd into the barracks. There was still power inside, and it was blissfully warm. They ended up in what looked to be the central dormitory. Everyone was milling around, looking for loved ones. When Anita finally found Andy, he hugged her tightly.

"Can you believe it?" he said. "We did it!"

"I guess so."

She could feel his heart beating so fast it was almost a flutter. He started to pull away, but then they were pushed back together by a shift in the crowd. For a moment, she thought he was about to kiss her.

"So what do you think I should say?" he asked.

"What do you mean?"

"When I see Eliza. I mean, should I take credit for this whole rescue thing, or should I play it cool?"

Anita made sure that no sign of disappointment appeared on her face. "Whatever you want."

"Be less helpful. Come on, Anita. This is serious. It's game time!"

"Isn't everybody going home?"

"No way! Golden brought a fucking party with him, yo. Tonight, the thrill of freedom meets a shit-ton of hard liquor. If I ever had a shot with Eliza, this is it."

Somebody switched off the overhead lights, earning a chorus of lascivious yowls from the crowd. A moment later some kind of huge curtain fell away from the windows, letting in a few pale strands of moonlight.

Andy cracked his knuckles and hopped up and down like a boxer waiting for the bell. "Okay. I'm gonna have one or two or six more drinks, then I'm gonna make my move. Wish me luck."

"Good luck."

And as Anita watched Andy skip across the room, she finally felt it, rumbling like a bone-deep hunger she'd been ignoring for weeks. A sensation somehow totally new and totally familiar at once. It was the glistening green blossom of jealousy, and deeper down, beyond the place where the stem met the dirt, the parched and greedy roots: love.

Eliza

IN THE SPACE OF FIFTEEN MINUTES, THE DORMITORY HAD BEEN COMPLETELY TRANSFORMED.
The place was still reverberatingly loud—echoes lingering in the corners of the room like cobwebs—and nothing could totally disperse the horrifying bouquet of a few hundred teenage boys packed into a small space. But by taping a couple of dozen flashlights to the walls (covered with sheets to diffuse the light), setting up a halfway decent DJ with a halfway decent PA system, and pushing the bunk beds back from the center of the room to create a dance floor, Golden's crew had actually managed to give the place a bit of atmosphere. An overturned bed frame served as a makeshift bar, where a great leaning tower of red plastic Solo cups was pared down one layer at a time as volunteer bartenders prepared drinks with a consummate ignorance of mixology. A stranger handed Eliza a brimming cup of tequila.

The music twitched like a tweaker coming down, thrummed like a subconscious thought. People began to dance, but Eliza stayed close to the bar, where there was a bit more light. She watched as Anita snuck up behind the "bartenders" and disappeared with a whole bottle of bourbon (and wasn't that a little bit out of character?). Soon after, Andy showed up to wait in line for his own drink. Eliza almost stepped out of the shadows to say hello, but some animal instinct told her to hang back. There was a wildness in his eyes that she didn't trust.

The tequila was already beginning to work its way around her body—loosening the muscles and lubricating the joints. She let herself sink down into the strange mixture of numbness and sensuousness that alcohol always brought on, and felt a familiar craving begin to assert itself, throbbing somewhere in the deepest, darkest crevices of her body. It was the same craving that occasionally led her out to the Crocodile to sit alone at the bar, waiting for one of the moony hormone synthesizers always revolving around her to break loose from his orbit and buy her a drink. The need to see some boy lose his shit because he wanted her so bad. Her sudden freedom was every bit as intoxicating as the liquor, and though she could pretend she was just wandering around, checking the scene, her eyes had an agenda. She knew she should get home to see her dad as soon as possible, but she couldn't leave yet. Not before she'd found Peter.

Of course, it was possible that he wasn't even here. Maybe someone else had worked out the location of the detention center and managed this whole rescue operation. Only that would have been such a gigantic failure on the part of the universe, Eliza refused to even consider it.

It was another two drinks and forty-five minutes before she spotted him, engaged in what looked to be a pretty violent argument with his sister. Eliza couldn't hear most of what they were saying, but it seemed like Peter was trying to get Misery to leave the party, and Misery was refusing. She grudgingly surrendered her beer ("God, it's not like I've never had a drink before!"), then darted off toward the dance floor. Peter moved to follow her, but Eliza caught hold of his elbow.

And then there they were, together at last. The darkness of the dormitory brought back memories of that day in the photo lab. She could remember the feel of his mouth on hers—rough with stubble but clean, clean as the good, clean boy that he was.

"Peter," she said. His flesh pulsed warm against her palm.

"I need to get my sister," he said, pulling himself out of her grasp and beginning to walk away.

"What's the rush?"

"Golden's here, for one thing. And Bobo. I just wanna get home with Miz, okay?"

Eliza followed him down a narrow path between two rows of bunk beds, past a couple talking in hushed tones in a bottom bunk.

"Peter, just wait up a second!"

He turned on her so suddenly that she flinched. "Why should I wait? What else could you want from me? I got you out, okay? Isn't that enough?"

They were alone now, hemmed in by beds and everything that beds stood for. Eliza had no idea why Peter was so angry, but she did know there was one way to make it all better. Grabbing him by the shoulders, she shoved him back against the frame of a bunk bed with the rough confidence of someone who'd never taken no for an answer, who'd never needed to. Peter dropped the bottle of beer, and the sound of it crashing down coincided with the crash of her lips against his. She slid her tongue along the tiles of his teeth, the taste of him weirdly familiar, even though it had been more than a year since the last time they'd kissed. She waited for his arms around her body, the pull tight and the tilt of the head, and then they would fall inward onto the bed and finish what they'd started in that darkroom. Only his arms weren't pulling her in; they were pushing her away.

"What's wrong?" she asked.

"What's wrong with *you*?" he spat back. "You think Ardor means you can treat people however you want?"

"No. I don't even know what you're talking about."

"Have you been with someone else, Eliza? Since we found out about Ardor?"

"I'm not sure I—" Her words caught in her throat. How could Peter know about the boy she'd hooked up with in the detention center? Or had he just guessed? Either way, he had no right to judge her for it. She'd been lonely and terrified, isolated from her dad and her home and what few friends she had, as the world outside kept spinning madly toward destruction. And so she'd allowed herself a moment of intimacy with a stranger. So what? Eliza felt herself ballooning with a sense of righteous anger.

"You're one to talk. You had a girlfriend when we first kissed."

"I know. And that was a mistake. But I broke up with Stacy a *month* ago—for you!"

"Then why didn't you say something? You had a million chances to talk to me and you never did! I'm the one who ended up writing to you!"

Peter slid out of her arms. "Well, it doesn't matter now, does it? Andy's my friend. I wouldn't go behind his back."

Eliza shook her head, confused. "Wait . . . this is about Andy?"

"Of course it is."

"But that's stupid. I don't care about Andy!"

Peter snorted. "I don't think you care about anyone."

He disappeared into the gloom between the rows of beds, a gloom that seemed to grow deeper and darker as Eliza stared at it, as if every single shadow on Earth were converging on this very spot, blotting out the light layer by layer, like shovelfuls of dirt tossed onto a coffin. They came from him and they came from her and they came from way out in space and they came from everything that drew breath. She gulped down the rest of her drink, then went back for another.

In the lot behind the barracks, Eliza walked the flaking paint line of an old basketball court as if it were a sobriety test—one that she was failing miserably. A few other people were outside, but they all stood under the eaves of the building, out of the rain, smoking. All she could see of them was the occasional golden flare of a cigarette. It was only drizzling now, but in the distance, lightning built huge electric blue sculptures in the sky, ephemeral trees that nevertheless left tenacious marks on the retina. Her skin didn't feel like skin, but an insensible little force field around her body. If the rain fell any harder, it would melt her down like the Wicked Witch of the West. She wondered what her death would be like. Would it happen fast—a lightning flash of pain and then nothing? Or would it be slow, choking on dust or starving to death under some collapsed building? She felt dead already; Peter had blown a hole in her pride and her faith and her hope all at once. What had gone wrong? Hadn't he come looking for her at Cal Anderson Park and held her hand tight as a mousetrap as they ran through the haze of tear gas? And why had he brought up Andy? Andy was just a friend. And as for that other boy, sure, they'd hooked up. But it wasn't as if she had a boyfriend or something. She hadn't had a boyfriend since . . .

I haven't ever had a boyfriend, she realized, followed by an even more terrible revelation: *And now I never will.*

There were a lot of countdowns that had haunted her over the past few weeks, from the totally mundane (how many breaths she had left to breathe) to the whimsically specific (how many more times she'd get to watch *Pitch Perfect*), but this was definitely the most depressing statistic of all: Between now and the end of the world, there would be no one else who would love her, and no one else she would love.

Thunder rolled across the flat expanse of Magnuson Park. Any second now, the real rain would come. That was Seattle all over. A goddamn perpetual drizzle, with occasional breaks for pouring rain. Just like life. Perpetual shit, with occasional breaks for pouring shit. And then, at the end, a big rock lands on your head.

She walked through a cloud of cigarette smoke and back into the barracks, then followed a hallway into some derelict dormitory, all rusted bed frames and moth-eaten mattresses. The room, like any place where lots of people used to be and now nobody ever was, felt haunted. Eliza would have been afraid, only she was floating a couple of feet behind her body now, a ghost herself, watching some faraway Eliza open a random door and walk into the darkness beyond, like that character in a horror film that you want to yell at—*Don't go in there, you dumbass!* She banged her knee against a table, then hurt herself even worse kicking the thing in anger. The heavy dubstep beats from the party melted away, exposing the quiet plinking of a distant piano. At first she thought the music was only in her head, but it got louder as she moved deeper into the room. Another door, and on the other side, the music expanded into presence. There was a bit of light from the red glow of an exit sign above the door. It bloodied the edges of a foosball table, a pool table, a couple of old pinball machines, and all the way in the corner, someone seated at an upright piano.

Eliza tiptoed across the room and landed softly on a scratchy couch. Her eyes began to adjust, just enough for her to make out Andy's slouched shape on the piano bench, tapping out a half-familiar tune—one of the songs he and Anita were always practicing, preparing for the Party at the End of the World. As if that were really going to happen.

When he stopped playing, Eliza gave a single loud clap. Andy's silhouette jumped.

"What the hell?"

She laughed. "Encore, maestro!"

"Eliza? You scared the shit out of me."

"And hello to you, too."

She stood up, almost tripping over the leg of her chair—even worse, almost spilling her drink. She gave a little bow in celebration of her superior balancing skills, then stepped gingerly across the room. The floor was a precarious log afloat in a rushing river.

"What are you doing in here?" she asked.

"I couldn't find you," he said. His voice was a drunken lilt. "I figured you were off somewhere with Peter."

"Nope. I'm right here, with you."

"So you are. Feel like a duet?"

She bent down to place her glass behind the piano bench.

"Little old me? Nope, nope. It's all you. Let's hear one of your favorites."

"All right. I'll hit you with some Flaming Lips."

Andy began to sing, his sweet little voice floating on top of the heavy piano like the scoop of vanilla ice cream on a root beer float: "*Do you realize that you have the most beautiful face?*" After the first verse, Eliza sat down next to him, letting her hip touch his. If he felt it, he didn't give any sign. But she wanted a reaction; the urge was still there, even stronger now with the exaggerating effect of the alcohol and the bitter taste of rejection in the back of her throat. As he started into another chorus, she let her left hand find the small of his back, ascend the ladder of his spine, and come to rest gently on the knob at the base of his skull. She watched her index finger wrap itself around a lock of his hair, spinning it like a strand of bubble gum. He choked on a syllable, choked on desire, though his hands kept playing the accompaniment.

"What are you doing?" he asked.

"Nothing."

"Doesn't seem like nothing."

"Something, nothing. What's the difference?"

"I can't sing while you're doing that."

"So don't sing."

When he hesitated, she turned his head to face her and kissed him with all the rage and appetite she had in her, finally putting a stop to the music. His hands slid up her hips, found the zipper of her jumpsuit, and pulled. Cold air on her skin, then his warm fingers, tingling, as if they were especially alive after playing. She pulled his hoodie and T-shirt up and over his head, scratched hard down his chest, felt at his jeans for the sign that she was wanted. He kissed her neck as he fumbled with the clasp of her bra.

Eliza allowed her eyes to drift open. Over Andy's shoulder, she could see where his hoodie had landed, in a narrow rectangle of gray light in the middle of the room. Strange—it had been completely dark in here a second ago. And now the silver line was stretching out, as if someone were taking a highlighter and underlining the floor. The line became a wedge, reaching toward them like a pointing finger. The shape of a person in the doorway, then darkness again.

Andy was facing the other way, so he hadn't seen it. But as Eliza felt his hand drop down between her legs, as she unconsciously ground against him with her hips, she felt the wrongness of what she was doing crash like an asteroid against the planet-size need to connect with someone, with anyone, and she pushed him off her with a fury that she knew he wouldn't understand, that wasn't even about him, so hard that he fell backward off the piano bench onto her cup, and then she was up and out of the room without saying a word, just in time to watch Anita throw open the door to the outside world as it exploded with lightning and thunder, like the warm-up to an apocalypse.

Andy

ANDY KNEW THE FAMOUS SAYING "BE CAREFUL WHAT YOU WISH FOR, BECAUSE YOU JUST might get it." But he'd always thought Morrissey's take on things made a whole lot more sense: *"See the luck I've had can make a good man turn bad, so please please please, let me get what I want."* Getting what you wanted, as far as Andy was concerned, was pretty much the most awesome thing in the universe.

For years, he'd imagined what it would be like to hook up with Eliza. To feel her arms around his shoulders, the warm pulse of her body curving into his, the soft skin of her breasts against his palms—innumerable hours had passed in contemplation of such wonders. By a standard like that, the event itself should have disappointed. But it hadn't. He felt as if he'd simultaneously nailed the groove of a new song, landed a sick jump on his skateboard, and snorted a line of coke (a drug he'd tried only once for fear another go would kill him—it made his heart want to go for a run outside his body).

Of course, it was hard not to read something worrying into her sudden exit, but Andy figured there were three possibilities, only one of which was truly terrible: (1) Eliza totally regretted what she'd done and now she hated him and wished they were both dead (the F possibility); (2) she was totally wasted and needed some time and space to clear her head (the C-minus possibility); or (3) she was so overwhelmed by her desire for him that it scared her (the A-plus possibility).

Andy couldn't solve the riddle on his own; he needed another girl to give him insight into the mysteries of girlish behavior. Unfortunately, he couldn't find Anita anywhere. Back in the dormitory, the revelry had reached a fever pitch. More than a few couples could be seen moving in slow rhythms under bunk-bed covers, and the dancing in the middle of the room was as close to sex as dancing could be. Andy grabbed a bottle of tequila from the unattended bar and went looking for someone else to talk to. He finally found Bobo and Misery grinding against a bunk bed just off the dance floor.

"Dude!" he shouted, slapping Bobo on the shoulder.

Bobo detached his octopus sucker of a mouth from Misery's. "What is it, man?"

"It's that I'm gonna get that grand, yo! I just made out with Eliza!"

"For real?"

"Swear to Baby Jesus."

Bobo put up a hand. Andy leaned back and prepared to land the most explosive high five of his eighteen-year-old life. But his palm got nothing but air; Bobo had pulled a too-slow on him.

"You do realize that making out isn't sex, right?"

"Yeah. But it means she's into me. The rest is, like, inevitable."

"Inevitable? Then why aren't you hitting that right now?"

"Well, that's actually why I'm here. Miz, I need your advice."

"You've got it," she said. Her face was red from rubbing up against Bobo's stubble.

"So Eliza and I were just getting into it, and then she jumped up and ran out on me. What does that mean?"

"That you suck at making out," Bobo said.

"I'm not asking you, asshole."

Misery laid a hand on Andy's shoulder with a drunkard's weight. "She's confused, man. She's not trying to be a cock tease or something."

"Yeah," Bobo said. "If there's one thing Eliza is *not*, it's a cock tease. More like a cock *lover*, right?"

"Dude," Andy said, but he still laughed.

Just then, some overexuberant dancer bumped hard against his back, sending him spinning. A black blur of movement, a meaty *thunk*. Bobo was suddenly bent over, holding his hands to his stomach. And there was Peter, appearing out of nowhere, like some kind of superhero.

"Did you just punch my boyfriend?" Misery said.

Peter knelt down low so he could look up into Bobo's eyes. "That was for being disrespectful." He turned on Andy next. "And you oughta be ashamed, letting someone talk about your girlfriend like that." Finally he addressed his sister. "Enough, Miz. It's time to go."

"Can't we at least stay until the end of the party?"

"No." He grabbed her by the arm and dragged her away.

Bobo finally caught his breath, straightening up with a wince. "That fucker."

"No, he was right," Andy said, mostly to himself. "I shouldn't have laughed. If I want Eliza to be my girlfriend, I have to stand up for her and shit."

But Bobo wasn't listening. He'd begun to stumble back toward the dance floor.

"Where you going?"

"To find Golden."

"Whoa, whoa!" Andy grabbed hold of Bobo's sleeve. "Just hold up a sec."

"You wanna let Peter get away with that? He *assaulted* me, yo."

"It's not that." Andy wasn't sure how to defuse the situation. A bad joke at Eliza's expense didn't give Peter the right to slam Bobo in the gut, but it also wasn't worth getting Golden involved. That dude was straight-up *nuts*. "I'm just saying we can take care of it ourselves."

Bobo smiled. "Now that's the Andy I like to hear! And I know just how to do it. Follow me."

He led Andy to an empty bed near the windows. Underneath the pillow were a couple of blocky plastic guns. Andy recognized them from television.

"Tasers?"

"For real. I found them in that gatehouse thing outside."

"You really think we need them? It's two on one."

"Don't be a pussy," Bobo said, handing him one of the guns.

Outside the barracks, the rain was falling in sheets. Peter had already made it halfway across the tarmac. Misery wasn't fighting him anymore, but they were still arguing loudly as they walked. The chill air combined with the downpour sobered Andy up just enough to make him wonder exactly what he was getting himself into. He didn't really have a problem with Peter, especially now that they were all tied up—one brief hookup with Eliza in a dark room to one brief hookup with Eliza in a darkroom. And as for the sucker punch, Bobo *had* been acting like a dick.

"Hey!" Bobo called out.

Peter turned around. "What now, man?"

"Misery doesn't want to go with you."

"Back off, Bobo. She'll see you later, I'm sure, whether I want her to or not. We're just going home to see our parents."

"You're not going anywhere."

Bobo raised his Taser and fired.

Nothing happened. The two tendrils of wire hung loosely from the barrel of the gun, like a couple of dead vines. They'd landed a good five feet shy of Peter.

Peter looked back and forth from the barbs of the Taser to Bobo, incredulous. "You stupid shit," he said, and began to close the distance between them in angry athletic strides. "I was holding her arm, you moron. You would have shocked her, too."

"Andy!" Bobo said, backing up.

"What?"

"Fucking shoot him, man!"

Andy had forgotten he even had the Taser. He found it now, like a tumor bursting suddenly from his skin. He didn't want to shoot anyone. But in another few seconds, Peter would be close enough to knock Bobo's teeth out.

"Stop there," he said weakly, pointing the gun, but Peter either didn't hear him or didn't care. Bobo threw his Taser at Peter's head and whiffed entirely. Only a few seconds left. If Andy didn't do something right now, it would mean the end of his friendship with Bobo. He didn't have a choice.

There was barely any recoil. At first, Andy thought Peter was playacting—quaking and quivering like a fish just pulled out of the water, little grunts coming out of his slack mouth. Then his knees buckled and his forehead collided with the pavement. His body went still. Andy dropped the Taser.

"What did you do?" Misery shouted, falling onto her knees next to her brother.

"That's what he gets," Bobo said. "Now come on. It's pouring out here."

Misery pulled hard at her brother's shoulder and managed to turn him over. She wiped away the hair plastered like tar across his pale white forehead. A rivulet of blood ran down from his scalp and was diffused into a bloom by the rain. "Just leave us alone, Bobo. This is all so fucked up. Everything's so fucked up."

"What, you're angry at *me* now? We only did this because he was trying to kidnap you!"

Misery didn't answer.

"Whatever," Bobo said, and headed back to the barracks alone.

Andy was still holding the bottle of tequila in his left hand. He set it down next to Peter's head, then looked to Misery for some sign of understanding or forgiveness. But she only blotted at the blood with her sopping sleeve, over and over again, waiting for her brother to come around.

Anita

THE DOOR SWUNG SHUT BEHIND HER. ANITA BROKE INTO A SPRINT, EACH SLAP OF HER sneaker like a tiny little gunshot against the wet pavement. She hid behind a big black Dumpster, then peeked out through shimmering curtains of rain.

"Anita! Talk to me!" Eliza was running so fast that she slipped, going down hard on her bony ass. So much less than she deserved. Anita had never approved of the way people described Eliza—that one word that somehow spelled shame for a girl and prestige for a boy: S-L-U-T. And yet now, she found herself muttering the epithet into her palm, like a curse.

Eliza rose shakily to her feet. "Fine!" she shouted. "Don't talk to me then!" She staggered back toward the barracks.

Anita realized she was crying, though the storm washed every tear away as soon as it slipped free of her eyelid. She was also intensely, unprecedentedly drunk, having imbibed most of a bottle of bourbon over the course of the last hour. The Earth turned perceptibly beneath her feet, revealing the vertiginous uncertainty underpinning reality itself. As if Ardor weren't evidence enough that there was no safety to be found anywhere on this doomed, malignant planet, she'd just walked in on Andy and Eliza making out, already half-undressed. Did that mean they were some kind of couple now? And would they end up sleeping together? Probably, given that Eliza was such a total, shameless, nasty-ass *slut*.

This was all Peter's fault, really. If he weren't so goddamn nice, he would've already confronted Eliza, confessed his undying love, and revealed Andy's deception. Didn't he realize this was the end of the world? There was no time left to be nice.

Anita stayed outside in the rain for a few minutes longer, punishing herself for something she couldn't quite name. Her shivers turned to outright convulsions. And sure, she could have just gone back to her car and left, but that felt too much like a surrender. Her presence at the detention center was the only thing keeping Andy and Eliza from getting married and starting a fucking family together.

The barracks had seemed cozy enough back when she was dry, but now it felt chilly and dank. Members of Golden's crew, drunk and menacing, skulked up and down the halls. Anita needed to sober up somewhere, preferably alone. She tried a dozen doors before finding one that was unlocked—a stairway.

"'*There's a lady who's sure all that glitters is gold,*'" Anita sang as she climbed upward into the dark, "'*and she's buying a stairway to heaven.*'"

The upper-floor windows, many of which had been knocked out by the fusillade of rocks, looked out over the whole naval base, a landscape of cracked cement and gnarled trees, illuminated in brief electric bursts like a strobe light set to the slowest possible setting. The rain drummed a metallic melody on the roof just above her head. Only after she'd unpeeled her socks and sweater did Anita notice the light at the end of the hallway. She crept closer, but the creaking floor gave her away.

"Is someone out there? You can come in. I sit in peace." It was a man's voice, his tone affable and mild.

The office was lit by a small green-shaded lamp perched on the windowsill and a half-dozen long-stemmed candles. Behind a large desk sat a rotund, ruddy-cheeked man wearing enough camouflage to tent a small house. In the glimmering, Anita could just make out his nameplate: CAPTAIN MORGAN. It was his name that kept her from immediately turning around and running away; somehow it seemed impossible that a man called Captain Morgan could be a threat. Only after she'd landed safely in a chair did she notice the mostly empty bottle of rum on his desk, and the mostly full glass in his hand.

"Hey there," he said.

"Hey."

"I'm Doug Morgan."

"Anita."

Doug raised his glass to her. "How you doing, Anita?"

"I've been better. You?"

"I, too, have been better." He drank, as if they'd just toasted.

"What are you still doing here?"

"Good question. I gave the order to evacuate, so I figured it was on me to stick around and make sure nobody burned the place down. I was meant to be keeping in touch with my superiors on that contraption, but it broke down on me yesterday." He rapped the side of a green metal box that squatted on the narrow table behind him. It was clearly a relic, corroded at the corners, with an old-fashioned black handset on the side.

"What is it?"

"A shortwave radio. Phones and cell towers are out, so we're back to the Stone Age." He polished off the rest of his glass. Just the thought of consuming more alcohol caused Anita's stomach to make a sudden and violent request to externalize its inner conflict. She swallowed it down.

"Your turn," Doug said. "What brings you up to the attic?"

"I'm not totally sure. Just wanted to get some space."

"I hear that. *Un momento.*"

He leaned down to open one of the desk's lower drawers. Anita's eye was drawn to the single photo frame propped up on a bookshelf—one of those digital things that played the same slideshow over and over again. It showed three babies becoming three toddlers becoming three elementary school kids, then only two teenagers. In photo after photo, just two, until the cycle restarted and a miraculous resurrection took place.

"Sometimes I forget that death existed before Ardor," Anita said.

Doug sat back up, already unscrewing the top of a fresh bottle of rum. "One of the many advantages of youth," he said.

"Those are your kids, in the pictures?"

"Yeah."

"Don't you wanna get home to them?"

"I would love to. But they live with their mom. In California."

"Why?"

Doug shrugged his massive shoulders. "Because there are no second acts in American lives." He didn't so much speak the words as recite them.

"Who said that?"

"F. Scott Fitzgerald. You know him?"

"We read *Gatsby* in English."

"Did you like it?"

Anita tried to remember the paper she'd written about the book. "Sort of. A lot of it was really beautiful, but I didn't like how he wrote about women. I got the feeling he didn't respect them very much."

Doug acknowledged this with another one-sided toast; rum splashed over the side of his glass, leaving rust-red splotches on the papers beneath it. "That's a fair read, Anita. I didn't love it either, to be honest—I was never much of a fiction guy—but I have a lot of respect for the character. Gatsby had a goal, and everything he did was about reaching it. That's admirable, even if it turns out your goal was a stupid one."

Anita was reminded of her own stupid goal, to make a little bit of music she could be proud of before the end came. She might even have achieved it too, if she hadn't allowed herself to get distracted by this whole rescue fiasco. And for what? On the off chance that her selflessness would be rewarded with love? Pathetic. The tragic truth was that somewhere along the line, without her even noticing, Anita had traded in her big stupid dream for something even stupider: a boy who didn't want her.

"And you know the funniest thing about that line, the one about second acts?" Doug said.

"What?"

"It never even got published. Fitzgerald wrote this one great book, right? And that was the finale of his first act. Then he drank himself stupid, cheated on his wife, and basically pissed away every opportunity he got. And that line comes from the book that he hoped would turn it all around. The one that would have been his second act. Only he died before he could finish it. So the book didn't get a second act, and neither did he."

A waver of the candlelight placed a living spark inside the droplet trickling down Captain Morgan's stubbled cheek.

"Are you okay?" Anita asked.

"Me?" He chuckled. "I'm fine. I'm over the hill. It's you I'm worried about. Your generation, I mean. Just look at you. So young and gorgeous and full of . . . life. You deserve a second act."

Anita stood up and walked around the desk. Maybe it was because Andy had done what he'd done with Eliza, or maybe it was because Doug had called her gorgeous and she'd really needed to hear that tonight. Whatever the reason, it seemed like the right thing to do. She bent down and kissed him gently on his rum-sweet lips.

"Who says the end of the world is all bad?" he said, smiling. Then he pushed up out of his chair with a groan and went to a cabinet in the corner of the room. "You're soaked, my dear." He fished out a pile of green fatigues and threw them her way. "Wear them proudly."

"Thanks. So how long you think you're going to stay here?"

"The generator should give out before morning. They'll all go after that."

Next to the broken shortwave was a more traditional radio, faux vintage, or maybe *real* vintage, with a brown metal grille for a speaker and a curved wooden top. Doug switched it on. The long, skinny bar of frequencies glowed the same butter yellow as the candlelight. He spun the dial, swimming across waves of static, until he found a lone voice, trembling above a cloud line of backing vocals and a ghostly rhythm section: "*I don't want to set the world on fire . . .*"

"Someone's still out there," Anita said.

"It's almost enough to make a man hope."

"Almost."

"It was nice to meet you, Anita."

"Likewise, Doug."

Once the door was shut behind her, she stripped off her wet clothes and changed into the fatigues. She was still half-naked when a flash of lightning revealed that she wasn't alone in the hallway: Eliza stood just at the top of the stairs.

"Hey," she said.

Anita quickly finished buttoning up the too-large shirt. "Hey."

"I followed you up here a few minutes ago. Hope you don't mind. I wanted to talk to you, but then I heard you in there with Captain Morgan, so I just figured I'd wait until you were done."

"You know him?"

"A little. Anyway, listen, what you saw downstairs, with Andy? It was a mistake."

"I know."

"I was pretty drunk—I still am, actually—and Peter had just basically accused me of having a boyfriend or something and totally rejected me, which really messed my head up. So I did something stupid, and I'm sorry for it."

"Why apologize to me?" Anita asked. "Why would I care what you and Andy do?"

Eliza frowned. "I'm not really sure. But I think you do. Am I wrong?"

The song was still seeping quietly out from under Captain Morgan's door: "*I just want to start a flame in your heart.*"

"Stay right here," Anita said. "I'm going to fix everything."

☦

She worried she'd be conspicuous walking back into the party in full military regalia, but nobody even seemed to notice. She saw Andy before he saw her.

"Dude, where have you been?" he asked. "The most amazing thing happened. Me and Eliza made out. And it was unbelievable." His excitement was an excruciating twist of the knife.

"And did you tell her what you told Peter?"

"Are you kidding? Of course not! Speaking of which, shit just got *crazy* with him. He punched Bobo. Like, out of nowhere. So we had to tase him. It was messed up."

"Peter punched someone out of nowhere?" Anita caught the brief flash of remorse in Andy's eyes. "I bet it was because of something Bobo did, wasn't it? And then he got pissed off, and you did whatever he told you to do. Like always."

"Peter was gonna kick his ass! What was I supposed to do?"

"You let him. You let Bobo get what he deserves. Because he's an asshole, Andy, just like you." Andy looked stung, but that only made Anita angrier. "And let's be honest here, yeah? Do you really think Eliza wants you? Because I'll tell you straight—she doesn't. You were just the closest warm body. And the funniest part is that she doesn't mean anything to you, either! The only thing you care about is winning your little game!" She wanted him to yell back, but he only stood there shamefaced, like a dog caught tearing up the couch cushions. "What is it even worth, huh? Would sleeping with Eliza protect you somehow, from what's going to happen?"

"She's all I've got," he whispered.

And that was the cruelest blow of all. "Is she? Fine. Then I wash my hands of you. I'm done. Now, where's Peter?"

"He's out on the tarmac."

"You left him in the rain?"

"Miz is with him. Wait, why do you want to see him?"

But Anita was already gone. Outside, her nice dry clothes were soaked through in seconds. A dark-blue dot in the middle of the runway came into focus—Misery sitting cross-legged with Peter's head in her lap. She raised a bottle of tequila by the neck as Anita approached, preparing to throw it.

"It's just me," Anita said.

But Misery didn't let her arm drop. "You here to finish the job?" Peter put his hand on his sister's elbow, forcing her to lower the bottle.

"She's a friend, Miz."

Anita launched straight into it. "Peter, Andy was never dating Eliza. He lied. I went along with it because . . . well, it doesn't matter now. Anyway, this is the truth. She likes you. And she's waiting for you on the second floor. The stairway's just outside the dormitory."

Nobody spoke for a good fifteen seconds. Then, imperceptibly at first, Peter began to smile. He stood up, and almost fell right back down.

"You're not going in there again," Misery said. "It's not safe."

Peter took the bottle of tequila out of her hand and began to walk back toward the barracks.

Misery looked to Anita. "I hope you're happy."

"Don't worry. I'm not."

But at least it was done. Eliza and Peter would get what they wanted—for all the good it would do them.

Anita left the navy base through the open front gate, then got in her car and drove as far as she could before she lost sight of the road entirely between the rain and her tears. She pulled over and dropped the seat back. Why not sleep here? There was no place in the world to call home anymore.

The rain was slowing. In a couple of hours, the sun would rise again. Less than two weeks left now, but Anita wouldn't have minded if Ardor came crashing down onto her car that very moment. What reason did she have to go on living? Andy would never forgive her for giving him away, even if he'd always known deep down that his stupid quest had been doomed from the start. It was the end of the first real friendship she'd ever had, and any possibility of something more than friendship. And beyond that, it was the end of the music they'd made together, which had lent some meaning to these last few desperate weeks.

Anita wouldn't ask the universe for a second chance, any more than she'd ask it for a second act. She knew now that no one was entitled to either one.

Peter

PETER WAS DROWNING. HE TRIED TO PUSH THE WATER AWAY, BUT IT KEPT COMING, HEAVY as stone. And now something had grabbed hold of his wrists, pulling him down even deeper. He was going to die here . . .

"Peter!"

His eyes opened. Not drowning, then: just the rain. "Samantha," he said, and let his rigid muscles relax. His head was resting in his sister's lap. "I got tased, didn't I?"

"Yeah."

"My head hurts."

"That's because you landed on it. Hold up." Misery stiffened. "Who the fuck is this?"

Someone was coming across the tarmac from the direction of the barracks. It looked like a soldier. Misery reached for the only weapon near at hand—a bottle of tequila—and held it by the neck like a hammer.

"You're gonna throw tequila at them?" Peter asked,

"Why not? I've got a good arm."

The soldier, blurred by the rain, finally came close enough for them to make out her face—Anita Graves, dressed head to toe in camouflage.

"It's just me," she said.

"You here to finish the job?" Misery asked.

Peter gently forced her to lower the bottle. "She's a friend, Miz."

Anita took a deep breath, as if she were about to try to lift up a refrigerator. "Peter, Andy was never dating Eliza. He lied."

Peter only vaguely listened to the rest of Anita's speech. If not for the throbbing pain in his forehead, he would've smacked himself. Of course Andy and Eliza weren't together! The little punk had only said that to get Peter out of the picture. It was a devious move, one that Peter should have been pretty pissed off about (to say nothing of the whole tasing thing). But how could he be angry now, when the path was finally clear?

He grabbed the bottle of tequila and swallowed a mouthful, both to numb the pain and to bolster his courage. Misery was trying to warn him away from the barracks, but nothing in the world could hold him back now. It took everything in his power not to sprint through the middle of the dormitory. Though most of the partygoers were so drunk they wouldn't have recognized their own parents, Peter played it safe, slinking slowly around the shadowy outskirts of the room. He suffered a bit of a dizzy spell on the stairs but managed to make it to the top without passing out.

On the upper floor, some kind of staticky 1920s music was playing. Peter took a final slug from the bottle and let it fall to the floor.

"Eliza?"

She was barely visible in the glow from the moon-suffused clouds—just a few silvery lines limning her cheeks and arms.

"Peter."

"That music . . . is someone else up here?"

"Just Captain Morgan. He's cool."

"Can he hear us?"

"Maybe. Come this way."

He followed her through a doorway and into an empty office, closing the door behind him.

"Eliza, I'm sorry about before. Andy told me you two were a couple."

"I don't care." She stepped toward him.

"But that's why I was such an asshole."

"Okay." Another step.

"Because I thought you had a boyfriend."

"Okay." Another step.

They were close now. Next to her, he felt gigantic and clumsy. He reached out and touched her face.

"I haven't been good tonight," Eliza said. "I've messed some things up." He leaned down to kiss her. "I'm serious, Peter."

"There's nothing you could have done that would matter to me now."

"That's a big statement."

"You want a big statement? I've been in love with you for a year."

She laughed. "Don't throw that word around. You don't even know me. We'll probably be dead in a few days."

"That's why I'm saying it now."

"This is the cheesiest shit I've ever heard," she said, but he could feel the smile against his palm, and then against his lips—warm and familiar, inevitable and profound: the sweetest collision he would ever know.

"The way I like to think of the universe, everything's an event. You, Peter Roeslin, are just an event. And so am I. And you and me, right here, is another one. On the right scale, a mountain is just an event. It's not a thing. It's a way that time manifests itself."

"Is that supposed to be comforting?"

"It is for me."

"More comforting than this?"

"Mmm. That's nice. But kissing's just an event too."

"So is this event over? Should we get up?"

"Not yet."

"But it's morning. The music's stopped. I think everybody's gone."

"Ten more minutes and I'll be able to handle all that. Just talk to me. Tell me something. About yourself."

"Like what?"

"The most horrible thing that's ever happened to you. Before all this, I mean."

"Seriously? That's what you want to know? Horrible things?"

"We don't have time to take it slow, Peter. How many more long conversations are we going to get? Twenty? Thirty? We gotta get to the deep stuff right away."

"I guess that's true. But I don't know what to tell you."

"Sure you do."

"I guess that's true too."

"So?"

"My brother, my older brother."

"What about him?"

"You know. He, uh, died."

"How?"

"A car accident. His best friend was driving. He went through the windshield."

"He was older than you?"

"Six years. What about you? What's your horrible thing?"

"My dad's dying."

"I'm sorry."

"Yeah."

"Your parents are still together?"

"No. My mom lives in Hawaii with some other dude. We don't talk. We, uh—shit, I'm sorry."

"Hey. It's okay."

"I don't know why I'm losing it now. It's just—she kept trying to reach me, before the phones went down. I didn't listen to her messages. There were, like, a hundred of them."

"I'm sure she understands. And you've still got time."

"No, I don't."

"You might."

"Let's change the subject, okay? Worst thing you've ever *done*."

"The worst thing?"

"You've ever done, yeah."

"Hmm."

"You can't even think of anything, can you? Mr. Goody-Goody—"

"Of course I can. It's just weird to say."

"Go on."

"It's you."

"Me? You mean what happened in the photo lab last year? That's the worst thing you've ever done?"

"It's the most dishonest I've ever been. How are you laughing right now?"

"I'm sorry. It's just so sweet."

"Stacy didn't seem to think so."

"I'm sure. So are you going to ask me now?"

"I'm not sure I want to know."

"I kissed Andy, Peter. Last night. I was so drunk, and you'd just shut me down. And I knew he wanted it so much, you know? He's actually a good guy, just kinda fucked up. Like all of us."

"Yeah. I probably would have done the same as he did. I mean, if I loved you and you didn't love me back."

"You know what, though? You wouldn't have. I think you may be the only good person in the whole karass. Or maybe you and Anita. I'm still not sure about her."

"Karass?"

"Oh, it's Andy's thing. Well, Kurt Vonnegut's thing. It's a group of people who are connected, but, like, spiritually. Andy thinks we're all in a big karass together."

"Even me? That's kinda sweet, actually."

"Yeah, he's a little angel, that one. Anyway, I'm just glad you're not mad."

"Nah."

"Then I guess I also wanna tell you one other thing. I hooked up with somebody else, here in the detention center. I didn't have anyone to talk to, and I didn't know if I'd ever see you again, and it wasn't like we had sex or anything, but I feel really bad because—"

"Eliza?"

"Yeah?"

"You're here with me now, right?"

"Yeah."

"That's all I care about."

"Really? Are you sure? Because I'm describing some pretty serious sluttery right here."

"Don't say that. We all do what we have to do to get by, right?"

"I guess."

"The only thing I'll say is that you might feel better if you apologize."

"I thought I did. You want it in writing?"

"Not to me."

"Then to who? To Andy?"

"Yeah."

"You want me to apologize to the guy who lied to you? The guy who *tased* you?"

"You kissed him. You led him on. I know how I'd feel if you did that to me and then ended up with somebody else. Why are you looking at me like that?"

"You're just so fucking nice. It's a little hard to believe."

"I'm not that nice. I have all kinds of terrible thoughts."

"Just thoughts, though. The rest of us have more than thoughts. Peter, are you religious?"

"Yeah."

"Like, a Christian?"

"Like a Christian."

"Seriously? That's nuts!"

"Why?"

"I don't know. It just is."

"Okay."

"You're offended."

"No."

"You are."

"I'm not. But do you want to hear *why* I believe, or don't you care?"

"Let's hear it, Reverend Roeslin."

"You sure? I might convince you, and then you'll have to start going to church and praying before all your meals and everything. It'll ruin your Saturday nights."

"I'm willing to take that risk."

"Okay. So, like, way before Jesus, there were all these different gods that people worshipped, and you had to do stuff for them—like burn baby lambs or whatever—or they wouldn't make your crops grow. And then all those gods became the one God, which made things simpler, but he still had all these rules—like you weren't supposed to love anyone else as much you loved him. But then Jesus comes along, and he's just a dude, but you were allowed to love him. You see?"

"Not really."

"Jesus made it okay to love *people*. So it's not really religion at all. It's just—"

"Humanism."

"What's humanism?"

"It's what you're talking about."

"Oh. Cool."

"All right, fine. You convinced me. I mean, I'm not giving up my Sunday morning cartoons or anything, but I *will* allow you to continue believing what you believe."

"How generous of you."

"You're welcome."

"We should probably go."

"Just a little longer. Just a little more of this . . ."

"Wait. I have a question for you now."

"So ask it while I'm kissing you. . . ."

"It's an important question! Stop doing that!"

"Making out and important questions are not mutually exclusive, Peter."

"Just listen for a second. This philosophy of yours, that everything is just an event, does that mean Ardor is just an event too?"

"Yep."

"Death?"

"Yep."

"Love?"

"Yep."

"I'm not sure I like that. It makes this all feel kinda meaningless."

"Well, let's be realistic. If Ardor lands, that's the end of you and me right there. And if not, then I'm going to New York in a few months, and you're going to Stanford. And you don't know me at all if you think a long-distance relationship is in our future. So yeah, this is just an event."

"Great. That's fucking great."

"Peter? Peter, lie back down. There's no reason to get worked up about it."

"So then what's the point? Do I even matter to you?"

"Of course! I'm not saying this event matters any less than any other event."

"Which just means you don't think any of it matters at all. It matters to me!"

"Okay, think of it another way. It also means you and me together, here, in this office, is every bit as important as a mountain. It's as important as the end of the fucking world."

"Yeah?"

"So come back to bed."

"You mean floor?"

"Bed, floor—what's the difference? Come back to me."

"Fine."

"Now kiss me one more time, Peter."

"Okay."

"One more."

"Okay."

"One more."

The barracks were empty but for the few people who'd stayed behind out of physical necessity. Peter did a quick sweep of the room but didn't see anyone left that he recognized. It was the first crack to appear in his newfound happiness, and he'd only been out of bed for a few minutes. Misery was gone. Hopefully, she'd gotten a ride home. He had no idea what he'd say to his parents if he had to show up without her. *Sorry, but I got distracted having sex with this girl I cheated on Stacy with last year. You're going to love her.*

Outside, the sky was a blank slate, and the air had that after-storm clarity to it. Peter let go of Eliza's hand only long enough to climb into the driver's seat of the Jeep.

"I have to go home," Eliza said. "I wanna see my dad."

"I should too." He put the key in the ignition but didn't turn it right away. "You know what's weird? After last night, I kinda thought it was all over. I thought if I could just be with you, everything would turn out fine. Did you think that too?"

She squeezed his hand. "Will you love me less if I say no?"

"Maybe a little."

"Then yes. I thought that too."

On the way to Eliza's house, they were stopped by a police officer in a battered cruiser. He looked like he hadn't shaved in a week, or maybe even slept. He told them to stay wherever they were going once they got there.

But that was easier said than done. As soon as Peter turned onto Eliza's street, she threw open the passenger-side door, crying out wordlessly. If he hadn't slammed on the brakes, she probably would have jumped out of the car while it was still moving. He undid his seat belt and ran after her, toward the burned-out husk of a three-story apartment building.

Police tape was stretched across the doorless doorway like a thick yellow spiderweb. Eliza tore it away, revealing the ravaged interior. Everything in sight was scorched and crumbling, and the ceiling above the stairs had collapsed in a pile of burned wood and blackened masonry.

"My dad was up there."

"I'm sure he's fine," Peter said.

Eliza turned on him. "You don't know that! I should have come home right away! What was I thinking?"

"This fire is at least a day old, Eliza. It wouldn't have made a difference."

"But what if I can't find him? What if I never see him again?"

Peter didn't know what to say. All he could do was stand there, on a bed of ashes, and hold her.

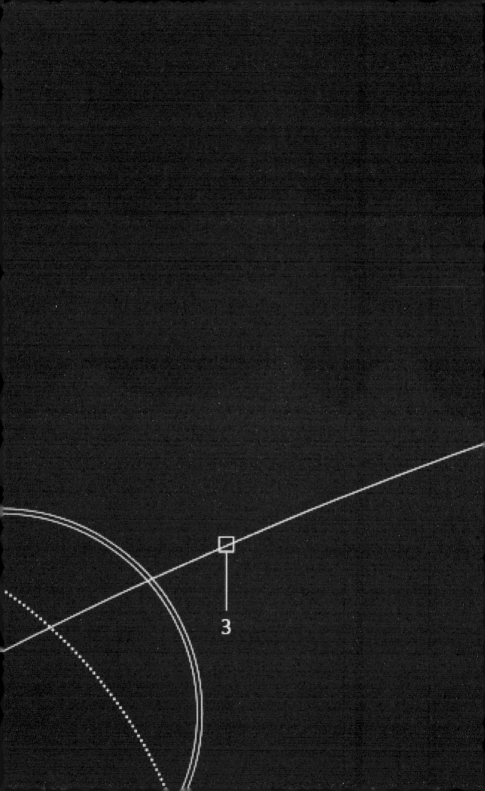

3

Andy

"TOSS IT, YO!"

Bobo's eyes were transformed by the flame of the Molotov cocktail into a pair of fiery asteroids. He was almost too drunk to make the shot. The neck of the bottle hit the edge of the window, but momentum carried it on into the store. It landed just next to a burial mound of building blocks and plastic figurines that they'd erected on the other side. A dozen SpongeBob SquarePants began to crinkle and blacken, sending up a plume of chemical smoke. The bottle exploded. A moment later the fire caught scent of the gasoline they'd poured all over the carpet. Orange streamers wrapped around the racks of candy-colored board games and Rubik's Cubes. They watched from the sidewalk as the place lit up like one giant firework.

"'Virtue needs some cheaper thrills,'" Bobo said.

Andy recognized the quote. "Calvin and Hobbes."

"Damn straight."

They drove back to the ma-in-law with their headlights on, fearless. It was past curfew, but there were basically zero cops left on the beat these days; why risk your life just to make the world infinitesimally safer for a couple more days?

"So, I know this may be a sore subject," Bobo said, "but now that you've blown it with Eliza, how are we gonna get you laid?"

"Who said I blew it with Eliza?"

"Well, it's been almost a week since you two hooked up, and you haven't seen or spoken to her. Plus, the world is ending next Tuesday. All of which means you've got about as much chance of nailing her as I do of nailing Taylor Swift."

"One man's opinion."

"One genius's opinion, yo."

Andy still hadn't told Bobo the whole story of the morning after the party. How he'd looked everywhere for Eliza, hoping that they might finish what they'd started on that piano bench. How he'd found the staircase to the upper floor. How he'd found her asleep in the pale light of sunrise, curled into Peter's chest. How he'd barely made it back out into the hallway before going down on his knees and vomiting up the whole night's worth of drinking—a seemingly endless cascade of all the hatred and sadness and rage that was inside him. He thought he would choke to death on it, on the harsh truth he'd been trying to ignore his entire life: that no matter how bad he wanted it or how he hard he tried to get it, he would never be worthy of anyone's love.

But he didn't choke. And when he rose to his feet again, he felt newly baptized in bitterness—the religion of Bobo and Golden and everyone else who'd discovered that there was no point or meaning to anything anymore. The karass was finished. Misery hated him. Peter hated him. Eliza hated him. Anita hated him. All he had left was Bobo.

They spent the next couple of days walking aimlessly around the city and smoking the rest of Bobo's weed. One night, just a few blocks from Andy's place, they found a house that someone had just set on fire. Crimson flowers bloomed from the windows, and the roof was one wide crown of orange and gold.

"It's kinda beautiful," Andy said.

"Yeah."

"If Ardor lands, the whole world may look like that. Could be worse."

The next day they'd started making their own flower arrangements.

Their first target was a Christian bookstore in Greenlake. Say what you would about the Bible, but it made for damned good kindling. They stood staring at the inferno for over an hour, passing a flask of Jack Daniel's back and forth and singing Pogues songs. Andy couldn't believe how long everything took to be consumed. You could almost imagine that you were liberating the material world somehow, as if every object had a secret desire to transcend its physical form and become light and heat, even if only for a few seconds. When everything was burning up right in front of you, you could imagine parts of yourself burning along with it—all your disappointments, all the things you'd done that you wished you hadn't, even all the bad memories (for example, things you might have seen on the top floor of a navy-base barracks). In his short time as a professional arsonist, Andy had become a lot less worried about the end of the world, because he'd become an agent of it. There was nothing quite like the feeling you got walking away from something on fire, knowing that it was disintegrating back into nothing, the way everything eventually did.

And it wasn't just the physical world they were burning up. It was time. Six days had gone by since the end of the protest. That meant there were only seven days left until the end.

"And a week without sex just ain't right," Bobo said. "I'm not gonna let you die as the Virgin Mary. Let's get Misery and Eliza off our minds tonight."

"And how are we going to do that?"

"The Independent, yo. Golden's always got girls around who are ready to go."

Since the collapse of the quest, Andy had stopped caring whether he managed to get laid before Ardor came, and he had no particular desire to hang out with the thugs downtown just for the hell of it. But he didn't have any desire to do anything else, either. "Why not?" he said. "It beats the shit out of sitting here."

Golden's home and place of business was well known to anyone who'd bought product from him: the Independent, one of Seattle's oldest apartment buildings—low-rent but with its own brand of faded glamour. Usually its name was lit up in bright-green neon above the awning over the front door, but without power, the tubes had gone dead and gray. Someone had decorated the lobby with about a million long white candles. Along with the high arched ceilings, the gaping maw of the marble fireplace, and a whole lot of dusky paintings and velveteen couches, they lent the place a distinctly Gothic feel. It would have been swank, if not for the fact that every single object and surface looked as if someone had gone at it with an electric sander. The sofas were all decrepit and moth-eaten, the Oriental rugs threadbare, the wood beneath them marred with scuffs and peeling varnish.

"Where do you think everybody is?" Andy said.

"Dunno. Upstairs probably."

The elevators weren't running, but there was a candle or two burning on every landing of the stairwell, like beacon fires. Andy opened the roof door to a blast of chill air.

"Hot damn," Bobo said.

A makeshift living room had been set up outside—shabby couches and coffee tables and beanbag chairs—all of which must have been sourced from abandoned apartments downstairs. There were a dozen gas-powered heat lamps, burning bright orange. A large generator was protected by a white canvas tent, with cables running directly to a nearby sound system and a couple of tripod-mounted speakers. Just outside the stairwell, a guy with a big red beard and a Slayer T-shirt stood smoking.

"Bleeder?" Andy said.

The lead singer of the Bloody Tuesdays grinned. "Fucking Andy? And Bobo! What's up?" They all bumped fists. "Welcome to the *casa*! There should still be some beers left in the cooler."

"And what about girls?" Bobo said. "You got any of them left?"

"You know it."

"Sweet."

"Hey, I'm glad you guys are here. You've got something to do with this thing at Boeing Field, right?"

For a moment, Andy didn't know what Bleeder was talking about. The Party at the End of the World—yet another grand idea that would end up coming to nothing.

"I think it's pretty much canceled," he said.

Bleeder looked genuinely dejected. "For real? I told my sister in

California she should drive up for it. Everyone said it was gonna be a rager."

"Don't know what to tell you, man. That's just how it is."

They walked on, through cumulus bursts of pot smoke, in and out of the rings of heat put off by the lamps. Golden stood all the way at the edge of the roof. He was looking into a telescope—one of those stumpy professional ones, rather than the typical skinny kind—and had it pointed at a fire burning down by the water.

"Shit's getting *crazy* out there. I swear I saw some guy jump out of a window." He raised his head from the eyepiece. "What's up, boys?"

"Nothing much," Bobo said. "We were looking for a party."

"Well, you found it."

Andy glanced around the roof. There were maybe a hundred people there, but most of them looked way too out of it to do much in the way of partying. It was a little sad, actually. "Where's that girlfriend of yours, Bobo? She know you're on the prowl tonight?"

"She's pissed at me."

"For what?"

"You remember her brother? The guy we ran into at the Cage?"

"Of course. The big man."

"Well, he and I got in a fight, and I won. Misery didn't like that much."

Golden laughed. "I bet she didn't."

"So I guess that means we're done."

"Just like that? Nah, man. You gotta tell her you were just doing what you had to do. Make her understand."

"I tried."

"Try harder." Suddenly Golden jumped up onto the narrow ledge of the roof. "Come on up here with me. Both of you."

Andy laughed nervously, "We're, like, fifteen stories up, yo."

Golden pointed right at Ardor. "And that fucker is, like, a week away from smashing your head open. So what are you afraid of?"

Bobo climbed up first. The ledge was only two or three feet wide, and slippery with rain. Andy's stomach turned over as he slowly stood. It hadn't seemed all that windy on the roof, but on the ledge, every little breeze felt like a tiny hand trying to topple him.

Golden inhaled deeply. "This is why I love that asteroid," he said. "We spend all our lives standing up on a ledge like this, but we pretend not to notice. Everybody working away at their jobs, saving their pennies, having their kids, when all it takes is one shove . . . and down you go. I felt like I was the only one who noticed that. But not anymore. Now everybody's up here with me."

He turned his silver-bullet eyes on Bobo.

"You don't wanna go out of this world with regrets. If there's something you want to do, you do it. You take this life by the balls and you tell it that you existed. You understand what I'm saying?"

Bobo nodded. "A hundred percent, yo."

Andy shivered, though he wasn't sure whether it was because of the wind, or the rain, or else because of the sudden fear he had that Bobo really did understand what Golden was saying.

Golden cupped his hands around his mouth and shouted across the lightless city, "I existed, goddamn it! Say it with me!"

"I existed!" Bobo said.

"I existed, goddamn it!"

"I existed, goddamn it!"

"Again!"

"I existed, goddamn it!"

"Again!"

"I existed, goddamn it!"

Then they were both saying it, over and over again, and then the call was coming from all around them, from everyone up on the roof, like a war cry. But for some reason, Andy couldn't bring himself to join in.

Eliza

WHEN SHE FIRST WOKE UP, SHE DIDN'T KNOW WHERE SHE WAS. A FOLD-OUT COT WITH striped flannel sheets. A low ceiling stickered with glow-in-the-dark stars, all of which had been colored in black except for one—Ardor, painted with sparkly blue nail polish. A bunch of posters on the walls: the Cramps, the Misfits, the Velvet Underground. A boy's room? No. Mirrored vanity in the corner, hung with cheap beaded necklaces and topped with a toolbox of industrial-strength makeup.

In the twin bed beneath the window, a flame-haired girl lay sleeping: Misery.

And it all came flooding back—her night with Peter in the barracks, her childhood home burned to the ground, driving in a daze of grief to Peter's house, and then the incredibly awkward getting-to-know-yous with his parents. They'd been friendly enough, but still insisted that Eliza and their son sleep in separate bedrooms. She'd been planning to sneak into Peter's room later on, but her exhaustion got the better of her, and a nap turned into a night. She hadn't even changed out of her prison jumpsuit yet.

The inside of Misery's closet looked like a Salvation Army bargain rack: T-shirts so old that you could barely figure out what they'd once advertised, hoodies with thumb holes bored into the sleeves and torn all the way back to the cuff, skinny black jeans so ripped up that they could practically pass for fishnets. Eliza paired an Iron Maiden T-shirt (*World Tour '88*) with a red leather skirt and black tights. She could only hope Peter wouldn't find it irremediably creepy to see her dressed up in his little sister's clothes. Or maybe it would be a better sign if he *did* find it creepy, actually.

She padded down the carpeted staircase and into the kitchen. Peter's mother stood at the stove, pouring a dollop of pancake batter into a small frying pan perched precariously on a butane stove.

"Hey," Eliza said.

"Morning, darling." Peter's mom turned around. Her megawatt smile flickered. "Oh, I'm sorry. I thought you were my daughter."

"It's fine. It's just I don't have any clean clothes."

"Of course. They look nice on you. Is Samantha still asleep?"

Eliza wasn't used to hearing Misery referred to by her real name. "Yeah."

"You girls up late talking?"

"Sure," Eliza said. In truth, she'd tried to make conversation with Misery, but all she ever got back were a few sullen syllables, followed by silence. Clearly, Misery was still upset over how things had ended with Bobo. It was a little hard to sympathize, given what an asshole Bobo had always been, but Eliza was trying her best to be understanding.

"Well, I'm glad you two are getting along," Peter's mom said. "Now, have a seat and tell me a little about yourself. What do your parents do?"

My dad dies of cancer and my mom runs off with other men. "My dad's a graphic designer, and my mom . . . I don't actually know these days. She used to paint a lot. And sculpt."

"You don't talk?"

"No. She moved to Hawaii."

"That must be tough for her."

"Hawaii? I hear it's pretty nice, actually."

"Not Hawaii, silly!" Peter's mom appeared to be 100 percent irony-proof. "I meant not talking to you. Samantha was at that prison for less than two weeks, and it nearly killed me. I missed her so much!"

Eliza knew there was no such thing as a "normal" family. Life, not to mention *Twin Peaks*, had taught her that something sinister was always to be found floating like a corpse somewhere just beneath any seemingly placid surface. Still, Peter's parents looked about as straightforward as parents could be. His dad had some kind of job that involved an office and suits and ties, and his mom stayed at home and cooked things and generally acted mom-ish. Eliza wondered how she would have turned out if her mom had been like that. Would she be better adjusted (i.e., not hook up with random delinquents in detention center bunk beds), or just less independent?

A creaking sound from the hallway gave Eliza hope that the parental interview was over, but it was only a doubling-down.

"Good morning, girls." Peter's dad was basically an older version of his son—tall and broad-shouldered, with the bearing and cheeriness of a Boy Scout troop leader. He crossed the kitchen and kissed his wife on the cheek. "I woke the young'uns. They'll be down shortly."

"Good thing. Pancakes are on the way."

"Yum." Peter's dad sat down at the table. "So, Eliza, you hear anything about old Stacy?"

"Steve!" Peter's mom said.

"What? Is that a weird question?"

"Yes, obviously."

"I don't really know her," Eliza said.

"See?" Peter's dad said, spreading his hands out wide. "She doesn't think it's weird."

"Sure she does. She's just too nice to say it."

Eliza smiled halfheartedly.

"Oh no. I've left you alone with them. Can you forgive me?"

It was Peter, thank God, still half in the throes of sleep, with pillow lines furrowing his face and a choppy ocean of cowlicks. Behind him came Misery, and for the first time, Eliza saw the resemblance between them, in this rare moment before they had the chance to sculpt their untouched morning selves into other shapes.

Peter ambled behind Eliza's chair, kissing her on the top of the head, unknowingly mirroring his father. "Sorry about them," he whispered. "You look lovely this morning." Just like a boy—he hadn't even noticed that she was wearing his sister's clothes.

"Don't apologize for us," his dad said. "We're delightful."

"Of course you are, Dad."

The pancakes had to be made one at a time in the tiny frying pan, so breakfast lasted for more than an hour. Misery didn't say a word during the meal and retreated to her room as soon as it was over. Peter suggested a walk, which Eliza assumed would be of the romantic, just-for-two variety, but his parents immediately invited themselves along. Thankfully, once they'd all made it to Volunteer Park, the kids were allowed to wander free, while the parents, citing hips and knees, located a comfortable bench.

It was the first day of spring. Dozens of families were out on the wet grass, tossing Frisbees and kicking soccer balls, pretending not to notice the overcast sky and the chilly air. A young woman with a newborn sat on a thin blanket beneath the verdurous spread of an evergreen. She gently poked the baby in the belly, drawing out little coos and giggles. Eliza wished she still had her camera. Seattle in springtime was a shadowless city; the constant cloud cover diffused the light, casting everything in the same silvery, washed-out shine. The baby glowed like an idol, reaching up toward the branches of the tree swaying overhead. It was the unofficial mascot of the Pacific Northwest, the evergreen—famous for staying the same no matter the season, eternal as a vampire. A metaphorically dishonest tree to grow up with. The sort of tree that made promises it couldn't keep.

"It's all so sad," Eliza said.

"What is?"

"The way everyone's acting like everything's okay."

Peter put his arm around her waist and pulled her tight to his side. Eliza had already noticed that he did this whenever he was about to disagree with her; it was yet another manifestation of his just-shy-of-ridiculous tenderness. "What do you expect them to do? Sit around crying all day?"

"No. I don't know. You really think it's healthy to live in denial?"

"Everybody out here is gonna die eventually, whatever happens a couple weeks from now."

"I know. But it could have been a couple decades instead of a couple weeks."

"So they should just stop living? Does your dad sit around being depressed all day, just because he has cancer?"

The mention of her dad pierced some thin-skinned balloon of pain inside her. "Some days he does."

A tennis ball rolled close to their feet, followed by a shaggy blond mop of golden retriever. The dog stopped in front of them and waited expectantly, windshield-wipering its tail.

"You wanna be like this thing?" Eliza asked.

"Are you kidding?" Peter picked up the ball and tossed it as far as he could. They watched the dog dash after it. "Right now, that dog is only thinking about one thing. I'd kill to be like that."

"You can't ever focus on one thing?"

"Sometimes. But it requires very specific circumstances." Peter let his hand drop down to her hip. "For example, we'd have to disturb a lot of these families to get me there right now."

"I'm in if you are."

He kissed her. "So I had a thought. If this Ardor thing doesn't happen, maybe we could go to Hawaii, to celebrate." He paused, waiting for a response, but Eliza didn't know what to say. "I mean, you've met my parents now. And I know how you wished you'd gotten to talk to your mom before the phones went out. This way I'd be there too. Stop me if this is a totally dumb idea."

"No," Eliza finally said. "It's not dumb at all."

She realized she was smiling so broadly and sincerely that it embarrassed her. But she couldn't make the smile go away. She was just glad no one could see inside her, because her heart suddenly felt so heavy, only heavy in a good way, like your stomach felt right after a big home-cooked meal. And then she noticed the knowing expression on Peter's face, and it seemed like maybe he *was* seeing inside her after all. She pushed his head away, so that he couldn't look at her.

"I'm glad you're not a dog," she said.

A week passed like that—walking and talking and touching. And it was good. Better than good. Better than great.

But it couldn't last forever.

In the middle of the night, in the middle of a dream—a cobalt-colored bird fluttering at the window, wings tapping against the glass—Eliza woke to the sound of quiet knocking, followed by the double whine of a door opening and closing.

She slipped out from under Peter's arm (spending the night together meant waiting until sister, mother, and father were all safely asleep, but it was more than worth it) and padded downstairs. Through the peephole of the front door, she watched a pair of silhouettes disappear behind the high row of pyramidalis around the front lawn. Eliza spun the knob, silent as a safecracker. As soon as she was outside, she could hear their voices. Misery and Bobo.

"But I miss you," Bobo said.

"I don't care."

"I know that's not true. Come with me."

"Why should I?"

"Because I need you to."

Eliza crept closer, unsure what her role might be in this scene, but glad she was there to watch over Misery.

"I needed you not to try and kill my brother."

"Your brother hit me first, Miz, and he was dragging you out of there by, like, your hair. I thought I was protecting you."

"Well, you weren't."

"Miz, I'm serious here. I miss you like crazy. Just come get a drink with me or something. Talk to me. If you're not my girlfriend anymore, I'll deal with it. But you can't totally disappear. Not when everything's almost over."

A pause. "Just a cup of coffee," Misery said.

"Yes. Thank you."

Just in the last day or so, Misery had finally begun to confide in Eliza. Afloat in the secret-prone darkness of her bedroom, she'd admitted that she knew she could never love Bobo again, not after seeing his face when he shot Peter with the Taser.

"He looked ecstatic," Misery had said. "Honestly, it scared me."

But now she was giving in—if not to love, then to pity. She had to be stopped, for her own sake. Eliza stood up, but her foot caught on a root, and she fell face-first into the hedge. By the time she extricated herself, an engine was already roaring to life. Eliza made it out to the sidewalk in time to see the car glide away down the tightrope of pavement lit by its headlights. She recognized Andy's station wagon.

Maybe it would all be okay. Maybe Bobo really did just want to talk.

But Misery wasn't back the next morning. Peter offered to check her usual haunts, but his parents begged him not to go. Misery was known to disappear without warning, even at the best of times, and they didn't want to lose him, too. They spent the entire next day perched nervously on the couches in the living room, drinking herbal tea and making small talk. But as the sun began to set without any word, Eliza knew she had to come clean.

She worried that Peter would be mad at her for not saying something sooner, but apparently love gave you a free pass on stuff like that.

"You're sure it was Andy's car?"

"Definitely."

Five minutes later they were on the road, heading for the ma-in-law. Peter was tense and taciturn, so Eliza just looked out the window—at the dead streetlights and the star-spattered sky. You could see so many of them up there, now that the power was out. Stars in thick clusters that twisted like ribbons. Constellations you could shape like clouds in your imagination. So many millions and billions of stars. Of course you couldn't dodge all of them forever. It would be like running out in the rain and hoping not to get wet.

There weren't any lights on inside the ma-in-law, or any cars in the driveway. They got out and knocked on the door anyway.

"No one's here," Eliza said.

"Maybe they're at Bobo's place."

"No way. Bobo basically lives in a trailer, and his parents are drunks. Nobody ever goes there."

Peter kicked the door in frustration.

"I know where they are," someone said.

Eliza turned around. Peter had already put his body between her and whoever it was that had spoken.

Anita raised a hand listlessly. "Hey, guys. Would you mind giving me a ride?"

Anita

THERE WERE ONLY A FEW RESTAURANTS LEFT IN THE CITY THAT WERE COMMITTED TO staying open 24-7, no matter what went down in the world outside, and Beth's Cafe was one of them. The place was so busy that people had to stand *between* the stools at the counter, the edges of their plates overlapping. And even if the menu looked like some classified document that had been heavily redacted—at least 80 percent of it was x-ed out—there was still enough fuel for the generator to make hot coffee, and toast, and pancakes, and hash browns, and that was enough right there to keep the sleigh bell above the door jingling.

Anita had spent most of the last eight days at Beth's, drinking unfathomable amounts of coffee, fortifying herself with waffles, and talking with strangers. When she got tired, she'd pad out to her car and pass out in the backseat. Sometimes she thought about going home, where she could trade a bit of groveling for a warm bed and some homemade food. But then she would remember her mother's face the last time they spoke—*you go and damn yourself*—and she figured she'd sooner sleep out on the street than go crawling back.

Maybe she would have spent the rest of her short-lived life like that—eating diner food and sleeping in the Escalade (which was just a dead hunk of metal now, as she'd accidentally used up all the gas when she fell asleep once with the engine running)—except that one afternoon she overheard something in the café. A couple, probably in their mid-twenties, were seated across from two huge camping-style backpacks. The waitress asked them where they were coming from.

"Portland," the guy said.

"What are you doing in Seattle?"

"We're here for the party," the woman said. "The one at Boeing Field."

"That's a long way to come for a party."

"I guess. We came with a whole caravan, actually. It's pretty much the only thing any of our friends have been looking forward to for the past month."

Anita had more or less forgotten about the Party at the End of the World, figuring it was every bit as dead as all her other dreams. But as she began to chat with other customers at Beth's, she discovered that a lot of people were still planning to go. In a way, it would happen even if it didn't happen. They didn't need Chad to turn it into an "event" or a "community space," they just needed warm bodies.

Anita knew then that she had to find Andy. Because what would the Party at the End of the World be worth without him there? Sure, she'd been pretty pissed at him that night at the navy base, but trying to stay angry at someone you loved was like trying to keep an ice cube from melting in a cup of hot chocolate: impossible.

Andy would be staying at either his place or the Independent, but while the Greenlake suburbs around his parents' house were still relatively safe, Seattle's downtown area had basically become one giant gang fight; Anita wasn't about to walk there on her own. And so she'd spent the last three days staking out the ma-in-law, waiting for Andy to show up.

The last thing she'd expected was to run into Peter and Eliza. It seemed the karass would not be denied.

The waitress forced her way to them through the crowd. "Hey, Anita. Table for one?"

"Three, actually. I brought friends."

"We're pretty packed, but there's room at Star Wars, if you don't mind the sound effects."

"That'll be fine."

"Star Wars?" Eliza whispered. "What does that even mean?"

What it meant was that their table was the slanted surface of a pinball machine. Every few seconds, it let out a little series of R2-D2 bleeps or a John Williams fanfare.

"This is where Andy and Bobo are?" Peter asked.

"No," Anita said.

"Then what are we doing here?"

"Eating," Eliza said. "I'm starving."

"The place where Andy and Bobo are isn't safe at night," Anita explained.

"Where's that?"

But Eliza interrupted before Anita could so much as open her mouth. "Don't say a word. If you tell him, he'll go, whether it's safe or not."

Peter glowered, but also looked a little pleased to be known so well. New love radiated off him and Eliza like quiet music. Anita had spent the last few days (and maybe even the last few weeks) resenting this girl, and now she couldn't for the life of her remember why. Eliza, scruffy and unwashed, dressed in what were clearly Misery's clothes, didn't look like anybody's archenemy. So when Peter excused himself to use the bathroom, Anita seized the moment. She hadn't had any girl talk in forever.

"Eliza, can I ask you something?"

"Sure."

"It's kinda personal. Like, weirdly personal."

"Go ahead."

"How many people have you slept with?"

Eliza laughed. "I don't know. I've lost count."

"Really?"

"No! Who do you think I am?" She laughed even harder. "Twelve. My number's twelve. Or wait! It's actually thirteen now. Jeez. Does that seem like a lot?"

"I'm not sure," Anita said, and she meant it. "I mean, I haven't found one person I'd want to do it with, so it's hard to imagine finding thirteen. On the other hand, there are seven billion people in the world. When you think about it that way, you've been pretty picky, actually."

"Well, if it helps, I regret most of them."

"So why do it?"

"Honestly?" Eliza looked toward the bathroom, to be sure that Peter wouldn't overhear. "There's this moment that comes when you're hooking up with a guy. Maybe you know what I mean. You become his whole world. Or maybe it's just sex that becomes his whole world, but that's okay too. I think we have this idea that it's bad, the way dudes are always thinking about sex. But to me, it's always seemed really pure. Like a puppy wanting a treat. And it starts to seem like such a little thing to do to make somebody so happy."

"So it's charity?"

Eliza grimaced. "It sounds that way, doesn't it? But don't get me wrong. It feels good too. Only not *that* good. Most of the time, anyway. But sometimes, when I think I must be the shittiest person in the world, sex lets me make somebody sublimely happy for a few minutes, and that makes me feel better."

Anita wondered exactly why she'd been so bitchy and judgmental about Eliza, who was just another girl struggling with the same stuff that every girl had to struggle with. "I realize it's way too late for this to matter," she said, "but I have to say it anyway. You are *stupid* cool. It's actively annoying how cool you are. You don't need to sleep with a guy to make him sublimely happy. I mean, you should've seen Andy after every time you hung out."

"Only because he thought something might happen. It was still about sex. You were the one he really liked. The way he talked about your voice, and the stuff you were writing together—that was love. He's just too much of a boy to notice."

Anita knew it wasn't true, but it was nice of Eliza to say it.

Peter came back from the bathroom, and then their food arrived, along with the bill. Then the waitress was rushing them out the door to make room at the pinball table for one more last-minute heart-to-heart.

The next day was Sunday, two days left before the end of the world. After spending the night at Peter's house, the three of them got up bright and early and headed for the Independent. Though Peter was all about marching in and demanding to see his sister, Anita convinced him that it would be safer all around if they waited for her outside. There was no way Misery would spend one of her last days on Earth in some dark old apartment building.

Around noon, they spotted Bobo and Andy leaving the building, skateboards in hand. They climbed into Andy's station wagon.

"Why isn't Misery with them?" Peter asked.

"Don't know. She could be inside, or somewhere else."

"They must be going to get her," Eliza said. "We should follow them."

Andy went north on I-5 and got off at the exit for Northgate Mall, gunning it so hard down the long ramp that there was no sign of him by the time Peter got to the bottom himself. He pulled the Jeep into the mall parking lot and they all got out.

It was the prettiest day Seattle had produced in months, totally cloudless, the sun a perfect white circle cut out of the blue. It made for a dramatic juxtaposition with the mall itself: Here was a burned-out McDonald's, there a blackened shell of a Red Robin, here a trashed Payless ShoeSource that, up close, didn't actually look all that much worse than a regular Payless ShoeSource. The whole complex had been torched—and recently, too. A charred odor lingered on the air.

"What's that sound?" Eliza asked.

From somewhere close by came a familiar clatter.

"Skateboards," Peter said.

In the back parking lot, Andy and Bobo were taking runs at a ramp built out of old phone books and a huge orange construction sign. Andy had just begun his approach when Anita called out, "Don't choke!" He turned his head at just the wrong moment and went down on his ass halfway up the ramp. Bobo already had his deck in his hands, swinging it back behind his head, ready to decapitate somebody.

"Anita!" Andy scrambled to his feet and ran to her. She'd prepared herself for any amount of awkwardness or anger, but not for a hug that was probably the longest she'd ever received from a boy, one of those hugs that made it clear how much the person hugging you was in need of a hug, or believed *you* to be in need of a hug. "It's so fucking good to see you," he said.

"Yeah."

A last tight squeeze before he let her go. He turned to Peter next. "Dude, I owe you an apology."

Peter seemed taken aback. "It's cool, man."

"It's really not. I was super drunk. And . . . there was a lot going on."

"Yeah, I know."

They shook hands, and then Eliza rushed forward and took all three of them up in one big hug.

"The karass," she said. "Together at last."

"What are you all doing here?" Bobo asked sharply, concluding the reconciliation.

"We followed you," Peter said. "We're looking for my sister."

"Oh yeah?" Bobo dropped his deck, then kicked it back up into his hand. His eyes studied the ground, as if he were looking for something he'd lost down there. "I think she's out with some friends or something."

"Which friends?"

"Who knows? I'm not her dad. That's you, far as I can see. And I don't like being followed."

"Too bad."

Violence still crackled around the edges of their words. Anita tried to defuse the tension. "So why'd you come all the way up to Northgate just to skate?" she asked.

"Because, up here, we can also set shit on fire," Andy said, grinning. "You wanna try it?"

"Don't be stupid," Bobo said. "These are the good guys right here. I'm sure they don't go in for arson."

Technically true, but Anita had found Ardor to be a pretty good incitement to uncharacteristic behavior. And honestly, what did it matter if a few more crappy stores burned down? The world hadn't needed this eyesore of a mall in the first place. "I could be convinced. Assuming you two left anything around here standing."

"Anita, are you serious?" Peter said.

"Why not?"

Bobo scanned the horizon. "I got a target in mind," he said, pointing. A Target store, just across the street.

"I always wanted to burn one of those down," Anita said.

Like just about everything else in this perishable world, the windows of the Target had been shattered weeks ago, and everything of significant value carted away. But they were still able to cobble together a halfway decent lunch of crackers and popcorn and potato chips—all the food that would not only survive the coming apocalypse, but probably still be crispy and delicious when the next phase of evolution emerged from the ooze.

"So how do we do this?" Anita asked.

"Well," Andy said, "thanks to the fine folks who run this state, Target is now licensed to sell hard liquor. And that shit *burns*. Of course, people jacked all the stuff on the floor, but Bobo and I found more in the back."

A set of double doors behind the linens department opened on a labyrinth of ceiling-high shelves stacked with boxes. They dragged a whole case of Goret vodka (priced to move at $3.99 a bottle) back out to the store.

"I'll pop this cherry," Bobo said. He pulled out the first bottle and swallowed a mouthful, then began to tear across the linoleum, streaming 120-proof alcohol behind him like a trail of bread crumbs. Anita had never been one for wanton destruction, but damn if that didn't look like fun. She unscrewed the caps of two bottles, flipped them over, and ran as fast as she could up and down the wide aisles. When they were empty, she chucked them at a display case full of hair dye. An explosion of glass and a tinkling aftermath. She hadn't realized how much she needed this—a chance to literally burn off all the anger she'd felt when she saw Andy and Eliza together, all the disappointment of getting run out of her own house by her shitty parents, all the frustration of a wasted life. She screamed an incoherent warrior scream and heard it echoed by the others, all across the store. Only Peter chose not to partake, standing stone-faced by the checkout line, waiting for the rest of them to finish.

Within a few minutes, they'd run slippery lines of vodka all across the store. They met up at the registers, where Andy produced a book of matches.

"You wanna do the honors?" he said, offering it to Anita.

"What a gentleman." She scratched a match hard against the strip. It hissed into life, white to blue to red. In the flame, she could see the store transformed into one enormous conflagration—the toys and the books and the CDs and the towels and the build-it-yourself furniture. It was the fate waiting for all of them, most likely, less than forty-eight hours from now. Ashes to ashes. Dust to dust. And even if this was all just a bunch of junk, Anita couldn't help but think it probably didn't want to burn any more than she did. They had so little time left. Did they really want to spend it impersonating Ardor? Was humanity's only legacy going to be wrack and ruin?

She blew out the match.

Bobo snickered. "I knew it. I knew she'd pussy out."

"I don't think I'll be able to enjoy my last few hours on Earth with the death of a Target on my hands." Anita looked to Andy. "Is that okay?"

He took the book of matches and put it back in his pocket. "Totally."

They'd gone only a few steps when Anita heard the flick of a lighter behind her. Bobo took a drag from a cigarette, then touched the orange tip to the floor. And there it went—the streaking arrow of destruction. The aisles lit up one by one, like lines of dominoes falling over. "Check that shit!" Bobo said. "That's like the Fourth of July right there!"

Anita walked out of the store, the heat already palpable on the back of her neck. She didn't know why she was so angry—it was just a Target, after all—but she couldn't help it. Why did boys always have to destroy things to feel alive?

"I'm sorry about him," Andy said, following her out. Peter and Eliza had retreated across the parking lot to lean against a savaged old Hyundai and watch the Target burn.

"It's okay."

"No, it's really not. That's not me, Anita. I don't want you to think that's me. And that didn't used to be him either."

"If you say so."

"I'm serious. Bobo's changed. And it's starting to freak me out."

"What do you mean?"

He gestured for her to follow him farther away from the store, so they wouldn't be overheard. Even then, he whispered. "I think something's gone seriously wrong with him."

"You're saying that like it's a recent development."

"This is different. He says that Miz is staying with him at the Independent, but I'm staying there too and I haven't seen her once. And he hasn't let me inside his apartment in days. It's like he's hiding something."

"What are you saying? Is Misery back there right now?"

"I'm saying I don't know where she is."

Bobo, momentarily framed in flames, emerged from the Target and made straight for the passenger-side door of Andy's station wagon. "Come on, Mary!" he called out across the parking lot.

"One sec!"

"So what are you going to do?" Anita asked.

"I have to figure out what's going on. I owe that to Peter."

Anita smiled. "You did tase him."

"I know. I can't believe he hasn't kicked my ass yet."

"Me either."

"Let's go!" Bobo shouted.

Andy took hold of her hand. "I'm gonna bring Miz home, okay? Just in time for our party."

"Okay."

Our party. Anita was so focused on the warm feeling these words gave her that she barely paid attention to Peter and Eliza's conversation in the car as they drove home.

"I don't trust him," Peter said.

"You mean Bobo?" Eliza said. "Who does?"

"We should keep following them."

"Your sister is a big girl, Peter. She can take care of herself."

"Maybe."

Anita reached between the seats and flicked on the radio, but there was nothing but a windswept desert of static now, all the way across the dial. And maybe she should have sensed something brewing in Peter's stoic stillness, in the resolve of that clenched jaw. But she was halfway to the front door of his house before she realized that he'd never left the car. Then Eliza was running back down the brick path, toward the driveway, screaming bloody murder at the back of the Jeep as it pulled out onto the street and sped off toward downtown.

Peter

THE LOBBY OF THE INDEPENDENT WAS EMPTY. DUST MOTES FLOATED IN THE FAILING LIGHT like dead insects in a puddle. The fireplace was one giant pile of trash. In the corner of the room, a genderless junkie was wrapped up in a dirty sheet, humming a wordless (and thus endless) version of "Ninety-Nine Bottles of Beer on the Wall." Peter stood at the abandoned reception desk, wondering what the hell to do next, when a couple of guys came through an arched doorway at the back of the room. They were dressed in ragged black leather and studded boots.

"Hey," Peter said.

"The fuck you want?" The guy's tone was less menacing than exhausted.

"I'm looking for my sister. Her name's Misery. Or Samantha."

"Never heard of her."

"What about my"—and Peter cringed inwardly as he said it—"friend Bobo?"

The other guy smiled, revealing a mouth full of mustardy teeth. "He's up on six."

"You know what room?"

"Why would I know what room? I look gay to you?"

"No. Sorry. Thanks for your help."

There were candles set up here and there on the stairway, though most of them had burned out. On the sixth floor, music from a battery-powered stereo slipped out from someone's apartment. Peter stretched his arms out wide and pounded hard on every door, left and right, as he jogged toward the window at the other end of the hallway. He heard a couple of them swing open behind him.

"I'm looking for Bobo," he shouted.

The sound of doors shutting, a scrap of muffled laughter. Then, just a few seconds later, something quieter, very close.

"Peter?"

It came from behind the door closest to the window, farthest from the stairway.

"Miz?"

"Peter! Get me out!"

He reached for the knob, but though it turned as if unlocked, the door wouldn't budge. Down near the floor, he found the culprit: a metal flap screwed into both the wall and the door, held in place with a padlock. Bracing himself against the opposite wall, he kicked out again and again, until the screws of the padlock were pulled out of the plaster and the door swung free of the frame.

Misery came running out of the darkness. Black mascara was streaked down the tear tracks on her cheeks. She grabbed on to him, sobbing. "I'm so sorry," she said. "He just told me to wait for a second, and then he locked me in."

"It's okay," Peter said. He stroked her hair, glad to be so much taller so she couldn't see the look of horror on his face. He'd always known that some people would turn desperate as Ardor approached, but he'd never expected that desperation to touch him so closely.

Misery pulled away, and in the wan light from the window, he saw her eyes widen. "Peter," was all she said, but the tone of warning was unmistakable.

He turned. A pack of silhouettes was coming down the hallway, amorphous and faceless.

"Who's down there?" one of them said.

"Get ready to run," Peter whispered.

There was no way they could both get past, but in the dark, in the confusion of limbs, he could make space for her at least. A running double clothesline, launched unexpectedly, took everyone down in a pile, and Peter watched from the ground as Misery disappeared back down the staircase.

They were just a bunch of kids really—not much older than Peter himself—but all of them had the hollow, haunted faces of drug addicts. They took him back into the lobby and through a door marked FITNESS CENTER. Down another set of stairs, Peter found himself in a pretty pathetic excuse for an exercise room—gray carpet, a few ancient stationary bikes, a set of scuffed-up iron weights—everything flickering and predatory in the candlelight.

"Take off your shoes," one of the guys said.

"Seriously?"

"Just do it. Socks too."

Barefoot now, Peter was prodded past the bikes and the weights, past a rack of threadbare towels and an empty watercooler, and through a swinging door into the locker room. The heavy smell of steam. A black plastic mat on the floor bit little hexagons into the soles of his feet. Then a frosted glass door opened with a whoosh of hot air onto a wide, low-ceilinged room, lit with a single battery-powered halogen lamp. There were half a dozen showerheads built into the walls, and all of them were turned on, sending their separate streams toward the single drain at the center of the room. The floor, walls, and ceiling were all tiled in a sickly yellowish brown, and everything was fuzzy with fog. The water was scalding hot, forcing Peter up on his toes.

On a long brown bench just inside the door, Golden sat back against the wall, wearing nothing but a towel and his infamous necklace. He smiled when he saw Peter.

"This guy kicked in Bobo's apartment door," one of the junkies said. "Says he came for his sister or something."

"Go get Bobo," Golden said. "He should be up on the roof."

The junkies left. As the door swung shut again, the steam swirled, revealing Golden a little more clearly. His skin was a dense sketch-book of tattoos: on his right arm, an upside-down cross, dripping blood; on his left, a naked woman stepping up to a gallows attended by a black-suited executioner. His entire chest was taken up with a depiction of hell—all faded-red flames and devils punishing the wicked with pitchforks. The eyes of the suffering men and women were aimed upward, toward the place where the tattoo finally ended, just below Golden's Adam's apple.

Peter considered making a run for it, but Golden was between him and the door. A snub-nosed pistol lay on the bench by his hip, like a pet.

"Hey there, big man."

"How do you still have hot water?" An inane question, but Peter felt stupid with fear.

"We rigged up the gas. Why, you want a shower?"

"I was just wondering."

"No, that's a great idea! Why don't you undress for me, big man? I'll get more comfortable too." Golden reached behind his head and unclasped the necklace, uncoiling it loop by loop.

"I'd rather not."

"I wasn't asking." Golden glanced over at the gun.

Peter knew it would be interpreted as a surrender, but the room *was* stiflingly hot with all that steam. He took off his sweater and the shirt underneath, if only to be better prepared for whatever was coming next.

"Peter!" Golden said with sincere amusement. "You've got ink!"

"Yeah. So what?"

He'd had it done a year ago, in Los Angeles, when the basketball team went to Nationals. After their last game, they'd all gotten thoroughly wasted in the hotel, then set out to explore the city. They couldn't find a bar that would take their fake IDs, but a tattoo parlor called Sunset Body Art was happy enough to have their underage business. While most of the team went for the usual stuff—Chinese symbols for victory, jersey numbers, girlfriends' names, and, in Cartier's case, an anachronistic MOM done in an elaborate Gothic script—Peter had wanted something special. He told the artist that he was looking for some way to honor his brother without being obvious or sentimental.

"What's it mean?" Golden asked.

"Nothing."

"Of course it means something."

"It wouldn't mean shit to you," Peter snarled.

Golden picked up the gun and fired it once into the ceiling. In such a small room, the sound was deafening.

"Try again," Golden said.

"It's just hard to explain," Peter said, his voice shaky. "It's a Celtic cross, like you see on gravestones. And the circle around it, the snake eating its own tail, that's a symbol for eternity. But a circle with a cross inside it like that is also a symbol for Earth. So I guess, for me, it's about the Resurrection. Or resurrection in general."

Golden nodded. "I like it. Resurrection. That's nice. You know, I got something similar myself."

He stood up and turned around, revealing the thick ropy muscles of his back, and also another, fresher tattoo. It reached all the way from his waist to the knob at the top of his spine. The colors radiated so bright and vivid that the whole thing seemed to be backlit. At the bottom left corner, just above his waist, spun the tiny blue marble of planet Earth. From there to the opposite shoulder stretched a vast expanse of pitch black—bespeaking dozens of hours of agony under the tattooist's needle—broken up by a handful of small white stars that were only Golden's natural skin tone shining through the ink. Then, taking up his entire right shoulder, a jagged, misshapen rock, blazing through the sky in reds and purples and oranges—divine fire—and just above it, a gigantic hand emerging from the clouds, shaped as if it had just thrown something. On the side of the rock, some words were carved: AND GOD SAW THAT THE WICKEDNESS OF MAN WAS GREAT IN THE EARTH.

"You know that line?" Golden asked.

"It's from Genesis."

"That's right." Golden turned back around. "It comes just before the flood."

The door of the sauna swung open. Bobo looked bone-tired, with bright purple crescents under his eyes.

"Peter?" he said. "What the fuck?"

Golden tossed his necklace over to Bobo, who just managed to catch the end of it. "You're never gonna guess what the big man here did."

"What's that?"

"He busted in your door."

Bobo's face twisted up, terror and rage competing for primacy. "Where's Misery?"

"She got out," Peter said, and didn't bother to hide his satisfaction. "She's gone."

The first punch was surprisingly solid; Peter was rocked back on his heels. A splash of red dripped from his nose onto the tile. He raised his fists to defend himself.

"Hands behind your back," Golden said. He had the gun trained on Peter's forehead. "Bobo, tie him up. He'll probably kick your ass by accident otherwise."

"You don't have to do this," Peter said to Bobo. "What's the point?"

"The point?" Bobo said, pulling the necklace tight around Peter's wrists and knotting it. "What point is there supposed to be? This is the end, man. There's no points left."

"This isn't the end."

Bobo shook his head. "We can't all afford to be optimistic like you, Peter."

"It's not optimism—"

"How about I prove to you that this is the end?"

—it's faith, Peter was going to say, only before he could, another blow had landed, and then he couldn't remember if he'd said something or if he'd only wanted to say something, because there was just the pain and the stifling steam and the feel of Bobo's skin as he bore Peter down hard against the tile floor, and then the fists falling fast and heavy as meteors, each one exploding in his brain like a supernova, until finally, gratefully, he let the agony overwhelm him and wash the world away.

2

Andy

ALL THE WAY BACK TO THE INDEPENDENT, AS BOBO BITCHED ABOUT PETER (THE ASSHOLE who sucker punched him) and Anita (the prude who wussed out at Target) and Eliza (the tease with the big ego), Andy felt the bonds between him and his "best friend" disintegrating, like the single sugar cube Anita always took in her coffee. He'd been so sure that he'd fucked up at the navy base too deeply to ever be forgiven, but then his whole karass had shown up at Northgate. Anita and Eliza had hugged him (and was it just his imagination, or had Anita's hug been particularly drawn out?), and even Peter, who had more reason to hate him than anyone, had made it clear he didn't hold a grudge.

Andy didn't have a lot of experience with forgiveness—Bobo had never pardoned his breaking of the pact—so he'd never realized how powerful it could be. It made him want to be a better sort of person, the kind who *deserved* forgiveness.

So now he had a new quest. He would find Misery and he would get her home, whatever Bobo had to say about it.

"I'm gonna go see if she's feeling better," Bobo said, once they were back at the Independent.

Andy followed him up the stairs. "Actually, I think I'll come along with you. I haven't seen Miz in forever."

"Can you maybe wait until later? I could use some time on my own with her right now."

"What for?"

"Just leave it alone, okay?" Bobo shouted, his words ricocheting off the cement walls of the stairwell. Andy's heart began to pound like a kick drum in his chest. For the first time in his life, he felt afraid of Bobo.

"What's going on, man?"

Bobo threw his hands up in frustration—and did he notice Andy flinch? "I don't know. I mean, I'm not supposed to say."

"Not supposed to say what?"

"I can't tell you in here. Anyone could be listening. Come on."

Up on the roof, Golden's perpetual party had dwindled down to a dozen people congregated around the one working heat lamp, like hobos warming their hands at a trash fire.

Bobo led Andy to a cold, quiet corner of the roof. "Okay. You ready for the truth?" He took a deep breath. "Misery's pregnant."

Andy's heart began hammering again. Not because he believed Bobo—the explanation was way too long in coming and way too soap opera to be real—but because of what the lie signified. If Bobo was willing to go this far just to keep Andy from talking to Misery, then something seriously fucked up had to be going on.

"Wow," Andy said, playing along as well as he could. "How long have you known?"

"A few weeks. She wanted to get it dealt with, but all the Planned Parenthoods shut down. That's why she left home. She felt like she couldn't hide it once Eliza moved in."

"She must be freaking out. I should talk to her."

Bobo shook his head. "Nah. She'd be pissed if she knew I told you. And besides, she's exhausted, like, all the time. I'm sure she's asleep right now. I'll try and get her to come out tomorrow, though, okay?"

"Okay."

"Good. Now let's drink a couple of beers and forget about all this shit."

Only there wasn't any beer left—just a few cans of room-temperature Sprite—and Andy wasn't about to forget anything. He was a sleeper agent, secretly working for Team Karass, waiting for just the right moment to activate.

And he didn't have to wait long. They'd only been up on the roof for an hour or so when some guy Andy didn't recognize burst out of the stairwell.

"Hey, Bobo!"

"What's up?"

"Golden says you should come downstairs. He's got something for you."

"Hopefully it's more weed," Bobo said. Andy had to grit his teeth to smile. "You wanna come along?"

"Nah. I'll hang up here."

"Cool. See you in a bit."

Andy gave it a couple of minutes, then headed straight for Bobo's apartment on the sixth floor.

He wasn't sure what to expect, but he had a distinct horror-movie feeling as he walked the long *Shining*-esque hallway. The door nearest the window had been kicked half off the hinges. On the ground, a latch and a padlock, still clamped shut. The room beyond the door was a wreck—mirrors shattered, sheets shredded, furniture in splinters—as if a wild animal had been imprisoned there.

There was only one explanation. Somehow Bobo had tricked Misery into coming to his apartment, and then he'd locked her in. Maybe he'd wanted to punish her for dumping him, or maybe he'd really thought that he could convince her to forgive him, if he could only get her to listen.

Andy was disgusted that someone he'd once called a friend could do something like this. But at the same time, he also felt strangely relieved. Ever since the night the pact went wrong, he'd been suffering under a lead weight of self-reproach. Now, at last, he was free to hate his best friend. And he did. As deeply and purely as he'd ever hated anything, he hated Bobo. It felt good, to finally arrive on the same page as the rest of his friends—Misery, Anita, Eliza . . .

And Peter.

The final piece of the story fell into place. The busted-in door. The "something" Golden had waiting for Bobo downstairs.

Andy sprinted back down the hallway, took the steps two at a time, moving so fast that he wouldn't even have noticed them in the lobby if they hadn't called out to him.

"Andy!"

It was Eliza and Anita.

"Hey!" His happiness at seeing them transformed immediately into fear for their safety.

Eliza grabbed hold of his wrist. "Is Peter here? Have you seen him?"

Andy knew that if he told her what he'd seen, she'd insist on coming downstairs.

"You need to leave, Eliza. Go back to Peter's house. I promise I'll bring him and Misery as soon as I can."

"We're not going anywhere."

"You don't understand. It's dangerous here."

"We don't care."

Every second he wasted arguing with her was a second he wasn't helping Peter. "Then just go up to the second floor, okay? Apartment 212 should be unlocked. It's where I sleep when I'm here."

"Is Peter there?"

"He will be."

Then Andy was off again, through the door and down the stairs to the fitness center. He caught Bobo and Golden just as they were coming out of the bathroom.

"Andy, my man!" Golden clicked the clasp of his necklace back into place. "You just missed the show!"

"What show?" Andy had directed the question at Bobo, but his former best friend didn't say a word. He looked as if he'd just been through a war. "Bobo, you okay?"

"Don't worry about him," Golden said. "He was a fucking champ in there. Unfortunately, we *have* lost track of his lovely little girlfriend."

"Have you seen her?" Bobo whispered.

"No."

Golden thumped Bobo on the back. "Then she's probably long gone. Oh well. Let's get you a drink, slugger. I keep the good stuff in my room."

"I'll meet you up there," Andy said. "I'm just gonna take a piss."

"Watch out for the occupied stall," Golden said. He laughed, and for once, Bobo didn't laugh along with him.

Andy already knew what he would find, even before he saw the wide swathe of smeared blood leading from the sauna to the bathroom. Peter was inside the rightmost stall, propped up against the toilet seat. He'd been fucked up in a way that Andy had only seen before in movies. One eye was swollen shut, and the other flew at half-mast. Dried blood caked the bottom half of his face. He wasn't wearing a shirt, and there were black bruises all over his ribs, each one haloed with a speckled starburst of vermillion. A string of gory perforations wrapped around both of his wrists. Worst of all was the wide patch of raw, ravaged flesh on his right bicep. At the edges, Andy could make out the flecks of black ink that had once been a tattoo.

Peter looked up at him, no emotion readable in his tumid features.

"I'm here to help," Andy said, and knelt down. They stood up together, as gently as Andy could manage. Peter groaned with each step. It took fifteen minutes just to get him back up to the lobby.

"Peter, I need you to stay here, okay? I'm going to get the girls, and then we can leave."

"Eliza's here?" Peter said.

"Yeah."

"Then I'm coming."

"But you—"

The whip crack of a gunshot from somewhere overhead. Andy had forgotten that Golden's apartment was also on the second floor. He'd *just* sent Anita and Eliza up there. . . .

He ran for the stairway, Peter limping along just behind him. As he reached for the door, it swung open from the inside. Golden came out, hunched over, holding tightly to a ruby wetness around his belly. He breathed out a constant stream of obscenity as he stumbled past them, oblivious to anything but pain, and out of the Independent.

Andy mounted the stairs in great blind leaps and threw open the door to the second floor.

Blackness, then a nebulous prickle of stars shining through the window at the end of the hallway. A couple of them disappeared, blocked out by someone's silhouette. What if it was Bobo? What if he had the gun? Andy ran at the shadow, full-tilt, taking it down to the ground with him. Hands clawed at his face, knees slammed around the sensitive target between his legs. He was about to start throwing punches himself when something caught his attention: a scent, of all things, familiar even in these unfamiliar surroundings.

"Anita," he said, trying to pin down her surprisingly strong arms, "stop mauling me!"

"Andy?"

He took his weight off her, put out a hand to help her up. "I'm so sorry. I didn't know who it was—"

He hadn't planned to do it. He'd only been trying to get her to her feet. Only they were closer together than he realized, and her face was coming right up at his face and in that split second he knew he had to, because what if they never got another chance? The kiss didn't last more than a few seconds, but that was time enough to open his mouth and breathe in a wisp of her breath. Time enough for everything terrible that had happened up to that moment—Bobo and Golden and even Ardor itself—to float a little ways out into space, for a few precious seconds.

"Is that Andy?" some other voice said. An orange-tipped ball crouched in a doorway just a few feet away.

"Misery?" Andy said. "Thank God." He reached out and hugged her in along with Anita.

"Who's out there?" Peter called from the stairway.

"It's Anita," Andy said, "and Misery, too."

"And Eliza?"

"I thought she ran out of the apartment with me and Misery," Anita said. "But I lost track of her in the dark."

"Eliza!" Peter cried out, then lost his voice in a coughing fit. The rest of them took up the call: "Eliza! Eliza!"

After a few seconds, the door to apartment 212 squeaked slowly open. Moonlight followed her out into the hall, illuminating the bare skin of her shoulders and stomach, reflecting off the lacy fabric of her bra. At first Andy thought it was just a trick of the light—that rusty shadow stretching across her abdomen and darkening the top of her jeans. But when he got closer, he recognized it for what it was.

"What happened, Eliza?"

"I'm sorry," she said, "but I had to."

"Had to what?"

She said it again, desperate this time, almost hysterical. "I had to!"

Anita

THE FREEWAY WAS BUSIER THAN SHE'D SEEN IT IN WEEKS, AND ALMOST EVERY CAR WAS headed in the same direction. If one of them got in an accident, there might even have been a traffic jam, just like in the good old days. Anita could remember hot summer afternoons gridlocked on I-5, air conditioner and KUBE 93 blasting.

Was it really possible to feel nostalgic about traffic jams?

"Do you think it's for the party?" she asked. "I mean, it's not supposed to be until tomorrow, but maybe they all wanna get there early."

"I don't know," Eliza said, distracted. "Can you drive any faster?"

"I'll try."

They'd been slow to get on the road. After Peter had torn off in the Jeep, Eliza had marched straight into the house and demanded the keys to Peter's mom's Jetta, but all she got in response was a barrage of anxiety-ridden Mom questions: *Why isn't Peter here? Is he with Samantha? Why doesn't he ask me for the car himself? What are you going to do with it? Is it safe?* Eliza raised her voice, and then Peter's mom raised her voice back, and then Peter's dad made both of them even angrier by refusing to take a side. While everyone else was arguing,

Anita rifled through the drawers near the kitchen sink until she happened upon a familiar VW logo.

"Never mind, Mrs. Roeslin," she said, dragging Eliza out of the house. "We'll just walk."

Just past the turnoff to 520, Seattle opened across their windshield like a pop-up picture book. *My city,* Anita thought. It was a shame that she'd never gotten to explore the wide margins of the planet—Paris and Rome and Timbuktu. But on another level, it made for a sweet sort of intimacy to have only lived in one place: geographic monogamy. She saw everything differently now, from the polychromatic nightmare of the Experience Music Project—a museum designed as an homage to Jimi Hendrix's melted guitar, but that better resembled what a kid would vomit up after eating a box of crayons—to the iconic Space Needle, looking even more solid and monumental now that those elevators weren't constantly inching up and down its sides like little golden pill bugs. So many memories: field trips to the Pacific Science Center, nights spent studying in the huge glassy greenhouse of the Seattle Public Library, austere family dinners at the expensive restaurants around the Market. She couldn't help but love it all now—even her parents, who'd been swept up in the general reminiscence and imbued with the golden light of retrospect. It occurred to Anita that hatred and dislike and even indifference were all luxuries, born of the mistaken belief that anything could last forever. She felt a pang of remorse. In spite of everything, she hoped her mom and dad were doing all right.

The white tablet of the sun sank beneath the watery pinkness of the horizon.

"I'm gonna miss this shit," Eliza said.

"I was just thinking the same thing."

The sky gave up its last bit of light just as they pulled up in front of the Independent. Stepping out of the car, Anita glanced up at Ardor. They'd all learned where in the sky to find it, just a few stars below the trough of the Big Dipper. It would never look particularly big, Anita could remember hearing, because it *wasn't* very big. More like a bullet than a bomb, they'd said. But a bullet could kill you just as easily as a bomb.

The lobby of the Independent was a throwback to another age. It would have been a particularly shabby sort of chic, if not for the piles of trash and the foul, enigmatic odor.

"Where are we?" Eliza asked.

"Feels like hell."

A door on the other side of the lobby swung open. Someone came sprinting out so fast that Anita raised her fists on instinct.

"Andy!"

He screeched to a stop like some kind of cartoon character.

"Is Peter here?" Eliza immediately demanded. "Have you seen him?"

"You need to leave, Eliza. Go back to Peter's house. I promise I'll bring him and Misery as soon as I can."

"We're not going anywhere," Eliza said.

"You don't understand. It's dangerous here."

"We don't care."

Andy sighed. "Then just go up to the second floor, okay? Apartment 212 should be unlocked. It's where I sleep when I'm here."

"Is Peter there?"

"He will be."

"Did he seem weird to you?" Eliza asked, after Andy had disappeared through some door marked FITNESS CENTER.

"He's always a little weird. But I'm sure he knows what he's doing. Come on."

They'd made it halfway across the lobby when something creaked over by the couches. A mop of orange hair lifted itself up from behind a patchy velvet settee: Misery. There was something deathly serious in her expression.

"What the hell are you doing over there?" Anita asked.

"You can't go upstairs," Misery said.

"What? Why not?"

She came out from behind the couch. Shadows slid off her skin, revealing where her pale arms had been studded with bruises, each one a little watercolor painting of a sunrise. She'd aged five years since the last time Anita had seen her.

"Bobo," Misery said, then shook her head. "He locked me in. And Andy must have known about it. They're in on it together. They have to be."

"Andy would never hurt you, Miz," Anita said.

"Oh yeah? He hurt Peter."

"I know. But that was a mistake."

"If you're wrong, and we go up to his apartment, he could lock all of us in. Or worse."

"He won't."

"How do you know?"

Because he's not Bobo, Anita wanted to say, but she didn't want to hurt Misery's feelings. Bobo's capability for cruelty had always been there, pooled just beneath the surface, like tattoo ink. But Andy was different. He was good. If there was one thing in the world that Anita knew for certain, it was that. She shrugged. "I just do."

"Me too," Eliza said, and Anita was grateful for that.

Together, they climbed the stairs to the second floor and entered apartment 212. It was decorated like a cheap hotel room, with the usual twin beds spread with the usual pinkish-red quilts laundered to a thready pulp, the usual two-seater couch, and the usual pointlessly gigantic flat-screen television on the wall. The only light came in through a semitransparent shade over the window. Anita pulled it open.

A lone white speedboat cruised Puget Sound like a symbol of something. Almost everything else that moved was moving south, toward Boeing Field. Cars passed behind the big sports arenas at the edge of the city as if crossing over into another world. Once upon a time, the Kingdome had sat over there, wide and squat as a cupcake, its segmented white top like the ribs of some enormous umbrella. Anita had only seen it in pictures; they'd knocked it down and replaced it with some other expensive athletic monstrosity when she was only three. Now Ardor would probably knock that one down too. There was some cosmic justice for you.

Anita turned away from the window. Misery lay across the bed with her head in Eliza's lap. She had a tragic grace to her, pallid perpendicular lines for limbs and a faraway, traumatized stare. Strange to think that Bobo wouldn't have done what he did if he hadn't found her beautiful. Beauty always made a target of its possessor. Every other human quality was hidden easily enough—intelligence, talent, selfishness, even madness—but beauty would not be concealed.

"Do you ever wish you didn't look the way you did?" Anita asked.

"All the time," Misery said. "I hate the way I look."

Anita smiled at the misunderstanding. She could remember what it was like to be sixteen—so uncomfortable in your body that sometimes it didn't feel like your body at all. Even at eighteen, she was only just beginning to be able to look at herself in the mirror without totally freaking out.

"No, I don't mean like that. I just meant—"

"Having to be afraid," Eliza said.

"Yeah."

No need to say more. No need to describe all the things you had to do to keep the eyes away. No need to discuss how hard it was to get the attention of the person you *wanted* attention from without being seen as desperate for *everyone's* attention. No need to catalog all the walls you had to put up; not just the walls that protected you from physical danger—though there were plenty of those, too—but the walls you had to build around your heart. They said no man was an island, and Anita figured that was probably true. But women were; they had to be. And even if someone bothered to sail over and disembark, he'd soon discover that there was always a castle at the center of the island, surrounded by a deep moat, with a rickety drawbridge and archers manning the battlements and a big pot of oil poised above the gate, ready to boil alive anyone who dared to cross the threshold.

"Boys never understand anything," Anita said, and though it didn't technically follow from what they'd been talking about, it was the kind of statement that was always appropriate—at least in a roomful of girls.

"Tell me about it," Eliza said.

"They understand boobs," Misery said sarcastically.

"That's the worst part. They actually don't."

And there in the darkness of the hotel room, scarcely more than twenty-four hours before the maybe end of the world, the three of them managed to laugh together. It turned out that no amount of terror could stop the great human need to connect. Or maybe, Anita thought, terror was actually at the heart of that need. After all, every life ended in apocalypse, in one way or another. And when that apocalypse arrived, it would be pretty cold comfort to think: *Well, at least I don't have that much to lose.* You didn't win the game of life by losing the least. That would be one of those—what were they called again?—Pyrrhic victories. Real winning was having the most to lose, even if it meant you might lose it all. Even though it meant you *would* lose it all, sooner or later.

And so they waited, together, for whatever was coming next.

Eliza

ELIZA SAT ON THE EDGE OF THE BED, FINGERING THE POINTY END OF THE BOWIE KNIFE AND wondering what it might feel like to stab someone with it. Like testing the temperature of a cooked turkey? Cracking the shell of an egg? Slicing the forgiving red flesh of a watermelon? Peter had given it to her this morning, just before they left the house. *Just in case,* he'd said. Light from Ardor glittered prettily on the blade. Eliza glanced out the window, to the wide, star-drenched sky. The asteroid looked as insignificant as it ever had—a tiny twinkle in the eye of a righteous god, the celestial equivalent of a sucker punch, practically invisible until the moment it smashed you in the face. A lot of things in life were like that: apocalyptic asteroids, late-stage cancer, love.

There was the sound of clumping feet out in the hallway.

"Peter!" Eliza said, running for the door.

"Hold up," Anita said.

Eliza opened the door, but it was so dark she couldn't make out who was there. "Hello?"

"Eliza?"

It was Bobo, and behind him stood a short, thick-limbed silhouette, dense as a neutron star: Golden, with a gun ostentatiously tucked into the front of his jeans.

Eliza improvised. "I came here to find Andy."

"He's downstairs. I can take you."

"Thanks."

She tried to slip out the door without opening it too widely, but some movement behind her must have given the game away.

"There's somebody else in there," Golden said.

"Run!" Eliza shouted, grabbing Golden's gun and chucking it as hard as she could down the hall. He took a wild swing at her, clipping her shoulder, but then Anita and Misery were there too, and everything got confused. Eliza bounced one way and another and ended up spinning back into the bedroom. There was the sound of a struggle in the doorway, then the door slammed shut. People running outside in the hallway, and somewhere much closer, a human sound, wet and whistly.

"Bobo?"

"It's all gone to shit," he said.

Eliza quietly slid the knife out of her waistband. "What has?"

"She hates me now."

"Misery? Did you lock her up, Bobo?"

"Only because she wouldn't talk to me. I just wanted her to talk to me, like a human being!"

In spite of herself, Eliza felt a little sorry for him. She'd heard his whole history from Andy—the alcoholic parents, the suicide pact, the antidepressants with their grab bag of side effects.

"You shouldn't have done that," she said.

"I know."

"But it doesn't make you a bad person."

"It does, though. We both know that. I'm just shit now."

The whimpering grew louder, closer, and then Bobo was hugging her, sniveling into her shoulder. His clothes smelled like gasoline, and his cheek was rough against the skin of her neck. He squeezed her uncomfortably hard, pinning her arms to her sides, and she realized too late that he was putting his weight into her, forcing her backward onto the bed. She had to let go of the knife to avoid plunging it into her own back.

"Stop it, Bobo."

"I always wanted you," he said. His voice had that thickness that Eliza knew so well, the voice of a man who was past the point of reason.

"You don't want to do this."

His hands were at her waist, unhooking the top button of her jeans. Of Misery's jeans. "You're so fucking beautiful," he said.

Eliza thought about the stranger who'd climbed into her bed at the navy base barracks. He'd been a thousand times sweeter and gentler than Bobo, but were they really so different? A couple of sad little boys, both desperate for love, both trying to get it any way they could. And it wouldn't have been that hard to let it happen. If she just lay back and went still as a corpse and thought about something else, she'd survive it. How much worse could it really be than getting plastered and sleeping with some guy she'd just met in a bar? A few numb minutes and everything would be over.

But then her free right hand, scrabbling wildly at the sheets, happened on the warm wooden handle of Peter's knife. And it seemed the culmination of his love for her, that it should be right there when she reached for it, like a miracle. All the time they'd spent together came to her in a single bright burst of memory—not just the last few days, but the whole year of silence, when she pretended not to see him even though his very presence in a room was like a highlighted sentence in a textbook or an overexposed section of a photograph. *You don't need to sleep with a guy to make him sublimely happy*, Anita had said. And it was true. After all, Peter had loved her after a single kiss. Maybe she'd loved him since then too. Maybe she'd been put on this Earth to love him, and their love would be the only thing in their short, stupid lives that mattered at all.

Bobo pulled her shirt up over her head; the knife caught on the fabric and tore it. "For the last time," she said, "don't do this."

He unzipped his pants. She could feel the skin of his belly on hers, and his breath was like a lit match in her ear. "We're all doomed anyway," he said.

It wasn't like she'd expected, hardly any resistance at all, and from the darkness came one small human noise, just a quiet moan— *ohhhh*—like a last-minute revelation. He slid off her, onto the floor, and she jumped on top of him, preparing for the next assault. But he didn't move. She'd aimed for the heart and she'd found it.

A moment of silence, then a gunshot sounded just outside the apartment. Eliza leaped up and flattened herself against the wall. She wasn't about to pull that knife out of Bobo, but she still had her nails and her teeth. She'd tear Golden's throat out with her bare hands if she had to.

"Eliza! Eliza!"

A chorus of voices: her friends. She rushed out into the hall. Andy was the first to see her. His gaze dropped to the red stain on her stomach.

"What happened, Eliza?"

"I'm sorry," she said, "but I had to."

"Had to what?"

"I had to!"

Andy ran past her, into the apartment. The others were standing close behind him—Anita, Misery, and a stranger. Even in the weak light, Eliza could see that his face was disfigured somehow. He was coming toward her now, a travesty of a smile twisting his mouth.

And she forgot about everything else as she recognized him, falling into his battered arms, sobbing.

In the echoey silence of the stairwell, Peter's breathing was painfully loud. It rasped and stuttered and gasped. They had to get him to a hospital, only there were no hospitals left open. Maybe the day after tomorrow there'd be hospitals again. It was possible. Anything was possible.

"What happened to Golden?" Peter asked.

"I shot him," Anita said, and there was no remorse in her voice.

They saw him for just a second outside the Independent, lurching around a corner. Maybe he'd survive, and maybe he wouldn't. It hardly mattered now.

"He'll be sad if there's no one there to catch his last words," Andy said. "He always loved to hear himself talk."

"That's not how people go," Peter said. "Most of us don't get last words."

Eliza wondered if he was thinking about his older brother, who'd died in that car accident. Or maybe he was talking about all of them. How quickly would the end come when it came? Would it hurt? Now that they were all together again, the fog lifted. Nothing stood between them and Ardor anymore but a few million miles of vacuum.

Andy climbed into the driver's seat of the station wagon. "Should we try and find a hospital?" he asked.

"Just take me home," Peter said.

They drove in silence through the dark, deserted Seattle streets. Peter was growing paler by the minute. Long coughing fits left his palm spritzed with blood, but he was still conscious when they pulled into his driveway.

Eliza squeezed his shoulder. "You ready to get up?"

"Can I rest a little first? Mom and Dad are going to freak out when they see me."

"Of course." She looked around the car, at the worried faces of her friends. "Do you guys mind going in without us? Say we're on our way."

"Do you want me to stay too?" Misery asked.

Peter shook his head. "Thanks, though. I love you, Samantha."

"I love you, too."

Eliza watched them go. Then she lifted up Peter's head and placed it gently on her lap. She waited for the coughing to stop.

"I wish we had more time," he finally said.

Peter

"MORE TIME? DON'T BE GREEDY, PETER. WHAT WOULD WE DO WITH IT?"

"I'm serious."

"I know. But don't be. I'll lose my shit."

"I'm not saying decades or anything. Just a year, maybe. Enough to give us a history."

"We have a history! Remember making out in the photo lab? Remember how we were at that riot together? Remember our first pancake breakfast with your family?"

"I mean real history. Like a language that nobody but us knew. My parents have that. I bet yours did too."

"You and I have a language."

"Yeah?"

"Yeah."

"Then say something to me in it."

"You have pretty eyes."

"That's just English."

"Most of the words in our language are pronounced exactly the same as normal English words. That's so people won't notice when we're speaking it."

"Are there any differences?"

"A few. Like *carrot.*"

"What's that mean?"

"Pumpkin."

"What else?"

"I love you."

"What does that mean?"

"It means 'I hate you.'"

"Aha. And what does *I hate you* mean?"

"Same thing as English. That one's not different."

"I see."

"Do you want to know how to say 'I love you'?"

"Sure."

Eliza leaned down. Her hair made a little bower around his face, and for a second he could ignore the pain that lanced through his chest every time he inhaled. Quickly, like a cat lapping milk, she licked the tip of his nose.

"Like that."

"That's not words."

"Our language is half sign language, half actual words. It's very complicated. That's why we're the only ones who speak it."

He heard the catch in her voice; somehow it seemed incredibly important that he keep her from crying for as long as possible.

"Remind me. That philosophy you've got, about events? How does that work again?"

Eliza shook her head. "I don't have a philosophy anymore."

"So make up a new one."

"Make up a philosophy?"

"Yeah. Like a bedtime story. Only it has to be true."

"Oh, okay. A true philosophy, invented on the spot. That's all."

"Yeah."

He waited. The pain in his chest was diffusing out to his whole torso now, weighing him down a little bit more with each exhalation, like the slow squeeze of a boa constrictor. He let his eyes close. It was all right. He'd protected them—his friends, his family, his karass. Even if it was only for a few extra hours, he'd kept them safe. No Pyrrhic victory, then, whatever happened. A real victory.

An infinity seemed to pass before Eliza spoke again. Peter was beginning to wonder if she'd given up, or else fallen asleep.

"So a really long time ago," she said, "this really advanced civilization had a science lab, right? And this guy who worked in the lab, we'll call him Todd, he was just an okay worker. Like, not totally moronic, but no genius, either. The specialty of this lab, I forgot to say, was making worlds. So Todd chose to make this world that was mostly water, which hadn't been tried before because everyone knew that water destroyed everything it touched, if you gave it enough time, and this lab believed in making things that were more permanent— like out of rocks and stuff. And at first, nothing really happened in the water world, except a lot of erosion and rust and stuff being damp all the time, and Todd's boss wasn't very happy. But Todd kept working away at it, and after a while, something amazing happened. There was life. Just a little bit at first, then more. Like, a lot more. And it started evolving. And then these little monkey things started learning new stuff and getting smarter, and everything was looking pretty good for Todd. But then, over just a few thousand years, the whole thing got totally fucked up again. There were these wars and terrorists and nuclear weapons all over the place. Todd couldn't understand it. It was like he'd built this really nice house for people to live in, but they'd decided to tear it down from the inside. And Todd's company, which was all about the bottom line, decided to pull the plug. Not every world could be a winner."

Peter felt a drop of cold land on his cheek, but he was too tired to wipe it away. It slid slowly down his face, tickling a little as it went. Every breath now was a victory. Eliza had gone quiet. Fear swept in to fill the silence. Fear of disappearing, of the dark, of the unknown. Fear of being somewhere without this love to define him. *Don't stop talking*, he tried to say.

And as if she'd heard him, Eliza continued her story. "So Todd brought the world home and tossed it in the garbage, just like he said he would. But then his son, who's called Chris, in a nod to your traditional Christian values, happened to find it. And right away, he fell in love with the little monkeys. So he pulled the world out of the trash and dusted it off and took it into his father's office. 'You can't just give up on these little monkeys!' he said. And his dad tried to explain about business and capitalism and everything, but Chris was having none of it. And here's the really miraculous part, because I know how much you religious nuts love miracles—he'd *just* learned about mercy that week in school. So he begged his dad to give the world one more chance to get better. He even came up with an idea for how they could make it happen. 'Let's scare them,' he said. 'Let's make them think it's all over.' And his dad was like, 'You mean with some kind of flood?' And Chris said, 'Floods are so old school, Dad. Let's do it with an asteroid. We'll tell them they're all about to die, but then, at the last second, we'll save them.' Then Chris's dad listed every horrible thing that the little monkeys had done throughout history. 'They don't really deserve a second chance,' he said. And Chris was like, 'Well, it wouldn't really count as mercy if they deserved it.' And once he heard that, his dad totally folded, and they went ahead with the plan. And at first it didn't seem like it was working. Actually, it seemed like things were getting even *more* horrible and ugly with every passing day. But Chris told his dad not to worry about the little monkeys. He said this amazing moment was going to come, when they all looked up from their tiny little lives at once, to see if that big fireball in the sky was really going to crush them. And maybe when they watched it pass them over, maybe when they felt that mercy, it would be just enough to convince them to change. Maybe . . ."

The droplets were falling every few seconds now, though Peter felt each one a little more distantly, as if he were falling along with them. Eliza didn't seem to know what else to say, so she just repeated herself, over and over, kissing him after each word, more and more lightly: "Maybe . . . maybe . . . maybe . . ."

He didn't feel anything when she licked her own tears off the bridge of his nose.

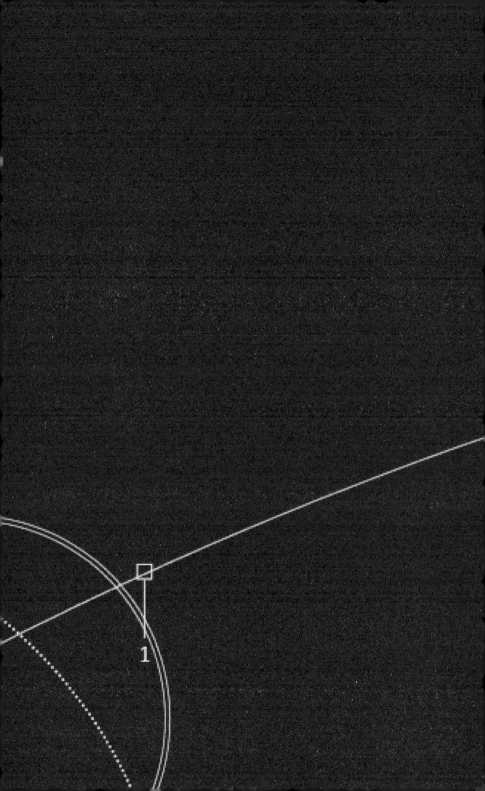

Andy

"HOW . . . ?" ANDY ASKED, BUT LOST TRACK OF HIS EXACT QUESTION AS HE STARED OUT THE window in astonishment.

From the freeway, Boeing Field glittered like some impossible fantasy kingdom. Hundreds of flames—tiki torches and huge blazing bonfires and even the delicate curl and flicker of individual candles—lined a long, snaking pathway that stretched from the empty runways (now a single unbroken ocean of parked cars) toward an inconceivably enormous hangar. There were electric lights, too: thousands of pale-white Christmas lights strung up like phosphorescent spiderwebs in an old attic; spotlights crisscrossing the sky as if they were searching for something up above the clouds; an ever-changing kaleidoscope of dance-club color coming out of the hangar; the red twinkle of brake lights providing a monochromatic fireworks show all the way across the tarmac. Andy rolled down the window. You could hear the music even up on the freeway, and a faint whiff of diesel sweetened the air.

If only the whole karass could have been there to see it.

They'd been up until sunrise talking with Peter's parents. Everybody had cried, though in his secret heart, Andy had been crying a little for Bobo, too. He couldn't remember falling asleep, but when he woke up again, the sun was already high in the sky, blaring like a megaphone. Peter's parents were passed out on the couch, looking grief-stricken even in sleep. Peter had been lucky to have them.

Andy found Anita in the kitchen, talking quietly with Misery and Eliza.

"Anita," he said, "we need to go see your parents."

He'd expected an argument, but she just wiped the crust from her eyes and nodded.

"Let me just get you something clean to wear, Eliza," Misery said.

Eliza looked down at her clothes and seemed surprised to find that the bloodstains were still there. "Right. Thanks."

It was past noon by the time they left Peter's house. Misery said she'd try to show up at Boeing Field that night, but Andy knew it wasn't true. Her parents needed her now, and she needed them, too.

The intercom at Anita's place wasn't working, so Andy had to nudge the gate open with the station wagon's bumper.

"They're probably not even here," Anita said.

But only a few seconds after she let go of the brass knocker, her mom answered the door. Wordlessly, she swept Anita up into her arms.

Inside, Andy and Eliza met Anita's dad, an imposing statue of a man with a hand like cold marble and very little to say. There was a ton of homemade food ready, almost as if Anita's mom had been waiting for them. After they'd gorged themselves, they fell asleep all over again, in a little heap on the heavy pile carpet of the sitting room, exhausted by the combination of satiety and sadness and shock.

They didn't come to until after sunset.

"Shit," Andy said, stretching like a cat, "we have to go."

"Just let me change," Anita said. "I don't care if it's vain. I've been wearing these clothes for two weeks." She ran upstairs, and a few minutes later, came back transformed. She'd switched out her T-shirt and jeans for a formfitting red dress, black tights, and tall leather boots. Her hair was brushed and pulled back, and a wide silver necklace glittered at her throat. She looked gorgeous.

"You look gorgeous," Eliza said.

Andy could only nod.

At the door, Anita's mom clung to her daughter like some kind of life preserver.

"You and Dad can come with us," Anita said.

But her mom shook her head, wiping the tears out of her eyes. "You know your father," she said.

"That I do."

As the three of them were descending the steps between the front door and the driveway, they all saw it at the same time—a bright blue bird with marigold eyes bursting out from between the white blooms of a magnolia and disappearing into the night sky, as if it were carrying a message straight to Ardor.

As the car approached the off-ramp, Andy was finally able to make out the shadows of people down on Boeing Field, walking two or three abreast toward the wide-open mouth of the hangar. They wore necklaces and bracelets of opalescent neon—the kind that you cracked over your knee to release the chemicals that made them glow—and tossed them through the air like Frisbees. They flicked open butane lighters and touched the pointed blue flames to the ends of joints and cigarettes. They made dancing white circles on the dirt with the cylindrical lightsaber beams of their flashlights. Beneath the dome of stars, they created their own constellations, like an endlessly variable reflection of the sky.

Andy followed a line of cars past a spotlighted sign: WELCOME TO THE END OF THE WORLD. By now, the dubstep had become another presence in the car with them, heavy as humidity. It took a good fifteen minutes to park.

The three of them walked toward the pathway that led to the hangar. Andy took Anita's hand, then Eliza's; if they got lost in a crowd like this, they'd never find each other again. As they passed one of the larger bonfires—a huge bowl of hammered bronze that glittered and danced with the flames inside it—Andy felt someone watching him. He glanced to his right, straight into a stranger's eyes. She was in her late twenties, walking with a man of about the same age and wearing a papoose on her chest. Inside, a baby bounced and cooed and looked generally unconcerned about the imminent apocalypse.

"Excuse me," the woman said.

"Yeah?"

"Um, your friend?" She pointed to Eliza. "Are you Eliza Olivi?"

"What do you want?" Eliza asked.

"I can't believe it!" Without waiting for the all clear, the woman wrapped her arms around Eliza, squeezing the baby between them.

The woman's husband lingered at the edges of the hug, looking as nervous as if he were in the presence of royalty. "Are you showing up late for your own party?" he asked.

"It's not really my party. I didn't even think it would happen."

"Everybody thinks you're dead," the woman said, finally letting

Eliza go. "They're going to freak out when they see you, like Jesus coming back on Easter or something. I can't believe we got to meet you. Thank you so much."

"There's nothing to thank me for. I didn't do anything." But the starstruck couple were already skipping off toward the hangar. Eliza shook her head. "I don't get it."

"Don't get what?" Andy said.

Eliza didn't answer, but her face was thoughtful in the firelight. They walked on, through the overlapping Venn diagrams of luminescence put off by the torches and past an empty stage equipped with a piano and a couple of microphones. Farther on, a small cadre of volunteers in red shirts stood outside the hangar, helping to manage the foot traffic. A big Hispanic guy was holding a clipboard and shouting at people, so Andy figured he must be in charge.

"Hey," Andy said, "we're looking for Chad Eye."

The guy gave them the once-over. "You're Peter's friends, aren't you?"

"How'd you know?"

He pointed at Eliza. "I saw you once, through the window."

"At Friendly Forks," she said.

"That's right. Actually, Peter's the whole reason I'm here. Just before he stopped coming into work, he mentioned you were putting this party together. I never forgot about it. So a few days ago, I drove up and offered to make some food. They already had plenty, so they put me on door duty. Beats moping around at home, anyway. Hey, Gabriel!" He called out to another volunteer, a tall black guy with a long scar across his chin. "Come over here."

"What's up?"

"These are Peter's friends. Can you take them up to see Chad?"

"Where's Peter at?"

A long silence. "He's gone," Eliza said.

Gabriel nodded. "I see. Come on."

He led them around the side of the hangar to an unmarked black door. Inside, a long staircase stretched upward into a darkness that was by turns purple and green and orange, shifting with the light from the faraway dance floor. Votive candles floated in glasses of water on every other step. They ended up on a latticed metal catwalk built into the very eaves of the hangar. Beneath them roiled a Pacific Ocean of humanity, rolling in waves, writhing in the shimmer of light and sound.

"How many people are down there?" Andy asked, but Gabriel couldn't hear him over the music. The thrum of the bass made the catwalk shiver like a ride cymbal. Halfway across the hangar, they came to another door.

"Chad's in there," Gabriel said. "You come back down and let me know if you need anything else." He took a few clanging steps back the way they'd come, then stopped. He turned to face them. "Peter was all right," he announced. Andy waited for him to go on, but apparently he'd said everything he had to say. He turned around again and kept on walking.

The office beyond the door was lit entirely with candles. Kora music tinkled out of a small set of speakers, though it was mostly drowned out by the beats from down below. Chad, dressed in a suit of off-white hemp, sat in a cheap folding chair in front of a window, looking down on his party.

"Yo," Andy said.

Chad swiveled his head toward them, and his face exploded with joy. Sid the beagle leaped off his lap as he stood up.

"You made it!" He took them all in for one huge hug. "I knew you would."

"That's a lot more than we knew," Andy said. He knelt down to pet Sid. "We thought you got locked up."

"I did. But the guards let me out when they found out I was in charge of the party."

"Seriously?"

"Seriously. There have been some nice surprises along the way, haven't there? Speaking of which, did you notice your stage on the way in?"

"The one with the piano?" Anita said. "That's for us?"

"Of course. You didn't think I'd forget, did you?"

"Kinda."

"Oh ye of little faith! Anyway, you better get out there soon—a lot of people are already skywatching out back. Now"—he put a hand on Eliza's shoulder—"let's talk about *your* performance."

"What do you mean?"

"You've got to say something to the crowd, Eliza!"

"Why would they want to hear from me?"

"Are you kidding? The only reason they're here tonight is your blog."

"My blog? What good was my fucking blog?"

Chad stared hard into Eliza's eyes, like he was trying to find someone he used to know in there. After a moment, he turned back to Andy and Anita. "I set up a little greenroom for you at the bottom of the stairs. Go get yourselves warmed up. I'd like to talk to Eliza alone."

354

Andy hesitated. It didn't seem right to leave Eliza behind. The end was only a few hours away; every parting felt like the last one.

"It's fine," she said. "I'll see you down there."

Andy walked back along the catwalk behind Anita, trying to make out faces in the crowd beneath them. There were more old people than he'd expected—little streaks of silver hair like patches of dead grass on a lawn. He wondered if Mr. McArthur or Mr. Jester or that security guard from Bellevue Mall had made it. And what about Jess and Kevin and the rest of the Hamilton crew? He liked to think they were all down there somewhere, surrounded by friends.

They'd almost made it to the bottom of the interminable staircase before Andy realized he was about to be alone with Anita for the first time since they'd kissed. He felt anxious and excited—her hips moved sinuously with each step, and that red dress clung in all the right places—but also weirdly guilty. Why had it taken him so long to figure out how he felt about her? How had he let himself get distracted by a girl who'd told him on day one that she wasn't interested? Why had he wasted so much precious time?

The "greenroom" was just an old office outfitted with a busted-up guitar and a couple of couches. Battery-powered "candles" with perfect flickering flames had been placed all over the room.

"It's nice in here," Andy said.

"Yeah. Totally."

"You want something to drink?"

"Sure."

There were a few bottles of water inside the dark, unpowered refrigerator. For just a second, Andy was gripped by the ridiculous fear that he wouldn't be able to twist off the cap. A drop of sweat dripped from his armpit down his belly. What if she hadn't even wanted to kiss him? What if she'd only let it happen because there hadn't been any way to stop him? He tried to remember if she'd really kissed him back, but it had all happened so fast. Maybe the best thing was just to forget about it. There were only a few hours left before the end of the world anyway. It was stupid to be worrying about love and sex at a time like this. He and Anita would just play their songs together and be friends and that would be enough—

"I don't want to die a virgin," Anita said. She immediately covered her face with her hands. "I know it's crazy to say that right now, with everything that's happened, but it's the truth." She straightened up, took a deep breath, and looked him straight in the eye. "I like you. If you're into it, then I'm into it."

Andy was speechless. He'd forgotten that there was actually another person in the room—someone with her own needs and desires and shit to freak out about. But it was funny, or better than funny, that sometimes two people could be feeling the exact same thing at the exact same time. He burst out laughing. Anita's eyes went wide, haughty and hurt for the one second before Andy was there to kiss her.

"We have to warm up," she said.

"Yeah," Andy said. "We should definitely do that."

Anita

ANITA HAD ONCE READ THAT ALL TRIVIAL QUESTIONS HAD A SINGLE ANSWER, BUT WHEN IT came to important questions, every answer was equally valid. Was life too short? Of course—there was never enough time to do all the things you wanted to do. And of course not—if it were any longer, you'd appreciate it even less than you already did. Was it better to live primarily for the good of yourself, or for the good of others? For yourself, of course—it was madness to take responsibility for other people's happiness. And for others, of course—selfishness was just another way to isolate yourself, when everyone knew that true happiness was all about friendship and love.

Did Anita feel any different after sleeping with Andy?

Of course she did—losing your virginity was always a big deal, and for her, it represented the end of a journey begun just six weeks ago (and how was it possible to fit so many lifetimes into six weeks?), when she left her parents' house with only a carry-on suitcase and a boatload of angst. More importantly, sex with Andy had brought her close to him in a way she hadn't even known was possible, a way that was grounded and wordless without being either mental (God knew she already spent more than enough time in her head) or spiritual (which she didn't really buy into). Their connection now was physical and human and earthly. It was the purest denial of death that there could be: the stubborn ecstasy of the body, the indefatigable heart. Anita felt like she finally understood why love was symbolized by that grotesque pumping organ, always threatening to clog, or break, or attack. Because the heart was the body's engine, and love was an act of the body. Your mind could tell you who to hate or respect or envy, but only your body—your nostrils and your mouth and the wide, blank canvas of your skin—could tell you who to love.

At the same time, it was silly to think of herself as totally transformed—she and Andy hadn't done anything that billions of other people hadn't done before them. It was just a few minutes on a plush purple couch. Only a hurried undressing and a bit of pain (less than she expected) and a bit of pleasure (less than she expected), some funny faces and some nervous laughter and then that sweet little shiver and something in his eyes that Anita imagined you only saw in boys' eyes at that exact moment, incredulous and vulnerable and masculine at once.

Did she love him?

Of course not—she barely knew him.

And of course—because her body told her so.

"Should I have been more careful?" he asked.

"I think the biggest morning-after pill in the universe is on its way. If we're still here the actual morning after, we can go find a real one."

"Cool. I mean . . . cool."

In spite of all the male bullshit she'd heard about "scoring" and "getting laid," Anita felt more empowered now than she had in a long time. In fact, it was Andy who seemed the more fragile one; maybe that's why it was always "getting laid" instead of "laying." In the end, girls had all the power, and boys were just lucky to receive some of it. Anita definitely understood Eliza a whole lot better now.

"Let's get dressed," she said.

"Okay."

Andy scrambled around the room like some gangly white spider, finding all her clothes before searching for his own. She helped him into his hoodie as if dressing him for the first day of school. The thought made her laugh.

"What?" he asked.

"Nothing. Just, you're great."

He smiled in an *I don't know what to do with my face* sort of way. "You wanna actually warm up?"

Anita shook her head. "I'm plenty warm."

Holding hands, they left the office and walked back down the torch-lit path. The stage was equipped simply—a grand piano, an acoustic and an electric guitar, a couple of microphone stands. Andy switched on the amplifiers and tuned up. People were still coming down the path from the parking lot, and a few of them stopped to see what was happening.

Was she nervous? Of course. And of course not. She'd been born for this.

The electronic music began to fade out. From where she stood, Anita could see through to the other end of the hangar. Two fifty-foot projector screens switched from a screen-saver-style light show to a live video feed. The DJ stepped away from his station, and Eliza took his place. She adjusted the microphone to her height.

"Um, hey. I'm alive." Applause built and crashed like a wave. Eliza spoke over it, clearly uncomfortable with all the attention. "I don't wanna keep you for long. I just thought I'd say a couple things. First, I wanted to thank my friends, Andy and Anita, who had the idea for this party. They're gonna be playing some music outside in a few minutes. So you should, you know, listen. Also, Chad, who made all this happen. Finally, to those of you who read my blog back when it started, thanks for that. All I ever wanted to do was show people some of what was going on where I was. I never expected it to turn into anything. But I guess the last couple months have been all about learning how to deal with the unexpected. I—" Eliza choked on the next word. She seemed about to cry, but then she smiled instead. "I fell in love," she said. "Can you believe that shit?" The audience laughed a complicit sort of laugh, as if Eliza weren't the only one.

"But everything ends," she said suddenly. "It does. And I don't want to bring you down or anything, because I know that's the last thing any of us need right now. But it's still the truth. There isn't very much I believe in. Not heaven, or hell, or that any part of us will survive if . . . if it happens. But I can say that, for me, it was still worth it. I mean, it was still worth being alive. I really do believe that. Thanks."

Even from way out by the little stage, the applause sounded thunderous.

"Not bad," Andy said.

Anita wiped at her eyes. "No. Not bad."

The DJ started spinning again, but much more quietly now. The moment had come.

"Ready?" Andy asked. Anita nodded. It had been a long time since they'd practiced, but that didn't matter. All that mattered was that they were here now, and together.

As Andy began to play the first few chords of "Save It," Anita wrapped her fingers around the microphone stand and closed her eyes. The audience was still pretty small, so it was easy enough to place herself back in her bedroom closet, singing just for the joy of it. When she opened her eyes again a minute later, the crowd had already grown. A dozen more unfamiliar faces, all looking to her. Before long, there were hundreds. But they couldn't all be strangers, could they? No one could say who was standing out there in the darkness. Maybe that girl from Jamba Juice who'd claimed to be the best thing since sliced bread, or the other members of student council, or Luisa and her family. Anita tried to imagine the crowd was made up entirely of people she knew. And here were a few that she *did* recognize, coming to stand just at the lip of the stage—lovely Eliza, along with Chad and his beagle. And next to them, another man, gaunt and totally bald, with his arm wrapped around Eliza's shoulders. Her dad. Anita smiled at him, and he smiled back.

Andy's thin voice reached for the high falsetto harmonies, so tight it sometimes felt to Anita as if she were singing both parts. She didn't speak between songs, while Andy moved from piano to guitar and back again. Eliza had already said everything there was to say, and besides, Anita was seeking a communion beyond words.

It seemed to end as soon as it began. She and Andy played every song they'd written together—maybe half an hour of music altogether. A few days ago Anita would have seen that as the sum total of her short time on Earth, and she would have been proud of it. But now she had something more to be proud of. She and Andy stood at the front of the stage, looking out over the crowd, bowing and coming up again. He pulled her to his sweaty side, kissed her in front of everyone. What a marvel it was—the body and its puppy hungers. She looked up toward the sky, toward the implacable sparkle of good old Ardor, and saw that the two of them—she and the asteroid—were caught up in a battle of wills. In that moment, she stopped being afraid of it, even dared it to come, because she knew there was no way it could crave death as much as she craved life.

Eliza

IF ELIZA HAD SAT DOWN TO WRITE A SPEECH—LIKE, IF SHE'D ACTUALLY PLANNED IT—IT probably would have turned out the exact opposite of the one she ended up giving. Even as she was walking off the stage, applause like a wash of white noise in her ears, she wondered who the hell this girl was, waxing poetic about love. It definitely wasn't any Eliza Olivi she'd ever known.

After Andy and Anita had gone off together—already something strange brewing between them—she'd been left alone in the office with Chad and his inscrutable beagle. And though Eliza had only spent a couple of hours with the weird old hippie, and that was weeks ago now, somehow he felt familiar.

"What's happened?" he asked.

"What do you mean?"

"You know what I mean."

Eliza considered dodging the question, or lying, but she was too exhausted to do either one. "Someone died. Someone I cared about."

"I'm sorry."

"Thanks."

"But you must know by now that the people you care about never really die."

Internally, she rolled her eyes. "I guess."

Chad watched her for a few seconds, waiting. When he spoke again, it was in the voice of a disappointed teacher. "Really? You're going to let me get away with that?"

"With what?"

"With that disgusting cliché." He put on Disney-big doe eyes and a cloying, high-pitched voice. "The people you care about never really die."

"What was I supposed to say?"

"The truth. That you don't believe that."

"Fine. I don't believe it."

"Say it again."

"I don't believe it."

"Again."

"I don't believe it."

"Louder!"

Eliza finally raised her voice, as much because Chad was needling her as anything else, "I don't believe that!"

"Tell me it's bullshit!" he shouted back.

"It's bullshit!"

"Tell me it's a load of goddamn fucking bullshit!"

"It is!" Eliza shouted. "People die! They die and they're gone forever!"

Somehow it felt totally natural that this last morbid statement made Chad laugh. "That's better," he said. "Eliza, why would you lie to me? I'm nobody. I'm just a tiny little character in the big book of your life. And you're right. People do die. All of them. Bar none. So what does it even mean? I call someone crazy because not everybody is crazy. I call someone brilliant because not everybody is brilliant. But everybody dies. Squirrels die. Trees die. Skin cells die and your inner organs die and the person you were yesterday's dead too. So what does it mean to die? Not much."

"That's a stupid argument," Eliza said.

Chad gave her a little punch in the shoulder. "That's the spirit!"

Eliza couldn't help but smile, but as soon as she did, as soon as she let even an ounce of joy into her heart, she remembered Peter. "The boy who died," she said. "I pretended to believe what he believed, at the very end."

"What did he believe?"

Eliza blinked hard, struggled to keep her voice under control. "I don't know. Crazy shit. Jesus. Forgiveness. Sacrifice and mercy and stuff. Love."

"You don't believe in any of that?"

"No."

"You don't believe in sacrifice or love?"

Eliza wasn't sure what she believed anymore. Tears tickled her cheeks. Everything blurred as the world turned to liquid, and then she felt a warm, shifty weight settle on her lap.

Chad's beagle.

"Give Ardor a hug," Chad said.

"I thought his name was Sid."

"I renamed him. I wanted to associate the asteroid with something loving."

Eliza petted Ardor, who wagged his tail once or twice, in recognition of her efforts, than resumed his usual calm beagality. She remembered what Peter had said in the park, about wanting to be like a dog. A happy memory—hers to keep.

"Feel better?" Chad asked.

And the weird thing was, she did.

Anita and Andy were only a couple of songs into their set when it happened. Gabriel, the guy who'd brought them up to see Chad, pushed his way through the crowd.

"Eliza?" he whispered.

"Yeah?"

"There's someone here to see you." For a second, her heart leaped up into her throat, because she thought it might be Peter. But that was impossible.

"Who is it?"

"He's over there."

She looked to where Gabriel was pointing. A ghostly white spot, like a halo—her father's pale, hairless head. He stood on his tiptoes, looking adorably old and out of his element. She ran into his arms.

"Hey, Lady Gaga."

"You found me!"

"It wasn't that hard. You're a celebrity."

"The apartment," she said. "It burned down."

"I wasn't there when it happened."

"Well, I know that now!" she said, laughing and wiping at her eyes.

After all the terrible stuff that had happened in the past few days, any good news seemed like some kind of miracle. They watched the rest of the show together, side by side. When it was over, Andy and

Anita kissed (and thank God for that—they'd been circling each other from the very beginning).

"Loved the set," her dad told Anita. "It was dope."

Eliza shook her head. "Please don't say that word."

"Never?"

"Never ever."

At some point during the performance, it had begun to rain. A typical Seattle drizzle, the drops like tiny puffs of cold air. Eliza realized she was holding hands with both her father and Andy, who in turn were holding hands with Anita and Chad. They were like Dorothy and her friends in *The Wizard of Oz*, skipping down the Yellow Brick Road to the Emerald City, Toto (a.k.a. Sid, a.k.a. Ardor) at their heels. Only in this case, the Emerald City was a 66.6 percent chance of ceasing to exist.

Chad led them out behind the hangar, to where an enormous crowd of stargazers sat on colored squares of blankets and cushions, a sparse but somehow unified checkerboard. They found a spot near the edge of the tarmac, where you could hear the faraway music only as a heartbeat thrum of bass. Above it floated the susurration of many thousands of people quietly talking, like wind on an empty beach. Chad had brought a couple of thick white quilts with him, and with one underneath them and another over their legs, it was almost cozy. Eliza leaned her head against her father's shoulder. Ardor looked slightly different now—more twinkly than before. Time passed.

"I wish Mom were here," she said.

"Me too. But we've got each other at least."

"Yeah. We do."

She considered telling him about Peter but decided against it.

There would be time for grief later. If there were time for anything at all, there'd be time for that.

"Hey, Eliza," Andy said. "Could I talk to you for a second?"

"Sure."

He walked away from the group. Eliza stood up and followed him. "What's up?"

"Uh, sorry if this is weird, but I just wanted to say, well, I'm sorry."

"About what?"

"I know I was the one who liked you, not really the other way around, but it still feels weird to suddenly be with Anita, after I was all in love with you."

Eliza laughed. "That's the dumbest thing I've ever heard."

She worried her honesty lesson from Chad might have been a little too well learned, but Andy laughed along with her. "Yeah, I guess it is."

"What am I missing?" Anita asked, joining them out where the pavement surrendered to the dirt and the weeds and the shadows.

"Andy's being an idiot," Eliza said.

"Sounds about right." Anita looked upward, toward Ardor. "It's such a little thing from down here."

"I bet it feels the same way about us," Andy said.

"Seen from the right perspective, pretty much everything looks tiny," Eliza said.

They were silent for a moment, then Andy sang a bit of some half-familiar song: "'*Can't believe how strange it is to be anything at all.*'"

Eliza thought about all the things she'd hoped to do in her life, all the lives she'd wanted to live. She could see them now, jagged paths cut into the shadowy future, lit up in small bursts of light: her first day at college, her reconciliation with her crazy mom, her first real boyfriend (something between Andy and Peter, maybe, or maybe something totally new), her first gallery show in New York (*Apocalypse Already: A Retrospective*), her wedding (if she wanted a wedding), her first child (if she wanted to have children), her divorce (because would she, of all people, really get it right the first time?). Magazine profiles. A professorship. Lovers. Living in Europe. A dinner table full of well-dressed friends. An affair. The Mediterranean. Grandchildren. An ashram. Her own garden, somewhere in Europe with light the color of wheat. Illness. Death.

Were Andy and Anita having the same sort of thoughts right now? Was everyone? And if they all managed to make it out of this alive, would the world be different when they woke up tomorrow? Would it be better?

Andy leaned over to kiss Anita's cheek. Maybe they'd stay together for the rest of their lives. Maybe they'd break up in a week. Maybe they'd both be successful musicians. Maybe they'd become record producers, or sculptors, or plumbers. Who could say? And even if Peter had survived, that wouldn't have guaranteed anything; he and Eliza might have turned out to be totally incompatible. Or maybe she would have ended up dying of leukemia a year from now. Whether Ardor landed or not, there was no way to know what would become of any of them. Eliza felt all her guilt and regret disintegrate in the face of this colossal knowledge. It turned out they'd been right here all along, standing in the darkness, appealing to the stars for some sign of what was to come, and never getting anything back but the shifting constellations of a swiftly spinning, precariously tilted planet. She let herself fall against Andy's side and felt Anita's arm reach around and come to rest on her hip. They were interlocked now, like the links of a chain.

"Red Rover, Red Rover, send Ardor right over," Eliza said.

They laughed. The asteroid was a little bigger now, brighter, and still they went on laughing. Laughing in the face of what they couldn't predict or change or control. Would it be fire and brimstone? Would it be Armageddon? Or would it be a second chance? Eliza held tight to her friends, laughing, and felt a pair of hands land soft as feathers on her shoulders, like the hands of a ghost, laughing and laughing as Ardor swept along its fated course, laughing and through that laughter, praying. Praying for forgiveness. Praying for grace. Praying for mercy.

A NOTE ON THE MUSIC

For a while, Eliza floated along with just the sound, until a few of the lyrics clarified in her conscious mind—something about the number of lovers someone would get in a lifetime. Eliza realized that Andy had written this song for her . . .

As a singer-songwriter and novelist, I've long dreamed of bringing my two passions together in one project. And as soon as I realized that some of the characters in *We All Looked Up* were going to be musicians, I knew I'd found my moment. *We All Looked Up: The Album* is my attempt to bring the songs

of the book—and a few others written on the general themes of the book—to life. Visit my website for a free song download or to buy the whole album in digital or physical form. The record is also available at all major online retailers, and probably some minor ones too.

Thanks for reading, and I hope you enjoy the record!

—Tommy

tommywallach.com

ACKNOWLEDGMENTS

First off, thanks to John Cusick, literary agent and fashion plate. You made me replace that terrible second half. Next up, Christian Trimmer, editor and humanitarian. You made me replace that only *slightly* less terrible second half all over again. Then there's Lucy Cummins, who designed my cover, for which she deserves a medal made out of chocolate. General thanks to everyone at Simon & Schuster, for being warm and welcoming.

A shout-out to the hundreds of coffee shops that have allowed me to sit and write over the last twelve years and seven novels ("I had a tea the other day!" "You couldn't pay." "Oh yeah . . ."), including Kávé, where most of *We All Looked Up* was written.

Thanks to my many forgiving mentors, especially Seth Kurland, who gave me sage advice about plotting that I should have listened to sooner. Also to Thomas Ertman, for all the notes, and to Jeanine Rogel, for the wild horse.

Love to my family: Stephanie Wallach (mom), Bob Dedea (alternating father/brother figure and artistic comrade-in-arms), Stephen Terrell (the distant fatherly type), Doug Myers (father and IT expert), and Ryan Davis (brother).

Finally and foremost, to Tallie Maughan. First you taught me to be an artist, then you taught me to be a man. Thank you, thank you, thank you.